"[One of] the most fascinating part[s] of the book is Naomi's child-hood remembrances. In addition to the difficulties of the Depression, the family must also deal with the turmoil caused by her father's attempted suicide and nervous breakdown... It's true Savannah storytelling."

—Rachel Mason
Connect Savannah

"This is not, repeat not, a fly-by-night literary whim of a Savannah debutante whose friends told her she 'rahts real purty.' *Scarlett O' Hara Can Go To Hell* is an entertaining, witty and cliché-free account of a Savannah woman's very extroverted journey through life in a city that prefers its sins behind closed doors…some hard lessons about family, love, sex and politics along the way, in the end she delights in the whole crazy experience of it all. And chances are you will too."

—Jim Morekis
Creative Loafing Entertainment News Magazine

Scarlett O'Hara Can Go To Hell

Scarlett O'Hara Can Go To Hell

Miriam K. Center

Good luck!
Mim Cent

Authors Choice Press
New York Lincoln Shanghai

Scarlett O'Hara Can Go To Hell

Authors Choice Press
an imprint of iUniverse, Inc.

iUniverse books may be ordered through booksellers or by contacting:

iUniverse
2021 Pine Lake Road, Suite 100
Lincoln, NE 68512
www.iuniverse.com
1-800-Authors (1-800-288-4677)

Originally published by Black Skylark Singing

Cover Author 1936
Author's Photograph Richard Sommers

This book is a work of fiction, though some characters have vague similarities drawn from life experiences

ISBN-13: 978-0-595-38382-5
ISBN-10: 0-595-38382-3

Printed in the United States of America

For My Parents

Rather than love, than money
than fame, give me truth

—Thoreau

Prologue

I sit looking down at the Grand Canyon, reflecting on how far my journey has brought me from Savannah. And about time, after fifty years of making some really dumb mistakes. Bound for California, like some throwback to the Gold Rush, I keep wondering if my grandfather, Zelig, felt the same way when he left Russia for his New World. Well, at least a 1984 white Cadillac convertible beats steerage class on a rotting immigrant ship.

Chapter One

It was a cool October morning, the kind that smells like crisp fresh linen. My mother had died the month before and my year long affair with a younger man had ended a week later. As 1980 drew to an end I found myself, a recently divorced, fifty-year old woman. Alone and hating it. And though there was a certain lightness, I realized that freedom is perhaps the hardest thing in the world to handle.

Opening my office that Monday morning I did my best to avoid looking down at the mail and real estate contracts that lay scattered on top of my desk. The sound of birds chirping from the branches of the live oak trees in the rear garden made me wonder if they knew secrets from the past.

I traced my fingers through the pile of papers, choosing only the ones that had to be dealt with immediately. I sat behind my desk longing for a call that might tell me what to do with the rest of my life. I jumped when the phone on my desk rang.

"Why you didn't eat the chicken you asked me to cook for you on Friday?" the voice calling from the kitchen upstairs said.

"I didn't tell you to cook a chicken."

"Uh huh you did. And now it's gone bad, and I throwed it away," Dora announced in exasperation.

"Damned if I remember telling you to do that."

In a few minutes, Dora shuffled into the office waving a grease-spotted piece of paper she had fished from the garbage. On it, clearly written in my scrawly handwriting was, "Bake a chicken, cook okra gumbo, make a pot of rice." The vegetables I recalled, had all been placed in the refrigerator. But I had completely forgotten the rest.

"Well, I'll be damned!" I sighed out loud. "There's been a dead chicken in my oven all this time. And I didn't even know it."

"Lord have mercy, Miss Naomi," Dora mumbled, throwing her

1

hands to the sky. Dora, always sweet, kind, comforting, Dora who had cared for Ross, my youngest son, since he was a little boy, now worked in my house on Mondays and Thursdays and at my ex-husband Bill's apartment on Tuesdays and Fridays. The agents in my office teased me that Bill and I shared custody of her.

Looking at Dora's disappointed face, I finally remembered that the poor chicken had been abandoned in my haste to meet an old boyfriend who had called on Friday. He had urged me to spend the weekend at Sea Island with him, and eager for just such a break, I had jumped in my car and sped away.

After Dora left I watched the leaves of golden autumn fall from trees in my backyard, as they floated then fell gently in a yellow heap to the ground, and daydreamed of being away from the familiarity of my surroundings and starting anew.

My eyes searched around the office, before locking on to the photograph of my grandmother, framed in silver. Her round Russian face massaged my wounded heart. Everything about my grandmother had been round, her nose, her feet, and her adorable face.

Perhaps my grandfather had felt the same as I did now when he left Russia searching for his new world.

America was the promised land for my grandparents. So much so that in 1904, when Zelig Racmanoff stood in front of the uniformed official who was processing the immigrants arriving on Ellis Island and was asked to tell his name, he let his fantasy fly into the world he was entering.

"I will be rich man," he said proudly. They were the only English words he knew. The clerk filled in the proper documents and on the line above the word "name," he wrote Zelig Richman. Zelig was a strapping young man with curly red hair, and a bushy red mustache lay above his protruding lips.

My grandfather had fifty cents in his pocket when he arrived in Savannah, Georgia. He started out working as a peddler, "klapping," or knocking on doors, supplying the basic necessities such as hammers, nails and bags of grits to devastated rural Southerners. Traveling by horse and wagon, he sold mostly to black families suffering from financial depression and immigrants like himself, struggling to support their families. After two years, he opened a small grocery store in a section of Savannah known as Frogtown. Savannah appealed to his Jewish heart. The poor black families who lived in clustered shacks near the railroad terminal reminded Zelig of his *shtetl* life back in Russia.

"Minna and Daniel are my two Europeans," my grandfather would laughingly refer to his children. But then he would hasten to add, "Sadie, Moses, Shirley and Ella, are my four Americans." Minna had been four and Daniel two when my grandmother, Eva, sailed with her children to the new country. Zelig adored Eva, giving all of his affection to her instead of their children.

My mother, Minna, was sixteen by the time the youngest, Ella, was born. Embarrassed at having a baby sister while she was approaching adulthood, Minna quit high school in a fit of temper. A week after she quit school, Minna went job hunting. When she passed Joe Cohen's Haberdashery, she saw a sign in the window advertising for a bookkeeper and walked in.

She glanced around the store, taking in the glass cases filled with shirts, socks and ties. Against the wall stood a tall wooden ladder, ready for a clerk to climb, in order to reach the round cardboard hat boxes stacked above. Then she noticed a young man in the far corner of the store leaning against a glass case. He blew out a puff of smoke from his cigarette and smiled at her. Though she had many beaus, she found herself curious about this dapper twenty year old immigrant. He had come from Russia with his father when he was twelve.

Avram Zipinsker wore his black hair slicked straight back from his high forehead. He dressed nattily, his knickers pushed over his bowed legs. He had a hook nose, and when he spoke, his *V's* sounded like *W's'*. Whenever he referred to the street named Victory Drive, he pronounced it, "Wictory Drive." Avram had an air of cockiness about him, as he leaned his arm, the one holding the cigarette, on top of the display case. Minna blushed as the young man continued to stare at her.

Mr. Cohen told her to report for work the following Monday. My mother left the store dreaming of owning a business just like that one, with a husband, a partner for life.

In 1918, the two rooms behind the grocery store in Frogtown were growing crowded now that there were six children. Zelig's business was

3

good and he had saved money during Prohibition when he stored whiskey inside the walls of the store, then bootlegged it for a handsome profit.

One afternoon as darkness filtered through the room, Eva lifted the top off the pot and tenderly stirred the matzoh balls with a wooden spoon. She wiped the perspiration from her forehead, then ran her hand across the front of her apron marked with X's, which she had sewn from old flour sacks. The summer heat was so oppressive you could almost touch it. Pungent cooking aromas mixed with sweat swirled together and filled the small room.

"It's time to buy a house, Mama," Zelig said, putting down his Yiddish newspaper, pushing his eyeglasses up over his brow to rest on his forehead. My grandmother nodded and agreed; she agreed with everything her husband said. They chose to live within walking distance of the B.B. Jacob Synagogue, which was especially convenient because Zelig never learned to drive an automobile.

My grandfather had established good credit with Rothfield, the German-born banker, who had built his bank by lending money to immigrant Jews in Savannah. They paid six thousand dollars for the house on West Charlton Street, overlooking Pulaski Square. It was just across from the Jewish Educational Alliance, which was the hub of Savannah activity for the Jewish community. Zelig would be able to walk to the grocery store and the family would, at last, have an inside bathroom instead of the small outhouse behind the grocery store.

Savannah, built on Yamacraw Bluff above the river, was one of the first planned cities in America. It had been laid out with tree-shaded squares of huge oaks that tossed off varied and magical light when the sun shone. The city had only one direction in which to grow — South.

The 1850 three story wood frame house stood on a corner. In back of it was a small confectionery store that would bring in extra income. The proprietor sold tobacco and candies. The ground floor housed several poor black families, who lived on dirt floors. They paid five dollars a month for rent. Zelig liked the idea that he was, finally, a social and economical notch above another class of people. A flight of wooden stairs led to the parlor and on the floor above the parlor were three bedrooms.

4

There was also a large attic in which Eva could store her straw trunks from Europe. My grandmother loved to take out her brass candlesticks and the hand crocheted tablecloth that had belonged to her mother. She would touch them reverently. Along with some photographs of her parents in dark oval frames, they were the few heirlooms she had brought from Russia, the only reminder of her lost family.

A class distinction cropped up among Jews in Savannah at that time. Those from Germany counted themselves a step above the Jews who came from Eastern Europe. Sephardic Jews were as high up as a person could get and still be Jewish. The affluent German Jews considered themselves more Americanized, scorning the sounds of Yiddish accents. Back in Minsk, buying a home such as this would have been unheard of. But here in America, my grandparents were feeling secure. They didn't have German Jews in the back parts of their mind. Their main reason and sole purpose in life was survival.

On Saturday nights Zelig had Eva fill the iron tub for his bath; the water tank in the bathroom had to be lit with a match so that hot water could run through the pipes. Then the rest of the family bathed one by one in order of their age. The same water was used for everyone. It grew progressively cooler and muddier with each bather. Zelig believed in saving money. Some said he was frugal, others called him downright stingy.

On warm nights when the family sat in cane rocking chairs and in a wooden swing on the side porch, laughter spilled through the air like the soft summer breezes as they talked about the day, about relatives, and about each other while evening stars seemed to be telling their own tales. It was on such an evening that Minna dashed up the front stairs, excited that she had just received her first pay check. Thrilled at having her own money, she had immediately visited B. Karpf's, a women's ready to wear shop.

"Look at this dress, will you?" Minna said as she pulled a green voile frock from the bag she carried and held it against her body. The bias skirt flared at the hem. It clung to every soft curve of her ninety-eight pound body. She had a date with Avram for Sunday afternoon and planned to wear her new dress.

That Sunday afternoon, as they walked in Forsyth Park through lawns of green grass surrounded by budding azaleas, Avram suddenly grew sad. He reached out to hold Minna's hand. Slowly, he began to talk about himself, for the first time.

"I never knew my mother. She died when I was an infant. My Papa left me with my grandmother while he looked for a second wife." With a tinge of sadness in his voice, Avram told of frigid Russian nights, how he slept against a brick hearth lined with burlap for the scattered warmth. He adored his grandmother, and she, in turn, doted on him. When his father returned with a new wife who would be stepmother to Avram, they sailed for America.

"I never saw my grandmother again," Avram said with a quivering in his voice that touched Minna deeply. His childhood had been one of misery and loneliness. He was taunted by the other children when he was enrolled in school upon his arrival in Savannah. A boy of twelve in the midst of first graders, Avram felt awkward and confused as he stumbled through the English language. Most of the time he would just sit in class and day dream, eventually dropping out of school at the end of the fourth grade when he was fifteen, barely able to read and write.

Every night after work Avram would walk Minna to Charlton Street. Soon, she was asking him to stay for supper with her two brothers and three sisters. He seemed much happier on the porch with her family than he did in the small apartment with his own family. Over the next year and a half, their courtship flourished.

One Friday evening, as my mother and Sadie helped clear the table after the Shabos meal, their youngest sister, Ella, climbed into Avram's lap. Her eyes were as clear as a lake. She giggled and shook her fiery red hair which was just like her father's. And like her father and her older sister, freckles covered every spot where the sun had touched her body. Avram hugged her and grinned at her mischievously. He whispered into her ear, "How would you like to have me for a brother, Ella?"

She slid off his lap and ran into the kitchen, squealing in a high pitched voice, "Mama, Mama, Avram wants to be my brother!"

Minna's face turned beet red. The entire clan of Richman women, no matter what age, would screech whenever they wanted to be heard. They seemed at such times to border on the edge of hysteria.

Upstairs in her bedroom Minna stared at the night through the small paned windows, and wondered if this was what if felt like to be a grown-up. The thought of sharing a bed with anyone other than Sadie, made her skin tingle and her heart fearful. Mysterious night noises slowly wrapped themselves around her.

On the parlor floor at Charlton Street the rain fell softly outside my grandparents' bedroom, the drops rolling into Eva's flower-bed of pale blue four o'clocks and bright orange marigolds. As Zelig and Eva made plans for Minna and Avram's lives, Eva made no mention of Minna's hesitancy about marriage that had come up earlier when they were clearing the kitchen.

Very soon after that night Avram moved into the attic on Charlton Street, and became part of the Richman clan. On Sunday mornings when the family was finishing breakfast, Zelig habitually scraped the oilcloth on the table with his bread knife, carefully rounding up every crumb and then eating them.

"Be sure, *kinder*, to always eat the crumbs," Zelig told his children, letting them spill into his mouth from the palm of his hand. "Crumbs will make you rich." Zelig had learned to save his money. He knew that pennies made nickels and nickels made quarters. He had saved faithfully to buy a house, even purchased other rental property in Savannah. He now fancied himself a successful man.

My parents fell into a routine of walking to work together every morning. At times they seemed like brother and sister. But late at night they sat on the swing kissing and hugging until dawn, listening to the rustling of trees, watching fireflies dart through the night.

The pair was wed at B.B. Jacob Synagogue two years later. The bride pulled her auburn hair into a soft bun at the nape of her neck. A veil with seed pearls clung around her forehead, as the tulle flowed down her back, trailing the ivory satin gown. The gown ended just above Minna's pointed satin pumps. My father would describe her for the rest of their lives as "a red-haired, ninety-eight pound freckled ivory doll dressed in satin and lace." Minna walked down the aisle between her parents, in true Orthodox fashion.

As Avram's and Minna's brothers held the *Chuppah* over the heads of the bride and groom, Avram smashed the small glass under his heel, and the Rabbi pronounced them man and wife. Everyone shouted, "Mazel tov!" Minna caught a glimpse of herself in the oval mirror in the hall, and in that moment she pictured their future bright and affluent, together building a successful business.

Minna felt as though they were the American dream come true. She wanted to work side by side with her husband. My parents faced their future, balancing the old world in one hand and hopes of the new one in the other.

Less than a year after their marriage, it was decided that Avram should open his own men's and boy's clothing store on West Broughton Street, which was the main business district in Savannah for retail merchants. While Levy's and Adler's, the more fashionable ready-to-wear stores, were housed on East Broughton, everything west of Bull Street was being developed by Russian Jewish immigrants. The trend in those days was to have a catchy name for the store, one that would hook the trade.

"I don't think you can call it Zipinsker's," my mother's sister Sadie said, "because it's too . . .well, too Russian." It was early spring of 1924. They were sitting on the porch trying to decide a proper name for the business.

"She's right," my father's brother Sidney said. "It's got to be short so everyone'll remember it. And easy to pronounce."

Minna looked at her husband tentatively. She didn't want to seem like she had the best idea of all. "Avram," she said shyly, "you could use your nickname. It's short and easy to remember."

Sadie's eyes lit up. "That's it! Call it Zip's."

Avram nodded, a slow smile spreading across his face. The others shouted "Zip's," everyone agreeing that it was the perfect name for his new store.

The two families agreed to advance enough money for my parents to rent a store and buy merchandise. My mother would keep the books, clerk when necessary, and act as cashier. She was excited about being a partner to her husband. It was one of her dreams coming true. My father, on the other hand, dreamed of becoming rich, sailing boats, racing horses, belonging to private clubs — all the things that he'd heard prosperous American businessmen filled their lives with. As my father sat at a table in Hirsch's Delicatessen, he stared across the street at the empty storefront that would soon have his name above the door. He bit into a hunk of halavah, washed it down with a cup of hot tea, and imagined that his name was hanging from a marquee over a theater on Broadway.

Chapter Two

When Rothfield's bank suddenly closed, Zelig was in shock that the banker had made off with some of his savings and the few dollars that my mother had been putting aside over the years. It was a sad day for the Jewish community to realize that the man whom they had entrusted with their hard-earned money was a thief. Papa became bitter when he heard the terrible news and it made his reoccurring headaches even more painful. After he retired from the grocery store, Papa began spending his afternoons at home. He would first make his rounds to collect the rent on his properties. His headaches became the center point of life on Charlton Street from then on.

When my older sister Ruth was born on New Year's Day in 1925, Avram was off on a business trip to New York. He received a wire telling him that he was now a father. Not much on sentimentality, he penned a note to Minna, the only letter she would ever receive from him. "Best of luck, with your baby," read the message. He signed it, "Yours truly," and affixed his full legal signature.

My grandmother offered to take care of Ruth while Mother went to work as soon as she finished her chores at home. She had to boil the diapers, feed Ruth, then sweep and dust their bedroom before she could rush to her job at the store. It was customary in the Richman family for every newly married couple to live with Zelig and Eva until they saved enough money to get a place of their own.

It didn't take long for Avram to discover that he hated the responsibility of owning a business. He had never wanted to be confined in a store, he felt trapped. He seemed jealous of Minna's attention to the baby. Since Ruth was the first grandchild on both sides of the family, everyone doted on her. Minna was tired, but she kept up her schedule without complaint.

Avram had begun chain smoking, lighting one cigarette from another. His fingers turned brown from the tobacco, and he constantly picked at the skin around his fingernails. He kept a bottle of rye whiskey in the stockroom in back of the store. Al, the black man my father had hired to do the tailoring for his customers, covered for him every time he slipped out the back door, through the lane, to the corner garage for a crap game. And even though my mother pretended to her family that business was good they knew something was wrong.

Because it was the custom in those days to have children two years apart, Minna got pregnant again. But she continued going to the store until her belly showed.

It was a sultry August morning when Minna's sharp pains began. She didn't think she could make it to the hospital. She screamed for Daniel to run to Solomon's drugstore, two blocks away, and phone the doctor. Avram had left for work early, to catch up on unpaid bills.

"You should've waited until I got you to the hospital," the doctor bellowed as he rushed up the stairs to my mother's bedroom. The delivery was swift, though painful. Minna felt she was being split in half with a butcher knife. She had nothing to ease her suffering, the way she had during Ruth's more civilized birth at St. Joseph's Hospital. Eva placed a rolled up towel in her daughter's mouth, so the rest of the family couldn't hear her screams. My mother fell asleep, angry that the doctor had scolded her, and too tired to even look at her new infant daughter.

I was named Naomi.

"Calls for a celebration," my father said, dashing to the back room to get the liquor bottle, when Daniel arrived to tell him he had another girl. He poured a jigger of rye into two glasses..

"L'Acheim!" they toasted.

It didn't take long for Avram to feel even more trapped. Two little girls — how would he ever make enough money to dress them, send them on fancy trips, or marry them off to rich husbands? He hadn't even tasted life, and here he was responsible for an entire family. He lit a cigarette, inhaled deeply, holding it in his lungs for as long as he could. He exhaled, sending a smoke screen up in front of his face. His fears did not disappear.

Though Minna wanted to be a stay-at-home mother, that was not the case, and she soon went back to work.

My parents knew it was time to find an apartment when Daniel became engaged. It was now my uncle's turn to bring his bride to live with the family. Even though the house on Charlton Street was bursting at the seams with adults and children, Minna hated the thought of leaving her mother's home. My grandmother's essence filled every nook and cranny of that house, and it had been known as Mama's house from the moment they had moved there and gotten settled.

Instead of happily anticipating the privacy that would now be afforded her growing family, Minna dreaded it, mainly because Avram's mysterious behavior had become a constant source of worry for her. She felt like half adult and half child, not wanting to accept full responsibility.

Angry and hurt, Minna finally told Eva about Avram's disappearances in the middle of the day. Eva patted her daughter's hand and sighed sympathetically then went into the kitchen to prepare supper.

The apartment that my parents found was only a few blocks away from Mama's house, over a row of red brick stores just around the corner from Zip's Men's and Boy Shop. Minna could slip back and forth to the store and still take care of chores. She hired Winnie Lou, a maid who would become as much a mother to my sister and me as Minna was. Winnie Lou was a large woman with wide spread nostrils. Her broad smile revealed several gold teeth, and her ebony skin was shiny and smooth. She wore her hair plaited and plastered close to her head.

There was a Methodist kindergarten housed in the basement of the red brick church two blocks from our apartment. Mother took Ruth there in the morning on her way to work, leaving me with Winnie Lou.

My mother thought Aunt Sadie the most glamorous person in the world and when Aunt Sadie married a dashing Rumanian immigrant, my mother, ever loyal to her family, offered him a job at Zip's. She felt that she would have more freedom with a family member working the cash register. But soon after my uncle started working there, Al, the tailor, confided to Minna that he didn't trust the man. When Mother refused to take his words to heart, Al grew impatient. Minna had a way of ignoring anything she didn't want to recognize.

"That man's got an evil eye. Somebody better take charge here, I'm telling you. If I was you I'd knock old Bob upside his Rumanian head," Al said. The bank account was dwindling due to Daddy's gambling and now there were also mysterious disappearances from the cash register.

In addition to the side porch at Mama's house, Mother found solace in sitting on a bench in Forsyth park on Sundays and holidays. She would take us there, where in happier days she and Daddy had spent much of their courtship. In the middle of the park was a large wrought iron fountain, spouting water from the trumpets of mythological figures. It had been fashioned after one in Paris and was a favorite place for young families to bring their children to play. Minna enjoyed watching her two little girls feed parched peanuts to the pigeons. Some days an organ grinder strolled among the bushes, his monkey sporting a red fez hat with a golden tassel. The monkey danced to the music at the end of his chain. Daddy never took part in our family outings; instead he spent his weekends with his cronies playing poker, hoping to make the big win of his life. Or sometimes he would stay alone in the apartment, smoking and reading murder-mystery magazines.

There was a vast difference between my sister and me. Ruth was always a sweet cherub of a girl, with a perpetual smile, while I was thin with a scowl on my face, constantly refusing to eat. From as early as I can remember I had trouble swallowing food. I had absolutely no appetite. At the noon meal, when my mother came home, she would push a forkful of lumpy mashed potatoes mixed with carrots down my throat, screaming, "Eat these vegetables, goddamnit!" As usual, I gagged.

"My throat hurts, I can't swallow," became the battle cry of the daily war between the two of us.

"You're too damned mean to eat," Minna shouted. I was determined to eat only what I liked. This show of early independence from her youngest child was something my mother hadn't counted on. And she had no idea how to handle it.

When it became my turn to be walked to Trinity Methodist Kindergarten I could hardly wait to climb up on the narrow raised concrete ledge that surrounded the cobblestone sidewalk and try to balance myself, putting one Mary Jane patent leather shoe in front of the other. I swung my arms from side to side to keep from falling and sang, "Swing Low Sweet Chariot." It was the spiritual that Winnie Lou sang. I loved the words and the beautiful melody.

"Don't fall, damn it! And quit singing about Jesus!" Mother would yell as she walked beside me. I'd begin to hum the song very softly and continue balancing myself on the concrete ledge.

Although Zelig and Eva's married sons and daughters had left their parents' home, the custom of spending Sunday afternoon on Charlton Street didn't change. It was almost sacrilegious not to be there. In summer, the family sat outside on the porch, waving paper fans to cool the humid air. When winter came everyone moved inside. There, the family gathered around the round, oak dining table and drank hot tea and ate Mama's *kreplach*. The warm, well seasoned ground meat, tucked into the hot crusty pastry, melted in my mouth. There was such warmth and family love in that house that I assumed it would stay that way for the rest of my life.

Our family, much like other immigrant families, stuck together through all kinds of adversities. Family loyalty was their backbone, no matter how angry they were with one another.

Usually, when the grownup talk started, my sister and I would sneak up to our aunt Ella's closet and play inside it. By then Ella was in high school, but she seemed like a grown woman to me. Other times I would announce, "I'm going down to ride the horse," a phrase which Mother never questioned but chalked up to my "wild imagination." In one of the downstairs rooms in my grandparents' house, lived a black man named John, whom I loved to visit. He was the oldest human being I knew and my genuine friend. John would hoist me high on his black leather lace-up boot, pausing to spit tobacco juice on the ground, and sing to me, swinging his foot back and forth. I pretended I was astride a Western pony. Although Savannah was a segregated city until the 1960's, I took for granted the bonding of blacks and whites. After all, Winnie Lou cooked my dinner, bathed me, and listened to me while my mother spent long hours at the store.

"Tell me your full name, Winnie Lou." That was my favorite question and every time she lathered soap over my skinny body I would ask it.

"Shucks, child, you don't wanna know that again." Winnie Lou invariably chuckled at my persistence. I knew if I didn't give up she'd finally tell me what I wanted to hear. Her voice was melodious.

"Well, my name is Winnie Lou Estelle Augusta Middleton Coleman Williams. My born name was Middleton. I got married to Mr. Coleman. And when he died, I married Mr. Williams."

While my sister and I had grown accustomed to the way Winnie Lou bathed us, we couldn't help but compare Mother's method of bathing us. It was altogether different. On the nights that Mother took up the task she would hand us a washcloth, and with an embarrassed look crossing her scrunched up face, carefully instruct us: "After you wash your tushy, be sure to wash your nasty tushy." She would then point between our legs and groan.

Winnie Lou would roll up the corner of the wash cloth and twist it inside my nostril and I couldn't stand it when she did that. But my questioning didn't stop at that intrusion. "How come you're a woman and my mother's a lady, Winnie Lou?" I said. I was eager to learn the difference.

"Black folk is treated different, Naomi. You just don't see that." It was true. Ruth and I had simply accepted the fact that our nurse served us lunch at the kitchen table while she stood over the sink eating. She never sat at the table with us. Our life was calmer with Winnie Lou around. because Mother was always angry at one or the other of us, no matter what we said or did.

"You're driving me crazy," Mother would shout when Ruth began complaining of frequent headaches. "You're going to send me to the insane asylum in Milledgeville!" She would then throw pots and pans across the kitchen. As the pots bounced off the walls, my sister ran out of the house and down the steps. Ruth dreaded our mother's open palm slapping her face. Being mother to two energetic daughters aged four and six while trying to run the clothing store and deal with her hus band's problems was more than Minna could cope with. She accepted her fate quietly as her lot in life, but inwardly she fumed. Her anger was taken out on us girls.

Yet when Ruth came down with scarlet fever and had to be quarantined, Mother sat next to her bed and for hours bathed her head with cold wash cloths. It seemed that only when we were sick did we receive genuine tenderness from our mother.

As soon as Mother would leave Ruth's room, I would sneak to the door, dash in and touch my sister's hand. I needed to know that she was still there, and I wasn't about to let them set rules for me about when I could see her. Chasing after Ruth one morning, I stumbled and fell down a long flight of steps in the backyard of our apartment.

While Winnie Lou went around to the store to get my mother, I sat at the bottom of the stairs shuddering. When Mother arrived, she took one look at me and screamed, "Why the hell don't you look where you're going? I can't take it anymore!" As I watched the veins in my mother's neck protrude like thick rubber tubes, I promised myself that I would never, for as long as I lived, forget falling down those steps. I etched it in my brain and for years I replayed the scene, and took a vow to never forget the incident.

"Come home with the *kinder*," Eva urged, even though the word divorce was never mentioned. She said that she and Papa would take care of us. Eva had begun to notice the sadness in her oldest child and after talking things over with Zelig, she made the offer.

"I can't, Mama. It would be a disgrace."

My sister and I spent every weekend at our grandparents' house because our parents worked late on Saturday nights. And occasionally we'd stay for an extra long weekend. Those days were special because I got to help my grandmother pull the strudel dough and watch her prepare the delicious Friday night meal. She would chop three kinds of fish, then grate onions into the mixture to make *gefilte* fish balls. The smell of fresh *challah* baking was better than the Evening In Paris perfume that Aunt Sadie splashed on her wrists. On the Sabbath my grandmother served a dairy meal, using special dishes. Theirs was a strictly kosher home.

"How do you make French toast, Mama?" I would follow Eva around the kitchen on Sunday mornings. She used the *challah* bread left over from Friday.

"You put in a *bisel* of egg, then a *bisel* of milk," my grandmother explained as she whipped the milk and the egg together. Then she dipped the slices of bread into the mixture, coating them well, and fried them in a thick slab of butter that had just melted in the black iron skillet.

More than anything, those times alone gave me a chance to ask the same question I always asked Eva. "Am I your favorite grandchild, Mama?"

She smiled tenderly and assured me that I was indeed special "because you were named after mine own mama." Then she took pennies from the Tetley tea box, shaped like a small red trunk and slipped two or three into my hand.

"Shh! Shh! Don't tell Papa," my grandmother whispered as she shut the top of the tin can and placed it back on the shelf next to the sack of sugar.

"Please, please, tell me you love me the most," I begged while putting the pennies into the pocket of my dress.

"Listen here," Eva explained. "I love your mother special cause she was mine first born." Then she went through the reasons why she loved each of her children in a special way, ending with Ella. "I love Ella special cause she was mine baby."

How I longed to hear those words coming from my own mother. I hungered for her affirmation, for her tenderness, for some private expression of a mother's love for her daughter. After all, I was her baby.

Chapter Three

One Sunday morning I was awakened by the sing-song chant, "Ere shrimp! Raw shrimp!" I jumped up from the hard, horsehair sofa that I slept on in my grandparents' dining room and ran barefoot to the window, as the newness of the day came through to greet me. The bells of St. John's Episcopal Church rang out in the air. My grandmother was already yelling down from the parlor window to the hucksters in the street below who carried straw baskets atop their heads.

"I want green butter beans," Eva shouted. "You got yellow squash? Maybe corn-on-the-cob?" But she never asked them for the raw shrimp. Shrimp was shellfish and not kosher.

Ruth and I were afraid of our grandfather but Eva was a champion at juggling the family. We could count on her to hand us coins and send us to Solomon's Drugstore for ice cream cones if the tension grew.

In 1930, Aunt Sadie and Uncle Bob were the married couple in residence. The family had been abuzz when Uncle Daniel and Aunt Rae had their first child, a blond girl. One cool May morning after kindergarten my curiosity and daring met its first challenge. I invited a girlfriend of mine to come see the new infant. I felt ecstatic that I now had something called a cousin. I told my friend that I knew the way and took her hand to help her cross the street.

We walked briskly through Forsyth Park, circled the French-designed fountain, and were stopped short by a police officer on a horse. "Where are you girls going?" he said, looking down at us. I put my fists on my hips and smiled up at him.

"I'm four years old and have a new baby girl cousin with blond hair. I'm taking my friend to see her."

"That's nice," the policeman said. "Now, I'm taking you two to your parents."

"My mother'll be proud that I know the way to Uncle Daniel's." I felt important walking along the side of the horse and looking up at the policeman.

But when I got home, Minna broke into one of her uncontrollable rages, ending with, "You make me sick!" It seemed, at least to my young mind at the time, that practically everything I did upset her.

Ruth was in the first grade at that time and she got sent home from public school during a lice epidemic. I hovered around the bathroom, watching Mother and Winnie Lou scrape the black double-edged comb through Ruth's dark, silky hair, meticulously picking out all the bugs. I would gladly and enviously have taken the cooties from my sister's head, so I could have my hair stroked.

Every night at bedtime Minna commanded us, *"Kiss the mezuzah."* She never strayed from that routine. It was her nightly order. As soon as we heard those words Ruth and I would take turns climbing on a kitchen chair, placing our right hand on the small metal object that was nailed on the doorpost. The oblong container (about the size of two cigarettes) held a tiny, rolled-up paper on which are printed verses from Deuteronomy. The inscribed passages contained the command to "love the Lord your God, and to serve Him with all your heart and with all your soul."

"Now kiss your fingers," Mother instructed. This was to bring us luck. Orthodox Jews never enter or leave a room without kissing the mezuzah. Just before we snuggled under our bed covers, Mother led us in the prayer that began, *Here O Israel, the Lord is God, The Lord is One.* Our father never took part in our daily lives, and refused to participate in anything that dealt with religion.

As a Jewish girl growing up in a small Southern town, with a healthy and strong appetite for life, I began to view my being different with alarm and with suppressed feelings. On stormy nights, when lightning crackled and rain slapped against the windows, after everyone was asleep, I liked to get out of bed and hide behind the sofa in the living room of our apartment. As the streaks of light came into the room, again and again, slashing at the living room floor, I would stare at the sky pretending that I was sitting instead, on the beach in the sunshine, and remembering how reliable it seemed in its blue purity and warm light. And I would wonder: *What does being a good girl mean? Do I have to do everything their way? Something's wrong with me because I think and see things differently than Mother's way.*

When it was time for me to enter the first grade, my family made its second move. This apartment was on West Fortieth Street. Other than Mother staying in a state of bewilderment much of the time, nothing much seemed to change.

Mother continued to scream at Ruth and me for making too much noise when we played tug of war with our blanket at night to see who could get the most covers on her side of the bed. Or she would yell nightly, when we lay on the floor listening to the radio or fingering a movie magazine, "Go to sleep, Ruth-Naomi, I'm tired." She ran our two names together as if they were one, hyphenated. And she was forever ordering us to be quiet.

But worst of all was the situation with my father. He continued to have dark, moody rages and he owed money to many creditors. He gambled, stayed away from the store more than ever, and withdrew from his family. There were hushed silences when he entered the apartment; there was terror in the hearts of his daughters. We were kept unaware of just how bad things were because he and Mother pretended that nothing was wrong. But late at night, when every one was in bed, Ruth and I could hear our parents through the thin wall that separated our bedrooms.

"Your gambling is going to bankrupt us," Minna said.

"I didn't cause the damn Depression."

"It's not just the Depression. It's your gambling and other things. My sisters can find time for fun, but all I do is work and clean up behind you and the children. I have no life. I'm like an old woman. I've lost my youth."

Then we'd hear her start crying in the night, and while my sister buried her face in her pillow, trying to block out the terrible sounds, I vowed to myself never to let any man hurt me, and in particular, to never make me cry.

And so, Avram, who hadn't wanted to run a men's clothing store or marry in his early twenties and settle into a life bracketed solely by work and children, grew more and more lost with every passing day. He did not confide in anyone. Sometimes he stayed out all night. Other nights, at home, he'd sit at a table, listening to the radio until dawn, a Lucky Strike in one hand, a glass of rye in the other. He had a good singing voice and liked music. Sitting there all alone, his wiry shadow cast on a wall, he would lift his hands, the skin on his nicotine-stained fingers torn to shreds from his habit of picking them constantly, and like an orchestra leader, conduct the musicians only he saw.

Chapter Four

My aunt Layle came to baby-sit for me and Ruth one afternoon because Winnie Lou had taken the day off to attend the funeral of one of her sisters who had choked to death on a pork chop. While I lay on the floor coloring in my Little Orphan Annie coloring book, Ruth chattered nonstop about choosing the right color for her ballet slippers for the upcoming dance recital.

First I smeared the orange crayon across Annie's hair. Then I smeared the brown one on the page, trying to get the exact color I had seen in the Sunday comic section when Mother read the funny papers to me. The Katzenjammer Kids were her favorite comic strip. I could tell by the way she raised her voice and used a fake German dialect to make the Kids' point of view.

"You know, Ruth," Layle said, "you could dye the slippers gold, or even silver." Layle gave us all of her attention, showering us in nurturing, almost as if we were her children.

Ruth dashed into the bedroom to get her new satin slippers. Layle fingered the toe shoes and stroked the long pink ribbons that would tie around Ruth's ankles. At age fifteen, Layle, my father's half-sister, had taken the surrogate job of counseling us. Layle was tall and heavyset and wore her brown wiry hair in a Buster Brown hairstyle. Due to poor vision she wore thick eye-glasses that looked like the bottoms of two bottles. It was she who took us to dancing school and she who insisted that we visit a dentist. She also urged Mother to have our eyes examined by a doctor. When Layle had noticed how often Ruth asked everyone to repeat themselves, she suggested that Mother make an appointment to have my sister's hearing tested. Ruth had indeed suffered some hearing impairment from her bout with scarlet fever.

As Layle carefully considered the color for Ruth's shoes, she became aware of my father's frequent trips to the bathroom. He had come home for lunch and was going to drive Ruth to dancing class. My aunt's eyes followed Daddy as he walked around us, muttering strange words and disappearing back into the bathroom.

"Good-bye, little girls," he said as he left the living room.

"What's the matter, Zip?" Layle asked. He didn't answer.

Just as Layle started to speak to Ruth about her satin slippers, my father came back into the room and patted Ruth's black, silky hair.

"I'm sorry," he said. His eyes were glazed. My stomach felt like a peach pit had dried up and was stuck there. The rain was beating against the window pane, and where the window was slightly ajar, little drops sprinkled in and bounced from the sill to my arm. The pink crystal candy dish, one of Mother's wedding gifts, was sitting on the floor, filled with Hershey silver tops. I peeled one and slipped it into my mouth, sucking it slowly. The melted chocolate soothed me as it slid across the roof of my mouth.

After another trip to the bathroom, Daddy came over to me.

"I'm sorry, I really am," he said. This time when he reached to touch my scrawny arm, his hand was clammy and cold. The smocking across the yoke of my dress itched my skin. He rushed to the bathroom and we could hear the toilet flushing. Layle followed him and put her ear against the door. There was loud coughing and retching sounds coming from the bathroom.

"Look," Ruth said glancing out the window, "the sun's coming out, but it's still raining."

"That means the devil's beating his wife behind the bush," Layle told us. I kept my eyes glued to Orphan Annie's head. I was determined to find the right crayon to fill in the outlined figure of her dog Sandy.

Suddenly, Layle headed for the bathroom. She pushed open the door and hurried in. There on the sink she found a bottle of opium tincture poison that had been emptied. My father was lying on the floor next to the toilet.

"Zip," she said, "please get up. You have to keep walking." She was bigger than him, and she slipped her arm under his while she held him around the waist, draping his other arm over her shoulder.

"Ruth!" Layle shouted, "Call your mother at the store. And tell her to send an ambulance!" My six year old sister did as told, and shortly after the phone call, sirens screeched to a halt at our front door. Two men ran up the front steps and into our apartment. Layle told them that her brother had swallowed poison.

I heard the two men discussing how to lift Daddy and carry him down the steps. Mother and Uncle Bob had gone straight to the hospital. Layle stayed with us. When Ruth began to sob, Layle pulled her onto her lap and hugged her.

I continued coloring in my book, pushing my head closer to the page, my black crayon bearing down harder and harder as I filled in the picture of Daddy Warbucks. The crayon dug a hole in his head. The paper ripped from the pressure of my hand. I clenched my slight shoulders and jaws so tight it felt as though my head was being stretched on a wire hanger.

Layle made us grilled cheese sandwiches for supper. When Mother came home she immediately rushed into the bathroom. Layle had already given the emptied bottle to the men who had come in the ambulance. In fact, my aunt had cleaned the bathroom thoroughly, leaving no telltale signs.

"Ruth-Naomi, go to bed," Mother said after she had inspected the bathroom. Her face was pale, she had eaten off all her lipstick, and her hair hung limp around her cheeks. No one talked about the incident, but within a few days I overheard my mother talking on the phone to an aunt. "Avram's had a nervous breakdown. We're sending him away."

My father was sent to a mental hospital in Augusta for six months. The stress his illness caused Minna was almost too much for her to bear. Many days, after she closed the store, she would come rushing into the apartment, tear into the bathroom, and lock herself in. I would quietly follow her to the bathroom door to peep through the keyhole. There I watched my mother dissolve into tears. I longed to comfort her, to absorb her hurts, and indeed I did.

Now, when I kissed the *mezuzah* at bedtime, I hoped the religious instrument would heal my family.

"When's Daddy coming home?" I asked.

My mother didn't answer.

"Where's Daddy?" Still no answer.

Mother rushed around the apartment as if she hadn't heard a word I said. And when I questioned my sister, I was met with a carefully orchestrated rejection.

"Just drink your chocolate milk and shut up," Ruth said as she stirred the thick syrup in my glass.

"But the milk better not have one drop of cream floating on top or I'll dump it right down the toilet," I said, sulking. My sister painstakingly skimmed the cream from the top with a spoon.

More and more Minna relinquished much of the store's responsibility to her brother-in-law, Bob. She needed a man to lean on and help her with business decisions. My mother longed for some peace. She longed for a husband as strong as her father, and she used every excuse she could find to avoid visiting her husband at the mental hospital. She dreaded seeing him in such a weakened state.

In response to Ruth's constant badgering to tell her where Daddy was, Mother finally called Ruth into her bedroom one night and shut the door. "Your daddy's sick. He's had a nervous breakdown, but don't tell Naomi." Ruth had now become our mother's confidante, but that didn't stop me from wanting to know the truth.

"Ruth, where's Daddy?" I asked one Saturday morning as the two of us lay sprawled on the floor, listening to "Let's Pretend," on the radio. Ruth knew that I had stood outside the room listening to her conversation with mother, so she told me the truth. But I wasn't sure what nervous breakdown meant.

I trusted Ruth and wanted to believe anything she told me. But locked away, inside a secret compartment of my mind, was an ominous shadow that I couldn't shake. Ruth took out an old family photograph album and opened it on the dining room table.

"Naomi, come here," she called out. "Come and see how beautiful Mother and Daddy looked when they were younger." Staring up at us was a picture, from the 1920's of our parents' faces caught in romance, as their eyes smiled across the glass merchandise case in Joe Cohen's haberdashery where they had met.

While my father was still in the hospital, Uncle Bob and Aunt Sadie moved in with us. They were the one bright spot in that dark period. Both of them did their best to make life as normal as possible for us. Best of all, they were fun. Ruth and I would sit every night on the brown overstuffed sofa, our feet barely peeping over the edge. Now that my two front teeth were missing I avoided smiling. I didn't smile that often anyhow.

"Aunt Sadie, do the Charleston," Ruth would beg.

Uncle Bob wound up the Victrola, and he and our aunt would begin throwing their legs and arms wildly in the air, doing the Charleston across the living room floor. Aunt Sadie's hair was finger waved and she kicked her T strapped shoes back and forth, her knees knocking each other, while Uncle Bob, nattily dressed in checkered knickers and wing tipped oxfords, matched her every step. It was impossible for me and Ruth to hide our giggles, and we always applauded loudly when the dance was over and Bob and Sadie collapsed breathlessly on the sofa next to us. Unfortunately for my sister and me, my aunt and uncle had a crazy habit. Every time they kissed us they would bite us on our cheeks, leaving teeth marks.

During this whole episode I clung to the belief that my father might call or write explaining what had happened. No one said a word about his absence, other than the whispers I caught sailing through the night with Aunt Sadie, Uncle Bob and my mother, or when the family was gathered on the porch at Mama's house.

But each time the name Avram was mentioned, Eva would suddenly purse her lips and whisper, "Shh, don't talk in front of the *kinder.*"

"He's seeing a psychiatrist," I heard Aunt Sadie whisper into the black mouthpiece of the telephone, her other hand clutched tightly to the long black stem as she pushed her red Tangeed lips close to it. Aunt Sadie was the tallest of the four sisters, and that in itself made her glamorous. I hid behind the door just outside the hall listening to her every word.

Then the day arrived when our father finally came home from the hospital. He had been away six months. Mother made us get dressed early with implicit instructions to run up to Daddy as he got out of the car. When the car arrived a very different Avram emerged from the vehicle. He walked slowly and had lost a lot of weight. His skin had a sallow color and his glance seemed to go beyond where we stood.

"Kiss your daddy," Mother insisted, shoving Ruth and me toward the car. I was afraid. He seemed so changed, so small, so sad, so lost. No one had told me that he had received electric shock treatments, but I could tell that my father had been hurt.

"How are my pretty girls?"

Ruth kissed him on the cheek.

My grandfather Zipinsker had hired a driver to take his son for a

25

ride every afternoon. It was part of the new routine that had been worked out for my father. He would go to his store for several hours in the morning then be driven home. Winnie Lou prepared his lunch, then he took a nap. The driver would take him for a ride in the country and then back to the store. It was meant to make him feel that he was actually opening his business in the morning and closing it in the evening. But Avram had lost all interest in his store, in his family, and in his life. Instead he dreamed, staring vacantly, out of the window, and smoked.

The family went about its life in the usual manner. In the summer of 1933, my aunt Ella, who was quite beautiful and extremely popular with boys, and whom I wanted to grow up to be just like, was elected to take me on a holiday for my seventh birthday. I liked watching her dress for a date, pulling on a clingy knit dress over her short, curvy figure. She would straighten the seams in her stockings, then slide on her high heels.

We went to visit family in Beaufort, South Carolina, where I discovered the hushed gentility that romantic fiction and the mimosa myths associate with front parlor life in the Low Country. The Beaufort women spoke with long vowel's, their *g's* casually dropped, and they spoke softly, lyrically. The middle register of my mother's speaking voice and that of her sisters was always near hysteria. But what was most thrilling was hearing the Beaufort kinswomen talk of music and books, of traveling, and plans after college.

The youngest of my three girl cousins walked me to the public library, a place of endless fascination for me. I gazed in awe at the shelves filled with books. I loved the musty smell that came from them. My cousin showed me how to check out three books, which was the maximum allowed, and then we walked home. I fingered the cover of Andersen's Fairy Tales, and imagined myself one of the two sets of Bobbsey twins. I planned to ask my mother to take me to the library as soon as we got back to Savannah.

The oldest of my Beaufort cousins had her own car and drove us to the beach to swim and picnic. It was a peaceful, carefree time. We'd only been there a week when I announced one day as I came out of the chilly river water, "Take me home, Ella." I felt a terrible pang of loneliness for my mother and father. I needed to be with them.

"We can't go home yet, Naomi," Aunt Ella said, as she pulled the white rubber bathing cap off her red curls, shook her hair loose, and kicked off the rubber slippers she wore to keep the mud at the bottom of the river from sliding between her toes.

"I want to go home, now!" I screamed. My wet bathing suit clung to my small frame. The shells on the beach were prickly under my bare feet. I was homesick and wanted to be home, to curl up on the over-stuffed chair in our living room.

"We came for two weeks, and that's how long we're going to stay." Ella spoke in a firm voice.

On the drive back to Beaufort, I threw a tantrum, complete with ulti-matum. "If you don't take me home right this minute," I cried, "I'm going to jump out of the car and walk to Savannah!"

The next day, Aunt Ella took me home. My Beaufort cousin drove us right to our front door.

"Mother, Mother, guess what?" I came rushing into the living room, anticipating hugs and kisses welcoming me home. Instead I found my mother and father in the midst of a family calamity. Avram had caught Bob red-handed helping himself to money from the cash register and had not only fired him, but had ordered my uncle and Aunt Sadie out of our apartment.

"Where the hell did you think he was getting the money to start a syrup factory?" my father yelled. "Why didn't you watch him closer?"

"You think I can do everything? Be a policeman, watch the girls, and keep the books while you're off in the booby hatch?"

Aunt Sadie was sobbing as she packed her clothes. Uncle Bob was in a huff, and I could hear him screaming through the wall, "That crazy S.O.B. doesn't know what the hell he's talking about. He's a goddamn crazy man."

"What do you want?" my mother said, looking up at me after my aunt and uncle had left the apartment.

"I went to the library. . . read books. . . Uncle Sam let me eat all the candy I wanted." I babbled on, hoping to sidestep my mother's anger. "Please take me to the library so I can check out three books. Please!"

"Don't be such a *nudnik* !" my father barked. I didn't know what *nudnik* meant, but I was sure it wasn't anything good. I guessed it meant ugly.

Then Ruth came into the room and slid her hand into mine. "I'll walk you to the library, Naomi." Ruth asked Mother for a nickel so we could buy a Baby Ruth candy bar on the way. Mother fished a dime out of her black pocketbook. After we got our library cards and checked out three books apiece we walked back home.

"I'll give you two Norma Shearers if you give me that Jean Harlow you just got," Ruth said on our walk home. Layle had given us a stack of movie magazines and we would sit for hours cutting out the ones we liked. Ruth tried to assure me that it wasn't so bad that Uncle Bob and Aunt Sadie were leaving.

"If you throw in that picture of Clark Gable, I'll swap," I said.

As vigorously as two Wall Street traders we began to negotiate and swap our cutouts even before we got home.

Chapter Five

My sister and I pretended we didn't hear our father roaring when the Jewish holidays rolled around. "Those bastards I do business with cheat me all week and then stand facing the east wall like religious zealots," Avram yelled.

"Well, just show your face at least," Minna pleaded, coaxing Avram to spend some time in the synagogue. She showed him her new brown shoes and the blue button up sweaters she had gotten for Ruth and me.

"You want me to go to *shul* with those *gonifs*, those hypocrites? Remember what that damned banker did to your Papa and you!"

"But it doesn't look right!"

"Who gives a goddamn what looks right!"

As far as my father was concerned, religion was for his wife and daughters, not for him. He was disenchanted with embracing God. It seemed to have gotten him nowhere. But despite my father's continued anger at other Jews and his railing at God, he and my mother still considered themselves to be Orthodox Jews. We observed Rosh Hashanah for two days, and once services ended, Mother walked Ruth and me to Mama's house to celebrate the holiday with a festive dinner of chicken soup with *matzoh* balls, roast chicken, carrot *tzimmes*, potato *kugel*, and the family staple, rice and gravy.

It didn't matter how hot the day was, if you were a Jewish child in the South it meant dressing in new wool clothes to wear to Shul. Being near the sea, on the banks of a broad river, Savannah swelters even in fall. It is beastly when the humid heat rises from the very earth one walks on. Nevertheless, it was socially unacceptable not to have on a new wool dress, a heavy sweater, and tight shoes for the holidays.

Dressed in our woolen outfits we all went to the Zipinskers' home for dinner on the second day of Rosh Hashanah. My father would be rude to Grandma, but she did her best to ignore it. Ruth and I loved the gentility and softness of our grandfather. He was a kind and patient man and always kept a jar of sugar cookies for us. He had many times baby-sat for us when our parents wanted to go out for an evening. We loved when he sat on the side of our bed and told us stories of the old country.

When we walked to the synagogue for Yom Kippur Mother always instructed, "Be a mensch, be sure to go upstairs and kiss Grandma, Tante Silverberg, and Mama." I didn't understand why the women sat in a separate balcony above the men. Grandma and Tante smelled of moth balls and bad breath because they weren't allowed to eat, drink water, or even brush their teeth until the twenty-four hour fast was over. After the day of fasting, the family met once more at Mama's house. This time, the meal at the end of a long day was herring and foods that contained milk products.

At the end of the fasting period Ruth loved to tattle on our uncles, who professed to observe Yom Kippur, but whom she had seen through the window of Lane's drugstore as they blatantly ate a ham sandwich. They not only ate, but ate something that wasn't even kosher.

Another hushed silence fell over our family in the late fall of 1933. Ruth and I were taken to Mama's house by Winnie Lou, she told us that Grandpa Zipinsker had died. We were not allowed to go to the funeral and were kept away from his house. Following Grandpa's death, my father grew more depressed and we saw even less of him than before.

A short time after that my mother wanted to move again. There were so many bad memories for her connected to Fortieth Street that she'd become superstitious. We rented another apartment, this time on Maupas Avenue, on the east side of Savannah. Mother arranged every piece of furniture in every room, catty-cornered. There was a shed in the backyard of the red brick building that I designated as a dollhouse where I could take care of a doll that my father had bought me on one of his trips to New York. I sat for hours with a make believe thermometer stuck between the doll's legs, wiping its forehead with a damp cloth.

"Let me kiss your *kepele*," I cooed to my sick little baby.

"If you puts just a pinch of salt on th' crown of th' baby's head, the evil spirit will be warded off." Winnie Lou stood over me and shook her finger in my face as she gave me sage advice for healing my wounded doll.

The summer that my father's favorite sister, Jean, was to be married, I was chosen as her flower girl. Her eight-year-old ugly duckling flower girl, so I thought, as I walked down the aisle in my pink, silk dress, tossing out only one pale rose petal at a time. I intended to save most of the petals for myself. I wanted to play wedding for days, with me as the bride. From what I had observed in my family I had begun to feel that marriage was the ultimate goal, that males were simply superior to females. I was growing up believing that my existence on earth depended on being the wife of a strong man who would scatter rose petals so my ladylike feet would never touch the ground.

I saved the fragrant rose petals and carefully hid them inside my bureau drawer at home, preferring to hang them around my neck.

Never having had a brother, my first awareness of little boys was my cousin Arnold. I was nine when aunt Sadie gave birth to him. She had tried to conceive for seven years, and after a miserable pregnancy, baby Arnold came along. They lived two blocks away from our apartment and after school I would run around the corner to see him. Uncle Bob's mother had just arrived from Rumania and she helped my aunt care for him. She wrapped his legs tightly in a baby blanket, restricting his leg movement. To me he seemed to be wrapped in swaddling cloth. I wondered if they thought they had brought a Jesus child into our family. They certainly treated him differently than my sister and I had been treated. They protected him from everything imaginable. And he immediately developed terrible asthma. Even as a ten year old I could see that he had no breathing room. In spite of it all, Arnold turned out to be an amazingly succesful law professor.

My mother had struck a bargain with Ebba Olson Thompson when Ebba opened her new school of dance in a space above an old store on Broughton Street, close to Daddy's store. Ebba had agreed to let both me and my sister attend classes for the price of one. It was my dream come true. That was the moment I'd been waiting for, and at last I felt almost equal to my sister Ruth.

The magical moment finally arrived. One afternoon, after school, Layle took me to buy tap shoes of my own. Our aunt Layle was very proud of her two nieces. She herself was in an adult tap dancing class at Ebba's because she had never had the opportunity as a small child.

When the special recital was to take place, Layle was to be in the performance with us. And our uncles and aunts would be in the audience to applaud. However, I would cringe, when in the dressing room, the non-Jewish girls, all wearing batiste underpants and frilly slips, sniffed the air, and pointed to the gauze bag hanging around my neck. I envied their prettie undies as I pulled off my boy's undershirt from my father's store. Uncle Bob's mother had insisted that my sister and I wear the stupid bag of brown, mushy asafetida tied around our necks on a string. It was believed by Eastern European women to ward off infantile paralysis. It looked and smelled like a wad of shit.

Finally the day of the recital arrived, and I was as excited as I can ever remember being. Pink tulle tutus flared out from our little bodies. The bodices were satin with silver sequins. Our new, shiny pink ballet slippers had been kept in boxes until the night of the performance.

I stuffed lambs wool inside the toes of my ballet slippers and slid them on, the pink ribbon crisscrossing and tying around my ankles. One of my numbers was a tap dance, to the tune of "I'm An Old Cowhand from the Rio Grande." As I tapped my little heart out, I searched the audience until I spotted Aunt Ella, Aunt Shirley, Uncle Moses, Aunt Sadie and Uncle Bob, Aunt Rae and Uncle Daniel, and my mother and father. Daddy's two brothers and Grandma also came. The entire clan was there, almost filling up two rows.

When my part of the recital was over I rushed into the dressing room where I joined my classmates in reliving the thrill of having just been on stage. Then, three of the girls who were to be in the next performance went into an adjoining room to change their costumes. It was a particularly cold night, and the girls huddled around the space heater for extra warmth as they were fastening the hooks on their costumes.

One of the girls brushed against the gas heater and her costume went up in flames. The sound — like a bomb explosion — shook the building. People began running frantically toward the exit. The child's desperate cry could be heard high above the room as she ran through the door like a whirling dervish to escape the horror of the fire. A sickening odor of burning flesh wafted through the air, filling our nostrils. As she darted toward the outside door she ignited two others. Screams pierced the magic of the night and ambulances screeched through the darkness to the back door of the auditorium.

"Where's Ruth?" Layle shouted as she grabbed my hand to run through the narrow passage leading to the outside. The cold concrete scraped across my bare feet like a potato grater.

"She already finished her last number and she's out front with Mother and Daddy," I said. Layle led me through the parking lot to where my parents were waiting with Ruth. The silence in the car was deafening.

Just as my father pulled his black Dodge away from the curb, I saw the mother of one of the burned girls leaning on the dancing teacher's shoulder, sobbing. Mrs. Jones, the school's piano player, had lost her only child. Ruth put her arm around my shoulders.

Two days later Ruth walked around the corner with me to view the body of my friend, Mrs. Jones' daughter. The living room was filled with people and one by one we walked up to the coffin to pay our respects. My friend was dressed in one of the costumes that she had worn in the recital. The dead child looked like a Shirley Temple doll in the blue satin sailor pants, white satin middy blouse with a blue collar, and a pair of black, patent leather tap shoes with large black bows. She looked as though she had been choreographed right into heaven.

I bit down hard on my lip so as not to cry in front of the others as I realized I would never again tap next to my friend.

Outside of the Jones' house a funeral procession of cars had formed to drive to the cemetery. But Ruth took my hand and walked me home. Within a week, the other two girls died.

Chapter Six

Just when our family was beginning to enjoy a semblance of normalcy, when my mother had started taking a day off every week to play cards with Sadie and her sister-in-law Rae, our whole world suddenly seemed to collapse.

Bankrupt!

That dreaded word that I'd heard whispered on the side porch at Charlton Street, at my grandmother's, had happened to us. My father was stunned that he had to close his store in order to satisfy creditors. It took several months to handle most of the details and during that time a mysterious fire engulfed Zip's. The money from the fire insurance helped tide us over for about six months. But eventually we were evicted from our apartment because the rent hadn't been paid for several months.

Ruth and I had to give up dancing classes. Our father sold his black Dodge. Mother denied herself clothes while making every effort to shield her daughters from the harsh truth. And Daddy's health was failing.

"Please Daniel, I have to have forty dollars." I cringed each time I heard my mother beg her brother for help. He had just driven us home from Sunday school. My uncle handed Mother a fistful of bills.

"I'm ashamed to ask Papa," my mother said, with a quiver in her voice. I sat in the back seat next to my sister and my cousin, all of us pretending that we hadn't heard a word. That night, my father sat at the kitchen table with his gambling sheets, bold letters marking the columns for his horse-racing picks the next day. My mother watched him but made no comment.

As my parents made plans to move to a less expensive apartment I was once again shipped away while the family faced a crisis. But I always knew and felt the pain of what was going on. It's just that I shoved my sorrows into that unknown secret place, the dark cave that my heart had become, so that no one would think I was afraid. I didn't understand why everything that happened in my family was such a secret.

This time I was sent off to my Aunt Jean and her Yankee husband in New Canaan, Connecticut, while my family moved. Getting there had been a feat in itself. Aunt Layle took me aboard a coastal steamer because in those days traveling by boat from Savannah to Baltimore, New York, or Boston, was cheaper than by rail. It took three nights and two days to get there, and one evening an Amateur Night was held. I got dressed up in my red and white polka dot costume from my last dance recital and entertained the passengers by tap dancing for hours, pretending I was Ginger Rogers waiting for bashful Fred Astaire. Lightning and thunder took over the sky, cracking through the room when a huge storm appeared. The boat started rocking and listing from side to side. I turned pea green, threw my hand over my mouth and made a quick escape to the rail. Layle said that the only food I would touch for the entire trip was pickled tongue and cupcakes, which in turn made her seasick.

My aunt and uncle owned a stationery store on the main street in New Canaan, and in the rear was a soda fountain. Aunt Jean told me to eat all the ice cream with sprinkles I wanted. She talked to me, explaining her feelings and encouraging me to share mine with her. She took me to Radio City Music Hall in Manhattan to see Martha Raye. I made a silent vow never to go back to Savannah again. I wanted to be Aunt Jean's daughter, to walk through the woods in the rear of their house, to read all the wonderful Nancy Drew books lined on the shelves of their store. It was so cool, so serene, walking beside the brook that ran across a pebbled bottom. Never had I been so happy.

On my eleventh birthday, Aunt Jean gave me a surprise party in the side garden. It was the first birthday party I ever had.

"Honey, I want you to go downtown with my friend's daughter and help her select something pretty," Aunt Jean said a couple of days before the party. I hated that girl; she was fat and talked with a Brooklyn accent. While we were browsing through the clothing store, I persuaded the nine year old to get the ugliest pair of socks there. Among the brightly wrapped packages at my party was that pair of socks.

"I hate them. I hate all of you. I want to go home!" I screamed. My aunt had every reason to slap me across the face, but instead she tried to explain to me some of life's more social graces. Above all, she knew that my outburst had to do with the fact that it was time for me to go back to Savannah, something I didn't want to do. I ran away from my party through the woods and hid under a clump of elm trees near the brook.

"You can always consider New Canaan your second home, honey," Aunt Jean said in a calm voice. "We'll write to each other often." Almost unnoticed, the summer came to an end. And with a lifetime of memories stored in my heart, Layle and I boarded the train for our trip back home.

Back in Savannah, I found my family settled into the Tomochichi Apartments, an eight-unit building on Habersham Street. Ruth had taken half the drawer space for her things and left the other half for me. My sister had also discovered through a schoolmate that lived in one of the apartments that she could buy cigarettes for a penny a piece at Ellerbee's confectionery. Winnie Lou now only worked for us two days a week. She helped me unload the boxes that contained my clothes, books, and other belongings. My father seemed relieved to be from under the pressure of running a business, and he liked working at Uncle Moses's pawn shop. My Uncle Moses was the clown in the family, and had a heart as big as the sky.

In the meantime Mother had taken a part time job working for Yacham and Yacham, a clothing store on West Broad Street. They referred to themselves as "Uncle Sammy's boys," because they had served in World War I. While our move seemed a notch down from our last apartment, there was a renewed energy. Most of the tenants were young families with small children who were embarking on a new life.

In the evenings the adults would gather under a large cherry tree in the front yard, sip cokes and visit, after the children had been put to bed. The smaller children followed me as though I was the Pied Piper. I could hardly wait to grow up, marry and have my own.

One night while the neighbors sat around, I heard them laughing as my father told them a story that had taken place in the pawn shop. He said that a young black boy around ten years old had come into the store to pawn an item.

"How old are you?" Uncle Moses said.

"I'm old enough to pawn something," the boy answered.

"You're not a legal age," Uncle Moses said.

"Well, Mr. Moses, I'm old enough to fuck."

Daddy assured the group that his brother-in-law had indeed taken the item in for pawn. There were many other amusing stories that took place at my uncle's pawn shop. Daddy talked about Southern society people who hocked their family heirlooms when times were tough. In fact, Uncle Daniel's wife had quite a collection of beautiful jewelry and silver serving pieces that had never been redeemed from his pawn shop.

It was on those nights that my father and mother seemed the happiest, and I began to absorb their lightness.

After the days of trading movie stars had run their course Ruth and I enjoyed piling up in our double bed at night, listening to the radio. We squabbled over whether to listen to Jack Benny and Rochester or my favorite, the big band music of Harry James, broadcast from the Meadowbrook Ballroom in New Jersey. And we'd spend hours in bed reading aloud from the novel, *Gone With The Wind.* An open box of chocolate Mallomar cookies sat between us. Those nine, divine, round, chocolate-covered marshmallows, perched seductively atop graham crackers, were divided carefully as we ate and read. The ninth cake always brought on a struggle.

One night, in the middle of munching and reading, there was a squeaking sound coming from the adjoining bedroom. Ruth said, "You know Mother and Daddy are doing it."

"Doing what?" I said, nibbling slowly on the Mallomar.

"Putting his thing in her," Ruth said. "Don't you know about having babies?"

"I don't believe you. Not Mother and Daddy. What thing?"

"All married people do it," Ruth insisted.

"You're a liar."

"What do you think all that squeaking is?" Ruth told me that sometimes at night she could hear our parents whispering, then our father would go into the bathroom after a few minutes and flush the toilet.

"I peeped through the door one night while you were visiting Aunt Jean. Guess what? I saw him kiss her titty!"

"Geeky!" I shrieked and grabbed the last cookie and plopped the whole gooey mound into my mouth.

My favorite family in the Tomochichi Apartment complex was our next door neighbors. They had a young black girl, Fern, working for them. She lived in, cooked for them, and helped care for their son. The husband was a traveling salesman who couldn't drive, so he took a chauffeur on the road with him every week. His wife worked at Lerners and was afraid to be alone in the apartment. Our front doors were not more than three feet apart and were often left open. It felt at times as though we were all just one big family.

Though Fern was only two years older than Ruth, she already seemed like a woman. She was tall and shapely and an avid reader, often suggesting to Ruth and me that we read the Bible. Ruth had grown quite tall and was only two inches shorter than Fern.

When Ruth asked Fern why she wasn't living with her family, Fern said, "I'm the youngest in my family. I have eleven brothers and sisters. My parents can't afford to feed all of us."

"What about school?" Ruth said. She was fascinated that Fern was earning her own living.

"I go to night school after I finish work." Fern had a deep religious conviction and took her church seriously. Several of her sisters and brothers had left the South and urged her to do the same, but she didn't want to be that far away from her aging parents, so she chose domestic work to augment the little they had.

To Ruth the inequity was that while she and I went to school, Fern washed and ironed clothes. And if we wanted to see a movie together, Fern had to sit in the balcony, which was reserved for "Colored." I couldn't help but compare it to my grandmother sitting in the balcony at the Orthodox synagogue.

I was glowing when Fern invited me to visit her parents in the country. They lived on the outskirts of Savannah and raised chickens. I loved gathering and holding the warm eggs in my palm. We sat on the back steps sipping fresh milk and eating warm corn bread with sorghum syrup. Fern's mother fixed us bologna sandwiches with mayonnaise on sliced white bread. I was struck by the tenderness that Fern and her mother displayed to one another.

Walking through the woods behind the modest frame cottage, we inhaled the fragrance of the tall pine trees. Being out in nature had a magical way of making our world more equitable. Fern pulled a long green pine needle and sucked on it. I walked rapidly to keep up with her long strides. I barely reached her shoulder. She turned to me and said, "My sister says that in New York, white children and Negroes go to the same school."

"Do you wish you could go to school with us?" I said, wondering how I'd feel if the roles had been reversed. June bugs flew around the trunks of the tall pine trees, whistling across our faces. Fern reached out and caught one in the palm of her hand.

"I quit wishing, Naomi. I've learned to take what comes. I read the Bible, and that's how I learn." It bothered me that on the bus ride home I had to sit up front while Fern sat in back. And though the black families had long ago moved from the basement beneath my grandparents' house on Charlton Street, I always felt that special bond that I'd formed with John.

When the little boy who Fern took care of came home from kindergarten with a fever and covered with a rash, Fern broke out with red spots up and down her arms and legs a few days later. She scratched incessantly. After a week of Ruth and me scratching ourselves continuously, Mother phoned the doctor to make a house call. She dashed around the apartment, polishing every table, throwing away the many newspapers scattered on the floor, and screaming, "Hurry and get dressed. The doctor's coming." He also planned to visit several other families in the Tomochichi apartments who had complained of "the itch."

When the doctor arrived, he carefully examined each member of our family, sliding his hands over the red splotchy spots on our arms and legs. When he got to me, he asked me to remove my underpants.

"No!" I screamed, in absolute horror.

"I have to examine you and those pants must come off," the doctor said.

I flew into the bathroom and locked the door. "You nasty old man, don't you dare touch me under my underpants!" I yelled at the closed door.

"They have chiggers," the doctor announced, closing his black bag, as he readied to leave. He prescribed a thick paste made with sulfur.

"Please understand," Mother said to the doctor as she walked him to the front door, "we have very little money now and just can't pay." I felt the sadness, the shabby humbleness of my mother's words. She was also mortified by my behavior and I could hear her apologizing to the doctor.

When he left she immediately turned on me. "You're the meanest goddamned child I've ever seen! You embarrassed me in front of the doctor." With that she threw a pot, then its lid, across the kitchen. They both hit the wall and immediately rolled to the floor.

I wondered if my mother forgot that she had warned me about the nasty part of my body between my legs. I was having a hard time trying to distinguish what was dirty and what was clean. Or what was love. Confusion and hurt overwhelmed me. I ran back into the bathroom, drew my knees to my forehead and sank against the bathtub, my head resting on my folded arms. The bangs across my forehead clung damply to my skin as tears rolled down my thin arms and legs, covering the itchy spots the doctor had examined.

In contrast to Mother's utensil throwing to discipline us, my daddy used the dark silent method for authority. He frowned, he scowled, and if that didn't work, he stormed about the apartment frightening us into believing he would hit us. "If you don't listen to me, right now, I'm going to get a big stick to you!"

Ruth hated him. I secretly adored him. In my secret compartment I told myself: *If I can just be good enough, pretty enough, smart enough, then Daddy will love me and we'll be happy.*

My thirteenth birthday meant that I was allowed to baby-sit for the young couples living in the Tomochichi. They paid me a quarter an evening. I always pretended that their children were mine, and fantasized about marriage and having a husband.

When my sister, Fern and I had the house to ourselves, Fern not only taught Ruth and me how to make fudge, she also taught us all the latest jitterbug steps. The three of us took turns stirring the hot, bubbly chocolate, and as one of us stood at the stove stirring, the other two danced.

"The dipsy doodle's the thing to beware! The dipsy doodle will get in your hair . . . !" we yelled and screamed, off key. And every time we heard Frank Sinatra singing on the radio, the three of us would swoon as if we were actually in the live audience, falling into a pretend faint on our living room floor.

One night, after much begging, Mother said that Fern could spend the night with us. She slept between Ruth and me. Mother yelled at us constantly to stop giggling and go to sleep. The louder she yelled, the more we giggled. Soon after we finally settled down, I heard Daddy fumbling with the kitchen door. The sounds were muffled and his voice incoherent.

"He's drunk," Ruth whispered.

I felt such shame. I didn't want Fern or anyone to hear Daddy coming home that way. The noise grew louder. We heard him stagger, slump against the wall, and fall. He vomited in the kitchen sink just before he made it to his bedroom. Mother rushed to the kitchen to clean up the slime before we could see it.

Fern reached over and took my hand.

"It's all right, Naomi. I won't tell anyone." There was a huge lump in my chest.

As Avram lay in bed, Minna screamed, "You lost all the money that my brother loaned us. What do you expect us to do?" He lay listless and unhearing. She never dared utter a word when he was awake and sober. I wanted to protect her but was unable to understand why she was so afraid of him. My anger was directed at her for being so passive.

Serving pancakes swimming in syrup the next morning, Mother announced profoundly, "Men are such babies, don't ever forget that." She poured each of us a steaming cup of hot cocoa.

"Why don't you divorce Daddy?" I said after everyone had left the table but Mother and me. My mother ignored me.

"Do you think Scarlett O'Hara would put up with that from a man?" I had taken Scarlett on as my idol.

"Scarlett O'Hara can go to hell!" my mother yelled after me, throwing a pot against the wall.

Chapter Seven

I was pubescent when I discovered that being popular was a necessary credential for a Southern girl. Scarlett had certainly used it to her advantage. When one of our neighbors at the Tomochichi Apartments noticed that there were a lot of teenage boys hanging around me while my mother was at work, she said to her one day, "Minna, your Naomi sure is popular." It was said the same way someone would declare that their dog had a pedigree. Minna shrugged her shoulders. She didn't pay too much attention to what my sister and I did with our free time.

When I bragged to Ruth that I had been kissed the most after an exciting evening spent at the Saturday Night Club, a social group to which my peers and I belonged, she warned me not to let any boy touch my bust. I loved those Saturday nights where we met boys, went for scheduled short walks in the neighborhood and played kissing games like Post Office and Spin-the-bottle.

"You know what? During Spin-the-bottle, Gloria let two boys run a hankie back and forth over her sweater," I said, tugging the blankets up under my neck.

"Well, you better not." Those were Ruth's last words before she fell asleep. As I lay there, I wondered: what bust? There was hardly anything there for boys to touch. My concern drove me to tell Fern about my lack of physical progress. I trusted whatever wisdom Fern would offer. Early Sunday morning, I dashed across the hall to her apartment where she was dressing to go to church.

Our talk about breasts was brief but enlightening. Fern told me that her mother had once tied a piece of gauze material tightly around her breasts so they wouldn't be too prominent and to discourage their rapid growth.

"It doesn't look as though I'm ever going to have any," I said, stretching my cotton blouse tightly across my upper body. I looked down dejectedly at my flat chest.

"You will," Fern said. "You're just a late bloomer." She grabbed her purse and Bible and left for Sunday school.

Trying to get my mother to communicate with me about anything personal was unproductive. One day when she came home from work I shoved a magazine with an advertisement for Kotex in front of her. "What's this?" I said. Even though I knew, I wanted her to be the one to tell me about menstruation.

"Don't bother me, Naomi, I'm too busy for your silly questions. I'm in a hurry."

Once more it was left to Ruth and Fern to educate me about impending womanhood. Theirs had already been launched and it now remained for me to start having "the curse." My sister and Fern suggested I get ready to buy a belt and that soon I could expect blood in my panties. One night I had watched my mother through the bathroom keyhole and I saw her step out of her droopy underpants and hold them inside the toilet bowl to rinse away the blood. Then she strapped the belt around her hips and fastened a pad in place. At least I knew now what the monthly ritual looked like.

Finally, when I reached fourteen all sorts of budding began to take place, including my breasts. But contrary to Fern's conclusion that I had nothing to worry about, and my sister's sole advice not to let boys touch them, I viewed my developing femaleness as a manifestation of my freakishness. When other girls confided that boys only liked girls who weren't too smart, I took this as further evidence that I was odd. I was smart, but I felt dumb. I felt like a klutz and a clod as hormones ran amok in my body.

Cramps seized me one day as I was walking home from school and I could feel the moistness between my legs. I rushed into the bathroom and called Ruth who verified that, yes, it was what I thought it was. Then my sister demonstrated how to loop the gauze of the Kotex onto the hook of the sanitary belt.

"Don't worry, you're not broken," Ruth assured me.

"Please," I begged, "don't tell Mother."

Of course, Ruth told her almost immediately and my mother smiled and said, *"Mazel tov."* Then she put a bowl of chicken soup on the kitchen table for me. Mother always fed us chicken soup when we were sick but I didn't think I was ill. The painful cramps convinced me that females, as men often said, were born to suffer. That night, I went across the hall and told Fern.

"Well, now you've got something to look forward to every month," Fern said.

"Don't tell me this happens every month!"

"Yes, that's when you ovulate and can get pregnant."

"Do you mean I can't kiss a boy when I have my period?"

Fern filled me in on the facts of life and how women conceived. She told me about condoms and that many modern women were using a diaphragm as a method of birth control.

Adolescence seemed filled with conflict and confusion, mood swings, loneliness and self-doubt. My childhood unhappiness had not been overcome and my mother's one big concern was whether or not the boys I brought home were Jewish. She was constantly letting us know that we were not to be interested in any boy who wasn't Jewish.

I usually told a white lie rather than incur my mother's wrath by admitting the truth, which was that I liked Gentile boys better than the ones I knew from B.B. Jacob Sunday School. I was very careful not to invite a non-Jewish boy to my house if my mother was home. When she did ask about some of the boys who visited, I automatically said, "He's Jewish. We were studying." If his name was McGilicudy, I didn't stop to explain.

I'd also begun to question in my own mind — since no one ever talked about it — what exactly religion was or the need for it. I started pulling away from some of the traditions that had been thrust upon me, not only becoming curious about the different religions my friends at school observed but also looking for a deeper meaning to life. Very little in the way of satisfactory answers came my way.

I lived in a city dripping with Spanish moss and antebellum charm. Just being close to the marshland is seductive. And yet, I was being taught to repress any sign of sexuality, to deny the sensual impulses that were a natural part of my emerging adult personality. What I desperately needed was a teacher, some sound advice from a person I could trust. Although my Aunt Jean and I wrote to one another and shared very intimate thoughts, she was still way off in Connecticut. And Fern and Ruth were not yet women themselves. In retrospect, I believe what made puberty so difficult were those long summers in the deep South which are accelerated by the fanfaronade and tensions of a region drenched in eroticism.

What I had developed, however, was a strong will to get what I wanted, when I wanted it, and I was tenacious about it. Anxious to have the pretty clothes that my wealthier teenage girlfriends had, I found a way to get them for myself. Every week Fern and I made the rounds from the house of one of my aunts to another with empty suitcases. We filled them with all of the family's discarded clothing. On Saturdays, the two of us would hold a rummage sale on the railroad tracks at the corner of Thirty Second and East Broad Streets. Even when the heat was 102 degrees, we lugged along a card table to display our merchandise and carried our lunch in brown paper bags.

When *Gone With The Wind,* was made into a movie, Ella treated Ruth and me. We stood in line at the Bijou Theater for three hours to see the film. At home I looked into the mirror and saw Scarlett. I decided that emulating the beautiful, willful, and determined Scarlett would be far more to my advantage than being like the docile, sweet and ever-accepting Melanie. In fact, I wanted to give Melanie a shove that would send her flying across the room. I thought about this one night as I tried to fall asleep while being bitten by tiny things crawling in the bed I shared with my sister. Just past midnight, I jumped out of bed, and began screaming.

"I'm not going to sleep with these damned bedbugs one more night." I carried my pillow to the big overstuffed chair in the living room and camped out, staging my first protest. My family didn't understand me. And I didn't understand their way of life.

"I'll sleep here for the rest of my life unless you buy us a new bedroom set," I screamed, waking my parents. "Do you think Scarlett O'Hara would put up with this?"

"Scarlett O'Hara can go to hell," Mother yelled back. My father smiled, walked back to their bedroom and said, "Mother, go downtown tomorrow, to Haverty's and buy new twin beds and a matching vanity."

At last, a victory.

Chapter Eight

The fact that Benedictine Military Academy was directly across the street from my junior high school meant that every Friday at noon, during recess, I could stand outside Richard Arnold Junior High and watch the boys of the Academy, in their gray uniforms, go through their military drills. Tootie Lamatta, a good-looking Italian, was one of them. His eyes were deep set and dark brown, like hot burning coals when he looked at me. His skin seemed to have a permanent suntan, and when he smiled, a set of even white teeth flashed behind his full lips. The sixteen year old Tootie also played football, so I was doubly impressed with him. One day he offered to tow me home on his bicycle.

I hopped up on the bar that ran in front of his seat. My legs hung side saddle. He held one arm around my waist. I could feel his muscular thighs against me. Tootie turned his bike around the corner and headed toward Habersham Street. Huge oak trees formed an arch above our heads, as their branches reached from opposite curbs toward each other. The branches were thick and extended at angles so long and so far, it defied physics. I wondered how high they would grow before they would fall. The leaves were full, rich, and green. The branches formed a lattice patched with blue sky, stitched with bluebirds and iridescent pigeons. Just as Tootie's bike started over the curb, we collided with a blue Chevrolet. The man quickly got out of his car and ran to us.

"My God, are you hurt?" he cried, as he pulled me to my feet.

"My bike has a bent fender," Tootie said as he stood his bicycle up to examine it.

"You want me to take you to a doctor?" the man asked. "Can I give you a ride home?"

After the man drove off, although I had some bruises on my legs and one arm, I begged Tootie: "Don't tell my mother." All I could think of was how Mother would have screamed at me for being stupid and that was something I no longer wanted to hear.

On Saturday night following the bicycle incident, Tootie drove me home in his old maroon colored Ford convertible. We had both attended the Saturday night ballroom class. My mother didn't know that I was coming home by car, with a boy. Worse yet, with a boy who wasn't Jewish.

I was fifteen years old at the time and had taken to wearing my hair long, covering one eye, just like Veronica Lake, I thought. I had seen her picture in one of Aunt Layle's movie magazines. Layle had become a beautician, which was considered declasse in our family. She had given Ruth and me frizzy permanents while practicing to get her license. But our hair had finally grown out. Ruth had shown me how to shave my legs for the first time just before I dressed to leave home. There were a few nicks on my calves to prove my passage into womanhood.

Even with my sexy hairdo, it was hard for me to believe that an older boy found me beautiful. At least that's what Tootie had said every time he tagged me when I was dancing with someone else. On the drive home Tootie pulled his car into the parking lot at Leopold's Soda Shop. We ordered curb service. He had a chocolate milk shake, I had a dope with vanilla, which was what we called Coca Cola. After Tootie paid the carhop, he headed the car toward Thunderbolt, a quaint fishing village on the way to Tybee Beach. He pulled the car to a stop in front of several shrimp boats that were anchored in the river.

"My family's in the shrimping business," he said. He pointed to several ships afloat in front of us. The Thunderbolt Bridge was barely visible through the moonlight, but I caught a glimpse of it shimmering on the water. It seemed so distant. The river's sheen cast romantic magic about us, like angel dust. Pools of moonlight flooded the car.

"Do you go shrimping on those boats?"

"We sell our seafood at a market on the docks," he said. Then Tootie took my hand and pulled me close to him. I felt my heart stop for exactly ten minutes. I knew that my mother would kill me if I kissed him.

Tootie's olive skin looked like velvet in the moonlight, with the Savannah sky as a backdrop. My head wanted to scream, "Yes! Yes! Kiss me, please. The way Clark Gable kissed Vivian Leigh in *Gone With The Wind.* " But instead, my brain froze. So did my vocal chords. No one had told me what to say or do. I suddenly realized I was on my own.

"Your hair is beautiful," the handsome Italian football player said.

I felt numb from head to toe. Except for a part of me that wasn't numb at all. There was a twitter of butterflies in my lower stomach, spreading toward my thighs. Only I didn't understand that part. Tootie put his arms around my shoulders, drawing me close. He turned my body toward him, leaned over and put his lips on mine. I sat frozen, like a popsickle. As he pressed his mouth harder on mine, I grew more frigid, like a stone of refusal.

Tootie pulled away, put one hand under my chin, and tilted my head up a bit.

"You know, girl," he said, kissing my hair and rubbing his cheek along the nape of my neck, "you're supposed to open your mouth."

I wanted to die that instant, while staring at the Thunderbolt River with the boats and their colored flags swaying overhead. My legs felt like the jellyfish I'd seen on the beach. This was the moment. I took a deep breath, leaned forward, closed my eyes and parted my lips. I didn't know about French kissing. This was my first kiss since the days of Spin the Bottle, when pecks on the cheek were the order of the day. My parents had no idea how many major changes had taken place in the dating codes since they were teenagers. My sister Ruth was only intent on warning me not to let boys touch me, although she was willing to help me cover up with intricate excuses when our mother got suspicious about my being away from the house too long.

"I think I better go home," I said.

Tootie didn't say another word. He fingered my hair, planted a kiss on my forehead and drove me home. All I could think of was how adorable our children would be.

When I got home and unlocked the kitchen door my mother was waiting. "Where have you been?"

"I was with my friends, having a coke after dancing class."

But Mother had called several of my girlfriends and discovered that I was not with them.

"What's the sense in Papa going through all the trouble to get to America, if I can't be equal?" I shouted.

"You might end up marrying a Gentile," my mother answered.

"So what?" I stormed around the kitchen, shoving the dishes out of my way while I mixed a glass of chocolate milk.

"That would embarrass me, that's so what! Don't you know that Jewish people are God's chosen people?"

"Chosen for what?" I screamed.

"You make me sick, Naomi!" The veins in Mother's neck began to poke out and I knew for sure that the discussion was over. I was constantly torn, wanting to please her and wanting to please myself.

Still, I dreamed that Tootie, captain of the Benedictine football team, would ask me to be his date when B.C., as the team was commonly known, played its arch rival, Savannah High. He eventually asked, and I said yes, but my mother said no. It was hard to pretend that Lamotta was a Jewish name.

"But what if his mother is half Jewish?" I reasoned. "Doesn't that count?" I couldn't think of another reason to augment my plea.

"No," my mother said with finality.

I went to the game, sitting alone in the stands, hurting in the pit of my stomach as the captain's pretty second choice walked across the football field, wearing a huge white chrysanthemum corsage, waving good luck to the team.

That moment was also an epiphany for me. With instant clarity I realized how different it is for a Jewish girl growing up in a small Southern town. The prejudices seemed to come more from within my family than from without. And I was being forced to suppress some of my enthusiasm for life in order to conform, to accept boundary lines drawn by my parents, and the Jewish community.

At the same time I found it too painful to acknowledge the truth about my father. I chose to believe a fantasy of him instead, choosing to deny his weaknesses, his human failures. I held on to this belief even as our family ricocheted from bad to worse and Ruth and I were given to understand that after high school we would be on our own. Any further education was out.

"Damned if I want my daughters to go off to college, then come home thinking they're smarter than me," Daddy bellowed at us any time we suggested higher education. One evening Ruth told us that she wanted to become a registered nurse because she had just started dating a pre-med student.

"Nice Jewish girls don't empty bedpans," Mother said as she clacked her knitting needles together.

My dream was to become a fashion designer. I had made several very stylish dresses in Home Ec. and for hours I would pour over magazines, finding the styles that would look good on me. I had even designed and made a few colorful outfits for the beach, without using a pattern. I chose fabrics in pale pinks and lavenders that glinted and glowed with gold threads woven through them.

"You two better learn to type; I'm not spending one more dime on you after you graduate from high school." Those were our father's words, while my mother had her own bit of wisdom to share. Every time we left home for a date, she would admonish us: "Be a mensch."

It was during a Sunday matinee at the Bijou Theater that Ruth and I first heard of our country being at war. We had gone to see the movie, *Moon Over Miami,* with Betty Grable and Don Ameche. Right in the middle of the film the theater manager cut off the sound and strode on stage. He announced loudly, "Japan has just bombed Pearl Harbor." We turned our heads, looking all around us, taking in the faces of the audience, hoping to understand what his words meant. Neither of us had ever heard of Pearl Harbor.

Then he made his second announcement: "All servicemen must return immediately to their posts."

"Come on, we have to go home," Ruth said. She steered me out of the theater. We climbed onto the Habersham streetcar and rode silently to our street. When we came into our apartment, Daddy was chain-smoking in front of the small radio, listening intently as President Roosevelt's solemn voice said that this was ". . . a day that would live in infamy."

Japan bombed Pearl Harbor, the United States declared war on Japan and Germany, and young men came to Savannah. On the streets one good-looking boy after another passed, and Southern girls did their best to make them feel at home.

I began to envy my sister going out with good looking boys in uniform every weekend. I counted the days until I would be sixteen. I became a Red Cross volunteer. I felt radiant in my perky uniform as I served coffee and Spam on white bread at two Red Cross canteens, one at Hunter Army Air Base and the other at the train station. I lied about my age, pretending I was sixteen and old enough to date.

One night just before the weekend was to begin, Daddy called Ruth and me into the dining room. I looked apprehensively at my father, wondering what kind of trouble we were in. Ruth was nervous too but not as scared as I was. I still carried his threat, "I'll get a big stick to you!"

in my head.

Our father looked at us with dead seriousness. "You two are going to be drinking when you go out on dates and I want my girls to be able to handle their liquor." He filled two shot glasses with his favorite drink of straight rye and two glasses with a chaser of ginger ale. He handed one to Ruth and one to me.

Ruth guzzled down her glass of rye. She didn't pause to swallow. She took several gulps of the ginger ale. She smiled with pride. I stared in disbelief as I picked up my glass. After taking one sip I choked, spitting the dark liquid across the table, splattering both my father and my sister. I felt like puking, but not my sister. She rose from her seat at the table as though she had just been crowned Miss America, proud of her accomplishment.

Even though Ruth's current boyfriend was now in medical school up in Augusta, our parents continued to discourage her dream of becoming a nurse. Mother constantly reminded her that it was better to become a secretary than clean up bed pans.

"You've been cleaning up after Daddy ever since I can remember," Ruth shouted. She slammed the front door and ran down the steps. But, of course, Ruth, ever the obedient daughter, graduated from high school and went to Draughn's Business College. She excelled in typing and shorthand and got a civil service job at Hunter Army Air Base as secretary to the Adjutant General. Every morning at six a.m., Mother protectively walked Ruth the three blocks to meet her ride.

When pay day rolled around Ruth would go to Broughton Street and buy herself new and fashionable outfits. I would wait for her to go to work, take out a new skirt, then double it over several times and pin it with a large safety pin. Ruth was a good four inches taller than me. I would return it to her closet before she came home.

At the end of the day, as we sat around the radio listening to the news, Mother invariably took out her large bag of yarn and knitting needles. Then she carefully taught us how to knit scarves and gloves for the servicemen. One night, while I counted my knit one, purl two, my sister opened the newspaper and showed me a picture of Bill Kramer, a local boy that she had once dated. He was a prizefighter in the Navy and the picture showed him in a boxing ring wearing only a pair of shorts. I cut the picture out and pasted it in my scrapbook.

"You're such a hero worshiper," Ruth said with disdain.

During the summer, before I became a senior, I began dating servicemen too. I preferred to date officers, because I liked their snappy uniforms, and I was exceedingly selective about who I went out with. It was possible to say no a dozen times before five o'clock and still have a handsome date for a dance at the Officer's Club at eight. Thanks to our father's dealing in black-market ration stamps, Ruth and I were assured of the latest fashions in shoes. And I always imagined that one of the handsome officers would offer to pay one hundred and fifty dollars in gold for a dance with me, just as Rhett had done to waltz with Scarlett.

Just about every person we knew did Red Cross volunteer work during the war years. The air of Savannah was filled with glamour, ugliness, and excitement. It was not unusual to read about a fighter pilot whom one of us had just dated being shot down. Some windows around the city had flags displayed for the number of family members serving in the war. A gold star in the window meant a son or husband had been killed.

However, down on Charlton Street things were not doing so well. My grandmother was sixty-three when it was discovered that she had lung cancer. My grandfather wasn't in good health, either. Nurses stayed around the clock in three shifts. My mother took Eva on the Nancy Hanks train to Atlanta for further diagnosis at Emory Clinic, but there was nothing to be done. Mama's face grew taut and gray, and her body began wasting away. That's when life at my grandparents house changed. There was no longer the merry Sunday afternoons, the Friday night dinners, or the family talks on the side porch.

The day my grandmother died I stood in the door of her room as the nurse leaned over her, her wasted body lost in the hospital bed that had been set up in the living room. Mama's eyes were glazed from all the morphine she had consumed. When she saw me, she let out a loud wail. "I love you most, little one, little one! You was named for mine own Mama. Oh, Mama! Mama!"

The nurse held my grandmother's hand gently and spoke to her in a soothing tone. After a few minutes had passed, she pulled the white chenille bedspread over her face. I closed the door behind me and walked out to the side porch. I sat and rocked in Mama's favorite chair. She had taught me the grace of feeling love from a person whom I loved. The fire of her love had fed my life. And now that fire was put out.

The family sat *shiva* on Charlton Street. They sat on wooden boxes during the mourning period, as was the custom for Orthodox Jews. Every mirror in the house was covered with a white sheet. My uncles each wore a black band around their upper arm. My mother and aunts had a small black ribbon pinned to their dresses. Each ribbon had been torn just before the funeral, the age-old symbol of grief, the rending of the garments. Life seemed to have drained from my mother. She was silent and isolated.

Zelig lived four months to the day after his beloved Eva's death. Throughout their lifetime, everyone had predicted, "When one of them dies, so will the other." They had always been one another's world. They had been enough for each other. Theirs had been a true love.

An era had come to an end.

Chapter Nine

When 1944 arrived, the reality that I would automatically be considered a grownup, and have to earn a living, was right in my face. My senior year of high school seemed to have happened overnight. That was also the year I met Van. It was a romantic meeting. I was serving as a volunteer at the Red Cross station at Hunter Field.

"I was up to my eyeballs in mayonnaise and hard-boiled eggs and had just finished spreading slices of Spam on white bread for sandwiches." That was how I explained him to my sister, framing the backdrop of my meeting with the Second Lieutenant.

We served sandwiches and crisp sliced carrots to the airmen when they took off and returned from their missions. Van was blond, divorced, soft spoken, and ten years older than I. His front teeth protruded slightly, and he wasn't very tall. He also wasn't Jewish. Van was the sweetest young man I had ever known. I no longer cared that my mother was incensed. Van adored me and we became an instant couple. We were together every night and on weekends. When he flew his route to China, Burma, and India, known as the Hump, we wrote to each other. I waited breathlessly for his letters and ripped open the envelopes when they came.

The minute I finished reading one of his letters I would grab my lavender stationary, bordered in flowers, and write to him. I filled my fountain pen with dark ink and sprayed perfume on the pages before I mailed them. I missed him desperately. From the moment we met I wanted to spend the rest of my life with him. When the envelope was sealed I would blot the back of it with bright red lip prints and write S.W.A.K.

During the Christmas holidays Fern came to visit. She was now living in Brooklyn,with her sister. As we walked down palm-studded Victory Drive, I told her that I was in love with a flyer, that I wanted to marry him right after graduation. I had already selected names for our son, Kenneth. And also our daughter, Carol Jo.

"You ain't fooling around are you? Can I be Godmother?"

When Fern heard of his non-Jewish origins and his divorce, her eyes widened. She wondered how my mother would react.

"Are you crazy? She doesn't know. I'll have to elope." I plucked a red oleander from one of the huge green bushes lining the sides of the street and stuck it behind my ear, signifying that I was spoken for.

"You ought to get out of the South, too, Naomi." Fern said that in New York, she went everywhere that white people went.

"I will when I marry Van."

For graduation, my father gave me a round trip ticket to Miami Beach. Van said he would go A.W.O.L. to be with me, but the thought of going away with him alone terrified me. So I talked Ruth into taking her vacation from Hunter Field at the same time. She and I stayed in one hotel, Van in another, across from us on Collins Avenue. Van was very nervous that he might get stopped by the military police. He had traveled without orders and didn't want to get in trouble.

Every day, after swimming, Van and I strolled Lincoln Road, shopping, and at night we sipped rum and Coca Colas, staring into each other's eyes across the tropical atmosphere. Miami Beach was being used as a training field for servicemen, and the few visitors other than us were mostly older Jewish people from New York, who were still drawn to its magic.

"I want you to marry me," Van whispered as he caressed my hair. We were lying across the bed in his hotel room. "You have the most beautiful breasts," he said, tracing his fingertips across the red jersey blouse that hugged my body like a second skin. Fern's promises had come true. I had given up all concern about reaching womanhood.

"Do you promise that we can have our son and daughter right away?" I teased. Up to that point, I had done everything to stall our first sexual experience. I wasn't willing to have intercourse before marriage. But now with the assurance that we'd soon be married, and the gentle coaxing by my second lieutenant hero, I took off my underpants. Van probed the inside of my thighs, fingering the spot I feared. Strange and new sensations stirred in me, and I agreed to let him ease himself inside, just a little.

"Stop!" I shouted. The pain felt as though a broom handle was being shoved up into my brains.

"That's okay, sweetheart," Van said, moving away. He assured me that he was willing to wait until we were married. I turned away and there on the sheets beneath my body were a number of brownish-red spots. My eyes told my heart that from this day on I was indeed a woman.

After five days, Van had to report back to his base, and my sister and I came home on the train. When we returned from Miami, Fern was back in Savannah to say good-bye to her family. She had joined the WAVES. That night, Ruth, Fern, and I sipped cokes and ate an entire tin of my mother's cookies, turned the record player up as loud as we could, and danced away the night with our budding womanhood fully ablaze.

"Tell me the truth, Fern," I asked, "did you resent Ruth and me?"

As Fern twirled me around, doing the latest dance step and lifting me off the floor, she said, "No, girl. I realized early on that white women just can't make it without us." There was a sharper edge to her voice than before.

"Yeah," I said, as if thinking aloud. "My mother, in her poorest days, set aside brown envelopes to budget her money. There was always one for electricity, one for water, and one marked 'maid'."

"You better learn to take care of yourselves," Fern warned. "The day's coming when black women won't be willing to clean up all your Southern shit." She looked us straight in the eye, glancing from Ruth to me. "And I'm telling you, girlfriend, your mother was right on target every time she told you that Scarlett could go to hell. Because when that day comes, you can bet your sweet white ass, that all of you Scarletts will be on your own."

After the holiday to Miami, when we came home, I went to Draughn's Business College just as Ruth had done. I also got a job at Hunter Army Air Base as secretary to Captain Warmkessel, who was officer in charge of the Post Office. I had met him during my volunteer work at the canteen. He arranged for me to pass the civil service test without actually taking the exam. I always had a cutting edge concerning political savvy.

In November of 1944, when Ruth was twenty and I was eighteen, we walked into the wooden warehouse just across from the Tomochichi apartment house and cast our ballots for Franklin Delano Roosevelt. He was running for his fourth term as president. A law had been passed by the Georgia state legislature allowing eighteen-year-olds to vote. It was thought by the legislators, in their wisdom, that if a man could fight for his country at age eighteen, then certainly he should have the right to vote. Our mother was working at the polls, as she did at every election. She smiled proudly as she watched her two daughters cast their vote for her hero.

Now that I was earning my own money, I could finally afford to take care of the physical problem that had plagued me for so many years. After all the suffering of sore throats and pain when I swallowed, and my mother endlessly yelling that I was too goddamn mean to eat, I went to a doctor and had a badly needed tonsillectomy. It was an excruciatingly painful recovery. I hemorrhaged when I came home and had to go back to the hospital.

A few months following my surgery, as soon as I could swallow, Ruth invited me to go to Morrison's Cafeteria for supper. Ruth was a stunning young woman, tall and shapely. People constantly told her that she looked like Hedy Lamarr. As we carried our trays to a table, Ruth said she had something important to tell me.

"Mother's been reading your letters from Van and tearing them up."

"I don't believe you." But suddenly I realized that his letters hadn't reached me while I was in the hospital.

"I caught her as she rummaged through your bureau drawer," Ruth said. "She had such a look of guilt on her face that I felt sorry for her. Then, when she read about your marriage plans, she began to meet the mailman when he came and destroyed them before you could get them." Ruth looked at me with deep understanding, realizing how deeply the wound had pierced.

It was a terrible piece of news. I was hurt, angry, bitter. My mother had deprived me of her love and now she was doing her best to deprive me of love from a man I wanted to marry. I immediately wrote to Van and asked him not to mail any more letters to my house. He sent them instead to my office at Hunter Field.

It was late in the afternoon on April 12, 1945, when I came home from my job to find my mother hunched over the radio and in tears. FDR had died at the Little White House in Warm Springs, Georgia. He had collapsed the night before while sitting for his portrait. The president had brought fame to that quaint town just an hour's drive south of Atlanta. He often traveled there to swim and bathe in the mineral springs to ease the pain of his crippling polio. My mother wept uncontrollably as she listened to the broadcast.

"My God, Harry Truman's our new president," my father said later that night after supper as we all huddled around the radio. His hands trembled as though he'd lost his closest relative.

A short time later, Eleanor Roosevelt told the mourning American population, "I am more sorry for the people of the country and the world than I am for us."

Chapter Ten

On August sixth, just after the atom bomb was dropped, the war ended. Almost immediately V.J. day was jubilantly declared. August fifteenth found strangers hugging and kissing, while dancing with one another on Broughton Street.There were street parties and celebrations, and American servicemen were coming home.Van was sent to Carmel, California to wrap up his tour with the Air Force. He wrote to me immediately.

Van told me that he was looking into the possibility of working with one of the commercial airlines as soon as he received his discharge papers. He had fallen in love with California and felt that I would also. He suggested marriage in a small chapel in Carmel-by-the-Sea. He had rented a Victorian house and was buying furniture, waiting for the day that I would arrive and become his bride. The end of the war was a strange time. A period of readjustment for the entire country.

I answered Van and told him that all of my thoughts were of the day when I would be his wife. In fact, my every thought was of the babies I longed to have. My visions were of our son looking like Van and our daughter like me. My entire life seemed to have been headed in that direction, waiting for the moment that I would be a mother.

My dreams seemed real until I thought of how I would break the news to my parents. In my heart I felt that Ruth would support me, but it was difficult to summon the nerve to confide in her. I had saved some money in war bonds. I knew that my father would never spring for a trousseau, since Van wasn't Jewish. Everyone I had ever known had gotten a trousseau when they were married.

When I finally raised enough courage to tell my parents that I was going to marry Van, I walked into the dining room where my father sat, playing solitaire. He deliberately selected each card, then placed the king on top of the ace, the queen, the jack, and on down, making sure that a black went on top of a red, and vice versa. My mother was clearing the supper dishes from the table.

"I'm going to move to California," I announced. "Van and I love each other, and we're planning to get married."

My father threw the cards across the table and buried his head in his hands, sobbing, "You can't do this to me!" I had never seen Daddy cry. Not even when Grandpa Zipinsker died.

"So this is what I worked all those years for, supporting you, feeding you, buying you clothes." Then he added, "To have you marry some *goy"*

My mother rushed into the kitchen and slammed the door shut between us. She shouted at the top of her lungs, "I'll never set eyes on you again! We'll sit *shiva* as though you were dead!"

I said nothing. Defeated, I went into my bedroom, threw myself across the bed, hugging Van's picture close to my heart. I knew what I had to do. I would abandon the plans I held so dear, if that meant, at last, that I might get the love of my parents. I pushed this disappointment into the deep dark secret recess of my mind, believing I could turn off my feelings as though they were a water hydrant. But some little part of me died that night. All my life I had confused love and approval. And there I was, still needing my parents' approval to proceed with my life. I had unknowingly taken the first step in learning to walk to the beat of another's drum.

Shortly after the war, our jobs came to an end at the base. Ruth and I made the decision to visit New York to look for jobs and start a new life. Fern had regaled us about the excitement of living in the Big Apple.

My sister and I were both ready to leave Savannah. Ruth was as unhappy as I was; she'd just broken off a four-year romance with her medical student. Although we were both dating quite a bit and had become attractive enough to have our father tell us that we looked like movie stars, we wanted to get away from our parents and life in the South.

Ruth had recently begun to date a young man who had survived a serious automobile wreck while he was returning to his Army base. He had been unconscious for two months after the accident and still wore a back brace. Ruth was a great typist; she agreed to write Ted a phony military pass so that he could get a free ride on the train to New York. As soon as our plans were confirmed, I wrote to Van and told him that we would be at the Astor Hotel in Times Square. But I told no one else of my secret. Not even Ruth.

I told Van that my parents had slammed the door of their approval in my face and I was masterminding plans without them. I said that I was too scared to come out to California alone and asked him to come to New York and get me. My heart was set on getting married at The Little Church Around The Corner. It seemed the perfect chapel for us to take our vows.

At the end of the letter I added, "I feel like a baby bird breaking out of its shell and can't do it alone. There's no one here for me, not even Ruth."

It was early October when we struck out for New York. It didn't take long for betrayal and disappointment to set in. Once we got to Manhattan, Ted monopolized all of Ruth's time, while I spent my days browsing through the bridal department of B. Altman's, fingering the selection of bridal gowns.

At the beginning of each day, I would rush to the front desk in the lobby hoping to find a letter from Van. I went into a jealous rage, throwing Ruth's clothes all over the floor of our room in the hotel and cried of being betrayed and that all my plans were ruined. Van never showed up. He never wrote.

Two weeks had passed and to keep myself occupied while waiting to hear from Van, I made up my mind to look for a job in the city. There was an elevator strike going on at the time. One morning I climbed fourteen flights of steps to apply for a position with a talent agency. Then I packed my suitcase, boarded the commuter special, and went to New Canaan to visit my Aunt Jean.

I never wrote to Van again. My love for him came to an abrupt halt. I chose to ignore any feelings of sadness. In fact, I chose to ignore any feelings at all. I deliberately pushed aside my love for him as though it was discarded clothing about to be taken to a rummage sale. I thought I could carve him out of my heart like the core of an apple. My aunt and uncle offered me a job in their stationery store.

"But, Aunt Jean," I said, "I want to work in New York. I've been assured a job there with a theatrical talent agency."

"That will not do, darling." She showed me how to display the dolls in their cases, as she rearranged all the toys in the showroom.

"What's wrong with my commuting to and from New Canaan?" I

could feel the electricity of New York pulsing through my veins.

"I'm worried that a young girl in a big city alone might become a prostitute," Aunt Jean said. She promised me that I would have lots of boyfriends and didn't need to live in Manhattan.

Aunt Jean had been right. There seemed to be plenty of boys infatuated with what they called my Southern charm. My dark brooding eyes took in every person I met. But when I accepted a date from the young handsome policeman whom I had met in the store, the old family prejudice reared its head.

"Honey, you know he's not Jewish."

"Not you too, Aunt Jean." I sighed with disappointment and immediately made a date to go ice-skating with the officer.

After spending three weeks in New York, my sister and Ted became engaged. They went back to Savannah to plan their wedding which would take place in January. And with them went the life I'd imagined Ruth and I would be acting out, a life as bohemian as we could stand in Greenwich Village. We would meet handsome, seductive men and gather in artists' bars among famous writers on Broadway.

In spite of Ruth's leaving, I loved going to New York with my aunt for the day and having her take me to the most fashionable department stores in the city. There was Saks, Lord and Taylor, and Bergdorf Goodman, where I bought beautiful suits, coordinating them with the proper blouses and shoes. Every penny I earned in the stationery store was spent on clothing. I felt very grown up, and I liked to think of us as equals when we ate lunch in Schraft's and attended Broadway matinees.

I'd been living in New Canaan for two months when Fern came into Manhattan one day, and we met at the Automat for lunch, something we'd never been able to do in Savannah. The two of us walked arm in arm down Fifth Avenue, and spent hours rummaging through Macy's Department Store.

"Why don't you stay here, Naomi? We can get a small apartment," she suggested. Fern was traveling around the country, registering young black people so they could vote in an upcoming election. She had taken up one of the early civil rights causes and was a dedicated worker. She told me of all the ugly treatment she'd been subjected to, the insulting remarks — even in the North — and the more dangerous incidents. On her most recent road trip, someone had hit her with a rock, and Fern had a large bruise on her forehead. She handed me her latest copy of *P.M.*

Newspaper, which detailed the story of how she'd been attacked by a Ku Klux Klan member. Fern's picture was on the cover.

"You've no idea how the South is about to change, Naomi," Fern said as we had coffee at a corner coffee shop. "And it won't be easy. My people are really hated." Fern's life more than whetted my appetite for adventure, and I longed for the autonomy that living in New York would bring.

Fern and I discussed how obvious it had become to all of us, that not only was the racial problem being addressed, but also the underbelly of class distinction that once existed among Jews was breaking apart now that Hitler had been stamped out. The German Jews were no longer a social notch above my ancestors. After the war, a Jew was a Jew was a Jew.

"My aunt Jean wants me to stay in Connecticut." Ruth was also expecting me back in Savannah to be the maid of honor at her upcoming wedding. "But I'll be back, and we can look for an apartment then."

Fern smiled warmly, a smile I had grown to love.

"Fern, I still miss Van, there's a hole in my heart, and I don't know how to fill it." I hadn't thought about him in so long, but seeing Fern brought back the immense emptiness of my loss. I suddenly wondered where he was, if he had married, and if I would ever fall in love again.

"Naomi, please don't let them live your life for you." Fern took my hand in hers as we left the coffee shop and walked uptown from 34th Street.

I lowered my head. "Every time I feel sad and lonely, I see his face and hear his voice, and I cry." Fern took a deep breath. She put her arm around my shoulders.

"Naomi, there's something I've never told you, and I feel I must now." She looked so serious. I felt my heart pound.

"Van wrote to your parents telling them that his heart was broken, that he would've been willing to convert to Judaism if they wouldn't take you away from him. He asked them for your address. They refused to tell him where you were living."

Shock swept over me. "How do you know this?"

"Well, when I went to visit the lady I worked for at the Tomochichi, she told me how sad she felt that your mother had deceived you."

"My God, who else knew about this?" Anger and hurt welled up in me from my head to my toes.

"Your Aunt Ella knew everything. But she promised not to tell you. Your mother made her swear." Fern said that my parents had never answered Van's many letters.

Chapter Eleven

When I went to Savannah for Ruth's wedding, I planned to get back to New York as fast as I could. As soon as I unpacked the dress that I was going to wear to her wedding, Ruth angrily accused me of having a prettier dress than her wedding gown.

"How did I know what your gown would look like?" I said. Ruth had told me to buy something white and I had bought, with my Aunt Jean's help, a beautiful white lace, off-the-shoulder dress. The truth was that it was far more stylish than Ruth's frumpy satin gown.

On top of that my parents were not too happy that my sister was marrying Ted. They didn't like his mother because she'd been twice divorced; they called her salty. But most of Ruth's girlfriends were already married, and Ruth felt pressured to follow suit.

"We must go to Fine's Department Store," Ruth said as she and I walked down Broughton Street after her bridal shower. One of the sales-clerks in the millinery department had offered her the use of any or all of their hats to wear to the many prenuptial parties being given for her. We stood there trying on hats with veils, small ones with big fluffy roses hanging limply over our foreheads. We put on tall cloches that hugged our heads and giggled uncontrollably when Ruth decided on one that our father would later say looked like she had "the whole damned turkey and its feathered ass on her head." We left the department store with so many boxes of hats in our arms that we could hardly see over the tops.

I stumbled on the sidewalk, then toppled, with hat boxes flying in every direction. When I looked up, I saw a familiar face. There stood Bill Kramer, a tall handsome man, grinning broadly. I'd seen his picture on the sports page of our local newspaper many times. He had been a well-known professional prizefighter, and I immediately noted his thick muscular arms bulging under his tight black turtleneck sweater.

In high school, I had developed a secret crush on him and had clipped his pictures from the paper and kept them in my diary. Ruth often teased me about being a hero worshiper. As a child I had begun to imagine the kind of man I'd marry and would do a mental inventory of every man that appealed to me from that time on. Bill was no exception. I was already casting him in a role that he would probably never understand, manufacturing exactly what he would mean to me.

"Your little sister has certainly grown up," Bill said to Ruth as he gathered hats and boxes from the sidewalk and helped me up. He had a slight lisp, and it made me smile. When Bill fumbled with the boxes I roared with laughter as his big hands grabbed the hat with the feathers.

"Naomi has just come home from New York to be maid of honor at my wedding."

"I'm only visiting," I added. I could feel the tight black dress that I bought with Aunt Jean in Bergdorf Goodman's melting against my thighs.

I nudged my sister, whispering, "Invite him to the wedding, please!"

"Bill, did you get the invitation to my wedding?" Ruth said.

"No. But I would love to see you and old Ted tie the knot, and to see how your baby sister strolls down the aisle before you." Like Scarlett O'Hara, my mind went to work, planning and manipulating how to get him.

Ruth made a lame excuse that there must have been a mistake in the delivery of the invitation, when Bill said he hadn't received one. She told him she expected to see him at the wedding. We thanked Bill and walked toward Habersham Street to catch the streetcar home.

"Are you satisfied that I asked him?" Ruth said. She struggled to keep her boxes from toppling again.

"Baby sister, his ass. I'm eighteen."

"You're still my little sister," Ruth said.

Bill's babyish face, sensual lips, and boyish grin stayed in my mind. His nose had been broken in the ring. He had recently been discharged from the Navy and was looking for a job. Bill lived with his mother in a small apartment not far from the municipal auditorium. His self assurance was appealing. He held himself high, exhibiting strength not only as an athlete, but I detected a warmth shining through as kindness. Savannah now looked a lot more inviting than I had thought.

At Ruth's wedding, part of me felt like a star returning to the South.

I sported a new hairdo, was expertly made up with the latest cosmetics from New York, and in my elegant off-the-shoulder gown, was a big hit. I flirted with every available male in the room, wondering which of them was the one.

Nothing seemed to stop the emptiness I was feeling, a deep sadness suffused me. And Ted was taking my older sister from me. I downed one bourbon and coke after another. I remembered how my father had demonstrated the way to open my throat to let the booze slide down quickly. I danced with every man at the wedding reception, glancing from time to time at Bill, who was watching me throughout the evening. It was so easy for me to be the belle of the ball, just as Scarlett had been.

When Bill asked if he could take me home, seeing that I was tipsy, I said, "I'm not ready to leave." But he insisted on getting me into the back seat of a friend's car just in time. I was feeling dizzy, then a wave of nausea came over me. Just as Bill leaned over to kiss me, I threw up in his lap. He took a handkerchief out of his pocket and wiped my face gently. I leaned back in the seat, closed my eyes, and instantly fell asleep.

The next week Bill invited me to watch him play in a local basketball tournament. After the game we went to Johnny Harris's restaurant and, while waiting for our food, Bill put a coin in the jukebox. We danced under the blue ceiling, designed with small lights that twinkled like a starry night sky. I snuggled against Bill's tweed jacket and felt safe.

"How's the job search coming along?" I asked after we returned to our booth. I bit into the juicy barbecued lamb sandwich, then licked the spicy sauce from my fingers.

"I'm starting next week as a traveling salesman." His mother had been nagging him since he'd come home from the service, but he needed to look around for a while before making a decision. Four years in the Navy hadn't prepared Bill for the civilian world, and he had little formal education. There was no family business for him to fall heir to. He and his older brother had learned at an early age that they had to work to help support their mother. "Ever since I was a small child, I would hang around the ports on the Savannah River, watching freight ships sail, longing to travel the world," he said. I liked him more and more. Maybe he, too, had a sense of adventure.

Bill's mother was born in Savannah, but his father had been an immigrant from Poland, and theirs had been an arranged marriage. His father had been both a fireman and a policeman, but when the land boom exploded in the 1920's, he had rushed to Miami. He had solicited everyone that he knew in Savannah for money to invest in land. The deals were fraudulent. Much of the land, it turned out, was under water. In 1926, when he lost everything, he shot and killed himself.

When I realized that Bill's father had died five months before I was born, my mind immediately flashed to the scene of my father's attempted suicide when I was four years old. I felt an instant pain as the long buried memory of his swallowing poison surfaced. And how he had failed in his attempt.

"How did your mother manage with two little boys?"

"She boarded with families just to keep food on the table for us." He spoke with pride when he added, "No matter how poor we were, she saw that we ate balanced meals. She would save the stale bread to make Apple Brown Betty for dessert." As Bill spoke, he seemed caught in a long-ago time and place.

The next weekend, I invited Bill to be my guest at the Ballet Russe de Monte Carlo. A friend, who was going to be out of town, had given me a pair of tickets. Bill said that his former boxing coach often said that male ballet dancers are the truest athletes of all because they're so disciplined and their bodies so well trained. Bill was proud of his body and kept it in shape by playing softball and basketball.

Bill was eight years older than me and seemed so worldly. He had toured the Pacific while serving on a P.T. boat during the war. He had boxed in Madison Square Garden in New York as a member of a Golden Gloves team. In his youth, he had often run away from home after his father's suicide. His mother worried about his graduating from high school because he skipped class so often. When she could no longer handle him, she arranged for him to attend a military school in Miami.

Since Bill didn't own a car, I arranged to borrow one from my neighbor, the one who didn't drive. He was Fern's boss. He needed the car because he was a traveling salesman. But his chauffeur, Fern's brother, did the driving. When the ballet performance was over, Bill and I drove out to Tybee, took off our shoes, and walked along the ocean's edge. As soon as we heard the growl of thunder we ran back to the car. The smell of the salty marshes drifted through the windows on our drive back to Savannah, and the night chill caused me to cuddle next to his warm body.

It wasn't long before Bill got a job as a traveling salesman with a notions manufacturer and bought a pale blue Nash. During his weeks on the road, he wrote long passionae love letters and often brought me small gifts when he came back for our weekend dates. Every Friday night we went to the movies and afterward we'd cuddle and neck on the sleeping porch of my parents apartment.

Bill made me laugh and his charm and friendliness were appealing. He was well-known around Savannah and I loved the way he'd stop and talk to people when we were out together. After we'd been dating for several months Bill asked me to join him and his mother for a movie. I felt awkward and believed that Bill's mother disapproved of me.

"She's a bit jealous, because she only has me. My brother's married and living in Jersey," Bill explained. It was rather obvious that since his mother had been born in Savannah, she felt a cut above my parents, socially.

Suddenly I was in no hurry to leave Savannah. When the time came for me to decide whether I wanted to go back to New York, to take an apartment with Fern, or stay in Savannah to be near Bill, I chose to stay. I would get a job and do what my family expected of me.

I'd heard of a politically appointed position that was available in the Chatham County Courthouse, and with Bill's help — he knew the butcher who was in charge of Jewish quotas for filling political jobs — I became a typist in the office of the Clerk of the Superior Court. Part of my job assignment was to attend Democratic political events, as the token Jewish employee in the Clerk's office. Bill was vitally interested in the Democratic party, so we went to these events together.

Bill worked on Harry Truman's presidential campaign, as well as local elections and I was very efficient in getting campaigns organized. We had more and more in common, I discovered. Bill had agreed to be in charge of a large voting precinct for an exceedingly important and rabidly contested election that was coming up in the city and I was given the day off from work to help out at the polling place. I would check the names off the list as each person cast his or her vote. Toward the end of the afternoon, Bill came over with a Coke, winked at me and whispered, "You can start voting the dead ones, now."

"What do you mean?" I asked, completely puzzled.

"They don't strike the names of the people who recently died. We can cast votes for them now."

"That's dishonest. I think I'll write a letter to the editor of the paper."

" Don't rock the boat, Naomi. Nobody likes a trouble-maker."

And with that, we voted for the recent dead citizens of Savannah. Then just before the polls closed, we cast votes for the live voters who had failed to show up. Bill's way of handling votes was the way Savannah had always handled elections. The candidate that Bill had so diligently campaigned for won the election by a landslide.

And it was clear that no one wanted to hear what I had to say about fairness at the polls. The South wasn't ready to change their voting habits.

I was so smitten with Bill that after we had been dating for six months I gave in. Bill picked up where Van left off. It took a bit of coaxing before we actually consummated the act. We would make love on the lumpy hide-a-bed on the sleeping porch. Its lumps, coupled with my father's nocturnal prowling, inhibited me, but not Bill. I often wondered if my father heard Bill flush the condom down the toilet. I dreamed of spending the night with him, lying next to his hard, muscular body. I dreamed of marriage.

During the summer of our courtship, we went for long walks on the beach. While sitting in the sand dunes, Bill often recited his favorite poem, "The Cremation of Sam McGee," by Robert Service. I would lean back as he relived the glory days of the Gold Rush, dramatizing the words he knew by heart.

Bill's tongue hit the front of his teeth at each word that had an "s" in it, and when his lisp kicked in, I had to restrain myself from giggling. He would deepen his voice and exaggerate the verbs as he geared up for the last stanza.

When it was my turn to recite my favorite poems, I almost always read excerpts from *The Rubiyat of Omar Khayam*. And I, too, was good at hamming it up.

A mysterious occurrence happened while Bill was away on one of his weekly trips. The newspaper was filled with sordid details. Pieces of a body were being dug up from locations not too far from where we lived. First a leg, then an arm. When the severed head was discovered, it became known who the dead man was. As soon as Bill called that weekend, I couldn't wait to shock him.

"Guess what part I found?"

We were in the back seat of a friend's car, driving home from a football game in Atlanta, November, 1946. Bill pulled me close to him and began stammering to find the words he wanted to whisper to me.

"I want you to spoil me and all my children for the rest of my life," Bill said. I took this to be a proposal. He cuddled me close to his chest. How easy it was to suddenly feel like Melanie Wilkes, protected and cared for.

"I'll call Daddy the very minute we get back," I said. "The wedding will be in December, and we can go to New York for our honeymoon."

"Wait, wait," Bill said, suddenly retreating. "I'm not ready. This is happening too quick. I may still want to date other girls."

"Too late!" I threw my arms around him and kissed him passionately. When we returned to Savannah, Bill sat across the room from my father. He opened his mouth to speak several times before the words came out. "I want your daughter's hand in marriage," Bill said with a nervous tone in his voice.

"Please, take all of her. It's a package deal," my father responded with a laugh.

When we shopped for matching gold wedding bands, Bill's had to be ordered because his fingers were so big. Inside of each ring was inscribed, "Til' death do us part."

I selected beautiful lingerie and the latest fashions for my trousseau. On one of our shopping trips Bill surprised me when he asked, "Can I take these suits to your house?"

"Why?"

"I don't want my mother to know I bought three suits." Bill blushed and turned away.

"Don't tell me you're afraid of your mother at your age?"

"I just don't want the aggravation and guilt," he answered sheepishly.

"You're paying for them, why do you have to hide them?"

"It's easier this way," he assured me. It struck me as odd that at age twenty-eight, a man would hide his clothes from his mother.

Late one afternoon as I was dashing around the apartment getting ready for my bridal shower, the phone rang. It was Van.

"I'm in Miami on a business trip and would like to come to Savannah, sweetheart."

My body felt paralyzed at the sound of his voice.

"No. You can't come."

"Why not?"

"I've met someone, Van. I'm getting married. I didn't know what happened to you." Old dreams flashed across my brain like bright neon bulbs.

"I tried to find you. Your parents never answered my letters. I should've come to New York for you," Van said. He said he had felt wounded that my parents were so against him, and had taken it quite badly. He wanted us to marry immediately.

I was confused, as though the two men had suddenly merged into one. There was a long silence between us. We said good-bye.

In December, a month after the proposal, Bill and I stood under the wedding canopy. A Jewish caterer had been hired. Mounds of chopped liver in the shapes of swans were piled on silver platters. Aunts, other relatives, and friends loaned their best china and silver serving pieces. My mother cried for weeks prior to the wedding and wrung her hands in frustration. She felt overwhelmed and burdened by the amount of work she had to accomplish in so short a time. My sister's satin wedding gown was redesigned and altered to fit my body. Seed pearls were sewn around the neck which made it quite elegant and sophisticated. I managed that month of preparation like a drill sergeant.

I walked down the aisle of the B.B. Jacob Synagogue between my mother and father, just as my mother had done. The long, elaborate lace veil trailed behind. Aunt Ella's two little girls served as flower girls.

As the violinist played, the vocalist sang in a sweet tenor voice, "Because God made thee mine, I'll cherish thee." Under the *chuppah,* I turned my eyes full into Bill's, the one I had chosen as my life partner, until death would part us. He stared proudly at his new bride.

We danced at our lavish wedding reception, courtesy of a small windfall my father had made in the stock market. Then we changed our clothes to board the train for New York. I flung my Aunt Jean's full length mink coat over my sleek black suit as I climbed the train's steep steps. My girlfriends thought I was the luckiest person in the world. My parents were happy. I had pleased them at last. They were relieved that Bill was Jewish and from a good family.

During the night, Bill climbed down from the single upper berth into the lower one to be with me. I awakened somewhere in Virginia, and wished I was eleven again, and that the face of the stranger next to me was the familiar one of my sister.

Chapter Twelve

I came into marriage certain that all my girlhood hopes and dreams would be translated into reality once I was mistress of my own home, once I had pleased my husband, and once I was the doting mother of healthy children.

Winnie Lou had come over to help me unpack the wedding presents and make the one-bedroom sublet apartment more livable for newly-weds. We scoured and scrubbed and mopped and shined every inch of the seventh floor apartment that overlooked Forsyth Park, while I planned the first dinner I would serve Bill. Winnie Lou and I fingered every piece of wedding china, with its gold borders and pale flowers in the center, the crystal goblets, and the Georgian Rose sterling silver-ware.

The first meal that I planned to cook for my husband that weekend was a challenge. I had shopped for hours, buying enough food to feed an army. Dinner was going to be roast chicken, rice and gravy, string beans, tossed salad, and a home-made chocolate layer cake.

When Winnie Lou saw my body halfway inside the oven as I was placing the chicken in its roasting pan on a rack, she pulled me out and said, "Move over, child. You don' know nothin' about cookin' no chicken."

"What's wrong?"

Winnie Lou shook her head. "Well, in the first place, you has to take the gizzards out, and you has to wash that yellow stuff off from around the chicken's ankles."

"I thought you just stuck it in the oven," I said wiping my hands across the front of my new white, organdy apron.

"You has to stick your hand up inside the poor thing and pull out the gizzards, liver, and heart, too. Lord, Naomi, you gon' kill your husband on his very first meal."

That evening, Bill whistled when he rushed into the apartment, his jacket slung over his shoulder, a huge grin across his face and a bouquet of roses in his hands. He swooped me into his arms, carrying me to the bedroom. We had rearranged the two single mattresses sideways so we wouldn't fall through the space between them.

"This is the best home cooked meal I've ever eaten." Bill devoured every morsel. As fast as I placed a dish on the table, Bill dug his fork in for second and third helpings.

"Well, honey, you ain't seen nothing yet," I said with a pleased smile on my face. All of my extra time was spent leafing through cookbooks and there was a pile of them stacked in the closet, ready to be explored. When I began washing the dinner dishes, Bill insisted on grabbing a dish cloth and drying them. This was something I'd never seen my father or grandfather do.

"Baby, I'll eat anything you feed me." Bill cupped his hands around my buttocks and nibbled at my nose. He kissed me and we danced around the kitchen floor.

While I was finishing up in the kitchen Bill announced that he had made reservations for the New Year's Eve dance. All of our newlywed friends would be at the customary celebration at the Jewish Educational Alliance. We were going to be at the same table as Ruth and Ted.

"Great. I'll be able to show off my handsome husband." I loved saying the words, "my husband." My face was beaming.

"And I can show off my latest dance steps." Bill laughed, shuffling his feet.

The night of the dance I put on the lace gown I'd worn as Ruth's maid-of-honor, Bill had on a rented tuxedo. He took much longer than me to ready himself. He primped in front of the mirror like a peacock, not quite satisfied with the way his suit fit. He twisted the cummerbund until he broke the hooks. I whipped out my sewing kit and repaired it. At our party table, the women talked about their wedding china patterns and what pieces they lacked to have an even dozen place settings.

Coming out of the ladies' room, I caught a glimpse of Bill rubbing his thick hand over the bare, tanned midriff of the only single girl at the dance. A visitor from California, her tanned flesh was an exotic contrast to the white crepe gown clinging to her athletic body.

I walked over and tugged at Bill's arm. "I don't want you to touch other girls."

"Oh, come on now, darlin', you're not jealous are you?" Bill winked, and gave me a flirtatious smile. In an instant, I felt old and worn, as if I'd been cast aside before I'd even gotten started. Bill told me that I could hardly expect him to stop looking just because we were married. He used "having too much to drink" as his excuse when we got home.

"You don't think I'd do anything like that if I was cold sober, do you, darlin'?" He pulled me into his strong arms, reassuring me. Bill loved to tease. It was his way of gaining power over me.

I took two steps back, hauled off and slapped him square across the face. "I probably wouldn't do this, either, if I were cold sober." Then I batted my eyelashes and smiled. "Happy New Year!" It was my first reaction. Too often I had used a quick repartee to protect myself. Now a great sadness engulfed me, my vision of marriage had not included feeling abandoned.

Bill stood staring at me, his fists opening and closing.

On the second day of January, Bill had to go back on the road, and once more I felt that nagging empty and alone feeling in the pit of my stomach. I called Ella and asked if her four year old daughter could spend the night with me. I didn't know how to tell her that I was scared of being alone. The truth was I sat alone in the apartment while Bill was away, studying exotic dishes in my cookbooks.

"What the hell are you cooking so much for? He's only home on the weekends," Ruth chided me. She laughed when I told her how often I went to grocery shop.

"I'm planning a cheese souffle."

"You wouldn't know a souffle if you saw one," Ruth said, teasing me. "Don't tell me you're going to have Grandma Zipinsker and Tante Silverberg over for a supper of kosher souffle?"

I planned those Friday night dinners for my husband as though they were the Lord's last supper. Bill's mother expected us to eat lunch with her every Saturday, and my parents took it for granted we'd be at their place every Sunday. My father especially liked to have us newlyweds around. Though his diabetes had progressed, Daddy seemed to have mellowed.

It bothered me that no matter how glorious a weekend I planned,

Bill always insisted that he had to play basketball on Sunday afternoons. I knew it was a great outlet for him after a week of driving around his southern territory. He raced and dribbled across the courts, running over whoever got in his way. He prided himself on the fact that he never hit anyone or got into public fights, but I noticed him elbowing players and then denying that he had even been near them when the referee blew his whistle.

"I want to spend more time together while you're in town for the weekend," I reminded him week after week. After being alone for the entire week I wanted us to do almost everything together. Bill always had an excuse when I wanted to go to the movies on Saturday afternoons. He said matinees gave him a headache.

What I adored most about Bill was his playfulness. When Valentines' Day rolled around and I handed him a frilly valentine but didn't receive one, I sulked. He excused himself from the breakfast table. "Cover your eyes, Poopsie." Then he yelled, "Surprise!" I opened my eyes, and he stood before me nude, with a large red ribbon tied around his penis and a box of chocolates in a red heart-shaped box in his hands.

My husband made fun of me because I would only make love at night, with the shades drawn, and in absolute darkness. I hated it if he even turned on a lamp. He teased me and said I was frigid, but actually sex seemed shameful, something hidden and forbidden.

Every month I would have to leave my job, wracked with cramps, go home and crawl into bed with a hot water bottle. During my adolescence, from the time my menstrual periods began they were intensely painful. My belly seemed to cry for a better healing, something to fill the cavity that cramped so badly.

It was in late April when I discovered my pregnancy. I was diagnosed by the same doctor who had treated my childhood itch. "Are you the good sister or the mean one?" he teased as he probed inside my body.

"I think I'm the pregnant one," I said, giggling. Bill arrived at the doctor's office just as the exam was finishing, and when he was told by the doctor that I was pregnant, tears formed in the corners of his eyes. I revered my husband for being so vulnerable and sensitive. He took me to Johnny Harris's for fried chicken to celebrate.

The medical world was changing in 1947, and I was referred to a specialist, a doctor who only treated women and delivered babies. I was so excited that I immediately asked Ruth to go shopping with me for a baby layette. There was little doubt in my mind that I would have a son for Bill. He would be the proudest father in the world, and I'd be the perfect mother.

"You're going to be a grandmother.." I said when I called my moher. Her obvious excitement thrilled me.

"I'll knit him a sweater and some blankets," my mother said, as we walked past the shelves of brightly colored yarn in Adler's department store.

"Don't buy anything that might suggest a girl." I only wanted soft blues, whites, and yellows. I ruled out any hint of pink. I was positive it was going to be a boy. Ruth couldn't wait to buy a white cotton romper, trimmed with a lace collar for her first nephew. We loaded up with six dozen diapers, batiste gowns that buttoned in front with pearl buttons, and selected the crib and chest of drawers that my parents were going to buy us as a baby gift. But we held to the Jewish superstition that it was bad luck to bring the furniture into the house before the baby was born. My mother said they would have it delivered while I was in the hospital.

"Can you have sex while you're pregnant?" Ruth wanted to know.

"I'm afraid I'll hurt the baby, so I'm not doing it." I patted my growing belly and smiled. I folded and refolded the baby clothes as we sat in Mother's living room, drinking tea and eating cookies.

"Jesus, if I was pregnant Ted wouldn't stand for that," Ruth said. "He can't get enough." She described all the different positions they had tried.

"Do you think Mother's disappointed because I'm having a baby before you?"

Ruth didn't hear a word I said. "When Ted was in the hospital after that last accident, we even did it in his hospital bed." When Mother walked in with another plate of cookies, and overheard my sister, she shouted, "Shut up, Ruth. That's the nastiest talk I ever heard." She raced back to the kitchen, her face a bright crimson.

In my fourth month of pregnancy Bill and I had to move in with my parents because our apartment's original tenant returned without notice.

Housing was hard to come by in the years following the war. I spent each day sorting out baby clothes and fretting that Bill, the traveling salesman, would only be a weekend husband.

"I don't want to be alone without a husband," I cried when we were in bed one night.

"I'm afraid to quit this job, darlin'," Bill said. "At least there is a sure income."

"What about a job with the city?"

"I've worked for political figures, and they want too much in return. That's not a good future."

"Well, what's wrong with getting a favor done in return for all that you've given?"

"I don't want to work for anyone," Bill said. He jumped from the bed, hurrying to the kitchen to fix a snack. We often got up at midnight to smear peanut butter and grape jelly between saltine crackers, washed down by a glass of chocolate milk. Especially after we'd just made love. When Bill came back with a tray, I put my arms around his neck. He was very seductive, using his boyish charms to bribe and manipulate me, the way he had always done with his mother.

"Ask your uncle to help you buy a business," I said. "I bet my Daddy would be willing to help, too."

"I've spent my life being at the mercy of my uncle for financial help. I want to be on my own."

"Well, it won't hurt to ask, you never know what'll happen."

Bill agreed to talk to both men, while interviewing various jobs that didn't please him. Several months later his wealthy uncle and my father were more than willing to lend him the money to buy into a partnership of a local furniture store. The present owner was a distant cousin of Bill's mother. My father's entire savings was three thousand dollars, but he offered it to my husband interest free. I planned to work there in the afternoons, as Minna had once done for Avram. I quit my job at the courthouse and began looking for an apartment, one with two bedrooms.

One afternoon a sea of nausea swept over me as I lay on the bed at my parents' house, gazing through the open window, counting the buds on the pink dogwood trees. The trees seemed pregnant with spring.

Once Bill was in his own business I went to work for no salary. That was simply what a wife was supposed to do. That's what my mother had done.

We moved out of my parents' apartment to one on Park Avenue when I was in my seventh month. I loved announcing to my friends, "I live on Park Avenue," although we were right next to a bakery. Paying no attention to Jewish superstition, I phoned and had the crib and chest sent out for the nursery.

Often at night, the delicious smells wafting through our windows were so irresistible that Bill would go down to the back entrance of the bakery and come home with a bag of hot sweet rolls. We picnicked in bed in the middle of the night. I was not only pregnant, but also working in Bill's store, doing the household chores, happily being a dutiful wife, and loving the struggle of beginning our life together.

But I remained terrified of the dark, a trait left over from my childhood, and many nights I imagined I heard noises. One night I shook Bill from a sound sleep. "I hear somebody at the back door." Without a moment of hesitation, he leaped naked from the bed, grabbed his softball bat and darted toward the sound of the noise.

He was back in a few moments. "There's nobody there, darlin'," he reassured me, nestling against my round body.

The next morning, Bill said, "You scared the hell out of me last night. I thought you were waking me up because you wanted to make love and I was exhausted. I said to myself, 'This is a hell of a time for her to want to get laid'." I scooped my back, like a spoon, against his hard belly.

"I'm bilious," Bill complained on days when he came home tired and irritated. Almost immediately, he began to question his choice of a business partner. When the bank refused his loan to expand the furniture store, Bill discovered that his partner had an outstanding police record and had served time in prison. Bill began to pace the floor at night, unable to sleep.

"Why don't you tell him you're not satisfied?"

"I'm embarrassed. Maybe I've made a mistake borrowing money from my uncle and Avram."

"You can't keep everything bottled up inside," I insisted.

"Don't tell me what to do!" Bill grew irritable and sarcastic. He asked himself how he could possibly afford a wife, a child, and the responsibility of caring for his mother. He longed to be carefree and play ball. He longed for boyhood.

My husband sounded more and more like my father and I questioned if this was how all men were. I was filled with suggestions, but my husband wanted no advice.

Once when Bill had arranged a fishing trip for six a.m., after a night of playing cards and drinking with his buddies, I was silently furious. He set the alarm to awaken him one hour before he was to meet his friends, and then he passed out in bed. As soon as he began snoring I got up and turned off the alarm. When Bill's buddies came to pick him up in the morning he was still asleep. They were annoyed that they had to wait for him and when he came home that night his face had a greenish tint. He had vomited the entire day and caught not one fish. What's more, his friends had chided him the entire day about my little trick.

As the time drew nearer, I was more and more certain that I would be cheating Bill if I had a daughter. My parents had never had a boy. I was an earth mother now, a bearer of the race, and I felt elephantine.

We were sitting in the living room one evening, choosing names for our son, when Bill suddenly jumped out of his chair and ran toward me in a fierce rage. The baby garments that I was folding slid from my hands as Bill grabbed me by the throat and started choking me. I gasped for air, my arms flailing at my sides. I couldn't believe the look I saw on my husband's face. He gritted his teeth, never letting go of me. His eyes formed narrow slits. Then he backed away, finally, with clenched fists.

Bill's hands were big and strong. I stared at him in horror and found my voice in a few seconds. "You're trying to kill me!" I screamed. I was scared that he might grab me again.

I threw a maternity dress and some clean underwear into a small suitcase, ran out of the house, and caught the bus to my parents' apartment. They were not pleased at what I had to tell them.

"You must've done something that provoked him," were the first words out of my mother's mouth.

"I didn't do a thing." It didn't matter what happened, she would always blame me. And it made me mad as hell.

"You better go home," offered my father. He seemed perplexed and most unhappy about my being at their house. Neither of them wanted to get involved in a problem between Bill and me.

My mother made me a cup of hot cocoa and plopped two huge

marshmallows in the steamy liquid. I spooned the white sweet stuff into swirls and drank slowly, just as I had done as a child. It didn't seem that many years ago. Now, my physical discomfort was matched by the emotional highs and lows I was experiencing. I had no one to discuss my feelings with, nor did I think I had the right to them. Somehow the burden of bearing life was giving me a knowledge that I had never been taught. It seemed to me that a woman could learn more about life because she gives it.

An hour went by before Bill telephoned to say he was coming over to pick me up and bring me home. When he arrived, not a word was said about what had happened. Bill seemed somewhat contrite and the ferocious look had softened. He was his old self again.

On the way home I asked why he had tried to strangle me.

"Oh, darlin', you just overreacted. I wasn't trying to hurt you. I was teasing. Anyway, I'm sorry."

During the next week I wracked my brain for reasons and excuses to understand Bill's behavior. When Winnie Lou came to clean our apartment, we sat at the kitchen table drinking coffee and I told her what had happened.

"You reckon Bill feels guilty 'cause his Mama has to live alone in that tiny apartment?" she asked.

"We give her a check every week to help her out," I said. Then I confided to Winnie Lou about Bill's father's suicide.

"You know, he jes' might be scared of the responsibility of a wife, a business, and child," Winnie Lou said. "He jes' might be afraid he'll put a gun to his own head." Bill had once told me that immediately after his father's funeral, he had stood alone, and noticed several of the Jewish women in attendance pointing at him and whispering.

"I felt such shame I wanted to disappear," he had said.

To add to the disgrace, his father had been buried in a remote section of the Jewish cemetery where people who couldn't afford to pay for a gravestone were placed. And since suicide was considered a sin by Orthodox Jews, the survivors were not allowed to observe a formal mourning period.

"I used to dream that the back door of our small apartment would open and my father would be standing there in his policeman's uniform," Bill once said. "I would jump from my bed and rush to the door, but then I'd realize it was only a dream."

The strangling incident was never again discussed. And, of course, I forgave my husband. In some strange and unbeknown way that occurance would be added to my collection of unresolved hurts. They would gather, like a storm brewing at sea, waiting to erupt.

Chapter Thirteen

The baby was due the end of December 1947, but it was two weeks late, and I was afraid I'd be pregnant and nauseous for the rest of my life. I begged the doctor to give me a dose of castor oil to bring on birth. He wasn't keen on the idea, but when I persisted he said, "If that's what you want, then go ahead and take two full tablespoons."

Bill complained of stomach pain after the particularly delicious meal that we'd eaten at Ruth's house on Christmas day. As usual he had overeaten. So I spent the early part of the night that my baby was born taking care of my husband. Just after midnight, I shook Bill awake.

"Bill, water is pouring from my body," I said in terror.

"What does that mean?" He ran to the bathroom and brought me a stack of towels. I wadded the towels between my legs to blot the water while he phoned the doctor.

At St. Joseph's Hospital, I shrieked in solitary labor. The needle inserted deep into my spinal column had sent excruciating pain throughout my body, and as I lay there alone for an hour, cold and cramped on a small table, I was frightened that I might fall to the floor, that I might die.

At last the doctor came in and patted my belly. "Now, be a good girl, Naomi." Then he disappeared into the doctor's lounge for a nap. He had just come from a huge family Christmas celebration and good cheer, lots of good cheer.

"Jesus Christ!" I screamed. "Please give me some ether for this goddamn pain." I last remembered inhaling deeply as I'd been told to do by the attending nurse.

I was so terrified of childbirth that my body froze the moment labor started. Heavily drugged, I went through the experience without knowing what was happening and without helping. I didn't realize that the drugs in my bloodstream could get into the baby, and he could be born too doped to suckle — even if I was awake to offer my breast.

Pink and white like a candy cane, Isaac entered the world. He was my first born, and he was a shining thing.

"Sugar," said the doctor, "here's your little boy." He winked. "But, you sure embarrassed me in front of the nuns with your vocabulary. You really cut loose, let me tell you."

"Listen, Dr. Kelly, if those nuns ever had to go through the kind of pain that I just went through, God knows what cuss words they'd shout."

My mother said Isaac was adorable. He was a beautiful baby, smart and cheerful. We named him for Bill's father, despite some family members saying it invited bad luck to name him after someone who'd committed suicide. It was another of many Jewish superstitions.

"I'm too young to be a grandpa," Daddy said with a twinkle in his eye. He was forty-seven. He immediately coined the names Amma and Ampa for Mother and himself. Isaac was my parents' first grandchild and the first boy in the family. It was indeed the one time in my life that I felt successful in my mother's eyes.

Bill was ecstatic. He looked at our baby and gently poked at his soft flesh until Isaac's grin erupted. He rushed out and bought his son a football. Ruth and Ted were delighted to be Isaac's godparents.

This was the happiest moment of my life. As I held my son close to me, my husband smiled at us from where he was seated next to my bed. I looked at the two men in my life and felt like the luckiest woman in the world. Bill reached over and touched my cheek.

Our baby's next hurdle was the *bris*, the Jewish circumcision ceremony. It takes place on the eighth day after birth. Since I was still in the hospital the *bris* was performed in a special room down the hall from mine. My mother and aunts baked cookies for weeks, storing them in tins so they would be fresh for the ceremony. A ceremonial loaf of challah was ordered from Gottlieb's Bakery. Bill arranged for the rabbi to conduct the service, and a *mohel*, a specialist in the Jewish community experienced in such matters, performed the circumcision.

"I'm a what?" I yelled as I struggled to fit into a white lacy gown and peignoir that I had bought for the occasion. My swollen breasts looked as if Mae West had loaned them to me.

"You're a *kimpatorin*," my mother repeated. In Orthodox Judaism, the mother isn't allowed to watch the circumcision being performed, it being assumed that she's in too weakened a physical and emotional state. A new mother is considered an invalid for six weeks following the birth and is protected by the family. She's even called by the Yiddish name which means helpless. It's supposed to be a way of honoring the one who has given birth. I sat in my bed with a corsage of white orchids that Bill had sent pinned to my peignoir and received the guests after they left the *bris* and visited my room to wish me good luck with my baby.

The day after Isaac's circumcision I heard shuffling in the corridor just outside my room. I could sense that something was wrong when I heard the doctor's voice from a small closet next to my room, adjacent to my bathroom. I heard him ask for sutures as he ordered the nurses around. I listened carefully, trying to piece together the urgency. Frustrated, I rang for a nurse to come to my room.

"What's happening in the room next to mine?"

"Nothing," the nurse said, rushing out of my room.

When the doctor came in he was wearing his green smock and a surgical mask hung loosely from his head.

"Honey," he said, "you're now going to know exactly how it feels to be a mother."

"What do you mean?" I sat up and grabbed my robe from the foot of the bed.

"Your baby has hemorrhaged, and I was called to stitch his penis."

"Where is he?" I cried. I leapt out of the bed, and without stopping to put on slippers, raced down the hall to the nursery. Unable to locate Isaac through the large window of the nursery I ran back to my room to telephone Bill.

"He's in the small room next to yours, by himself," the doctor assured me.

"Let me see him. Let me hold him," I begged.

When Bill arrived with my parents we made the decision to call for a private duty nurse to stay with Isaac until we were sent home. The hospital's policy was to keep Jewish male babies in isolation the doctor informed me. The baby might be contaminated because he had been exposed to other people during the circumcision. So Isaac had been put in a room the size of a broom closet and at feeding time he had been forgotten. His hungry cries had caused his incision to open.

I didn't think to ask if non-Jewish babies, after routine circumcision, were removed to broom closets. I didn't ask if infants taken out of the nursery to their mothers for feeding were then isolated to prevent them from contaminating the babies who had stayed in a sterile environment.

Later, when I did think of such questions, I came to the conclusion that Isaac had been stuck away and forgotten because he was Jewish and for no other reason. It wasn't my first time to doubt the Jewish customs being thrust upon my young family.

Bill brought me home and up the stairs to our apartment after ten days. Winnie Lou carried Isaac and settled him in his new white crib. She wrapped a soft white mohair blanket about him.

Breast feeding Isaac didn't last very long. His hungry little mouth sucked and gummed my nipples until the pain was unbearable. And I had always been ashamed of my breasts; now they seemed dirty and sloppy. When the doctor ordered weekly shots to dry the milk and told me to bind my breasts with gauze I felt like a mummy who had fled an Egyptian crypt.

Bill was a wonderful father and I realized how lucky I was when he sterilized bottles and learned to make the formula for Isaac. He sang to his infant son as he walked around the apartment showing him his new home. Patiently, he diapered his baby boy, rubbing his fat little bottom with baby oil and sprinkling baby powder all over him. When Isaac peed in his face, Bill broke into loud laughter.

Isaac was barely two weeks old when I heard that the Ballet Russe de Monte Carlo was making an appearance in Savannah. I was feeling sentimental because one of our first date had been to the ballet. And ever since my days at dancing school, ballet had been my favorite art form.

"It's too soon," Bill said. "Isaac isn't old enough to leave."

"The ballet company will only be here for one performance," I said.

"I'm supposed to play in a basketball game."

We argued half the night. Bill finally agreed to go with me but his attitude was so hostile that I almost wished he hadn't. Several of his friends cursed at me for making Bill miss the game.

My dreams that marriage meant we did things together were fading. I wanted a husband to spend more time with me. But even with that bit of disappointment, when I was at home with my son I felt a God glimpse, and that compensated for anything that I didn't have.

Chapter Fourteen

"Eat *aynnekel*, eat *boychikel*," were the words my father sang every time we took Isaac to see my parents. Daddy loved having his grandson over for a visit and feeding him. He lapsed into his long-ago-past, remembering songs he hadn't sung since his childhood in Russia. He would sit with Isaac on his lap, smiling and singing. My mother was constantly placing a chicken bone in Isaac's hand. She very carefully spooned chicken soup into his mouth, blowing on the spoon to cool the broth. They were doting grandparents. It seemed as though my parents had lived through all their troubled times eagerly awaiting this moment. I felt that I'd given them something to make them happy, like a present they'd always wanted and now finally had.

My marriage and family life were beginning to fall into the comfortable pattern and typical routine of the married couples I saw around me. And though I wanted Bill to spend more time with me, doing what I considered adult things, like going to art galleries and attending the symphony when it visited town, he routinely took me out to eat once a week at Morrison's Cafeteria and to a movie. Frequently we visited our young friends for dinner on weekends or had them over to our apartment.

Ruth had a frown on her face when she came to visit. She told me that Ted was sulking and not happy that they were going to have a child. The cousins would be nine months apart.

"He's just like Daddy," she said. "He stares at the stock market pages while dreaming of being a millionaire. I swear, sometimes I ask myself why I married him."

"Because you two cha cha so great together or maybe you wanted to screw Daddy," I said, trying to cheer her. When Ruth and I were alone we could be just as silly as we had been during our teenage years. That didn't sit well with Minna. She insisted that her two married daughters act married, and I couldn't figure that out.

Mother urged us to join Hadassah and various other women's organizations. She even paid our membership so she'd be sure we joined. Once in a while I'd attend a meeting with her, but I was bored. It wasn't my cup of tea; my interests leaned more toward politics.

Life with Isaac was bliss; he was such a sweet baby. Bill and I hated to leave him for an evening or an afternoon so we took him with us whenever we visited friends. I only trusted my parents or Winnie Lou with Isaac. Twenty months later, while I was in the hospital giving birth to our second son, Alex, I had my twenty-third birthday. Things were different with the second birth.

"I'm not going to have a *bris*," I protested to my mother. The thought of some barbarian slicing my baby's penis infuriated me. I had changed doctors but the new one refused to honor my request to perform the circumcision in my room or in the operating room. He said he wouldn't go against Jewish culture in Savannah because it would hurt his practice. To me Orthodox Judaism was beginning to feel like a thorn in my flesh.

In the end, I acquiesced. My mother had been nagging me for days. She even solicited Bill's mother in persuading us that it was the right thing to do. But this time when I left the hospital I hired a practical nurse to stay with us for three weeks. I was experiencing postnatal depression and was unprepared for the blues that caught up with me.

I loved Isaac so deeply that a fear engulfed me that I might not have enough love for another child. Alex cried far more than Isaac had. He would wake us all through the night, interrupting our sleep and exhausting us. One night I was so tired and filled with anxiety that I threatened to slap him. Bill had to stop me.

"Mommy bed, Daddy bed," Isaac would cry. He wanted to sleep in our bed every night. The physical exhaustion and frayed nerves were very new and scary to me but I ignored them.

"Baby boy Alex," was Isaac's first sentence. He stood over the crib and tickled his infant brother, loving the fact that there was a new baby in our family. Now I wanted to swallow them both, and Bill to swallow me, so all of us could be just one.

Once more, I went back to work at Bill's store in the afternoons, still without compensation. My husband took it for granted that I'd oversee the office and keep his books just as I was doing in our personal life. And though I found his business boring, I desperately wanted us to be partners and equals.

Both children loved Winnie Lou who now divided her time between my parents' apartment and mine. She cradled them, singing the same songs she had sung to their mother. My two boys were dressed alike most of the time and every night when I came home from work I stopped to polish their little shoes so they would be perfect and white the next day. Daddy teased me about having two dolls to play with.

Everything about my sons delighted me. They brought joy to my heart, proving that I had enough love in my heart for twelve children, if I so desired. Everywhere I went I talked about them.

"You're not supposed to brag about your own children," Ruth chided me. How could I not talk about the two that brought my life such joy? That didn't make sense to me.

On the other hand, Ruth's son, Gary, was given to tantrums. He would bang his head against the concrete sidewalk. He was trying to tell his parents something that they just weren't hearing. My sister's patience wore thin.

"Ted's cruel to him," Ruth said. It was hard for me to understand this because Ted was always kind to Isaac and Alex. My sister was sad that her son didn't have a loving father. She was amazed how the boys loved to climb all over Bill. and how extremely affectionate he was to them. Bill never had trouble kissing his sons.

From the start, Alex seemed to feel he had to live up to his older brother. Isaac was built more like Bill with a large muscular frame, while Alex was like my father, small and wiry.

When the furniture store began showing a profit Bill and I started planning a vacation to Miami Beach. Bill's brother, Elliott, who had moved back to Savannah with his wife and daughter, was having financial troubles and asked Bill if he could come to work for him. I wasn't too happy about this, since I'd always pictured myself and Bill as equal-partners in life and in business.

"My uncle says he'll help me buy out my partner with the understanding that Elliott go into business with me," Bill told my father, when he went to him and asked for another loan. My father thought it would be a better idea for his two daughters and their husbands to build a business together.

"My uncle insists that I take in my brother, and besides, he's not making a decent living." Bill felt terrible that his older brother was struggling in his job. Added to that was the guilt that their mother was living with Elliott.

I was angry because I had thought all along that the reason I worked without making a salary was so I would become the other half. When I mentioned it to my father, he agreed.

"Don't let them push you out of the store," Daddy said.

But I had little to do with any of Bill's business decisions. It was taken for granted that I'd continue to work for free while I taught Elliott the business. The accountant, Bill's business advisor, said to me, "It's not a good policy for a wife and husband to work together." It was hard for me to believe one word of advice about marriage being offered by the accountant since he was on his third wife and cheating on her, too.

"Why don't you consider selling real estate?" the accountant suggested. The only thing I knew about real estate were the stories and the memory of my grandfather Zelig and his slum properties. My parents had never given one thought to owning their own home, though all of their sisters and brothers were homeowners.

"It's a booming industry," the accountant said. "Hardly any women are in that field, and many couples are buying homes under the G.I. Housing Bill, which helps finance veterans in purchasing homes."

A few weeks later, I went to talk to a local Realtor. He was a builder who had a terrible reputation within the Jewish community. No one trusted him. However, he did an enormous business and built gorgeous homes. Mr. Rosen seemed delighted to meet me. I sat across the desk from him in his well-appointed office, taking in his infectious smile and silvery gray hair.

I couldn't help but notice that his nails were well manicured and how well he was dressed. Mr. Rosen leaned over and handed me a small brown pamphlet and told me I'd have to study it, then go to Atlanta and pass an exam in order to get a real estate license. I was ecstatic at the thought of having a career of my own. Bill offered to lend me his car when I needed it.

Ella and Ruth agreed to go with me to Atlanta, when the time came for me to take the real estate test. We decided to make it a fun shopping trip as well. The Nancy Hanks train took six hours. We spent the night since the real estate exam would take another four hours and was to be given at nine the next morning. I got up early so I could catch a bus there. Then I met my sister and aunt at Rich's Department Store. We shopped for three more hours buying skirts, sweaters, and shoes. We looked like he original version of country-come-to-town.

"My God, Ella," I said, laughing and pointing to my aunt's shoes. Ella was short and had very small feet. Her feet were swollen from all the walking they had done. "You've worn your feet down to stubs. I swear, it looks as if you have only heels with toes protruding."

The three of us stood around pointing at Ella's puffy feet, doubled over in laughter. Ella had a habit of wetting her pants when she laughed too hard. We watched the trickle run down her legs and into her black patent leather pumps right there in the middle of the shoe department.

The day that I received my real estate license, I was nervous but excited. I felt like a woman of the world, ready to step out and claim my independence. The piece of paper seemed very official and important. I went to work for Abe Rosen who welcomed me to his company. He eyed my curvy figure from top to bottom as he showed me to my desk. Then he took me through the office and introduced me to the rest of the staff.

I scheduled my appointments so I could be at home with the children in the afternoon. Immediately I became friends with Catherine, a cheerful Irish woman who worked as the office manager. I turned out to be a dedicated employee, often working until midnight to make a sale and devoting weekends to seeing walk-ins at open houses.

"You seem to be a natural for selling, Naomi," Mr. Rosen said. He asked if I would like to hold an open house Sunday afternoon on Brandywine Road, a new development that he had started. I jumped at the opportunity. I hadn't given one thought to who would take care of my boys. But I knew that either Winnie Lou or my parents would.

On Sunday I slipped into a beautiful chocolate brown sundress with spaghetti straps; it had a tight skirt with a ruffle running down one side. I strapped on a pair of high heeled multi-striped sandals and readied myself to drive to Brandywine. Carefully I smoothed my hair into a pageboy, then applied lipstick and eye makeup. I was a bit overdressed; I looked more like I was going to a cocktail party than to sell real estate.

When I got to Brandywine I unlocked the door. The house had been furnished with superb taste. I settled into the soft beige cushions of the living room sofa. Every time someone walked in I hurried to show them through the rooms. The kitchen had aqua appliances and the square tiles on the floor were color coordinated. It was my dream house but too expensive for Bill and me. Two hours had passed when Mr. Rosen stopped by to see how I was handling things.

"I have a list of interested buyers," I said. I was excited about the way the afternoon was going.

"You're learning quickly," he said as he sat next to me on the couch. His white teeth shone when he smiled. He wore a well tailored brown flannel suit. As we discussed the new house that was being built just across the street he put his arm around my shoulders. Just as he leaned over to kiss me the front door swung open and a young couple entered. I felt saved by the bell but I had to admit that I was somewhat titillated. The man was a charmer. Older, handsome, and successful.

I made the first sale of my career in 1950. It was a small house in a new subdivision. It sold for thirteen thousand dollars. My commission was three hundred and twenty-five dollars. I decided right then and there to open my own checking account. I was feeling quite independent and glowing with pride as I stared at the check made out to me, not to my husband.

"I'm going to buy a secondhand car," I announced to Bill. "I need it for my work." I had been using his Nash and had to return it to him every time he needed it. The used, black Plymouth two-door coupe that I purchased couldn't have meant more to me had it been a Rolls Royce.

By summer the real estate business was flourishing and I began to make bigger sales. However, I grew suspicious when Abe, as Mr. Rosen now had me call him, told me that he could handle the closing of a particularly large sale of mine without me. When I met him in his office to pick up my commission check, he was most cordial.

"Let me look at the closing statement," I said. I had made it a practice to always examine the documents concerning any sale that I had been involved with.

"Oh, I've already filed them away with the secretary," he said.

"I want to see them."

"Don't you trust me?" He flashed me his capricious smile.

"It's my responsibility to check all papers. It's my duty. And frankly, I have a right to see them." He asked Catherine to bring in a copy of the settlement sheet. I quickly glanced over it and when I'd finished looking at the figures, it was quite obvious that he had shorted me by two hundred dollars.

My hands were shaking. "You owe me two hundred dollars," I said.

"Well, I made concessions to them by swapping a gutter over the front porch, that's why the figures reflect that way."

"Give me my money, or I'll tell Bill," I demanded. I picked up a small metal file case with the names of his prospective clients in it and slung it across his desk. He was surprised, but he knew I couldn't be pushed further.

"You don't need to call Bill, darling. We'll work this out. Remember, we're sort of like a married couple. Just because we don't agree, it doesn't mean divorce." My boss had always been a fan of Bill's athletic prowess, ever since his boxing days, and the mere thought of Bill knocking him in the jaw was the clincher for getting the money that was rightfully mine. He had Catherine draw a check for two hundred dollars and gave it to me.

Several weeks later when Catherine asked me to meet her for lunch at the Pink House, I found that she'd already been making plans to leave. Catherine had decided that she could no longer work for a man she didn't trust and would open her own office. She rented an historic brick building overlooking the murky Savannah River.

"You know, Naomi, Mr. Rosen was scared to death that you might tell Bill what happened and that Bill would beat the hell out of him. If there's anything that man's scared of, it's being hit," Catherine said. Then she asked me to consider transferring my real estate license to her new firm. She planned to open her office the early part of 1953.

"That'll be a welcome change," I said. I liked the idea of going to an office on the waterfront. I would hike up the cobble-stone path in my high heels every morning, gazing at the boats that were sailing up the Savannah River, as they made their way to the ocean.

"I used to be a waitress at Leopold's Soda Shop," Cricket Jones said when she joined the firm. She was short, stout, and wore her peroxided blonde hair in a beehive. "I can make a lot more money in real estate and not have to take all that damned chiding." Every time Cricket crossed her legs, her nylon stockings whistled against each other.

Soon, other women began to join our real estate company. It was an all-woman office and, therefore, a unique experience for all of us. We shared our domestic lives, our frustrations, and traded stories about our husbands. We ordered hamburgers smothered in onions and shrimp salad sandwiches from the Crystal Beer Parlor and ate a communal lunch at our desks.

When Nancy Bragg came to work for Catherine, she had been a practicing attorney, and at one time had owned an accessory shop in the downtown business area. But now she was anxious to try her hand at real estate. "I can do anything a man can do," Nancy said. "I think I can do it better."

Nancy had married late in life, to a successful insurance man ten years her junior. They had two sons. Nancy was a good agent, but if a sale fell through that she'd been working on, she would bury her head in her hands and cry. Nancy felt that she, not the property, had been rejected.

"Remember, Nancy," Cricket comforted her, time after time, in an attempt to make her take the blame off of herself. "As they say in Hollywood — fuck 'em if they can't take a joke."

Another agent, Dawn Keating, was a suburban housewife with two children who had graduated summa cum laude in biology from Emory University in Atlanta. When Catherine hired her, Dawn candidly told us, "At first I liked staying home and raising the children. But when they were able to do more for themselves, my household duties became a mindless habit. I was growing more and more frustrated. Something I used to have was missing."

I nodded in understanding, stuffing the hamburger into my mouth. Every one of us was in pursuit of our true identity. It was as though we were all links in the same chain.

"Ever since I was a young girl," Dawn said, "I've been pro-grammed by family and society in general to think that marriage is a woman's greatest calling. There's got to be more. If I sell real estate, at least I can replace some missing parts."

And yet another one of our office staff taught us not to take any bullshit from a man. "I was nursing my fourth baby," Joan Halligan said, "when that son of a bitch husband dumped a plate of spaghetti on me, down my breasts." Joan got up, put the baby in his crib, and after cutting her husband's best suit into pieces, flushed it down the toilet.

Then she left him, taking the baby, the crib, and the other children with her. She was hellbent on taking care of herself and her children.

Chapter Fifteen

In spite of the fact that I had become a successful real estate agent it took a great deal of talking, nudging, and coaxing to finally convince Bill that we should buy our first home, a three bedroom, two bath ranch style bungalow just across from a golf course and adjacent to a farm. The house on Bacon Park Drive had a double carport, and Bill immediately hung a basketball hoop so he could play ball with his sons. I was asked to be president of the Fairway Oaks Garden Club almost as soon as we moved in. Planting my garden gave me a sense of being rooted, especially as I watched my prize-winning roses grow. Bill gladly left the decorating to me, which pleased me. But I still wanted more sharing of it with him.

"Digging in the dirt makes my skin crawl," Bill said when I begged him to work in the yard with me. I began to realize that Bill left almost everything up to me. Sometimes I wondered if I had invented him so that I could pretend to have the man of my dreams, rather than accept him for who and what he really was. My husband had his own vision of what our life as a married couple was supposed to be. He just wanted to play a little ball and earn enough money for his family. For Bill, that was enough — a full life.

It wasn't long before entertaining in our new home became a hobby for me, giving lavish dinner parties so that I could attract new clients. It was natural for me and I thoroughly enjoyed showing houses to young couples who dared to dream of their ideal home. I liked spending time shopping with them, helping them decorate their dream houses, and often guiding them to my husband's store, which helped Bill's business.

Real estate was very satisfying. While most of my women friends in the Jewish community thought working to be declasse, I felt a sense of personal accomplishment. I was now earning money of my own. And I was doing something I liked. I was lunching with bankers, accountants, attorneys, and other important business and professional men. They liked me and offered advice and strategies for expanding my sales. And I found that I liked working in a man's world.

I had established a rhythm to my life, working in the morning, being home when my sons came home, running from sales meetings to Cub Scout meetings, serving as an officer in the local real estate society, as well as president of the P.T.A. Like a human firecracker, I was moving faster than time. It gave me a feeling of being successful. And as fast as I ran, I attempted to make Bill run at the same speed. But he didn't have the same ambitions that I had.

My self confidence grew as I developed a reputation for being a salesperson who could find exactly what someone wanted in a very short time. I had people calling me constantly. It pleased me to find someone the home of their dreams.

In September of 1953, before Isaac's sixth birthday, he was enrolled in a private school called Pape, where Savannah's elite sent their children. The Chatham County Public School system used September lst as the time frame and we didn't want him to lose a year. Because Isaac's birthday was in December, he missed the cut-off date for entering first grade. Of course Bill and I considered him ready for Harvard from the time he was two.

Isaac had a keen thirst for knowledge. He came home from school one day and, having been told to play a game of phonetics for his home-work assignment, tried it out at the dinner table that night. As plates of food were being passed around, Isaac said, "Think of a vegetable that starts with the letter 't'."

"Tomato," I said.

"Nope," he said, his round face broadened into a grin.

"Turnips," suggested Bill.

"Nope." Another grin. "Give up?"

"Turkey?" Bill said.

"Oh, Dad! Be serious!"

"I've got it! I've got it!" I shouted. *"Tzimmis,"* I said as I broke into laughter.

When we had exhausted our answers, Isaac shook his head from side to side. "Tater salad!" he announced proudly. His dimples and smile could light up the darkest sky, just as they did inside my heart.

But there came a time when I felt that Isaac was ashamed of me. I had gone to his school to see his teacher, and he had looked away from me. I had just come from an important real estate luncheon and was wearing a slim black wool dress, a large hat, and long, black gloves. I thought I looked attractive. But my son was critical.

"Why don't you dress like other mothers?" he asked that night as I helped him with his homework.

"I had on my best dress, honey."

"You looked too dressed up, Mommy."

I couldn't help but notice that most women attending school functions at Pape wore simple short-sleeved cotton frocks, a uniform of tiny floral prints on shirtwaist dresses. These young mothers took pride in their sameness; I didn't want to look like everyone else. One of my favorite things to do was to study fashion magazines and experiment with makeup and hairdos. In every part of my life I was striving to be independent, and it seemed to always bring on criticism. That night, as I hung my clothes in the closet, I wondered when, if ever, my family would stop trying to change me.

Only when I was working did I truly feel a sense of self-worth. As I and the women in my office soon discovered, work became far more than about earning money. It established our identities as productive and independent people. We felt a camaraderie, a feeling of trust and mutual support. I learned to be more assertive. And I had long ago stopped worrying about a boss who would try to cheat me out of a commission I had just earned. The wrenching resentment of thinking I was alone finally disappeared.

As the women in the office talked about preparing for their Christmas holiday, I remembered how as a child I had wished I could have Santa visit. I wanted Isaac and Alex to experience Santa Claus. It seemed unfair for all of their friends to get toys under a tree, while they didn't. It was a few weeks before Christmas when I stopped by to inspect a new shipment of carpeting at Bill's store. Bill had recently opened a bigger store there near the corner of Barnard Street.

The downtown area was aglow with decorations. Christmas was a happy time, and I'd dreamed forever of having a tree with lights and tinsel. The closest I had come was the time my mother hung up an old pair of Daddy's argyle socks and filled them with Hershey kisses, tangerines, and pecans.

"Bill, I want the children to have Santa Claus," I said as I flipped through the carpet samples.

"My mother'll have a fit, if she sees a tree in our house," Bill said. He lit a big cigar and showed me a piece of carpet that he particularly liked.

"It'll be fun."

"Fine with me. I'd love to play Santa."

And so our boys observed both Chanukah and Christmas. It felt very natural to light the candles of the *menorah* and at the same time decorate the pine tree with colorful ornaments. Little by little, I was letting go of the traditional Jewish upbringing I'd known and beginning to embrace more of the modern customs. I didn't observe kosher dietary laws in my home. In fact, I often questioned whether I even felt like a Jew.

And what exactly did that mean? Did one have to feel like a martyr or suffer to practice Judaism? It seemed to me that all religions were actually reaching for the same thing, and that we should all learn about each others' beliefs. I wanted and needed a more positive approach to life. I was tired of thinking that I had inherited the right to suffer.

Just before Christmas, I sat with my boys in front of the T.V. set, watching an Arthur Godfrey program where he was showing the latest in toys. Then afterwards, as the three of us were busy dripping silver icicles and hanging colored balls on our tree, the children made notes of what they wanted.

"I want that jigsaw puzzle, the one of the entire world that's shaped like a globe," Alex said. He was good at following intricate instructions.

Suddenly Isaac started to cry.

"What's wrong, honey?" I asked. He turned his face away from me to the wall.

"If I tell you what I want you'll think I'm a sissy," he sobbed.

"Well, just tell me." I sat next to him on the sofa and put my arms around him.

"I want the cookie baking set, so I can make cookies like Amma's.

"That's fine, Isaac. Don't you know some of the greatest chefs in the world are men?" I wanted my boys to have just a few years of fantasy, of believing that Santa Claus would bring them whatever they wanted.

And that men had the right to enjoy domestic bliss.

The clock in our house could be set according to Bill's behavior. He came home every afternoon from the furniture store, went into the kitchen, opened the lid of every pot, smiled, and then went in to wrestle with his sons. They would pretend to have him pinned on the floor and yell, "It's beat-up-Daddy day."

"I hear your brother's going to buy a house," I said to Bill one night as he sat behind the newspaper picking his nose. Bill opened the *Savannah Evening Press*, while I creamed the potatoes for our dinner.

"Why didn't you tell him to use me as his agent?"

"I can't butt into his business." Bill spoke as though to dismiss my remark. He had a different attitude when he talked about the sales of his business. I was pissed off.

"That stinks! Where is your loyalty? I get pushed out of your damned business so he can be your partner, and neither of you even think of my career?" I felt betrayed and hurt. We ate our dinner in silence.

When Isaac was seven, and Alex five, there was a deep-seated restlessness stirring inside of me; something was missing. Work didn't seem to be the complete answer. I longed for something new, something different.

"Let's try for a daughter," I said, one night lying snuggled next to Bill. I was in my late twenties, and had always expected to have four children, ever since I was a child and fell in love with the *Bobbsey Twins*.

In the last eight years, Bill had become less and less decisive, leaving it up to me to make the family decisions that I had hoped would be mutual ones. So I really didn't need his approval, just his cooperation. At first I didn't tell the others in the office that I was pregnant. But as my belly started to protrude and maternity clothes were necessary, I announced it. Catherine threw a baby shower for me at The Pink House restaurant, and most of the gifts had a tint of pink in them.

Six years had passed since I held a baby next to me, and the arrival of Ross in October, 1955 awakened not only my adoration but also my parents' and that of the baby's older brothers.

While I was giving birth to our third son, Bill stood outside the delivery room with his brother. Elliott and his wife had just had their third daughter a few weeks earlier.

"It's another boy," shouted the doctor. I was exhausted, but I could hear the yelling just outside the room.

"Well, Doc, what can I do to change our luck so Naomi and I can have a daughter, and my brother and his wife can have a son?" Bill asked loudly. The doctor's chuckle floated overhead. The loud voices mixed with mirth continued to race back and forth through the hospital corridor. I was too tired to make sense of what they were saying. But I managed to catch the doctor's words.

"Well, you and Elliott could try changing wives next time, Bill," he answered.

"Hell, Doc, that's what we did this time," Elliott said as the two brothers broke into laughter.

A terrible secret had been kept from me while I was in the hospital. My father had tried to kill himself again. He was given shock treatments to relieve his chronic depression.

My mother telephoned Ruth the morning she found Daddy unconscious in the bathroom. He had slit his wrists with razor blades. There was blood all over the sink.

"I don't know what to do," Mother said.

"I'll come right over and take him to the hospital." Ruth agreed to drive him to and from the mental ward in St. Joseph's Hospital for his bi-weekly shock treatments. The psychiatrist who presided over him was a cousin of Bill's and the only practicing psychiatrist in Savannah.

"He's like an animal," Ruth told Mother each time she brought him home. "I hate seeing him like this. He's unable to speak, and he dribbles at the mouth."

Over a period of twenty-five years, my father had attempted suicide three or four times. And each time my family tried to hide it from me. I wondered if they thought I was wearing diapers and still asleep in the wicker bassinet on Charlton Street. Ruth bore the responsibility of Daddy's mental care, while Mother took care of him physically. Ruth had come to feel like she was the parent to Minna and Avram.

Despite my father's fragile physical and psychological health, he was a good grandfather. Ruth's daughter and son and my three sons brought more simple pleasure to his last years than he had ever known. It seemed the children prolonged his life, giving him strength after illness overtook him, even after a leg had to be amputated from the complications of diabetes.

We sat around the waiting room after that last operation, wondering how he would respond to having one leg. Hours after the surgery, when I walked into his hospital room, my eyes rested hesitantly on the sheet that covered the leg that now ended just above his knee.

"I'll bring Ross up to see you tomorrow," I said, fumbling for words. My father smiled. We were silent. Because of our silence, the noises in the hall sounded like a roar.

Eventually he was fitted with an artificial limb, and even with the phantom pains he felt in the leg he no longer had, he never lost his sense of humor. It saw him through the difficult days of crutches, walkers, and canes.

Daddy instructed us that when his time came, he wanted engraved on his tombstone, the sentence: "I told them I was sick." Bill went back and forth with Avram to Atlanta for fittings on his artificial leg and many afternoons took him to watch Alex play Little League baseball.

It didn't take long for me to rediscover that a new baby in the house meant a deluge of domesticity, which I had certainly asked for, but which failed to satisfy that gnawing hunger. Bill was preoccupied with his business and political meetings. And though Bill was expanding his furniture business, my dissatisfaction was acute.

I never seemed to think we had enough money. God only knows what would have been enough for me. Nothing ever seemed to satisfy me for any period of time: there was always a higher goal to be met. Only I wanted Bill to meet it.

Bill had become an avid golfer, and any spare time he had was spent on the links. I knew by now that I had the talent and skill to sell real estate, so I decided that when Ross was four years old, I would return full-time to my career. Besides, I wanted a bigger house, more clothes, a fancier car, and expensive jewelry.

By now my dreams had become quite grandiose — maybe a swimming pool, a trip to Europe. Yet, whatever it was I was searching for, I seemed to face enormous obstacles finding it. I hungered to have someone I loved tell me how to infuse my life with purpose and meaning.

And while I faced inner turmoil, my father's health was getting worse. Because the needle frightened him, my mother, reluctantly got the job, of giving him insulin shots.

"I hate to come home from work; I never know if I'll find him dead," Mother complained to me on the phone one evening. She worked full time as a check-out clerk at a neighborhood supermarket. Daddy was unable to work and was receiving disability pay.

At the end of his life, back in the hospital, Avram called for his wife and daughters to come into his room separately. Later, I found out that he had said to Ruth the same words he'd said to me. "I'm sorry if I didn't do everything right. I always loved you."

Mother didn't say what he told her.

My father died in the hour before dawn in late October. I was in his hospital room, alone with the nurse. My mother waited in the lounge. I walked out of his room and went to her. "It's over," I said, putting my arm around her shoulders. "Daddy's dead."

She fixed her eyes on the floor, her shoulders fell into a slouch. "Now I'm a widow," she murmured. Her voice was filled with self-pity. I was stunned at my mother's reaction and sensed that not only was she weary but perhaps glad, or at least relieved, to have this ordeal over. Her life with my father had certainly not been an easy one.

I felt an immediate rush of guilt that we hadn't let him have the chocolate ice cream cone he had wanted just two days earlier.

Avram was buried in the Richman family plot in Bonaventure Cemetery, next to my grandparents, Zelig and Eva. When the services ended, Mother nudged me and Ruth toward the water spigot. It's a Jewish custom to wash death off your hands after the cemetery services. I invited my mother to stay at my house during the week of Jewish mourning. All the aunts and uncles arrived each day to receive friends who came to offer sympathy and pay their respects. Huge meals were served daily. Mother thrived on being the center of attention, probably for the first time in her life.

One night when everyone had gone I turned to Bill with a sudden reality that I would never see Daddy again. "There were so many things I wish I'd said to him."

"You had him a lot longer than I had my father," Bill said. At that moment, he looked as I imagined he must have looked as a boy of seven, when his father put a gun to his head and blew his brains out in their living room. I felt a small sense of relief that despite his attempts, my father hadn't died by his own hand.

I was exhausted from having a continual group of people in our house for every meal. As I readied myself for bed one night I noticed a few strands of gray peppered throughout my hair. Glancing at my face I saw that my eyes had lines that seemed to have appeared suddenly.

"Thomas Wolfe says of George Webber speaking to his editor, 'For I was lost and was looking for someone older and wiser to show me the way, and I found you, and you took the place of my father, who had died.'" I was reading aloud, from *You Can't Go Home Again*, while my husband snored noisily, not hearing a word.

Sighing, I sank into the soft pillows and turned out my bed lamp. Tears ran down my cheeks in the darkness and I clung to my pillow for comfort.

At the end of the required week of mourning, my mother went back to her apartment. She was sad and lonely, yet, I thought, very brave. The family saw to it that she spent very little time alone. She'd have dinner with Ruth one night every week and one night with me, and visit her sisters and brothers on the other evenings. She returned to her job at the supermarket which was within walking distance of her apartment. She welcomed the chance to be around people all day.

Chapter Sixteen

I was over thirty when I became curious about who I really was, before I began to see the role of the American house-wife as soul-rotting and intellectually barren. I had been married for twelve years and had begun to discard the diehard enthusiasm for domesticity that had shaped my dreams as a young bride. But I, unlike most women, had begun a career. And though I loved creating a lovely home, I intuitively knew that just being a housewife wasn't enough for me.

Preparing the huge picnic lunches for the family outings on Sundays fed my sense of family. Bill would fix his famous waffle and bacon breakfast while I pranced around the kitchen packing the picnic basket. Bill was traveling a great deal of the time, opening furniture stores in Charleston and Brunswick, but on Sundays during the summer we would drive to the beach and enjoy the sunshine while the boys played ball. It was such a happy time, even with the normal boyhood squabbles over lost games and toys.

Isaac, like Bill, praised everything I cooked. On the other hand, Alex had the strange habit of partitioning his food into separate piles. The peas were not allowed to touch the mashed potatoes, the meat was not to mingle with anything else on his plate, and God forbid if the salad was anywhere near any of the above. He ate each pile separately too, finishing one before starting on the other. It drove me mad, but at least he was eating the whole meal.

Ross also had peculiar eating habits. For one whole year, he ate only peanut butter and jelly sandwiches, three meals a day. Then suddenly he made the switch to bologna and white bread, spread thick with slabs of mayonnaise for the following year.

Once when we were on a family vacation in Florida, Bill and I insisted that one member of the family order pancakes each morning at the restaurant because Ross was now eating only pancakes. I felt that if he ate only one pancake out of the stack, that he'd have some nourishment for the day.

"He's spoiled!" Alex said, protesting the way we ordered breakfast. But Ross got his pancake, and we ate the rest of the stack.

When Winnie Lou remarried at the age of seventy-two and added the name of Jones to Winnie Lou Estelle Augusta Middleton Coleman Williams and moved to South Carolina, she arranged for her niece, Dora, to come to work for us. Ross was three years old and Dora was wrapped around his little finger in no time. So was the entire family. Ross was sweet and cuddly, and very affectionate, like his dad and his brother Isaac. Alex didn't have time to be bothered: he was always reading or working on an intricate science project. Our middle son asked far more questions than his brothers. He asked more questions than God.

There was little doubt that Isaac was the athlete in the family: he excelled in most sports, which pleased Bill to no end. Alex fought constantly to keep up with his brother and his father. Ross, the mascot was overly indulged.

Once we moved to the suburbs we become pioneers in the new way of life that was sweeping across America, with look-a-like houses and manicured lawns. On Saturday nights, when the weather permitted, we'd gather in the backyard with our neighbors, drink gin and tonics, and party. We stuffed ourselves on barbecued chicken and steak, told dirty jokes and got drunk.

"That Patsy was one great *nafka* (whore)," I overheard Bill say to one of his buddies. I was busy in the kitchen arranging hors d'oeuvres on a tray during a dinner party. Bill didn't bother to change the conversation when I brought in the tray of food. As they took hot cheese puffs off the tray and popped them into their mouths, Bill and his friends blatantly continued to describe their youthful visits to St. Julian Street prostitutes, which had been Savannah's red light district. It was easy for men to talk about women as sexual objects, and about having flings or one-night stands or even, God forbid, affairs.

It had never occurred to me that as Bill's dutiful wife, I could have an affair. That was something men did, not women. A man's sexual needs were greater than a woman's I had been told. The guys acted as though it were a great accomplishment when my husband crowed that a prostitute had offered him pleasure at no charge during his days as a boxer, so well endowed was he.

"I don't understand those men; it's as if they're not satisfied with a good wife who caters to them," my sister said. "I may not have much with Ted, but I'll tell you one thing, sex is delicious. We've done it in a hospital bed, on the kitchen table, and standing up in the shower."

I got a big kick out of my sister's candor. Maybe I was missing something. And though I didn't acknowledge it, sex to me remained a taboo subject. Minna had taught me well, as though she had forged her sexual inhibitions into me, like the grooves on a record. For the first time, I began to wonder about sex with some of the men I'd met through my real estate work.

Our lives were filled with childhood growing pains and traumas never ceased. Someone was always hurt for one reason or another. It was part of raising a family, I was told. Once while Alex was playing "Davey Crockett" with one of his playmates the two started fighting and rolling on the lawn. When Alex pulled away the other child reached out to bite his leg. Alex came flying into the house with blood pouring from his penis.

He had managed to squirm from the child's attempt to bite him on his thigh, but the boy had missed his mark and Alex's urinary tract had been injured. The doctor said it was a miracle that he wasn't injured for life.

And Ross, at age four, anxious to be independent like his brothers, climbed on a stool one Saturday afternoon to reach the cord that pulled down the attic steps. The stool slipped and he fell and broke his left arm.

"It's your fault," I screamed at Bill when he came home from the golf course. "If you'd ever stay home with your children like you're supposed to, this wouldn't've happened." Bill had grown accustomed to me blaming him for everything bad that happened. He stood in the kitchen and shook his head, then mixed a martini.

Our boys adored their father. He knew how to joke around with them, and he also was a big tease. One day as he prepared to barbecue in the back yard, he called the boys together.

"There's something I want you fellows to know." He was actually trying to squelch an argument that was going on between Isaac and Alex.

"What is it, Dad?" Alex said.

"This is a very serious matter," Bill added. He leaned over the grill and wiped the grate with oil. And then with his most somber voice he said, "I must tell you that one of you guys was really born a girl, and it's time for the other two to know." The boys glanced around from one to the other, waiting, wondering. Bill broke into a loud roar.

"Dad, that's not funny," Isaac said. But his brothers and father couldn't stop laughing and finally, Isaac joined in, too.

Religion had puzzled me most of my life. Everything seemed to be run by rote. Yet Bill and I felt a sense of obligation to have our sons experience their Jewish rite of passage.

Due to tradition we were members of the Orthodox synagogue; our families had always gone there. As Isaac was approaching thirteen, and though his schedule was full, he would come home from school in the afternoon and then go straight to Hebrew school, while he was preparing for his *bar mitzvah*.

In the fall of 1960, Bill and I were in Atlanta. We had been invited to have cocktails aboard a houseboat on Lake Lanier, a huge man-made lake named after the nineteenth century Georgia poet, Sidney Lanier. Our host drank too much but insisted on driving us back to Atlanta. His black Thunderbird collided with an oncoming car. One of the passengers in our car broke her pelvis, another an arm. Bill and the driver escaped injury.

I was pulled from the wreck and placed in the middle of the rain-drenched highway to await the ambulance. My collarbone was broken. I felt paralyzed. I wondered if I would ever walk again.

"What about my three boys?" I cried from the highway. "Who will take care of them if I'm a cripple?"

Bill's wealthy cousin, who lived in Atlanta, came to visit me in my postage-stamp sized room at Piedmont Hospital.

With him was A.D. Levy.

Chapter Seventeen

With my shoulder wrapped in a figure-eight bandage, my feet virtually jutting into the hallway, because the hospital room was so small, I was a mess.

"Naomi, do you know who I am?" A.D. said. I chalked that up as one of the more curious questions ever put to me. But, as it happened, I did know he was a corporate lawyer from Atlanta, and success radiated from his pinstriped three-piece suit like neon lights. He was semi-bald with a fringe of gray hair and he wore metal framed eyeglasses. When he put out his hand to shake mine, I noticed a solid gold watch on his left wrist, a bracelet of gold linked chain on the other.

"You're the lawyer who was written up in *The New York Times* for bribing politicians in Washington," I said. Nothing like some hospital drugs to bring out the truth. I remembered that the paper had reported how he had offered certain public servants their pick of deep freezers or mink coats. "Do you happen to have a freezer on you? I need one." My eyes were glazed, my speech slurred. I didn't know what the hell I was saying, as the words spilled from my mouth like popped corn.

"You're a *mazik*," A. D. said, referring to the Yiddish word for a bright, mischievous, imaginative child. He laughed at my wild accusations.

He offered to represent Bill and me against the driver, who now claimed he hadn't touched a drop. A.D. sent bouquets of roses to my hospital room every day with a card signed from his wife and him. Three months later, I saw A.D. again. We had invited him to Isaac's *bar mitzvah*. He came alone.

I had to rely on others to get the celebration organized because it took so long for my shoulder to mend. Ruth drove me back and forth to the doctor's office for physical therapy. My mother baked exquisite cookies and cakes. Aunt Jean came for the occasion and helped out. Ella gave a lovely brunch for the out of town guests. Alex and Ross participated in the religious ceremony, and Ruth's son, Gary, almost another brother, stood by his cousin on the pulpit. Each read a portion of the Torah.

Bill had given various adult male family members an *aliyah*, an assignment, which is considered an honor. They were called up to the *bimah* by their Hebrew names. Women sat in the upper level, fashionably dressed, observing and gossiping. Because A.D. was a distinguished guest, Bill had also given him an *aliyah*.

During the weekend festivities, A.D. told me that he wanted to talk to me about the accident case on his next visit to Savannah. Then he said, "I have a better idea, why don't you join me in New York? I have a business trip coming up in two weeks, we can discuss your case and see a show or two."

His invitation caught me off guard, and I didn't know whether he was joking or not.

"I'm going to New York next week," I said. "with my husband."

"When you get back, call me so I can come down and go over the case with you," A.D. said.

"When you're here, I'd also like to discuss representing some of your real estate acquisitions in Savannah." I saw this as an opportunity to develop a new client.

I had never been involved in a lawsuit before and I felt that I could rely completely on A.D.'s expertise and outstanding reputation. Bill left the business details to the two of us. Soon, A.D. was phoning me several times a week, to joke and tease. I coaxed him back to the subject of the accident.

"I wish you'd settle the case. I need the money," I said.

"Isn't Bill doing well in his business?" he asked.

"He's not making money fast enough for me." I told A.D. that I had suggested to Bill that he open another store in Atlanta, but he didn't want to locate in a city that size. Bill complained that I drove him too hard, that I was never satisfied. My mother said the same.

"Well, I'm coming to Savannah on an important real estate matter," A.D. said. "I'd like for you to represent me." I was excited at the chance to deal in commercial real estate. That night as we were eating dinner I was anxious to tell Bill about my coup.

"A.D.'s going to list an office building with me when he gets here next week. Let's have him over for dinner."

"Isaac, did you pitch a no-hitter today at little league?" Bill asked. He ignored my enthusiastic comment.

"Won't that be wonderful? This could be a chance for a big commission. Maybe we can take a trip to Europe," I said, wondering if Bill had heard me.

"I can't afford a trip to Europe," Bill said.

The day that I went to meet A.D. for lunch, I passed him in the lobby of the DeSoto Hotel, but didn't recognize him.

"Hello, *mazik*," A.D. said. He took my elbow and steered me to the cocktail lounge. "What would you like to drink?" he asked with a playful smile on his face. He ordered Dewars and water. We were seated at a small table in the Tavern, located on the lower level of the hotel. The wood paneled room was very dark, as though it were night.

"Make mine a Bloody Mary," I said, as I let the mink stole, borrowed from my next door neighbor, drop from my shoulders, placing it carefully across the back of my chair. The day I met A.D. for our first business lunch was also the first time I drank a cocktail in the middle of the day. To add to my pseudo sophistication, I had worn a large black picture hat.

He held his glass, leaned over the table, and touched the rim of mine. He smiled, then handed me a small box.

"What is it?" I felt flattered that he was offering me a gift. It was obviously a jeweler's box, and I also felt confused. I'd never gotten a present from another man before. In fact I'd never gotten a piece of jewelry from anyone. Inside was a gold watch on a thin chain.

"What's happening with the settlement of the accident?" I asked. I fingered the chain of the watch for a few seconds.

"If you don't go to court, you can get several thousand dollars," he said.

"What do you think I should do?" I discreetly tucked the gift inside my purse.

"Take it." He touched my hand with his soft white one. "My law firm won't charge you a fee," he added.

The man fascinated me. A.D. had been born in Savannah and left at the age of twenty, the year I was born. He had lived in Washington, D.C. before moving to Atlanta. Now he enjoyed returning to his hometown, rich, famous, and successful. He bought companies, liquidated them, dealt in real estate, owned shopping centers, restaurants, motels. He'd come a long way since night law school.

A.D. was a big spender, a bon vivant, a tycoon. While he was elegantly dressed it was obvious that he was a bit paunchy. He wasn't good looking but he was exciting. He offered me a large company's property to sell, and he called every day to discuss either the real estate or the accident case.

"What are you going to do with the big commission you're about to make?" A.D. looked at me with a twinkle in his eyes.

"I'm going to buy a pair of black alligator shoes and a bag to match."

"I'll buy them for you," he said. Then he hastened to add, "You can save your money from the sale." He talked to me as if I were a little girl. This was nothing new to me. As a Southern woman I'd grown accustomed to men who thought the way to get me into bed was to talk to me as if I were still in diapers.

Later I would connect my father's death with A.D.'s arrival in my life. A.D. was old enough to be my father. I teasingly called him "Daddy" on the phone several times. He called me "Baby" and "Mazik." I almost fainted when A.D. told me his first name.

"It's Avram."

"And your middle name?"

"I gave that one to myself," he said. "When I finished law school, I thought it would be more impressive to have a middle name. I took Dayan, which in Hebrew means a rabbinical judge. Actually, God is called Dayan Emes, 'the righteous judge.' " A sly smile slid across his lips.

On his numerous trips in and out of Savannah I often invited A.D. to have dinner with my family. Bill was as enthralled with him as I was. The man was a charmer. He always arrived for dinner with flowers for me, toys and books for the boys, and a bottle of scotch for Bill. He and Bill liked each other, joking easily and frequently. They would slap their thighs and double over at each other's dirty jokes. A.D. told Bill that Atlanta held great potential and mentioned expanding his business there.

One evening when he was at our dinner table A.D. talked about the legal language of our accident case. I never felt more like chattel than when A.D. explained "lack of consortium" to us.

"You can sue the bastard for lack of consortium," A.D. advised Bill, as he held up his glass of wine to be refilled.

"What's that?" I asked.

A.D. leaned over to whisper, "That means Bill could not indulge in sex with his wife for an uncomfortable period of time."

"A million dollars couldn't make up for what I've missed," Bill said, a huge grin on his face.

"That good, huh?" A.D. said.

I felt like the used goods in my long-ago rummage sale. Who gave them the right to tell me when I can and cannot have sex? Where was it written that his rights to sex were more important than mine?

"You can both go straight to hell," I said, getting up from the table and scurrying to my bedroom. I slammed the door as hard as I could. Their laughter slid through the night like a poisonous snake.

With so much time spent on his business's expansion, Bill had to be out of town often. He was in Charleston on a business trip when A.D. arrived in March to liquidate a large company. He gave the property to me to sell for him. We met in his suite at the DeSoto Hotel.

"You can make some decent money on this piece of property." His voice thickened as he moved closer to me on the sofa. He put his arm around me, leaned over and kissed me. I froze just as I'd done when Tootie Lamotta kissed me for the first time.

A.D. cupped his hands under my breasts. He had removed his shirt and a gold chain with a large Star of David hung loosely over his fleshy breasts.

"I can't," I said softly. "I have my period." It was a lie. I certainly wasn't ready for this. A.D. smiled at me and put his shirt back on.

"You're a real *berrieh*, baby," meaning that I was a woman of remarkable energy, talent and competence. But my words had cooled him down.

A couple of months later, he called again. "Lunch?"

There was something different about that Monday. I was to pick up A.D. at the airport. I had arranged a meeting for him with some investors who were buying a warehouse that he owned.

The night before, Ruth, Ted and their children had invited Bill and me along with our sons and Minna to join them at the Officer's Club at Hunter Field. We were going for a sumptuous Mother's Day buffet of

114

roast beef and lobster thermidor. Minna glowed at having her two daughters and their families dote on her. Bill had downed one too many martinis and had immediately gone to sleep when we got home. I picked up my favorite book of Emily Dickinson's poems and flicked on my bedside lamp. My eyes caught the words, *"That love is all there is, is all we know of love."*

The next morning, I donned a tight black skirt and cashmere sweater, and painstakingly applied my makeup. At the airport, I sat in the waiting room that faced the landing field. My heart paced inside me, like a caged panther, dying to get out.

When A.D's plane landed I went to the gate to greet him. He was carrying a brown alligator briefcase. "Mazik, you look wicked." He leaned over and kissed me on my cheek. I had recently colored my hair black, and had it in a bun at the nape of my neck. I wore large sunglasses with tortoise shell frames.

We went to lunch at The Purple Tree in the Manger Hotel. I ordered a gin and tonic with a twist of lime. A.D. ordered a Dewars. He raised his glass to mine in a toast. "May this be the beginning of many more commissions!" Then he added, "I'm proud of you."

I could feel my heart melting at his words. After lunch, we went to a meeting in the lawyer's office. The deal went smoothly. A.D. asked me to stop by his hotel suite. He was going to write a check for my commission, plus whatever expenses I had incurred. He sat on the sofa in the sitting room and removed his jacket. He reached into his briefcase and handed me a brown velvet pouch. I opened it and took out a gold ring with two cultured pearls. He slipped it on my finger.

"Are we engaged?" I giggled.

"You could say that," he answered. He pulled me to my feet and slipped his arms around my waist. He kissed my lips, hot and passionately. I didn't resist. I knew that to keep him in my life, I would have to succumb. I couldn't play any more games. And I knew for sure that I wanted him in my life. A.D. took my hand and led me to the bed in the adjoining room. As I lay back against the pillows the familiar view of Savannah stared at me through the window panes.

He unbuttoned my jacket and fumbled with the back of my bra, then ran his hands around my breasts and lowered his head to kiss them. His tongue made circles around my nipples. He was tender and slow. I was sure he could feel me trembling. He was warm and sensitive to my feelings. He kissed my eyelids, the tip of my nose, and again my lips.

His naked skin rubbed against my thighs, as he explored every part of my body. He didn't seem hurried, and I let him take the lead. This was new for me; its thrall was intoxicating, but it also made me terribly uncomfortable. I was confused about what was morally wrong and what my heart desired. It was as if we both knew — that up to this moment everything in my life had been a dress rehearsal. A.D. and I would be the main event.

Another part of me was born that late spring afternoon. Something was awakened I hadn't known existed. I could document that very moment when I fell in love with A.D. I felt his imprint. I belonged to him, just as though he had swallowed me whole. I was hooked by the drama.

"How can I face my family?" I said afterward as tears filled my eyes.

A.D. comforted me. "Don't cry, honey. You've just come of age. You're now a mature woman." I believed him when he said this was the way of the sophisticated world.

"Everyone in Atlanta takes it for granted," he assured me.

After that, at eight o'clock, every morning after Bill had left for work, A.D. called to sing my praises, to promise me trips to exciting places, to help me expand my limited horizons and my real estate sales. He would fly to Savannah for the day, take me to lunch, spend several hours making love, and then fly back to Atlanta. He took the time to satisfy my needs as well as his. Too often, I'd been little more than a quickie to Bill. But A.D. loved romance and foreplay. Sex between us became tender and necessary. Being with A.D. was too fascinating and exciting to give up. And I was desperately in love.

"I want us to spend the whole night together, Daddy," I said during one of our morning chats. I wanted to cuddle with him for twenty-four hours. That was fine with A.D., he told his secretary and his wife that he was leaving on a business trip and arranged a hotel room for us. He suggested I say there was a real estate seminar to attend.

While Bill was driving me to the Savannah Airport he said, "I've talked to A.D. and he said that we could count on a settlement very soon." When the plane landed, A.D. was there to meet me. He took me to the Atlanta Cabana, the newest hotel in the city. The blue velvet chaise lounge in our room smacked of a 1930's movie.

"Baby, let's stay here and have room service," he said. "How about it?" I had never ordered from room service before and thought the whole business terribly glamorous.

"You can go shopping tomorrow and buy yourself some pretty clothes," he said, handing me a fistful of one-hundred-dollar bills. "Get something sexy!" My wildest fantasy was coming true. I had dreamed all my life that someone would love me this way, and being indulged by A.D. was the icing on the cake.

"Come here, baby, and give Daddy what you know he likes," he said, guiding my head downward. I was unaware of how needy I was, how quickly I was forming an intimate bond with this man. Hungry for love and acceptance, I only felt alive when I was with A.D. If I didn't see him for two weeks I became desperate and terrified. I wanted to hug and kiss him at the corner of Bull and Broughton Streets in broad daylight.

And while I enjoyed the glamour of hotel rooms I abhorred the fact that our love was in hiding. He was the first man I had come to know intimately who had worldliness and power. That part of him appealed to me almost immediately. He blended this powerful persona with intellectual pretensions. He seemed to be sensitive, literary, and at home in the manor houses of old moneyed families.

"Let's each get a divorce so we can get married," I said one morning when he had spent the night in Savannah. Bill was away on one of his constant business deals. I had gone home to spend the night after dinner. In the morning, as soon as I got the children off to school, I rushed back to have breakfast with him in his hotel room. A huge rose sat in the vase in the middle of the serving table.

"We will, baby, soon." He handed me a cup of coffee.

In Washington, while handling a legal matter before the Supreme Court, A.D. took me along. I feigned a trip on behalf of the Democratic party, using as an excuse my committee appointment with the state chapter. Bill never questioned it. While we were in Georgetown, the most elegant section of Washington, I watched with amusement as A.D. romped like a little kid through the French market and then, later, so easily slid into the roll of sophisticated lawyer. He asked me to go with him to buy a pair of shoes.

"Watch me, baby, and learn how to bargain." He selected six pairs of the most expensive shoes in the shop, then said to the clerk, "What's my ministerial discount?" He got the shoes for ten percent less than the sales price. Back in our suite at the Four Georges he opened a bottle of Dom Perignon and poured us each a glass. I was being seduced by glamour coupled with romance, something I had never experienced. That night as we dined with several of his friends from the Senate he regaled them with one joke after another. I was so proud of him that I laughed at the same joke I'd heard a dozen times.

Later, when we returned to the hotel, A.D. said, "You should think of going into business for yourself." I knew that I functioned best when working, and the encouragement he offered me was something I'd never gotten from any other person in my life. It was utterly thrilling.

"I'll have to pass a state exam to get my broker's license. I'll count on you to get me going." I gave him a warm kiss. I liked his promises and his juicy, passionate kisses, and especially the way he believed in me.

Not long after that trip to Washington, Bill asked me to drive with him to Atlanta, to attend a national furniture convention. He was serving on one of the committees. The banquet was held in a private room at the Diplomat Restaurant, close to our hotel. We arrived early and stopped in at the lounge. Across the room I spotted A.D., who along with a group of investors, owned the restaurant. He rushed over to Bill and me, shook Bill's hand and gave me a conciliatory peck on my cheek.

"Come on over to my table," A.D. said, leading us to the table where he was sitting with his wife. Irene, who appeared to be in her mid-fifties, was an attractive woman. On the shoulder of her blue brocade suit was a huge diamond brooch. Matching earrings adorned her ears and there was a large diamond on her hand.

"Irene, this is Bill Kramer and his wife Naomi." A.D. sounded as if he were presenting ordinary clients to his wife. I felt uncomfortable and conspicuous. He practically pushed us into the chairs at his table. He waved his arm to call a waiter to take an order for our drinks. As he chatted on I could feel his hand sliding up the inside of my thigh. My knees felt weak and I felt faint.

To make our meeting sound legitimate A.D. turned to Bill. "I've finally settled the accident case and the check'll be sent sometime next week."

I said nothing. He'd given me the check three weeks earlier.

The cocktail lounge was paneled in dark walnut, the red banquettes were upholstered in a rich dark leather. On each table there were two silver bowls with goldfish crackers in one, and in the other, plump black olives. I reached for a handful of fish.

"I've heard a lot about you from my husband," Irene said as she turned to face me. I felt as though I was being X-rayed from head to toe.

"Yes, we've done business together." I toyed with the goldfish in my hand, and plopped one between my lips.

"Have you ever seen such a man? He's up talking on the phone at seven-thirty every morning. The man never sleeps," she said, as though she were asking a question. I felt a tingle of guilt crawling up my backbone.

Back in Savannah, I told my sister about A.D. I desperately needed to confide in someone.

"Well, Naomi, you know what they say. When a man has a mistress it's not unusual for the wife to try and make friends with his lover." The term mistress made me squirm.

It was obvious to me that A.D. was starved to have a young woman who listened to him. He said his wife cut him off in mid-sentence and changed the subject if what he was talking about didn't interest her. Rarely did he have the chance to trumpet his triumphs or even to express his fears. With me, he talked and talked. I probably knew more about the interior of his mind than any other person. And I relished the fact that I did. He promised to take care of me, to get me anything I wanted. All I had to do was ask. And sometimes that wasn't necessary.

As it turned out, what I would come to want was beyond the power of any man.

Chapter Eighteen

The summer following Isaac's *bar mitzvah* found the country enthralled with the dreams, youth and vigor of John Fitzgerald Kennedy, the newly elected president of the United States. In July, Isaac and his cousin, Gary, went to New Canaan to visit my Aunt Jean. Isaac was an easygoing child and a very good student. After school he attended football practice and Boy Scout meetings. He had done the required years of Hebrew school. He enjoyed puttering in the kitchen, helping his grandmother bake cookies and had recently taken up golf.

Before his trip to New Canaan Isaac seemed nervous, which was unusual for him, and his right hand shook slightly. When he complained of headaches, I attributed it to a fall he had taken in a neighbors yard. He had fallen off of a trampoline. Aunt Jean phoned my sister while the boys were visiting her and said she was worried. But not a word was said to me.

When Isaac returned his right hand had an exaggerated tremor. I saw it the minute I picked him up at the train station. I immediately called our pediatrician and made an appointment. The doctor was a close personal friend and had treated all three boys. They didn't want to switch to another doctor even when they got older.

When he had finished examining Isaac an appointment was made to see a neurosurgeon that afternoon. The doctor put Isaac in the hospital at once. After a spinal tap, there was no conclusive diagnosis.

"It could be muscular dystrophy, multiple sclerosis," the doctor said, "or something else." I wanted to rip the surgeon's arms and legs from their sockets. Bill and I were both frightened. Isaac was a perfect patient. As soon as the doctor left the hospital room, Bill rushed to the public library while I stayed with Isaac. He checked out the book, *Death Be Not Proud,* by John Gunther. He stayed awake all night reading the author's story of his son's brain tumor and the heart wrenching sorrow their family faced.

"I don't think you should read that book," Isaac's doctor said when he saw Bill pouring over the pages. Tears filled the corners of my husband's eyes.

"My head hurts, Mom," Isaac said, as we boarded the Nancy Hanks train for the trip to Atlanta four days later. We were going to Egleston Children's Hospital at Emory University for further examinations by neurological experts.

"Put your head in my lap, honey," I said comfortingly. He seemed to go in and out of a sleep as we went the distance to Atlanta. We went by train because I was afraid to fly. I'd always been afraid of planes, preferring travel by car or rail. But now I was doubly afraid with my precious Isaac. Bill stayed home in Savannah. Instinct told me to telephone A.D. He met our train, took us to the hospital, and waited during the agonizing hours of tests. After each test, with yet another doctor, A.D. held me in his arms.

"I'll never leave you," he said.

The neurosurgeon called me into his office at the end of the day to tell me that they had discovered a tumor. He said that an exploratory operation was needed immediately to determine whether the tumor they had detected in Isaac's brain was malignant, and to call my husband to come to the hospital as quickly as he could. They scheduled the surgery for early the next day.

Bill arrived just after midnight. The two of us stood silently in the hall outside our son's room, taking turns so that one of us would be in the room with Isaac at all times. I filled Bill in on everything that the doctors had said to me. We looked into each other's sad eyes, but we had nothing to say to each other.

Early on the morning of the operation, an orderly came to get Isaac to roll him in to surgery. While I held one of his hands, Bill walked along on the other side, holding Isaac's other hand.

"They're going to have to shave your head, son," Bill said, leaning down to kiss him on his forehead.

"Stay with me, Dad," Isaac said, showing his fear for the first time.

"Your mother and I will be right outside waiting. I promise."

A tall, heavyset orderly wheeled him through the double doors. I fell into Bill's arms, sobbing against his chest. His tears spilled down onto my face.

The Egleston doctors drilled through Isaac's skull.

Four hours after Isaac was rolled into the operating room the lead surgeon called us in. "Shall we go for the tumor in his brain or sew him up and put a shunt in his spinal column?" That meant a choice between rendering Isaac a total vegetable or the uncertain promise of a few more years of life. There was no guarantee of what either would bring.

"The shunt," Bill said. I had slumped to the floor.

"Time's running out. I don't have time for a hysterical mother," the surgeon barked as rushed back into the operating room.

I ran toward the small hospital chapel crying, "God, don't take my child from me." Soon, A.D. came in and found me curled up in one of the pews like a frightened puppy. He held me close.

"I promise I'll always be here for you, baby," he said and comforted me as no one else could have. "If that's what you want, then I'll take care of you forever. You're my baby."

That was exactly what I wanted.

We waited throughout the day and late into the night for Isaac to come out of surgery. A.D. never left us. His wife, Irene, came to the hospital. She brought sandwiches and cokes for us and other friends of ours who had come to be with us during that terrible day. Irene comforted me, offering to take me out to run errands if there was anything I needed or even to take me to her beauty parlor. I couldn't deal with it. I felt like a character in a bad play.

The first thing Isaac wanted to know, after he'd awakened, his head wrapped in endless white bandages, was how he looked. He asked for a mirror.

"Darling," I said, "you're the most beautiful boy in all the world." His eyes were glazed from the drugs and surgery. Isaac was hospitalized for a month. At the end of the first week, Bill went back to Savannah and I continued staying at our friend's house. Trained pediatric nurses stayed around the clock with our son.

During those nightmarish days, I came and went in a fog of absolute sorrow. I slept with the help of a pill. I couldn't eat and lost fifteen pounds in three weeks. A.D. picked me up every morning from my friend's house, which was just around the corner from where he lived, and drove me to the hospital, insisting that I eat breakfast. He stopped regularly at a restaurant and ordered for me, but I could only swallow black coffee. At the end of every day A.D. came back to the hospital and brought me vials of tranquilizers and sleeping pills. One of his clients was a wholesale druggist, and he had no trouble getting whatever he asked for.

Bill drove up on weekends to be with us. He was trying hard to be brave for Alex and Ross the days he was in Savannah. He was torn in his attempt to be a business man while worrying about the weakened condition of Isaac. Bill's back caused him terrible pain and he was experiencing extreme indigestion.

A cousin of Bill's in Hollywood told his celebrity friends about Isaac and dozens of autographed photographs of film stars began arriving at the hospital. The mayor of Savannah wrote Isaac to say the city missed him. Aunt Jean asked the Ambassador to Guinea, a frequent customer in the stationery store, to send a carving. He sent a wooden bust of a Guinean tribeswoman. Coins and stamps came from a friend in Israel. The room was filled with flowers and candy sent by well-wishers. One friend even sent a large aquarium filled with tropical fish.

I was at Isaac's side in the hospital for a month. Then Isaac and I got an apartment on Ponce de Leon, not far from the hospital, where he had daily cobalt treatments for two months. Bill called every day. On the weekends that Bill came he insisted on me going out to dinner and a movie with him and friends. The practical nurse that we had hired stayed with Isaac.

A.D. came by every morning on his way to his office. He brought records from a radio station he owned. He bought Isaac a small record player. He fixed a fresh pot of coffee for the two of us. We held each other, made love, talked. His daily visits were my anchor. He was strong, resourceful, wise.

"I know you're worried about not having a car," A.D. said one morning. "Here's a check, get one. Just consider it as part of the commission on the last piece of property." He told me to let him know if I needed money.

"No one has ever taken care of me like you do." I threw my arms around him and cried. It was so safe and comforting to be close to him.

Ella came. Ruth came. Aunt Jean came from Connecticut. Ruth had brought her son Gary, and Alex, with her on her visit. The boys were speechless when they saw Isaac so listless, his head bald from the treatments. Alex did everything in his power to keep from crying. Neither of the boys had been prepared to see Isaac in this condition.

My mother never came nor did she telephone. The fact is, Mother felt helpless; she couldn't face the possibility of losing her precious grandson. She thought if she didn't talk about it then surely it wasn't happening. The reality of our tragedy was too much for her to bear.

Ruth finally put her foot down and said, "Listen, Mother, I think you should move into Naomi's house. The boys are being shifted from my house to Ella's and they'd be better off in their own home. It's not fair to them. Why can't you offer to stay there?"

"I don't think I can get them to listen," my mother said. Mother was afraid of the responsibility. But Ruth kept insisting until Minna moved in. Alex and Ross were back in their familiar surroundings in time to prepare for the beginning of school in September. And Bill was with them some of the time. My sister took Ross to school and got him registered for the first grade. But not without incidence. Ross had grabbed a butcher knife and threatened his grandmother for making him get dressed for school.

Every day I would take Isaac's drained body in and out of the hospital for his treatments at Emory. I stood outside the large glass window and watched as he was placed on a table while the cobalt machine was arranged against his head. He was so brave, so uncomplaining. He was God's special child and I didn't want to lose him.

The treatments ended. The tumor was malignant. It was time for us to go home. Bill and I had a final consultation with the neurosurgeon before we began our drive to Savannah.

"How long will we have him?" I asked.

"No one knows these things. Just take him home, and live as you always have."

"Can he go to school, or play golf?" Bill asked.

"Let him do whatever he wants. Your doctor in Savannah will check him regularly."

As Bill drove toward Savannah, Isaac's strength began to renew itself. His younger brothers stood on the lawn waiting to greet him, not knowing what to expect. Isaac wore a small plaid hat to shield his baldness. My mother was also standing there, her face a study in fear and bewilderment. She was so frightened she couldn't speak.

That night when Ruth came to visit we sat on my bed. I burst out in anger against our mother. "Christ! Why doesn't she stop staring at me and show some motherly support? She just stands there, frozen. Why can't she offer a single comforting word?"

"You know how she is," Ruth said, putting her arms around me.

I wanted life for Isaac to be as normal as possible, as normal as I could make it. He had a tutor, his friends came by in the afternoon, and amazingly, he played eighteen holes of golf twice a week for quite a long time.

For me, normalcy meant Valium and sleeping pills. I took a leave of absence from my office; I'd lost interest in selling real estate. I neglected Ross and Alex. I gave all of my attention, my love, and energy to Isaac. Bill made every attempt to prepare breakfast for our other sons but he wasn't good at coordinating the morning routine that they were used to and Alex and Ross soon resented me for not being available to them. Bill couldn't break through the tension that had developed between his sons and himself. None of them could talk to one another about Isaac's illness. Neither Bill nor I could bring ourselves to discuss death. We lived in a state of urgency and disbelief.

After his brothers had gone off to school I would painstakingly prepare a leisurely breakfast for Isaac and me. I took him to his doctor's appointments, summoning every ounce of courage available to me, to be cheerful and to keep his spirits up.

"When will I be well, Mom?" Isaac asked me the same question at least once a week.

"Soon, honey." But I had no idea because the doctors didn't know either.

Several months later, I took Isaac back to Egleston Children's Hospital for his checkup. The doctors were pleased that he was doing as well as he was. They warned me that he could begin to lose his eyesight and experience numbness in his face. A.D. had gotten us reservations at the Atlanta Cabana. He met us at the hotel and took us out to dinner. During dinner, he gave me a ruby and sapphire ring and Isaac a pocket calculator.

I sensed Bill's mounting frustration about the relationship between myself and A.D., but he couldn't confront us. A.D. was so generous to Isaac and our son was very fond of "Uncle A.D." Bill didn't want to do anything that might hurt Isaac, even temporarily.

Late one night after the boys were asleep, while Bill and I were watching television, he put his arms around me. "I'm so glad Isaac's doing better," Bill said. He ran his hand across my breast and pulled me closer.

"Bill, I just can't." Like an actress trained for the role, I went into my headache routine.

"Naomi, I need you," he said. "I'm not made of stone, you know. You seem to have time for lunch when A.D. comes to town." There was a caustic tone in his voice. Any time he tried to start a discussion about A.D. I would change the subject.

"That's different. That's business."

Within four months Isaac began walking with a slight limp and needed glasses to correct his weakening vision. Still, he took it in stride. When his eyesight began to fail, he patiently exchanged his hobby.

"Can you find me a book about coins?" Isaac asked. He had come up with the suggestion during one of our trips to the public library. On one of the programs he'd watched on television, the host had discussed rare old coins.

"Let's go to the bookstore," I said. My heart felt a sigh of relief that he'd thought of something to substitute for his golf game. Friends from around the city hastened to bring him special ones while Bill and Alex read him the dates on the coins and helped him catalogue them.

Isaac began to deteriorate gradually but steadily. I monitored every move from my peripheral vision, careful not to alarm him.

"There's rice sticking to Isaac's lip," Ross said one night as we sat at the dinner table. I looked at my oldest son, my heart colliding with my stomach. What the doctors had told us to fear was happening — he was losing the sensation in his face. Bill and I made plans to take him to a specialist in Boston. Isaac's glasses had to be stronger and he needed a cane. My mother gave him the one that my father had used when his leg was amputated.

"Tell me how your father died, Dad?" Isaac asked Bill. As Isaac's health continued to decline he began asking more questions about our family's history.

"Well, son, my father shot himself with his policeman's gun. He lost all his money in the Miami land boom of nineteen twenty-six and he was very depressed."

"How old were you?"

"I was much younger than you. But he was my hero, you know. He was a policeman and a fireman and that's hard to beat." Bill laughed as he recalled having seen his father in two kinds of uniforms.

"Where were you when he shot himself?"

"My brother and I were in the bedroom when we heard a shot. My mother rushed into the living room, screaming for us not to leave our room." Bill's face looked tired and haggard as he spoke.

"I'm sorry you didn't have a father when you were growing up," Isaac said, leaning to hug his dad.

The doctor explained that due to the tumor, Isaac's censorial system was changed. He thought purely and clearly, and when members of the family visited, he would ask deep and curious questions.

"I want to call Aunt Ella," Isaac said when he heard that Ella's oldest daughter was getting a divorce. He asked for the phone.

Bill dialed and handed the receiver to Isaac.

"I heard about Sally's divorce, Aunt Ella. I'm sorry about what's happened." Bill and I looked at each other without saying a word, wodering why we couldn't be so totally honest. But we answered all his questions.

Dora, Winnie Lou's niece, helped me with Isaac, often coaxing me to spend some time away from the house. "Miss Naomi," Dora said, "you gotta take care of yourself, too. A cheerful heart's good medicine, you know. But a downcast spirit dries up the bones."

A.D. would come to visit and I'd have lunch with him for an hour or two. I needed his arms around me to sustain me through the days and weeks of fear, helplessness, and bewilderment. He brought me more and more jewelry — a jade pendant with spirals of diamonds, a matching pair of diamond and jade earrings, and a ring with eight old mine cut diamonds set in gold. I shoved everything into a dresser drawer, not caring about any of them. Bill never noticed my jewelry. And A.D. felt frustrated that he couldn't ease my suffering.

"Why don' t you let me take you away for a few days, baby?" A.D. pleaded. "We could go to Jekyll Island and you can walk along the beach."

"I can't leave his side," I said.

"He'll be cared for while we're away."

"How can you possibly know what it feels like to watch a son die? To see him wake up in the morning, to pour my heart and soul into his very breathing, and still not know if it will be enough to keep him alive?" I felt as though Isaac was still in my womb.

A.D. took my hand and kissed my fingertips. There were tears in his eyes.

Bill began to ask more questions about my relationship with A.D. One night as we sat in front of the television, after the boys were asleep, Bill said, "Naomi, I know you're tired, so am I. But I don't see why you have to talk to A.D. every day. That's too much time to be spending with him. I don't like it worth a damn."

"He comforts me," I said. "Please understand that he's my best friend." I was telling the truth but Bill didn't want to hear it.

Life was certainly not ordinary. Dora did her best to get me to relinquish some of my duties but I felt compelled to do every-thing for Isaac.

"Come on now, Miss Naomi, I can bathe him good as you can," Dora urged, trying to get me out of the bathroom where Isaac sat on the edge of the bathtub filled with warm water. But I didn't want anyone else to touch him. Isaac and I were one, I thought, not two. I ceased being myself and lived only for the sake of keeping him with me. I carefully dressed in my best clothes every day and made up my face to perfection. Isaac would never see me looking tired, unkempt, or distraught.

By the summer of 1962, Isaac was in a wheelchair and his right arm began to shrivel. Bill moved into Isaac's bedroom to take care of him, because, periodically at night, he grew nauseous and vomited. Bill was gentle, loving, and very patient with his son. And Isaac still managed not to complain, not to despair. He still brought joy to our family. I marveled at my son's spirit. I locked my stomach into a tight knot, tying off my anguish to hold it away from the encroaching brutal reality.

"Dad," Isaac asked one night after Bill had lifted him from the wheelchair into his bed, "am I dying?"

"We're all dying every day of our lives," Bill answered. He tried so hard to be hopeful, cheerful, yet honest.

"When will I be well, again?"

"By your birthday, son." Bill straightened Isaac's blanket and kissed him goodnight.

Alex had his bar mitzvah late that summer. Instead of a joyous time during his rite of passage, a somber cloud stood over our family. During the services Isaac had to leave frequently, to lie down in the rabbi's office.

Secretly, I wondered if he would live until his fifteenth birthday. Friends and family came to visit, yet I felt utterly alone in the world with my precious first born. If I could just give him my breath, my blood, my heart.

During Isaac's last weeks he sank into a coma. Alex stood for hours by the side of the bed, waiting to hear his brother speak. Bill took the two younger boys aside to share the truth with them. Alex was thirteen, Ross seven.

"Your brother's dying," he said, his voice trembling slightly.

Alex looked straight at Bill. "No, there'll be some miracle. He won't die, Dad. He's not even fifteen, yet!"

Ross stood silently, looking unsure as to what his father's words meant. Alex ran from Isaac's room, slamming the door as hard as he could. He sat high in the branches of the big oak tree across the road from our house for hours until Bill coaxed him down at midnight. Alex's eyes were red and swollen.

Two days before Chanukah, I took Ross shopping for holiday gifts for his cousins, while I bought Christmas presents for his and Alex's classmates. The December day was cold and gray. We stopped off at Ruth's house to wrap the presents. My sister was at work but her maid gave me the needed gift paper and ribbons.

The telephone rang in the kitchen. I heard the maid say, "Yes ma'am, she's here. Okay. I'll keep her until you come."

I knew. Isaac was dead.

"Get your jacket, Ross, we're going home," I said.

I paid no attention as my sister's maid tried to get me to wait for Ruth. I rushed to my car, locked the door next to Ross, and started the engine.

"Your brother's dead, baby."

"How do you know?" He moved closer to me and nestled against my body.

I put an arm around him as I drove. I ignored the red traffic lights and just kept going. We came into the house. I slowly removed my coat and gloves. Dora was slumped over the kitchen sink, her head bowed. She didn't move. I walked toward Isaac's bedroom. The door was slightly ajar. At the foot of his bed stood Bill and the doctor, empty expressions on their faces. I walked past them.

"Goodnight, my angel son," I said as I reached to pull the covers up under his chin and smoothed the pillows under his head.

Ever so softly, I kissed his forehead.

Chapter Nineteen

In my raging grief, I turned away from God, not to Him. The God of my childhood was the all-knowing, omnipotent figure who would treat me like my grandmother had, or better. If I obeyed, I would be rewarded. If not, punished. Somehow I knew that human tragedy was part of the fabric of life but I hadn't connected myself intimately to the blasphemous curse.

I had never questioned God's mercy. I believed He would see that the innocent children I had brought into the world would be safe. Why had He taken my son in the bloom of his youth? A benevolent God would not have interrupted my son's life, I reasoned. And why had He delivered such unrelenting pain to those who loved Isaac? Finding no answers, I withdrew from God and from life.

People acted as if Isaac had not lived. No one spoke his name to me for fear of igniting the pain more fiercely. I felt completely alone, trying to bridge the primal stage of grief — the time of anger and guilt and incomprehension — with the succeeding stage of acceptance, which never seemed to come. No one has made room for death in our culture, as though it only happens in the movies and in books. Denial of my own grieving was something that all of my friends and family had scripted for me.

A.D. had flown to Savannah for the funeral. But he didn't come into the cemetery because he said he was a Kohen, that he belonged to a special tribe of Jews who were forbidden there. It was one of the proscriptive laws circumscribed to a tribe who looked upon themselves as a priest of Justice. Bill had asked six of Isaac's young friends to serve as pallbearers. I looked at their innocent faces as they struggled with Isaac's coffin and remembered how they had stood by him during the two years of his illness, honest, caring and loving. They represented the truth that his life had been and we wanted them to carry him to his grave as they had supported him during his last days.

Once more my mother nudged me toward the water fountain to wash my hands. This time I refused. Bill took Alex and Ross by their hands to follow my mother. My sister sat next to me, her arm protectively around my shoulders. The moist lushness of the large trees and huge camellias and azaleas in Bonaventure Cemetery sent chills to the marrow of my bones.

When we returned from the cemetery I went to my bedroom and closed the door. I wanted no part of what seemed to be a party. Groups of people were preparing a meal for the family and I didn't want to eat it if my son wasn't there. I wanted to be in the grave with him. Instead of him. He hadn't sinned, I had.

A.D. came into my bedroom. He sat on the side of my bed and asked what he could do for me. Inside my head I screamed, *Bring back Isaac, make my mother love me, marry me!* But the words didn't come.

"Here, baby, take these," he said, as he left two large bottles of pills on the night table.

I ricocheted from days of intense, debilitating frustration to endless, sleepless nights. Bill continued sleeping in Isaac's bedroom. I could hear him crying during the night or sometimes when he was in the shower.

I felt helpless when trying to offer comfort to my sons. Our meals were silent, our lives empty. My heart had a hunger that I was unable to feed.

A heavy rainstorm fell a few days following Isaac's funeral, making me want to rush to his grave.

"I have to hold an umbrella over my child. It's too cold and lonely for him there," I told Dora. She agreed to go with me. We sat together in the rain, next to the soft earth of his newly dug grave for several hours before Dora persuaded me to go home.

Ross had developed a talent for mimicking stars that he had seen on television. His latest was Crazy Guggenheim, the character who appeared within a bar scene in a popular comedy weekly during the sixties. Every night Ross would come to the table wearing Bill's old gray-brimmed hat pulled down over his ears.

Every time someone came in to pay a condolence call, Ross would say, "Hello, Joe! I'm Crazy Guggenheim." He spoke as if he had a wad of mush in his mouth, his lips contorted.

None of us could resist his comedic performances. He craved the attention. So wrapped was I in my cocoon of sadness that it was hard for me to realize that Bill and the boys were suffering as much as I. My thoughts were of my own pain and the cruel death of my child. People would look away from me when I mentioned Isaac, and I would feel so left out and lonely, in a way I'd never felt before. My family's pain was lost to me.

Ross had been pushed aside during Isaac's illness at one of the most crucial points in his young life. Not only was he the youngest of our family, he was hurting, too. Ross had started first grade while I was in Atlanta with Isaac. As a result, he rebelled and became a clown for attention to hide his fear and confusion. His teachers pampered him because they felt sorry for him. Dora gave in to his every demand.

It took all my willpower to keep from crying as I spoke, while asking Alex what he wanted that had been Isaac's. Alex chose the golf clubs and held his brother's favorite putter. He chipped at an imaginary golf ball.

Like me, Alex withdrew from the family and stayed in his room alone much of the time. He had no one to share his feelings with. He ran through the empty fields across the street with his dog, Thunder, and lavished all his attention on the playful grey Weimaraner.

When Dora urged me to clean out Isaac's closets I refused, I didn't want one thing disturbed in his room. I couldn't accept that he wasn't coming back. Isaac's golf shoes, slightly pigeon toed, looked as if he'd walk up and step into them at any moment. Nothing in Isaac's room had been touched for six months when Bill and I sat down to discuss plans. I wanted to sell the house and build across the street, where the farmland was being subdivided.

"Alex wants to move into Isaac's room," Bill said. "He wants his own bedroom." I knew that meant Bill would be sharing my bed again.

Day after day, I sat in my bed, blinds drawn, not wanting to get dressed or face a world that I no longer felt a part of. Dora brought breakfast to me on a tray. Ross cuddled next to me, rubbing my arms with rosewater and glycerin lotion. Alex never failed to run into my room when he got home from school. He wanted to tell me about his day, but emotionally, I wasn't there for him.

An entire family was crumbling and none of us knew how to stop the disintegration. A.D. became my only refuge. His daily calls helped me survive though they had less meaning than before.

"You and I are the ones that have sinned. We should've been taken," I said one day when he called. "When can we tell them the truth?"

"As soon as the time is right. You know we can't now."

It had been no secret to A.D. that I wanted to be his wife. Almost from the moment we'd fallen in love I wanted us to get divorces at the same time. I wanted him to work out all of the details and legalities.

To assuage my grief, A.D. brought me a three-karat diamond ring surrounded by baguettes. He said it was for our soon-to-be-announced engagement.

Well meaning friends gave advice to end my grief. Some offered, "Get out of town." Others said, "Perhaps you should move." I spent my time dreaming of being A.D.'s wife. It seemed to me that A.D. was giving me what he could in material gifts in lieu of what he wouldn't give me.

"It'll be good for all of us to get away from the house," Bill said, insisting that the boys and I drive with him to Florida for a week. He thought a quiet place on the beach near Tampa would be relaxing.

"Dad, can we look up the guy that knocked you out in Madison Square Garden?" Alex said. The children loved the picture in Bill's old scrapbook showing him sprawled on the floor of the ring.

While we were in Tampa, Bill visited the fighter in the photograph and introduced him to his sons. For the first time I had begun to feel a bit like my old self. My vanity surfaced when I dressed for dinner, brushing and teasing my hair into a bouffant. Later that night, at a seafood restaurant, Bill stared at my hand and asked about the huge stone on my finger. I told him it was a zircon. He didn't know the difference.

Out of the discomfort of the days and the numbness of the nights that followed our return to Savannah, I learned how to smile while feeling pain, to go out with Bill for dinner, though food had no taste, to shop for beautiful clothes although wearing them held no joy. I was learning to talk about the latest fashions with Ruth and other friends, to pretend that my life was coming back together again. My Russian heritage had instilled in me the ability to become a stoic. And Southerners have always pretended that everything is fine, even when it isn't.

I began to create a new facade for myself. I decided I'd be the best dressed woman, no matter where I went. When Bill showed me the invitation from his cousin in Atlanta to attend his daughter's wedding, I began preparing my wardrobe with dedication and focus, as though I were Elizabeth Taylor preparing for the Academy Awards.

I bought a magnificent bright, yellow Malcolm Starr gown. The midriff was bare. A large rhinestone 'X' in the front of the garment connected the top to the flowing skirt. Bill and I drove to Atlanta for the weekend, staying at the newest, trendiest motel on Peachtree Street. I lay around the pool and sunned myself as though I were a chicken on a rotisserie until my body had the perfect bronzed glow to offset the bright yellow gown. I had eaten nothing but tossed salads for the past six weeks. There'd be not an extra ounce on me.

I went to the best known hairstylist in Atlanta, who wore his own hair in a high peroxide pompadour. When he asked how I wanted him to do my hair, I replied, "Different."

"Well, all the rich ladies who will be at the wedding are wearing their hair in a bouffant." It was the most popular style of the day, the one Jackie Kennedy had made famous. He ran his comb through my long, thick dark hair.

"Let's give you the new sexy Italian cut," he suggested.

The dress, the suntan, the hairdo, all worked. I had no trouble getting all the attention I craved. But at home, the days began to cast long, loathsome shadows. Bill and I avoided each other because unaware to the two of us, a confrontation would confirm the loss of our son which neither of us was willing to accept.

So I turned more and more to A.D., and my need for him grew stronger.

Chapter Twenty

When A.D. took Irene on a vacation to Europe I went to the doctor and explained my situation to him. He was kind and patient, suggesting that the painful cramps in my legs were the physical manifestation of the emotional terror I was in. I felt that all I had was A.D. With him, I knew a sense of well-being. Without him, I experienced withdrawal not unlike that of a drug addict. A.D.'s possession of me was total, his control over me was present even when he wasn't.

"Have you told your husband?"

I shook my head. "Please, tell me what to do."

"Why don't you confess all this to your husband?"

"I could never tell Bill. He'd kill me," I insisted.

"I think it's worth trying. Confession's good for the soul. He might be far more understanding than you give him credit for."

"No," I said, flatly. "Bill wouldn't understand." All I could think of was the night that Bill had put his hands around my neck, choking me, hating me.

"You have lover's syndrome," the doctor said. "Don't you know that love can be like narcotics and alcohol? It's like any number of things you put into your body, mind, and heart. It can be habit forming."

When my neighbor, Andrea Welbourne, asked me to have tea with her one afternoon, I felt that if I didn't tell someone what was going on in my life, I would burst. Andrea listened as she served tea and home-made lemon squares. It was much easier to talk to a stranger than to family.

"So what?" Andrea said. She had been having afternoon love affairs ever since she married her second husband. She talked about them as though it were just another pleasant way to pass an otherwise boring afternoon.

"But you don't understand how much we love each other," I said.

Andrea spoke in a hushed tone, almost a whisper. "Naomi, I've never had a man love me and I've been married twice. And I'm counting all my lovers, too."

Andrea smiled and said she wanted to meet this man who had enough power to cause my legs to ache.

It wasn't long before the two of us became confidantes and playmates. We started each day with a phone call. Andrea helped me get through the long, empty days of grief. My house had turned into a private fortress and my prison.

A.D. called from Europe to tell me he wasn't having a good time, but I missed him and hated the idea that he was with Irene. His three-week trip seemed like three years. Andrea's companionship became a great solace to me.

Fern called me from Alabama, where she had joined the forces led by Medgar Evars to abolish segregation on public buses and in eating establishments. She was saddened to hear of Isaac's death.

"I'm sorry I wasn't there with you," Fern said. "Please get interested in the civil rights movement, Naomi." Fern knew that I had long questioned the injustices toward black people in the South and urged me to look for a cause that would not only be something I believed in but would release me from the personal agony that was consuming me.

"Remember, the gift is in the giving," Fern said. "I've always told you there's such a thing as a Christian heart."

After my talk with Fern I told Andrea that I was going to join the NAACP and work for desegregation in the public school system. There was a long silence on her end of the phone.

"You're crazy," she said. Andrea had learned, in that most Southern of fashions, to subdue her emotions. What you did, did not matter so much, if you didn't tell anyone, even yourself, that you had done it.

At an early age, she had married a young man who beat her regularly and had once even stuck the end of a rifle down her throat. After her first baby and divorce, when she couldn't manage alone, she had run home to her parents — Andrea's family had money and privilege — who helped her find her present husband, an older man. Even though he belonged to all the right clubs, as she put it, she found he was incapable of fulfilling her sexually or emotionally.

Her current lover was a banker in Charleston, a quick two-hour drive door to door. The banker, she indicated, was hardly a meaningful relationship. He did business with her husband. She was also having an affair with her husband's best friend in Savannah.

"Maybe in a few months I'll go back into real estate," I said. "But I can't live in the past. The South is changing. Or at least it should. It has to."

"Well, Naomi, do you want darkies to live in our neighborhood? My husband wouldn't stand for it," Andrea said. What I wanted was for Alex and Ross to be a part of the new South, not separate from life in the universal world.

There was a convention in Las Vegas that Bill wanted to attend and he asked me to go with him. He said after the convention we would go to Los Angeles. A good friend of Bill's was producing Hollywood's biggest night, The Academy Awards, and had offered us a pair of tickets. Bill was trying hard to create some measure of fun for us. I agreed to go. Dora stayed at the house and Ruth promised to check in on the boys and drive them wherever they needed to go.

During a candlelight dinner at the Dunes Hotel, peopled with celebrities, we ate to the sound of thirty violins around a waterfall of glittering turquoise. Suddenly, without any warning, I burst into tears. Our fantasy surroundings and the ultra-artificiality of everything in Las Vegas had been unsettling. People around our table went on eating, pretending not to notice me. Bill sat dumbfounded, then he, too, began to cry. We had left the scene of our grief, but the pain itself, like baggage, came with us. Bill rushed to the men's room to cry alone. I wished that he had stayed with me. We had, by then, so little to share, at least we needed to share our hurt.

Bill's business associates were solicitous and we managed to end the Vegas trip without another breakdown. But it took a big effort on both our parts. When we arrived in Los Angeles, in the presence of film stars and the aura of glitzy Hollywood, my sadness lifted for a while. The Awards ceremony was held in Pasadena, the banquet at the Beverly Hilton Hotel. I danced with Danny Thomas and joked with Savannah's native son, Johnny Mercer, who received an Oscar that night for his musical score, *Days Of Wine and Roses*.

The next day Bill and I went sightseeing. After visiting the Farmer's

Market and lunching at the Brown Derby we walked down Rodeo Drive, looking into the store windows filled with extravagant merchandise.

"Nothing appeals to me," I said in a tone that surprised myself.

"Yeah, I've noticed that you like flabby men instead of movie stars," Bill said. Despite the fun and glamour, with Bill's smug remarks about A.D., I was ready to go home when the time came.

Back in Savannah, in the house where Isaac died, amid the many souvenirs of his childhood, I went back to my grief, embracing it as if were an old friend. I decided to throw myself back into selling real estate just to be near people.

The morning after we returned to Savannah, Andrea came over for coffee and gossip. She wanted a blow by blow description of everything I'd done and all that I had seen.

"What did Sophia Loren have on?" Andrea wanted to know what everyone wore when I mentioned the names of those stars I'd had a close look at.

"Oh my God, she's unbelievably exquisite. She wore a design by Dior. A white chiffon dress that ended just above her knees."

"Who else did you see?"

"I talked to Cary Grant. I was tongue-tied, and he laughed at me."

I reached for my bottle of Valium, Andrea frowned. "Why do you have to take those pills?" Her conservative attitudes belied the mess that her own life was in.

"Because I need them."

"You just need to develop a hobby,"Andrea said in a soft voice. She spent a great deal of her time gardening, baking wonderful delicacies and knitting beautiful sweaters in an upstairs room of her huge house. She had started a small mail-order business to sell her sweaters. When we first met she had suggested I work with her.

"So, how's the great love affair with Mr. Bribery," Andrea teased. My spine stiffened at Andrea's name for him. She had given him that label because every time I made demands on him I came away with an expensive gift.

"He says as soon as he winds up the law suit he's working on in Chicago, he's going to get a divorce and then arrange mine."

"Sure he is." Andrea's lips pursed. "And I'm going to walk on the moon." The clandestine aspect of my relationship with A.D. had been part of its attraction, but now I had become anxious and embarrassed about constantly making excuses for why his divorce hadn't taken place, why we were not yet a married couple.

"A.D. is my mentor."

"No, Naomi. He Svengali, you Trilby. He has tremendous power over you. You've given it to him."

When I showed her some of the exquisite pieces of jewelry A.D. had given me Andrea's look turned from admiring the rings and bracelets to one of sadness and longing.

"That's more than I get. I seem to be the one to give gifts to lovers." She said that no one had ever loved her for herself.

"I do, Andrea. Why, I tell you things I've never told another living person. I trust you totally."

"It's the same with me," Andrea said. "My mother said you're the first friend she's ever known me to have."

As time went on I became more and more aware of the curious and sometimes disturbing role I played in A.D.'s life. "You are," he said many times, "the love of my life." He admitted to being miserable with the woman who had shared his name since they both were twenty. A.D. saw his meetings with me as his elixir. Every time we were together he told me he was able to conquer yet another business challenge. He told me things he never confided to Irene. He had lovers before me, but I was the one who lasted.

In our times together he went from being the boulevardier showing off his lovely possession, me, to the guilt-ridden cheater who deserved only the wrath of God. The latter was usually reasoned away when he realized how lonely and barren his marriage was. And how well I knew that feeling. My own marriage had turned into a contract between two strangers.

One afternoon when A.D. had taken me antique shopping in Savannah, where he bought me an outrageously expensive Sevres porcelain tureen for my dining table, I looked up at him and said, "I want to marry in November or December." The year of mourning for Isaac was about to end. He took my arm and put it through his as we continued walking in the direction of his hotel.

"Baby, I have some major problems with my law firm. I can't concentrate on anything else right now." His firm was getting ready to merge with one of Atlanta's leading legal groups. He was worried about his seniority. His problems took precedence. It was maddening not being a part of the important events of his life on a day to day basis. I felt like an appendage. And I was jealous of Irene, who loved her role as the wife of one of Atlanta's most wealthy and prominent men.

"You make me feel larger than life, baby," A.D. said when he showered in the hotel room before I drove him to the airport. At the airport he kissed me and said he would call every day. He was leaving for Florida the next morning for a vacation, with Irene. Before he said good-bye he handed me a Tiffany box with a silver desk clock and matching pen in it. Beneath the cotton in the pale blue box was a gold sculptured brooch set with diamonds. Andrea was right. A.D. bribed me. And I let him, every time.

A few days later the phone rang on the night table next to my bed and I reached to answer it. Bill and I were dressing for a Christmas party. I had hardly said hello when I heard A.D., his voice hysterical.

"My son has died!" he sobbed through the receiver. "It's all my fault! I should have never bought him that BMW. Oh, baby, God is punishing me."

"Daddy, slow down. Please tell me what happened." Disbelief engulfed me and I began to cry with him.

"My son and his wife were attending a football game. They had a head on collision as they were leaving the stadium." He again broke into loud sobs. Then his voice became inaudible. He caught his breath in a few seconds and said, "We're catching the next available flight out of Fort Lauderdale to Atlanta. The funeral will be day after tomorrow."

"Do you want me to come?"

"I need you, baby."

When Bill got out of the shower and walked into the bedroom he saw me sitting on the side of the bed with my head in my hands. There was no way I could pretend about the telephone call.

"A.D.'s son is dead," I cried. "A car accident. It happened this morning while A.D. and Irene were on vacation."

"Where did he call from?" Bill asked.

"The airport. He's hysterical."

"What did he think you could do?" Bill looked angry.

"Comfort him. Just as he's done for me through the last couple of years."

Bill continued to tie his bow tie, straighten his cummerbund and slip on his patent leather shoes. He fumbled with his cufflinks as he finished dressing.

"He said he needs me to help him through the funeral." I asked Bill if I should make plane reservations for him, too.

"No, he seems to value your friendship more. You go." Bill's hurt at what he suspected, perhaps knew but didn't want to acknowledge, continued to emerge in often sarcastic comments. I ignored his remark and went on dressing.

At the funeral A.D. threw himself across his son's coffin, wailing in remorse. I went to his house after the services. Irene seemed surprised to see me there. Her decorum was perfect. She stood at the front door of their home, greeting guests. Perhaps the sudden shock of her son's accident brought on a different reaction than my watching Isaac's prolonged death.

"Stop blaming yourself, Joseph's death wasn't your fault," I said. Seeing A.D. sobbing was difficult for me. I leaned over and kissed his forehead. He had been, in fact, an indulgent father, trying to live his son's life for him, taking unpleasantness on his own shoulders, sparing Joseph. A.D. had wanted to take charge of everyone's life he shared.

Seeing my lover confront his pain made me realize just how vulnerable we all are.

In a strange way, I began to realize that a life that knows some suffering can never grow complacent. My acceptance of this began to move my heart for the first time toward recovery. I began to understand the role that tragic events play in our lives. How they help us to grow, to master our own fate. How they can teach us the truth about ourselves.

For four months A.D. struggled to get to his law offices each morning. His enthusiasm was at an all time low. The idea of time in the sun, to rest, to let his soul catch up, as the Irish say, would help him the way the California trip had helped me. Grief is so draining, and A.D., in his late fifties, needed to lie on the sand and gently exhale. When a friend of Andrea's offered her his home in Freeport in the Bahamas, she asked me to join her there for two weeks. A.D. saw this as the perfect opportunity to spend time with me and to be far enough away from his work and personal life so that he might renew his energy and emotional strength.

The Hotel Lucaya in Freeport was having its grand opening when A.D. booked a room there. Andrea had said it wouldn't look right for him to stay at the house with us. And true to form, the first night A.D. was at the hotel, he met someone in the elegant bar who knew of his reputation and the two began planning an intricate business deal together. For the next three days he lavished Andrea and me with expensive gifts and fabulous dinners.

"You're really lucky," Andrea said to me. "No man has ever indulged me the way he does you." But along with her admiration of A.D. and his generosity, Andrea accused him of being dishonest, a briber. She said his taste was very Jewish, yet she accepted every gift he presented her.

"I must go back to Atlanta, tonight," A.D. said to me one morning while we were walking on the beach. He had only been there three days.

"Why? What happened?" I asked, my heart sinking.

"I just spoke to Irene. She said that I'm the biggest son of a bitch in the world to be here, vacationing only four months after Joseph's death."

He took the next flight out.

"We'll have fun without him, you'll see," Andrea said. She put her arm on my shoulder. "He's never going to marry you, so you better get used to this. He likes having you as his baby doll." Try as I might, it was hard to deny what Andrea was saying. If A.D. really wanted me he would have left his marriage. I began to resent Irene and the hold she had on him, the hold A.D. let her have on him.

That night, dressed in our prettiest outfits, we went to the Hotel Lucaya to watch the international backgammon tournament, with celebrities descending on the tiny island for the social event.

"Face it," Andrea said. She turned to me with her lips pursed tightly, her shoulders pulled back like a drill sergeant's. She stared directly into my eyes. "A man who's unfaithful because 'my wife doesn't understand me' is often blaming her for his own shortcomings."

"But it's different with us," I said defensively.

"Naomi, grow up."

We spent the wee hours of the morning in the casino of the hotel watching the backgammon tournament. But all I wanted to do was leave the Bahamas and get back to the States. Andrea obliged. As we drove toward St. Augustine, on the way to Savannah, I said, "Stop. I have to call A.D." I needed to know he was there. It took four or five calls from different pay phones before I located him.

"You're the most insecure woman I've ever known!" Andrea yelled out to me from the car just as I was about to make my last call. She was growing impatient with me, but I was determined to talk to him. When I finally reached A.D., he was curt, distracted, not happy I had called him. He talked for less than a minute. He said he had to get back to the business meeting that he was in when I phoned.

That night when Andrea and I checked into a motel I dialed Bill, a call I dreaded. It made me feel like I was reporting to my truant officer. Bill got quickly to the point.

"I found a love note written on a napkin, hidden in a locked box at the bottom of your shoe closet," he said. "It's in French."

My stomach flipped over. A.D. had trained me to lie so well that the words came without a second's hesitation. "Well," I said, "it just so happened that one day I was at Hilton Head. A.D. was there with some attorneys, and he wrote me that note. He had a waiter deliver it to my table." A.D. had written *je ta'ime*. Bill understood that it meant, "I love you."

Andrea grabbed the phone from my hand and yelled, "Damn it, Bill, you could've waited for us to get home. You didn't have to upset Naomi this way. What the hell's the matter with you?"

"Hurry home, drive safely." Bill sounded very contrite.

I phoned A.D. early the next morning. He apologized for having to cut our earlier conversation short. After I explained Bill's discovery, he said. "Just be calm. Bill can't possibly say anything happened because of a simple little napkin. And tell him he had no right to go through your personal belongings. It violates your right of privacy." Ever the tough lawyer on the offense, A.D. instructed me to "deny, deny, deny." Bill would have no part of that.

"Tell me exactly what's going on," he demanded as soon as I reached the house.

"Just because A.D. wrote that on a napkin doesn't mean anything. You know how he likes to joke around," I said as calmly as if I were ordering groceries. Deceiving Bill had become a part of the life that I had sculpted for myself.

"I want to know what the hell is going on between you two. Tell me if you've fucked him." His anger rose, his voice shook. "Tell me!"

I couldn't answer him. He suddenly grabbed me so hard it threw me off balance, knocking me up against the wall. I slid to the floor, my head throbbing.

"Bill, we're good friends. I love him—like a father."

He pulled me to my feet and began shaking me. I felt as though I was going to pass out. I didn't fight back; I felt that I deserved punishment.

Bill stormed through the house cursing and flinging things from the tables, smashing china objects, including a prized wedding present and throwing them out of windows. His hand swept across the bedroom dresser sending bottles of perfume against walls and onto the floor. Broken glass was everywhere.

"How dare you let another man *shtup* you!" Bill raged. "How could you go to bed with him? His body is soft and pale." Bill couldn't imagine that I could love a man who didn't have an athletic body. Bill was frustrated: he had come to feel that no matter how hard he worked he could never please me, never do enough.

Much later that night Bill tried to make love to me. He wanted to bury himself in me, to cling to me. He always felt that a little sex would cure anything unpleasant that happened. My lessening sexual response to him reflected my growing separateness, which permeated the conflicts in our marriage. I knew, if he did not, that the disparity of sexual desire between us was a result of our disaffection, not its cause.

As he reached for me across the bed, I recoiled. "Please, Bill, I'm hurt and angry." My head ached, there were bruises on my face and I felt sick to my stomach.

"The hell with you," he yelled. Bill jumped out of bed, hastily put on his clothes and stormed out of the house, slamming every door on the way. I desperately wanted my relationship with A.D. to be out in the open, but somehow I knew confession is not always a mature and loving act. And A.D. had instructed me to always deny.

Bill did not return the next day or the day after that. A week passed, then another. It was getting harder to explain to the boys. I took refuge in my real estate work, diving back into it with a vengeance. A.D., in Savannah on a brief trip, was shocked that Bill had been away for so long without contacting me.

"You need to find out where he's living or file for divorce," A.D. advised. He offered to buy me a house in Atlanta and to help move me and the children. I declined his offer.

"One thing I'm sure about. I don't want to be your kept woman, A.D. Either you get a divorce, too, or I stay here." I no longer loved the man I was married to nor could I marry the man I loved. Instead, I began to create new fantasies. I would own a luxurious car, a beautiful new house, my own business.

One day Andrea suggested that we follow Bill from work. We found him living in a dilapidated shack at the beach that belonged to one of his golfing buddies. I was consumed with guilt at the thought of him living in such a rundown place. The next morning I phoned him at his office.

"Bill, the boys miss you. Please come back for their sakes. There's a terrible sense of loss without you." He returned, but his unspoken anger continued to seethe, barely contained. His more violent reactions had turned into caustic comments in response to almost everything I said. When I told him that we'd been invited to the Savannah Symphony Ball his reply was typical.

"Why don't you get your rich lawyer to come to town and go with you?" I changed the subject and told him about a sale that I had closed that day.

"Did Mr. Rich Bastard Lawyer buy it?" He treated my real estate sales as though they were some ridiculous waste of time. And when he did, the guilt would begin to eat at me like soil eroding at the edge of the river.

Bill turned toward me with an empty smile. "And don't worry, Naomi. I wasn't alone at the beach." He stomped out of the room.

At that moment my pity for him — for both of us — pierced my heart.

Chapter Twenty One

Early in 1965 I confided to Andrea that I suspected I was pregnant.

"Whose is it?" Andrea said, when I told her that I had missed my period. I surprised myself when I realized how happy I felt at being a mother again.

"A.D.'s, of course."

I could pinpoint the exact moment of conception. It was during an afternoon that A.D. and I had made love in his room at the Hotel DeSoto. At the height of our passion, I knew without the slightest doubt that I had conceived. Six weeks later, the rabbit died.

A child, I truly believed, would change A.D.'s life. We both missed our sons so desperately. Isaac's death was not that far in the past and this pregnancy seemed like the perfect vantage point for A.D. and me to begin our life together. And A.D. could replace the pain and guilt he had never lost after Joseph's death. The child would make him decide to marry me. I was sure of it.

"You better tell A.D.," Andrea advised. She didn't trust him or how he would respond. I wanted the two of them to be friends because they were my closest allies but their worlds were too far apart.

I called A.D. to tell him the news. He said: "Abortion."

"I want to have this baby!"

"I don't want another man to raise my child!"

"Marry me, then," I said.

"We can't get married right now. "It's not time."

"What better time than now, Daddy?"

"Half a loaf is better than none," he said. "Remember that."

"Remember it! You've said it to me so many times it's imprinted on my brain!" I wanted to slam the telephone against his head. But instead I began to cry.

"I have to see you. I can't handle this by myself," I sobbed.

A.D.'s solution was to take me to a psychiatrist in Atlanta.

"If I were A.D.," the doctor said, "I would certainly marry you and have the baby."

"You're not A.D."

I went to see another of A.D.'s friends, a gynecologist, who said I should have an abortion.

"I really do want this baby." I looked at him with pleading eyes.

"Honey," he said, smiling, "if it were me, I'd marry you."

"It isn't you."

A.D. held me in his arms, kissing me sweetly. "If you love me, sweetheart, please have the abortion. I'll make it up to you in a million ways. My word of honor, we'll be married soon."

Arrangements were made for me to have the abortion in Atlanta. My mind was filled with horror stories. Abortions still weren't legal in 1965. Fifty percent of maternal deaths resulted from criminal abortions. The papers printed the story of a seventeen year old girl in Los Angeles who had been rushed to a hospital, hemorrhaging. Her temperature was 105 degrees. Surgeons performed a hysterectomy. An amateur abortionist had injected a toxic solution into her uterus. Part of a needle had been found by doctors; it had punctured her uterus and perforated her intestines.

I asked Andrea to come with me to Atlanta. I needed her support more than ever. "Naomi, I can't go with you. I've got my hands full." But I knew that a big part of the reason was that Andrea was disgusted with me and my obsession for A.D.

"My family doesn't know about this. What if I die?" I said to A.D. as he drove me to meet the abortionist. I sank against the soft tan leather of the car seat holding my hand to my stomach.

"We'll think of something," he said in a patronizing voice. He suggested we ask a mutual friend to cover for me, to say I was her house guest and to also say that I was out shopping in case Bill phoned. A.D. was such a master of the lie that he couldn't understand why it bothered me. He had built his entire marriage and law practice on lies. I had heard it said that he was a ruthless lawyer who manipulated and bribed his way up the ladder. Yet, to me, he was the gentlest man I'd ever known.

"Trust me," he said as he drove more rapidly toward our appointment.

"Daddy, do you know how much I wanted this child?" A.D. drew me to him, and put his arm around me.

Gladys, a registered nurse, met us in the parking lot of a shopping center. She was coarse, inhumane and sloppy. A.D. had found her and she was willing to perform the illegal abortion. Mothers with babies in their arms walked by and the clamor of children competed with Gladys's small, grating voice.

"Put her suitcase in the back seat," she ordered. A.D. was nonchalant, as if he'd come to this dreadful place with other women to hand them over to his favorite abortionist. For a few dollars she would hack life from my body. I felt reduced to nothing. The man I loved thought solely of his image and reputation.

"Please, A.D., don't make me do this," I said clinging to him before stepping into Gladys's car. I felt so tiny and incomplete. Gladys drove away with me on the seat beside her, chain smoking.

When we arrived at her house in Tucker, a suburb of Atlanta, Gladys ordered me to lie down on a bed in a dimly-lit room that seemed to be furnished in K-Mart rejects. My mind raced. What if she killed me? Only A.D. knew where I was. Would he cover up my death so his wife and daughter wouldn't find out? What about my children? My mother? Bill?

"Lay across this here bed and spread your legs just as far apart as you can get them," Gladys instructed. Boxes of rolled gauze were piled on the floor next to the bed. I lay with my legs open. Maybe Andrea was right, it was time to give up A.D. It seemed that if he really loved me he wouldn't have left me to face this alone?

"Please, stop, it hurts. I just can't take it," I begged, as Gladys pushed rolls of gauze into my body. This was an attempt to suffocate the embryo and cause me to abort.

"You women are such big babies," she snapped. She belched repeatedly and kept barking at me to shut up the crying. Then, in her best cracker-redneck accent, she added, "I don't know why you mess around with some rich ol' man like him. He ain't gonna marry you."

My head was throbbing. I was afraid to cry, but the tears came on their own.

"You just weak, that's all," she said. It was the last thing I needed to hear as the gauze stripping tore at my dry vagina. Sharp pains stabbed and ripped through my lower back.

Gladys blamed me, not A.D., for the life inside.

"I didn' quit my job as head nurse in obstetrics for charity," she said. That was certainly obvious.

For three days I stayed there. Gladys informed me that I was not to use the telephone nor leave the house. I had to remain inside with the shades drawn until I aborted. The house had roaches in every corner. Gladys's husband sat in the kitchen in a sweat-stained undershirt. The gray hair under his armpits, matted and wet greeted me at every meal.

The cramps increased. The pain became unbearable. But still I did not abort. I told Gladys I had to talk to A.D. She let me use the phone.

"I'm dying," I moaned on the third morning. A.D. told me to put Gladys on the phone. He said that he wanted his gynecologist friend to talk to me. When the call came Gladys listened on the extension. She warned me to be careful of what I said. I didn't describe my agony so he really didn't know what advice to offer. But he sounded upset when he heard the quiver in my voice, and he had known others who had used Gladys. He promised to call A.D.

One miserable day dragged into another as I paced the floor of the dingy house, stepping over the cracks in the linoleum filled with stale, hardened bacon grease. The husband attempted conversation, but I had no interest in hearing anything he had to say, except when he mentioned the fact that he had known A.D. from his gambling days, when A.D. had kept him from serving time in prison. This was their way of paying A.D. back. Gladys now performed abortions for his wealthy clients. She even named a few.

A.D. finally came to see me. He told me that Bill had phoned our friend and when she answered, for the third time, that I was out shopping, he screamed at her and accused her of being a liar. Five days had gone by. I had on the same pink cotton house coat that I'd worn for the last three days. It hung loosely about my body. My hair was damp and uncombed. AD. looked shocked when he saw the wretched state I was in.

"I can't live like this another day," I said, embracing him.

He was genuinely worried. "I'll take care of things, baby."

"Get me out of here as fast as you can." I felt like a murderess, attempting to kill the baby, who was hanging on for life and refusing to leave my womb.

A.D. told Gladys to take me to a doctor right away, that I needed medical attention. His gynecologist friend had obviously given him this advice. He slipped two one hundred dollar bills into Gladys's hand. I was bundled into the back seat of Gladys's blue Plymouth and taken to a doctor who put me on a table and then pulled out the gauze packing. He was young, kind and patient, talking to me softly, reassuring me that I'd be all right. My terror lessened for the first time in days.

With an instrument that resembled a small vacuum cleaner, the fetus was removed. I floated in and out of consciousness, no longer caring what happened to me. All that mattered was that the pain had diminished thanks to the shots the doctor had given me. I was only vaguely aware of Gladys standing very close by. When it was over, like a limp rag doll, I was helped off the table.

"Three hundred dollars cash, please," the doctor said, with his hand outstretched.

"I have no money," I replied groggily.

Gladys said, "Her rich ol' boyfriend'll pay, don't you worry. I'll have him send you the money." With that she supported me by the arm and walked me out of the doctor's office.

Gladys drove to the same parking lot where A.D. had deposited me in her car. He was waiting, sitting in his car with a huge box of Godiva chocolates on the seat next to him. Without looking me in the eye, he handed me a black jeweler's box. There was no doubt that I had grown accustomed to his gifts borne of guilt. But now I felt as though he were tossing a quarter to a lice-infected pickpocket down on the Savannah wharf.

Inside the box was a diamond pin in the shape of an oak leaf. "It's very beautiful," I said, dropping it beside me on the seat. I slumped down, physically exhausted, unable to hold my body upright.

A.D. drove to the Airport Motor Lodge, a motel that he owned. He had arranged for the best suite. He got me settled in, explaining that he had to rush back to the office for a meeting. And then Irene was having a group of people for dinner that evening at the Mayfair Club.

"You can't leave me alone tonight!" It was the first time I had been assertive with him.

"But I'm the host of this very important client," he said.

"If you're not here with me, A.D., I'm calling Irene and telling her exactly what happened."

A.D. phoned Irene and said that he had to leave town on an emergency. Later in bed, he held me close to him. "Come on, baby. Give daddy a little *kepele*." This is the Yiddish word for "head."

To me, our loving each other meant marriage. To A.D., it did not. But he continued to make the promises that I longed to hear. "This time things are different," he said. "I'm going to marry you. On my granddaughter's life, I swear it." He was swearing on the life of his dead son's child. He couldn't possibly lie about this.

But he did. His promises were like echoes in icy mountain air, and compounded with the lovelessness of my own marriage, made me feel a sense of desolation like nothing I had ever experienced.

While leaving Bill and seeking a divorce skated through my head at all times, I didn't have the courage to take my sons from their father, not knowing what lay ahead. The fear of fighting out in the open, in the courts, crippled me. I still wanted A.D. to be there waiting to catch me when I dared to take the leap. As hard as I tried to convince myself, I still wasn't my own woman.

Chapter Twenty Two

When I told Bill that I wanted to build a big, beautiful house, in an area of Savannah that was very upscale he asked where the money would come from for such an expensive lot. I lied and said I had some money from the accident settlement in a savings account. But in fact, A.D. sent me a check to purchase the half-acre parcel. I convinced Bill that it was time for us to leave the sad memories behind and move on. "A.D. owes me a huge commission on a piece of property and that will pay the balance," I said.

Although Bill was concerned that A.D. would be part of the financial arrangement for our new house, once again he didn't press the issue.

"You're the agent in the family, you handle it," Bill said, and turned over all the responsibility to me. Bill was a creature of habit, a man who liked his routine. On the days when he was in town, he'd come home from his store, mix himself a double martini, reach for the newspaper, watch television, and pick his nose. I wanted to talk to him, to share my day, the sales I made, the people I met. But Bill seemed deaf to any conversation I tried to start. Eventually I stopped trying, stifling the part of myself that wanted to communicate.

And our sex life had become an absolute farce. Often on Monday nights, during half-time in the televised football game, Bill would rush into my room expecting a quickie before the third quarter. I wondered if watching grown men smashing into each other for an hour had turned him on. When my body froze in anger at his advances Bill would tear into the kitchen for another beer.

"I bet you're not that way with your rich old lawyer," he shouted one Monday night as he slammed the refrigerator. This was as close as we came to discussing my affair with A.D. I wanted to shout back in defense of myself but I never said anything, choosing to ignore his accusations rather than deny or defend myself.

Of course A.D. no longer came to visit us at home. Bill knew that A.D. was investing heavily in real estate with me and he knew the money was helping to pay for the new house. His attitude seemed to say that for now he seemed willing to let the old fool invest in a home that would enable his family to live more prestigiously.

When winter ended, construction began on the new house. We hired an architect to draw plans for a two-story brick home that would fit into the cluster of trees surrounding it. A.D. and I selected bathroom fixtures and furniture. He bought me everything I wanted. Manufacturers who were A.D.'s legal clients arranged special purchases that he would pay for, but on his books, would become business deductions for him. A.D. knew how to turn every deal to his advantage.

While Bill was in the Bahamas on business one weekend, A.D. and I went to Hilton Head. Alex and Ross were staying with my sister. We drove back to Savannah before A.D. had to leave for the airport, I wanted to show him how the house was coming along.

As we drove through the Carolina Low Country near Blufton I spotted Bill's car; he had returned home sooner than expected. When he saw me driving, A.D. on the seat next to me, Bill swerved his car in front of mine. I slammed on the brakes to avoid crashing into him. He waved his fist and motioned for me to pull off the road.

"Be calm," A.D. said as I steered the car to a stop in the dirt alongside the shoulder of the road. "Remember, just stay calm. My luggage is in your trunk, so he won't see it." The Spanish moss from the trees brushed the top of my car. Through my rearview mirror I saw the fury in my husband's eyes.

Bill jumped from his car, leaned through the window, and slapped A.D. hard across the face. "Come with me!" he ordered. Then he shouted, "You goddamned murderer. You killed your son with your prick!"

"No, Bill, A.D. is not going with you. He's staying in my car." I spoke in a calm voice as I started the engine. I believed that the truth would put our lives in order; I felt like a tree freed from suffocating vines that had been wound too tightly, for too long. A.D., sitting beside me, started to cry, then pulled out his handkerchief and wiped his eyes. Bill got back into his car and followed us as I drove A.D. to the airport.

"Don't worry, baby. I'll call Bill and talk to him. I'll smooth everything over. Just don't worry."

"It's time to tell everybody the truth, A.D. You tell Irene and I'll tell Bill." My voice grew firmer as I spoke.

"Not now, baby. Just be patient." A.D. looked at me with pleading eyes. "There are problems with the children, the grandchildren. It won't be that much longer, I promise." He touched my arm. "Remember, half a loaf —"

"Is better than none." I spit out the words, all the while knowing in my heart, that even if A.D. couldn't keep his promises, I couldn't stop loving him.

When Bill got home that evening I was on the phone with Andrea. I had asked her why she hadn't tried to protect me when Bill called her. She told me that seeing newspapers in our front yard, Bill had telephoned her. When she told him that I had gone to Hilton Head with a friend, Bill immediately drove there hoping to catch us. His rage had turned violent when he was unable to find A.D. and me at the resort.

Bill walked into the room very quietly, overhearing every word. He grabbed the phone out of my hand and pushed me across the bed. "You whore, you goddamned whore!" I lay there overwhelmed with remorse that I had brought on so much hurt and misery, especially to myself.

Later that night I decided yet one more time that my marriage had no future and that I would have to be the one to leave. Bill was never going to leave his home. Whether or not A.D. was going to be there for me, the time had come for me to make a decision. I packed a few things in a suitcase having no idea where I would go.

Bill screamed for the boys to get up, he shook them awake. He pushed them toward the door. "Your mother is leaving you!" he shouted. I lowered my head, unable to look at the frightened faces of my sons staring incomprehensibly at me.

Alex ran to me, threw his arms around my waist, pulling and crying. "Please, Mom, don't go. Come on back, please." I put my bag down on the floor and folded Ross in my arms. I said nothing.

"She can't stand being with us," Bill railed.

Ross snuggled against my shoulder as I wiped the perspiration from his forehead and kissed him on the top of his head. I was disgusted that Bill had used the children to stop me. I decided I would see a lawyer the next day. At that moment I felt manipulated by his self-pity and whining. I went slowly to my room, put the suitcase on the bed, and unpacked the few things I had hastily thrown into the bag. I was defeated, but only temporarily.

The lawyer, a mutual friend of mine and Bill's, thought I should not get divorced. "Playing around is a fact of life," he said. "Tell him you're sorry and stay married till the boys are older."

As soon as I called my sister to tell her of the incident, Ruth shocked me with her news. "I'm divorcing Ted. Mother can't handle two." My sister was leaving her twenty-year marriage, but since she was the oldest, she had priority. And she was right, our mother probably would be too devastated.

But the longer Bill and I lived under the same roof, the more his jealousy grew. He stood around the phone no matter who I was talking to, questioning, demanding to know who was on the other end. Andrea waited until he left for work to telephone. So did A.D. And Ruth was afraid to call if she knew he was going to be home. Any time I met a male friend or business associate for a drink after work Bill would fly into a rage the moment I got home.

In fact, one time a good friend of ours asked me to join him for a drink at the end of the day because his father was very ill and he found comfort in my ability to listen. This same friend had been at our side all through Isaac's sickness and at the end. As couples, the four of us often had dinner together. We had even traveled to Europe as a foursome

"Where the hell is my dinner?" Bill bellowed as soon as I opened the front door that night.

"Didn't you get my message that I'd be home a bit late?"

"Yes, but you were with a man," he shouted.

"I was with Johnny, for Christ's sake!" He reached for the phone, dialed Johnny's home and shouted at him, "How the hell would you feel if your wife didn't have your fucking dinner ready when you got home?" He slammed down the receiver. Bill's wrath was out of control. It consumed him.

The next morning when I approached Ruth, hoping to find a sympathetic ear for my unhappiness, she topped every story I had to tell, so I shelved my own tale of woe and listened to my sister's.

"Mother said Ted is exactly like Daddy and she's glad I'm out of this. She told me that she never had the guts to leave Daddy because of us."

"That's just what I need to hear, that we're the reason for Mother and Daddy's miserable life together. She couldn't take responsibility herself, huh?" I knew my mother would never understand my wanting to leave Bill, unless she could see enough similarity between him and my dead father.

It seemed that we had reached a stalemate. Bill spent longer hours at his golf and gin rummy games and attended boring good-old-boy activities at his club. But I was no longer afraid of Bill, of what he might say or do. Indifference has its own subtle way of punishment.

With my professional experience and A.D.'s capital, I thought it reasonable that I'd be able to open my own office within a year or two. I took refuge in my work and poured my heart and soul into it. Owning my own business became a top priority for the future. A.D. was supportive and the fact that he was now propelling my career meant he was still in control of me.

"Just think, Mazik, you can deduct everything that you spend on travel, even if I'm paying for it." A.D. knew every angle. He told me he often billed three clients for one trip and then deducted it from his firm as well.

A.D. liked to have an entourage when we went out to dinner in New York. I suppose he thought there was safety in numbers. Our favorite hotel in New York was the Regency. Whenever we were there he instructed the piano player to immediately begin playing *Fascination* the moment he saw me enter the bar. So I continued to give him sex, romance, excitement, and youth. And he gave me bliss, panic that he wouldn't always be there, and a renewal of the yearnings I'd carried from my childhood for parental love, my mother's approval and my father's indulgence. By now, A.D. had taken the place of both Minna and Avram — he was my mother and father. The ones I'd always dreamed of having.

"Tell me, baby," A.D. asked one evening after I'd been shopping on Fifth Avenue, "has Bill noticed your fur coat or said anything about all your jewelry?"

"He's never mentioned any of it. He still thinks the diamond you gave me is a zircon." A.D. was surprised at my remark.

"What's wrong with that man? If Irene came home with a full length mink coat and I hadn't paid for it I'd wonder where the hell she got it."

"Darling, if Irene came home with mink, you'd know damned good and well that she charged it to your account."

When I returned from New York Andrea listened intently when I told her about our conversation. She said her husband never noticed a thing she bought or wore, that he cared only for martinis, his business, and The Oglethorpe Club.

"Naomi, I have closets overflowing with clothes. You know I'm a shopaholic. I ask Gordon at least once a week if he loves me. Do you know what his answer always is?"

I shook my head.

"Of course. I love you, like a hog loves slop."

Andrea accepted the fact that her marriage was empty; she kept it a secret from no one. She accepted the fact that she had no companionship in exchange for a wealthy husband who paid all the bills. Her own trust account was used exclusively to satisfy her extravagant tastes. At the same time she was fascinated by my ambition and ethnic qualities. She yearned for some of the wild passion and romance she saw in my life.

"Doesn't look as if either of us has the perfect marriage," I said.

Andrea shrugged her shoulders. "Why don't you give up. What's holding you to him?" She was referring to AD.. Andrea could understand staying in a bad marriage, but not a bad love affair.

"You may never understand, I don't either. But all I can tell you is that my heart has a mind of its own. And as much as I struggle, my heart has reasons that my mind can never understand. That's just the way it is."

When moving day rolled around Andrea came bursting in, barking orders like a drill sergeant. She had offered to oversee the packing. The new house wasn't quite ready but we had sold our house and the new owners needed to move right in.

"Get off the damned phone with Mr. Bribery! Your movers'll be here any minute." I obediently told A.D. I had to hang up.

"Look, you haven't even taken pictures off the walls." Andrea scolded me as she began lifting paintings off their hooks and wrapping them in heavy brown paper. "For God's sakes, Naomi, get a move on. Dora and I can't do it all."

"I know how dependable you are," I teased. "You really are the paragon of organization. You are my official *mavin*."

Andrea nodded. "Good thing too, because somehow your husband always manages to be out of town when you need him most." My friend ran the moving operation with military precision. She even seemed to be enjoying it. Which is more than I could say for myself. I had a sense of foreboding. I may be moving into a lovely new home, I thought, but I was not leaving my troubles behind me.

Because the new house was only two blocks from where we were moving the boys kept the same friends and went to the same school. Troy, Andrea's oldest son, by her first marriage was causing her a lot of worry. He still lived with them but often didn't show up for school. Her two younger boys played ball with Ross.

Our new house was twice the size of the one we left and ever so much grander. Bill stocked his built-in bar with every conceivable brand of whiskey. He bought Bombay gin and Apricot brandy, lining them up next to the Smirnoff and Seagrams. I had my linen closets in order, while every pot and pan in my kitchen shone like a precious jewel. With a place for everything it was easier for me to organize the boys activities and leave for work.

At holiday time Andrea threw an extravagant Christmas cocktail party. I was in the middle of a boring conversation with one of her guests when I noticed Andrea leaning to whisper something in Bill's ear, then run her tongue around it. It was widely known among our friends that Andrea was restless and enjoyed openly flirting in front of Gordon.

"I saw you kissing Bill," I said casually to Andrea the next morning as we discussed the details of her party.

Andrea didn't miss a beat. "He grabbed me under the mistletoe, and do you know what he did? He stuck his tongue in my mouth!"

I wondered if perhaps Bill was attempting to get even. We were both miserable, avoiding confrontation, playing a game that was dangerous, possibly deadly

Chapter Twenty Three

When Andrea's oldest son, Troy, ran away from home she was beside herself. Andrea didn't know where he was, but she did suspect that he was using marijuana and other drugs. She had even gone to members of the Board of Education to talk about her son's drug use as well as that of many of his schoolmates. They all thought Andrea was crazy to think there was a drug problem among teenagers in Savannah. No one did anything about it and drug use continually increased among students.

A month later Troy ran out of money while living on the beach near Key West. He called and asked Andrea to wire him enough money to come home. He was extremely thin and his skin was yellow when she met him at the bus station. Troy's drug addiction had resulted in a deadly bout with hepatitis. Doctors suspected that he had used an unsterile needle. The boy developed double pneumonia and had to be hospitalized. Andrea called me from the hospital pay phone, her voice shaking. I said I would be right over. The moment I saw my friend I sensed the worst. Andrea's voice sounded far away and hollow as she said, "The doctor told me that he might die."

"I don't believe it." I could barely get the words out. I didn't want to believe it. It couldn't be happening. I called A.D. He came to Savannah for two days and went with me to the hospital. We sat in silence, the three of us, stunned by the common realization that each of us was sacrificing a son.

I felt as though I were delivering a soliloquy as I drove A.D. to the airport. "God should've passed over our houses and left our firstborn sons alive. He should've seen our front doors smeared with the blood lost and the tears shed while giving birth and raising them."

"Baby, no promise of gain, or knowledge, could ever be worth the pain of what we've sacrificed. The price was far too precious." There was a symphonic note of sadness as he spoke.

Andrea's two younger sons were having dinner at my house when she called from the hospital a few days later. "Naomi." She spoke in a voice hardly audible. "Please tell Gordon, Jr. and Lance how sick their brother is." She didn't know how to talk to them.

I invited the two boys into the den and sat across from them, explaining that Troy's illness was extremely serious. Gordon, Jr. and Lance looked bewildered and asked if they could visit him. An eerie sense of deja vu suddenly swept over me. I had the urge to run into the woods behind my house, to hide under the huge flame colored azaleas. But Andrea needed me and I certainly wasn't going to let her down. Alex and Ross had come into the den and awkwardly listened to what I was saying. Young and innocent, the four boys now shared a tragic bond.

At the hospital, Andrea met us in the hall then walked down the corridor to stand at the door of Troy's room. He had slipped into a coma. His slender, tanned body lay against the white sheet, his eyes closed peacefully, Christlike. A week later, he died.

When Andrea came home from the hospital the afternoon of Troy's death I tried to hug her in order to hold all the pieces together so she wouldn't fall apart. But Andrea fled past me into the kitchen, grabbed the mop, and began to clean the floor. Then she took her finest cups and saucers down from the cabinets. She snatched up her polished silver and fine crystal, and began giving me instructions.

"Naomi, please put out all of my best things when people start to come." She ran a bath to soak in the warm water, as if to wash away the film of death.

"You want me to stay with you?"

"No, just see that my house looks proper."

At the funeral, as I stood at Troy's grave, seeing the ineffable sadness on Andrea's face, I once again questioned God's motives.

Morning coffee now took on a different meaning for Andrea and me. She said, "I need some time to understand what's happening. I don't know what to believe or not believe." She said she was going to rest and spend more time in her garden.

"I wonder what Troy was thinking," Andrea said, staring at his picture in a solid silver frame.

"He absolutely adored you," I said.

"We never talk about love in my family," Andrea said. "Could that be the difference between Jews and Christians?"

As she spoke I remembered life in Eva's house on Charlton Street. And suddenly even my mother's automatic kisses seemed generous compared to what Andrea had.

"Do you know why we're being punished?" Andrea said.

"Why would I be punished?" I looked at Andrea with anger in my eyes.

"Maybe because you love A.D., God took away Isaac."

"You're nuts. What kind of God would punish me for loving a man who's so wonderful to me?"

"You know, a lot of people in town talk about you and me behind our backs. I mean, women as well as men scoff because they think we're too independent, that you shouldn't be leaving your home to go to work. My mother said you're trying to force your way into a man's world."

"Andrea, I need to work. Just being a housewife and mother has never been enough for me. I have a good mind, it must be used."

Now that Andrea and I shared the common tragedy of having lost the eldest of our three sons, that uniqueness gave us an exclusive friendship. We phoned each other every time we had a thought to share. We had become each other's alter egos.

"How long does this suffering last?" Often my friend spoke as though she were in a trance, then would let out a deep sigh.

"It never ends for a mother. We have to learn to live with the scar tissue. It's sort of like learning to live with a clubfoot, or being born with one arm. It takes practice." Yes, I had learned that the hard way.

My mother's pride in our new house was something else. Whenever she came to visit with one of her sisters she loved showing them around. They admired the two-story living room and the wrought iron balcony, where I had hung some of the paintings collected on my trips to Europe and Mexico. Bill and I had taken our first European trip on my fortieth birthday. We had stalked the silver vaults of London and numerous art galleries and I had instantly become a collector. But, intuitively, my mother saw beyond the home's beautiful interior to the trouble that she knew no amount of style and comfort could hide.

"Why are you and Bill sleeping in separate bedrooms?" She was in my kitchen, grating potatoes into a glass bowl. She had come over for our annual Chanukah dinner. She preferred to grate the potatoes by hand; I liked using the electric blender. We each made half and then mixed the two batters together. Every year the two of us made potato *latkes* together, a bit of Jewish tradition that I clung to so that mother and daughter would have something to share.

"His snoring keeps me awake," I said and wiped the tears from my eyes. The raw onion burned intensely.

"*Oy gevalt*," my mother said, not looking at me. She spooned apple sauce and sour cream into serving bowls. Suddenly, she looked over at the grated potatoes. "Cover that bowl. You know the potatoes will get brown if you don't cover them with plastic wrap." She liked being in the kitchen with me and especially liked ordering me around.

I longed to tell my mother about my disinterest in Bill and my love for A.D. But sexuality still remained a taboo subject between us. Mother and daughter stood in the kitchen, neither one able to mention the word "sex." My mother chose instead to search for reasons for my marital rift by assuming I was to blame.

"You spend too much money," Mother said accusingly.

Hoping to avoid a confrontation I went to my bathroom and began touching up my make-up. When I came out she was going through my closet.

"What in the world are you looking for?" I asked.

She stood inside the huge walk-in, pushing one garment aside after another, stopping to examine the price tags still hanging on some.

"You throw money away on expensive clothes." I couldn't tell her that A.D. had paid for most of them. Rifling through my wardrobe, she demanded, "Why do you have to buy so much?"

"I've always loved beautiful clothes, you know that." I tried to ignore her remark and to not yell at her.

"This is no *shmatte*. This suit cost over two hundred dollars!"

"Have I asked you to pay for any of them?"

Ignoring the question, my mother bore in. "You should be saving for your old age. You're more extravagant than Ruth." For some reason, the more upset I got the more energized my mother became. She seemed to enjoy driving me to the point of explosion.

"Can you guarantee me old age," I asked defensively, wanting to scream, "Did anybody guarantee my precious Isaac a long life?" But I held myself back.

"Ted never made a decent living, Bill does. Ted's a *shikkerer* (a drunk). It's too bad Ruth didn't marry someone like Bill."

"It's too damn bad she didn't marry Bill," I shot back. "And stop trying to make me feel guilty because I have more than Ruth. Why the hell can't you ever be satisfied with me, show an ounce of enthusiasm for my good luck, the fact that I work hard? Nobody handed me anything, especially not you."

"Don't talk to me like that," my mother said. "I don't know why you get so mad." She never seemed to be satisfied until she had driven me to the point of explosion.

Contrary to my arguments with my mother, Bill and Ross had their own way of handling Minna. Once when Ross's dog was hit by a B.B. from a neighbor's gun one of her hind legs had to be amputated. Ross lovingly nursed She, his dog, back to health and was so proud of the way She got around that he often bragged that his dog was better with three legs than most were with four. Ross had named his dog She because Lyndon Johnson had a dog named Her.

One Sunday evening a neighbor rang our doorbell while Mother was visiting. The woman said she had been knocked from her bike by our dog running into her.

"You're going to cause some of our most prominent citizens to be crippled," the woman yelled. My mother did not know how to respond.

When the woman left, Mother turned to Ross and shouted, "See, I told you nobody likes a dog with three legs. You better get rid of the damned thing."

Ross looked straight into his grandmother's eyes, and said, "Why should I, Amma? You were married to a man with only one leg and you didn't get rid of him."

Then she turned her anger toward Bill. "Why do you let him talk that way?"

"I tutor him to talk that way. I insist," Bill said, not blinking an eyelid.

That night, Minna went home earlier than usual.

Whenever A.D. came to Savannah, he liked for me to drive him around his native city so he could reminisce. On one of our tours he pointed to a two-story green house on Bolton Street. "Movsovitz, the *shochet*, used to live there," he said. "He was the kosher butcher and killed all the chickens." A.D. was having a grand old time allowing himself to take a sentimental journey into his past. He loved to point to houses that he remembered from his childhood. It was amazing how he still recalled the names of the families that once lived in them and he had a personal history for every one.

"There's a house I'm dying for, Daddy," I said as we drove through a block of restored homes. Savannah was in the midst of being reborn; a number of old houses were being restored to their original splendor.

"Drive by and show it to me." A.D. broke into a broad smile.

I loved Savannah's historical district. These were the streets, squares and parks in the original city plan, dating back to 1733, and many of the houses had been built in the eighteenth and nineteenth centuries. I had sold a number of these beautiful old homes to young married couples who had seen the architectural grandeur behind the surface grime and decay. The glory that once existed was being returned with the help of favorable interest rates, tax incentives, and encouragement from local preservationists. Property values were reasonable. National magazines sent writers who were unanimous in their praise of the landmark district.

"How much?" A.D. said, when I slowed my car down to point to the house I wanted to buy.

I pulled over to the curb, switched off the engine, and jumped out of the car. I had admired the house all of my life. It was built of brown brick, shaped like a crucifix, stately on its corner, mysterious like a beautiful woman with a past. Though other structures edged up to it, the house possessed the isolated air of England's Devonshire moors.

"Look, A.D., the entrance is over here!" Through the windows I showed him the ground floor apartment that I wanted to turn into my office.

I ran, like a little girl, up the wooden steps to the second story porch yelling, "Come up here, Daddy, come here! It's a terrific investment." I stared into his eyes. A.D. didn't need convincing. He smiled at me proudly, lovingly.

I dashed back and forth all over the house, pointing out which rooms would be the bedroom, the living room, and kitchen of a great rental unit. It only took me ten minutes, gesturing wildly, to lay my plans for complete restoration. It was there on East Gaston Street that

A.D. purchased the 1857 Italianate house for me.

"Let's write a contract right now, Mazik, and take it to the owner." I pulled a form out of my briefcase. We sat on the steps of the house while I filled it out. Then we drove to the owner's antique shop, and A.D. wrote a check for the down payment, and agreed to pay off the mortgage by the end of the first year. He bought me a desk, a typewriter, and a chair. I was overjoyed. After years of selling real estate I was about to become my own boss. A.D.'s enthusiasm matched my own. He alone knew how I felt. He alone was my champion.

Bill pretended to know so little of the realities of my life and work that he never asked how I had come to own such a lovely house. When we filed our income taxes, he would automatically sign whatever forms were thrust in front of him, never questioning my earnings, never curious about my new business.

I loved sitting in my office, setting up my filing cabinets, installing the phones, printing cards and stationery with my name. When I made three large sales immediately, my self-confidence soared for the first time in years. Two months later I interviewed agents who wanted to join me. Andrea became my first sales associate. Due to her social connections throughout Savannah, our sales began to triple. We agreed that it was time for me to hire a secretary.

Then two new agents joined our firm, Zelda Goldberg and Dawn Keating, whom I had worked with before. I structured the office staff loosely so that the women could plan their days around their family activities at home. Andrea became jealous, complaining and arguing every time I fed a lead to Zelda. I found that much of what I had to do in my office with my employees, was very much the same things I had to do at home with my children. I was den mother, mediator, nurturer, disciplinarian, problem solver and decision maker. A.D. was my financier and business advisor.

When I told him about Andrea's rumblings, he warned me, "She's jealous of you, I've always known it." He told me not to let her have access to the files or to any privileged information. One evening when the three of us were having dinner together Andrea flirted with A.D. When he told her that he wasn't interested she suggested slipping me a pill so that we could all indulge in a *menage a trois*.

"She wants everything you have, baby. She wants to be you," A.D. said. "Promise me you'll be very careful with her." I promised.

"Until you have both a satisfied purchaser and a satisfied seller, you have not been successful," I preached over and over to my sales force during our weekly morning meetings. I impressed upon them my belief that the commission was not the most important part of a sale. "Doing a good job is the best feeling there is and your greatest accomplishment."

"I want my commission, first," Andrea demanded. "I don't feel satisfied until you write me a check." Zelda and Andrea had an ongoing rivalry. To separate them I gave Andrea her own private office away from the others. Zelda was sweet and accommodating, though not very ambitious and assertive. She was willing to stay in the office and chain smoke while waiting for that one sale she hoped would come her way.

We had developed a ritual in our office. As soon as the weekly meeting was finished, we'd all walk to Clary's Drugstore for breakfast. Putting aside real estate matters, Andrea would tell Dawn and Zelda and me about her marital problems.

"Gordon doesn't think I can ever make it on my own. He says my commissions are just enough to pay for my clothes."

"Andrea, underneath that sexy southern accent of yours is a strong, capable business woman," Zelda said. And even with A.D's warnings about her in the back of my mind, the fact was Andrea had become the number one producer in the office, proving to her husband just how successful she could be.

At another meeting Andrea complained about the lawyer who was handling a sale for one of her clients, a prominent banker. "He's giving me the run-around, and time's running out. I know he's avoiding me."

"I'll talk to him and see if I can expedite matters," I reassured her. I was beginning to feel that most of my time was spent easing the anguish between agent and client, client and lawyer. I asked for A.D.'s advice. "Stand up for your rights, baby. Those yokel lawyers down there are *shmucks*," he said.

I went with Andrea to the attorney's office at the appointed time for the closing of the sale. Andrea said, "He's very rude. Be prepared." I told her not to worry.

"Who the hell do you think you are coming here when I didn't tell you to?" he shouted upon seeing the two of us sitting in his outer office. His elderly secretary winced. He turned to her. "You had no right to let them into my waiting room, damn your old hide."

Wasting no time, Andrea got up and walked out of the office.

I followed the man into his private office. "How could you talk to Andrea like that?" He and I had known each other for twenty years, since the days when I worked at the courthouse. I thought we were friends.

"Get out of my office, you damned Jew-bitch! Shoo! shoo!" he hissed at me, waving his arms in sweeping motions as if trying to rid his office of a flock of chickens. "My own wife doesn't have the right to ask me questions, so who the hell do you think you are?" He shook his fist in my face.

Outside the lawyer's office, I looked at Andrea and burst into tears of sheer frustration. I remembered how the same lawyer had once bragged to me, years ago, when we were having lunch in a little Greek restaurant just outside the courthouse, "I plan to be known as the absolutely meanest son of a bitch in this town."

"Why?" I had asked.

"Because nobody wants a nice lawyer representing him in a court-room," he replied.

I had stared right back at him, without blinking, and quoted Shakespeare: "The first thing we do is kill all the lawyers."

"What smartass said a stupid thing like that?"

"Henry the sixth," I replied. "Shakespeare."

During those years a new phenomenon was beginning to face the housing industry in the South, racial integration. Federal laws were passed to insure that people could not be discriminated in housing because of race. It wasn't readily accepted in Savannah, but the law prevailed. While on a trip with Bill in Miami to see the Orange Bowl game, a ruddy-faced man with a beer belly, turned to me and asked about the real estate conditions in Savannah. He sold real estate in Augusta, Georgia and was sitting on the seat behind us as we rode the bus from our hotel to the game.

"Y'all having trouble with the coloreds wanting to move into white neighborhoods, sugar?"

"No," I answered, then paused and looked him square in the face. "We're having trouble with whites who don't want black people to move into their neighborhood."

That night in the hotel overlooking Miami Beach Bill put his arms around me. "I was really proud of the way you handled that *shmuck!*" Then he said, "I've been asked to appear on the Democratic ticket, as an alderman." Bill had talked it over with his brother and now wanted to know how I felt about his entry into the city's elections.

"You'll be good for the city," I told him. And I meant it. Bill was far more honest than the politicians I had known. "Do it. I'll support you wholeheartedly." I felt a twinge of jealousy since I also had worked all these years for the Democratic party. But what the hell, I thought, being an alderman's wife would serve as next best. I had grown used to next best.

When Bill and his team campaigned for election, I haunted the black churches on Sunday mornings for my slate of candidates, asking some of the ministers to "hoop" — stir up enthusiasm — in their churches. I solicited funds from real estate associates and members of my family. Everyone seemed to share the enthusiasm over Bill's entry into politics. And he was great at handshaking and baby kissing. The campaign livened our communication at the end of each day.

The night of the election returns, I took Dora and Ross to head-quarters to await the results. Bill had run a tough campaign. Along with the freshness and vitality that the new Democratic slate exhibited, Bill and his team pledged to lower city taxes and to annex areas outside the city that were benefiting from the city of Savannah.

Bill and the rest of the candidates running on the Democratic ticket won the election. It was a very sweet victory, finally ousting the Republicans in the district. Bill also gained a renewed sense of self-confidence and purpose. And it coincided with our son Alex's election as president of his fraternity at the University of Florida where he was in his sophomore year.

In the mean time, Alex had registered for the draft. I vowed to whisk him off to Canada if he was called up. I was determined not to let him serve in Vietnam.

While my real estate business continued to flourish, I began waking to anxiety. Facing the fact that I was now living three separate lives was unnerving. I was lover to one man, from whom I received income, gifts, support and nurturing and wife to another, who begrudgingly doled out a hundred dollars a week to me although it cost three times that amount to live the way we did. Most importantly, there was my work, my career, the one thing that allowed me to carve out my own identity and independence. I didn't know how much longer I'd be able to juggle the three lives. Sooner or later one of them would have to come crashing down.

It began with another tragedy. Somehow tragedy has its own way of sending everyone involved a wakeup call. Irene had been ill with what, at first, seemed to be bronchitis. After months of visits in and out of the hospital, the doctor told A.D. that she had lung cancer. He held me in his arms and cried. At times, I felt like I, too, was married to Irene.

Ironically, my beloved Aunt Jean had recently died of lung cancer, and during the long months of her illness, I had commuted between Savannah and Connecticut to spend time with her. On my last visit, Aunt Jean had said, between those terrible dry hacking coughs, "Darling, I don't care what people say about you, I love you very much. I've always felt that you were my daughter." I construed this to mean that my aunt hadn't passed judgment on my relationship with A.D; that somehow gossip had made its way up north and Aunt Jean knew about us. I so wished that I could have discussed it with her, but I didn't know how.

During Irene's long illness I kept my patience with her husband of forty-two years, listening, consoling, sympathizing, trying to cheer him up. The last week of Irene's life, A.D. invited me to go with him to his Palm Beach condominium, saying that he needed a rest. It was too painful for him to see Irene suffer. While we were there the phone call came. I helped him pack so that he could catch the next plane back and begin making funeral arrangements.

I looked around the ornately decorated apartment and began to conjure up visions of how I would change the place, make it much lighter and brighter, as soon as we were married. As soon as I became Mrs. A.D. Levy. Finally, I was going to be whole. And happy.

I drove A.D. to the airport knowing that in a few months we'd have everything we both wanted. And, until then, I would coast, say nothing, wait for his mourning to end. I felt a sense of peace. The anxiety of leading dual lives would soon be over.

My life was business as usual, office duties, house responsibilities and my morning calls. Many mornings when A.D. made his call Ross picked up the phone before I could. "Why does Uncle A.D. call you every day?" he asked.

"He's my business advisor."

Once when Ross found an airline ticket that I was planning to use to meet A.D. he threatened to tell his father. I talked him out of it still using the old deny tactics that A.D. had taught me.

When our youngest turned thirteen, Bill and I spared no expense for the extravagant party in honor of his bar mitzvah. We rented a lavish hall and friends of ours came from as far away as England. I relished the fact that I had more time to spend with Ross during the years that Alex was off at college.

One weekend, a few months after his bar mitzvah, I decided to take Ross to New York by train so he could experience travel by rail. A.D. had arranged for us to have a suite at the Plaza Hotel. He had also arranged theater tickets for us, to see a performance of *HAIR*, the wildly popular musical about the hippies and flower children of the "make love, not war" generation.

At the end of the show, the audience was invited to come up on the stage and dance with the cast. Ross had on his favorite outfit, purple pants, purple shirt, and purple socks. He even had on purple shoes. He looked more like a miniature pimp than a young lad entering manhood. I watched as my baby rose to the stage shaking his rear end without a shred of self consciousness. I beamed up at him from the audience.

"Mom, I don't think you understood that play," Ross said, looking up at me, as we walked toward La Caravelle for a lovely French dinner.

"What makes you say that, honey?"

"Well, there were some words that I don't think you know what they mean."

"For instance?"

"Well, Mom, I don't think you know what fuck means."

I tried to keep a straight face. "Well to tell you the truth, I think I've heard it once before."

Six months after Irene's death, while I was attending a real estate conference in Charlotte, N.C., A.D. flew there to meet me. I was there to attend a seminar on syndication. But when he arrived I suggested that he get a room of his own. Not once in that time had he mentioned the word marriage to me and I had made up my mind never to ask him again. My days of begging were over. Somewhere, somehow, the magic seemed to have disappeared, like a fading sunset under a thunderous sky.

"How do love affairs like ours end?" I asked him. We were in the bar having a drink and I felt stronger than I had in a long time.

"They just do."

"Have you made any plans for us?"

"No." The look on his face, his language, everything about him, said "no."

"You took up nearly fifteen years of my life with broken promises and all you can say is no?" I ordered some water to chase down the bourbon I had brought in a brown paper bag. North Carolina had laws requiring that you bring your own liquor to a restaurant. I had come prepared.

"I just can't do it now," he whined. "My daughter's jealous of you."

"A.D., you knew that for years. I lied for you, left my family and business, while you were dishonest with me the whole time. You made a joke out of my life. You even promised on your granddaughter's life." I downed another glass of bourbon.

"Baby, I need time to think."

"You've had all of my time that you will ever have."

I walked out of the lounge not asking or caring what his plans were. He took the next plane back to Atlanta. It was time for us to part, the end was obvious. I was sick of waiting for him and above all, sick of my obsession for him. His power and wealth no longer tempted me.

In retrospect, I thought, as I flew home to Savannah and looked at the whole picture, it appeared as a depressing portrait of betrayal, lies, broken promises, and secrets. And of course, sexual obsession. But then I took a look at the bottom line: By God, as my mother would have said, I had profited. I may not have gotten what I wanted, but I had certainly gotten what I needed.

Chapter Twenty Four

In the middle of January, 1973, a party was given by my firm to create more sales for our office. Each sales agent was asked to make a list of prospective clients, men and women who could bring business to us. We called the event the Rollicking Ripple Party, at which cheap Ripple wine was served as a gimmick to emphasize the residue left from the 1971 recession in the real estate market, to get us out of the slump.

A.D. had called that morning. He had never stopped calling; the old habit was hard for him to break. After Ripple, beer, and champagne, several of the women cornered clients in secluded spots to plan the rest of the evening. They were just like good old boys leering at their secretaries, except the roles were reversed.

I, too, behaved like a fourteen year old girl waiting for the boy of her dreams, anxiety gnawing away. I had discovered that men who shared the business arena with me were attracted to me, as if my equal footing created a sexual challenge, just as women had always been attracted to powerful business executives.

"I see you have your white sexmobile parked out front," my special guest said, referring to my white Cadillac. He winked, then saluted me with his glass. Bruce, eight years younger than me, had definitely been number one on my list of prospects to invite. Just under six feet tall, with sandy hair and a slight gap between his teeth, Bruce was the manager of an investment firm. He wore his navy blue Brooks Brothers blazer, gray flannel slacks and Gucci shoes, like a badge of honor. His striped shirt sported a solid white collar, and his tie was from one of the ultra fashionable men's boutiques on Madison Avenue. Bruce collected fine art, read all the "in" books and magazines, and worked out daily. His voice was husky with a resonant ring to it. He knew every play on Broadway. In the midst of our conversation Bruce invited me to have dinner with him after the party.

"I'm the hostess, it would be unsociable for me to leave," I said, flashing him my most demurring smile. I wanted to be pursued. Bruce's laughter had a sexy ring to it. We made a date for the following night. He would pick me up at my house.

When she called early the next morning, Andrea went through a recap of the party. "I swear to God! that man had the biggest thing I ever saw." Then I remembered that Andrea had left the party with an executive from out of town. They had ended up in his hotel room.

"He stood in the corner, at the side of the bed, undressing," Andrea said. "I just hollered when I looked up at him. There ain't no way that thing will fit in me. It was like a watermelon, I swear to God!" Her description of the evening spent with her husband's out of town client sounded like an off-Broadway comedy. Andrea explained that Gordon had referred him to her because he was looking for an apartment in Savannah. And besides, her husband never questioned a thing she did.

When Bruce took me to dinner, supposedly to discuss real estate, we talked of everything else but. We sat in front of an open fire at the restaurant sipping Irish coffee. He told me that he wasn't happy working in Savannah since his divorce, two years earlier.

"I've made inquiries into offices at Hilton Head and down in central Florida," he said. Bruce had all the confidence that was needed to move to another city and begin a new life. I admired him for that. When we finished discussing his moves he leaned toward me and smiled. He toyed with the ring on my finger, and asked how many carets it weighed.

Since Bill was still in Atlanta, attending a furniture show, I invited Bruce in for a brandy. I had purposely planned the office party at a time when Bill would be away. I walked over and slipped a Johnny Mathis record on the player, while Bruce poured the drinks at the bar. While Mathis crooned in velvety tones, Bruce slid his hand up the back of my sweater. He kissed me long and slow, deliberately sliding the sweater off my shoulders. He asked no questions. Our clothes flew around the room like paper kites, landing all over the place. Our bodies slid to the floor in unison, melting into the thick, white carpet.

"What about same time next week?" Bruce said, as I stood on my tiptoes to kiss him goodnight. He nuzzled me to his chest.

"Where are your sons?" Bruce glanced around the room, taking in the framed pictures on the end table. He told me that his son and daughter lived with their mother.

"Alex is off at school, and Ross spent the night at Andrea's."

I reveled at the thought of having the house to myself for a night. My mind was racing to make the comparison between A.D. and Bruce and Bill. Soon, Bruce and I met often for lunch, for drinks after work, and for dinner whenever Bill was out of town.

For years I'd mastered the art of deception, so Bruce fit right in where A.D. had left off. However, the intensity was gone, and what a relief. And I was discovering that what I'd recently read in *Cosmopolitan*, about older women and younger men as lovers was true. That women reach their sexual peak at a time when men years younger than themselves are reaching theirs.

Bruce told me that I was more sophisticated than most of the Southern women he knew. His words touched off a spark of thinking that perhaps I could use a change in my life. And while I dared not admit it to myself I had begun to feel alive because an interesting man desired me. And I was terrified of being undesirable.

While Savannah was buzzing with excitement surrounding the opening of its new Civic Center, Bruce and I volunteered to work together and head up a committee for the gala opening. Before one of the organizational meeting to discuss the planned festivities, the two of us stopped at a bar on River Street for a drink late one afternoon.

"I've met a woman. The mother of two small children, who wants to marry me," Bruce said as we sat at the small cocktail table sipping a Chablis cassis. A sinking feeling suffused me.

"This comes as quite a surprise. How do you feel?"

"You know I've been wanting to move to another location. And she's anxious to go with me. Besides, I don't like living alone."

Bruce had been my immediate antidote to A.D., and from the start I felt myself transferring to him the love addiction that had consumed me with my older lover. Whenever we met I felt at ease. Bruce, like A.D., possessed an endless zest for fun and life. He smoked pot, he had all the money he needed. Bruce made me realize that I could love again, no small accomplishment. I had started to feel more vibrant and sexy. Despite the emotional roller coaster of our affair, I never regretted it. Bruce encouraged me to exercise and get my body in good shape. We played like a couple of college kids. I convinced myself that I was in love, thereby avoiding the sense of guilt that inhibits most Southern women, which keeps them from admitting that they want and need sex.

"You're just asking to get caught, Naomi," Andrea said after seeing Bruce's car parked overnight in my carport. "The initials on the back of his Alfa Romea blast from your carport like a billboard, for Christ sake!"

That summer, Bruce asked me to go to Jekyll Island, a hundred miles south of Savannah, for a romantic weekend among the cottages that America's richest families had built on the nine mile long island. For nearly seventy years, the Astors, Rockefellers, Morgans, Vanderbilts and Pulitzers maintained Jekyll as an exclusive hunting preserve. I announced to Bill that I was going antique shopping over the weekend.

"I really need your moral support," Bruce said as we nestled against a large piece of driftwood on the beach. The tide was high. The surf slapped at our feet. "There's a job offer I want very much." And though he was well established in his Savannah office, he was doubtful that he could create the same success for himself in a new city.

"Where is this job offer?" I asked, imagining myself often visiting him there. Since Alex was studying law at The University of Georgia and Ross was preparing for his freshman year at Chapel Hill, my nest would soon be empty.

"The Tampa Bay area," he said.

"If you need me to help you get settled, don't fail to call on me," I said, out of sheer practice. It was odd how the words that came from my mouth didn't correspond with what I was feeling. I felt emotionally drained and alone again when Bruce got ready to leave the next morning. I burst into tears.

"What is this about? The Great Lady Realtor cries?"

I wished him luck and suddenly realized that I had gotten good at taking care of everyone who needed caring for except myself.

Bruce moved to Tampa right away; as soon as he was settled in he called and asked me to come spend a few days with him. Naturally, Bill took it in stride when I said I'd be at another real estate conference. And I still labored under the belief that without a romantic partner in my life, I really didn't have a life at all. Bruce took me to elegant restaurants and introduced me to his new associates.

The house that Bruce bought overlooked a lake and in the back was a gazebo. The night before I was to leave he placed an ice bucket with a bottle of chilled champagne on its floor. Next to the bucket was a crystal bowl filled with fresh strawberries. Bruce laced each berry with powdered sugar and fed them to me one at a time.

He had rolled several joints for us. As we inhaled deeply, any inhibition that either of us might have had, vanished. We rolled naked in the grass, laughing and loving. When we tried to walk into his house in the wee hours of the morning we were so stoned we had to crawl on our hands and knees.

All I could think of was Bruce when I returned home. And once again I became a romance junky. I called his house in Tampa two nights after I got back from Florida. His voice was strained.

"Is someone there?" I asked.

He didn't answer but made a lame excuse to get off the phone.

The next morning Bruce phoned. "Naomi, I'm sorry about yesterday. Yes, someone was with me."

It was the woman with the two children who wanted to marry him. She was irate that I had been there to see him and gave him an ultimatum.

Six weeks later, he married her.

Slowly I began to give myself some of the support I had given others. For years I had worked on various political campaigns. I had paid my dues, knocked on enough doors, solicited enough funds, and licked enough envelopes. I felt that my time as the token woman in the smoke-filled back room was becoming history. I wanted my turn as candidate. There were no women in the Georgia state legislature in January, 1976. I told Andrea that I planned to run for the State Senate.

"Jesus Christ, Naomi!" Andrea screamed, suggesting that I begin with an office someplace less grandiose and challenging. "Why don't you run for the school board first?"

"Because I know I can do this, and I'm ready to."

Andrea pledged her support. So did all the other sales people in my office, which was up to eighteen agents. I called some of my friends in the Democratic Party and rounded up a dozen loyal supporters. Bill offered to do some fund raising but made it clear that there wouldn't be a whole lot of time in his schedule. He had already promised to work on Jimmy Carter's presidential campaign. Bill professed to be proud of me but I knew he felt some jealousy. I was going for an office with more political clout than the one he held.

"Someone introduced me as Naomi Kramer's husband today," Bill said when he came home from work. Though he smiled at the words, I sensed his irritation. I called a news conference to announce my candidacy. A time was set for the cameras to roll. Bill stood on one side of me in Forsyth Park with the fountain and azaleas serving as backdrop.

"Standing before us, in the sunlit shadows of the beautiful pink camellias, is our newest candidate to announce for State Senate, rather like a camellia herself," said the announcer on the TV news that night. I wanted to throw up.

When I answered the phone the next morning, it was my mother telling me that I looked cute on television. Exasperated, I told her that cute wasn't what I had in mind.

"Well I don't know why you want to do a man's thing," my mother said. She made me stop and wonder if I really did want a man's "thing." Mother had grown more dependent on me ever since my sister had moved to Atlanta. Ruth had met a man and they planned to marry at the end of the year. It disappointed me that not one member of my family in Savannah offered to help with my campaign.

The theme of my campaign was "common sense in government." Being a businesswoman, I felt attuned to the problems and needs of the voters in my district. There were speeches to be made before organizations and civic clubs. I had learned early on that most of them were male-structured, so I wasn't too surprised when I wasn't invited to speak before them. But Bill managed, through his alderman connections, to get me before a few of these groups.

"For many years, lawyers and special interest groups have controlled the legislature. It's time to bring representation to Atlanta for the consumer citizen," I said, speaking to a group of firefighters. I was delighted when I received their endorsement.

As I went from one group to another, my self-confidence returned, my energy revived. I felt motivated in a way that I hadn't been in a very long time. Alex came home from Atlanta, where he was practicing law, and Ross from N.C. on weekends to help distribute my campaign literature at shopping centers. They were proud of their mother.

One weekend Alex brought along a young woman he had been dating. He told us that he was getting engaged. I had often wondered when and if Alex would fall in love. He was in his late twenties and I'd already had three children when I was his age.

Among my first close political allies was Fern, who had come back to Savannah briefly, after a painful divorce. Her husband had been cheating on her and it broke her heart. She was glad that they had decided against having children. When Fern undertook a campaign she ran all over the opposition, but she said that my bid for office would be her last political involvement here in Savannah or anywhere else. Fern was tired of giving her time away and never having it pay off for her personally.

"Girl," Fern said, "you ain't seen nothing of political fighting until you've seen Niggers in politics." Her high cheekbones were shining, her eyes snapping as she described the fight that was taking place within the ranks of the NAACP. While she and others were pushing me as their candidate for my senatorial district there was a huge in-house fight going on within the group.

Fern had worked tirelessly for voter registration in Georgia; she had traveled through much of the South taking voters to the polls in her car. Four years earlier, when Shirley Chisholm ran for president, Fern worked long and hard on her campaign. Fern had invited me along to be part of the caravan of supporters who met the congresswoman at the airport. We were whisked through the musky Savannah night, driven by a man who piloted the local Negro funeral parlor limousine. As the police-escorted motorcade rode us through Savannah I was thrilled to be sitting in the car with the first black woman presidential candidate.

In my senate race my opponents were the crooked powerful incumbent and a rich WASP lawyer, a self pronounced alcoholic, who was a member of a prominent Savannah family. I begged Bill for more support in my campaign. Although he agreed to escort me to the Elks Club, where he was well-known from both his business enterprises and his city administration post, he was tired of campaigning. In spite of that, we worked the room well together.

"Hell, I'm already doing more for you than I did for myself when I ran for alderman," he complained. It was, of course, expected that a wife would always help her husband campaign and be tireless in her support. But it certainly wasn't the same when the situation was reversed and the wife was the one running for office.

"Let's go, Naomi," Fern urged, grabbing an armful of brochures. We were setting out for one of our daily walks through neighborhoods in the senatorial district.

"It's a hundred degrees, Fern," I protested. Insult was added to injury when, after trekking in the blazing noonday sun, the good citizens of the district slammed doors in our faces. One old man shouted, "You nigger lover! You support bussing." Then he slammed his door so hard it almost split.

Fern insisted that I ring his bell again. It took all the courage I could summon to say, "Sir, I'm also for the elderly getting extra tax benefits!" This time, he closed the door more gently.

The Savannah media either ignored my candidacy or trivialized it. The mainstay of my campaign committee consisted of Fern, Andrea, Dawn, Zelda and myself, and a handful of volunteers. Then, Beckie, a young magazine illustrator, joined our group.

"Why don't you tackle an area where you can get to the mothers?" she suggested.

We concentrated heavily on a section of the city that had strong family activities. There, I sponsored the first all girl Little League baseball team in Savannah and donated pale blue jerseys with my company's name, Naomi Z. Kramer Realty, ablaze on them. The mayor and other city officials could hardly ignore me now, I thought.

Midway into the campaign Fern held a garage sale behind my office to help raise funds. One of my friends, a dentist, played the guitar while people ambled through the garden in the humid month of July, inspecting the household goods, clothes, and cast-off belongings that friends and family had brought to the sale.

"Do you have to have so many *shvartzers* for friends?" my mother asked me, as she sat at the gate collecting the money.

"Please, Mother, people can hear you," I said, trying to shut her up.

"Well, for God's sake, it's different if it's just Fern. But you've got a whole bunch of them here." Minna didn't budge. She had assumed an air of authority, being the money taker. I walked away before I lost control.

When the Political Action Committee of the NAACP held its final meeting to endorse a candidate for the race there was a bitter fight. The lawyer running against me offered a great deal of money to get their endorsement, which was considered a swing vote, an almost certain victory. The president of the Savannah Chapter of NAACP stood up at a closed meeting and said that they would be betraying a true friend if they didn't endorse me. The fighting continued but I finally won their support.

The incumbent candidate was furious. He had received the NAACP endorsement in his previous election and was counting on it again. He summoned the ethics committee from Atlanta, claiming that my campaign had not properly filed the amount of contributions received at my garage sale. The local newspaper ran a bold black headline, "Candidate Kramer Under Investigation." The words made me cringe.

The ethics committee investigator from Atlanta met Fern and me in the lobby of the DeSoto Hilton to discuss the ridiculous accusations.

"Does the committee know that the person filing the charges runs illegal bingo games?" Fern said.

"We're well aware of his activities," the man said. He advised us to go on with our campaign and wished us luck. However, when the Savannah Morning News printed the committee's retraction it was a very small and insignificant paragraph buried in the middle of the last edition.

A.D. called the morning of the election to wish me well. He offered to send a check to help boost my campaign funds. "I was wondering what it would be like to sleep with a Senator?" He laughed softly. His voice sounded frail and shaky.

"I'm afraid it's too late for that." But I did accept his offer to feed the campaign kitty.

Ross had arrived the night before from college. Alex was coming with Dianne, his fiancee, to lend moral support.

A bouquet of red roses appeared that morning. Attached was a note that read: "You're the greatest, dear lady. I wish you fame and success." It was from Bruce. I telephoned to thank him.

"I'm unhappy," Bruce said. "Will you meet me in Atlanta?"

"When the election's over."

The election was held on August 10th, 1976 — the day I turned fifty. It was the first birthday party anyone had given me since the one Aunt Jean had surprised me with during that long ago summer in New Canaan, Connecticut, when I was ten years old, This surprise was from my office. We drank wine and ate birthday cake. My office staff and my family all gathered around the television set that we'd set up in my inner office to watch the returns. I lost the election but had forced the two male candidates into a runoff.

That night, in bed, I cried like a lost little girl. Ross came quietly into my room and lay next to me on the bed. "I'm sorry, Mom. Next time I'll work harder for you." Once more it was a man who soothed my hurt, only this time the man was my own little boy.

"As a woman, I would've brought a new dimension to government," I told the local reporters the next day. It wasn't easy to be a gracious loser. How clear it was that Savannah, that beautiful and sensual lady, with moss dripping like an outdated hair style, wasn't ready to make the changes I wanted. Timing was everything.

I went back to work, Fern went back to New York, and my life resumed its familiar pace. As'I had promised Bruce, we met at the Hyatt Regency Hotel in Atlanta.

"Sorry about the election," he said. "The city wasn't ready for you."

"Perhaps I'll wait and run for the oval office," I joked.

"You've been miserable for a long time," Bruce said, as he encouraged me to file for divorce. His new wife had left him and he needed to pour out his heart to me as much as I needed him to hear my lament.

"I know I've talked and talked about it. I've often acted like I'm single, especially when I'm with you."

"Look, sweets, don't beat yourself up. You have to start somewhere and it's time to talk about divorce." He assured me that divorce is not pleasant, and hardly ever easy, but not entirely traumatic either.

After a few drinks and a superb dinner at Nikoli's, we fell into each other's arms with wild abandon. The friendship that we had formed coupled with the chilled vodka was like an aphrodisiac. We parted the next morning after breakfast promising to stay in touch with one another.

For old times sake, I phoned A.D. at his home when Bruce left.

"Where are you, little Mazik?"

"In Atlanta."

"Where?" He paused. "Where are you staying?"

"I'm with a young lover."

"Who?" He paused. "Is he Jewish?"

"You sound like my mother."

A.D. had once told me it was a known fact that women cheated on their husbands. It was, however, a cardinal sin for a woman to cheat on her lover. I could hear an echo of this belief in his shaky voice. That minute satisfied my need for retaliation for A.D.'s having consumed about fifteen years of my life.

Chapter Twenty Five

When my sister phoned to tell me that she and her husband were planning to spend a long weekend at Hilton Head, she asked Bill and me to drive to the island for dinner on Saturday night. Ruth had remarried, she and her second husband were living in Atlanta. Saul was twelve years older than Ruth but at last she had found the security that she hungered for. He was a quiet man, tall and thin. They went dancing at the Elks Club every Saturday night.

In the car, driving to Hilton Head, I began crying, for what seemed no apparent reason. Tears poured down my cheeks. I couldn't seem to stop.

"What's bothering you?" Bill asked, reaching to hold my hand.

"I don't know."

"Something must be."

"I want to be a child. I'm tired. I want a mother." I was as shocked as he to hear those words.

"I'll baby you, Poopsie," he offered, which made me cry harder. They were the first affectionate words I'd heard from him in so long.

I walked into Ruth and Saul's room at the hotel, hugged my sister, and burst into tears again, falling on the bed.

"What's wrong?" Ruth said, worried.

"I don't know," I sobbed.

"You never used to cry," she said. "I was always the crybaby."

"I know, I know. That's what's wrong. I need to cry."

"But you were the popular one, the one the boys chased," Ruth said. "You didn't have anything to cry about."

"You were always told you were pretty, and I wasn't," I sniffled. "Mother always said how smart you were." I blew my nose in the tissue that Ruth handed me

"You have a beautiful house, a handsome husband, and your own business. You have a hell of a lot more than me!"

Saul stood at the doorway, listening. "It wouldn't be a bad idea to take some time," he suggested, "just the two of you. You really need to get to know one another again."

"Let's go to the bar and have a gin and tonic," Bill said. Ignoring the rivalry between the sisters, our husbands left the room and went light-heartedly on.

When my crying continued into the next week I realized that I needed professional help. My life had become unmanageable and confusion had taken over. Bill, unintentionally, made the decision for me to get help. It came about one night when Andrea and I had gone with several clients for drinks and dinner at the Boar's Head, a riverfront restaurant. Bill was at one of the many political meetings that took up most of his spare time. A mutual friend stopped at our table. He had just left the hotel bar at the Hilton where Bill was rip-roaring drunk.

Worried that Bill might drive under the influence and get into trouble, I suggested that we stop by the Hilton on our way home. When we got to the Hilton, someone said Bill had just staggered out and gone home. Andrea's current boyfriend suggested we go to the Park Lane Lounge, a latenight spot frequented by politicians. We got into Andrea's car and drove there.

Suddenly Bill appeared.

He marched straight to our table. There was a very fierce look in his eyes. He slapped me across the face. "It's one o'clock in the fucking morning, you whore! Why aren't you home? You god-damned bitch. You better get yourself a fucking lawyer!" Bill grabbed my arms and began to drag me from my chair and across the room.

"I'm not going home with you!" I screamed back.

"You can't talk to that lady like that!" A stranger had grabbed Bill, to pull him away from me. Bill swung a punch at him.

"Come on, let's get out of here," Andrea said, tugging me gently by my arm.

"She's my fucking wife," Bill screamed as he was being ousted from the club. The bartender, who knew Bill, offered to drive him home. Bill left sheepishly.

"I'm not going to stay under the same roof with him," I said. But Andrea soothed me and talked me into driving home with her.

"Everything'll be fine in the morning, Naomi. Just let him sleep it off." Andrea pulled her car up to the front of my house.

I dreaded going into my own home. It was a terrible situation. Bill couldn't admit his unhappiness; his jealousy was the only thing he seemed to be in touch with. The next morning Bill was filled with remorse and embarrassment. He telephoned everyone he could remember having seen at the bar the night before and sheepishly apologized for his behavior.

"You better see a psychiatrist. Your jealousy is completely out of control," I said to him. Surprisingly he agreed, but added, "There's nothing wrong with me. You're the one with the problem." Still, he made an appointment with Dr. Henderson Grant.

When Bill came home the night after his visit to the psychiatrist he said that Dr. Grant wanted to see me, too. "I'm going to have one more appointment with him and that's all the bullshit I'm willing to listen to. If you're so dead set on shrinks you keep the appointments. I'd rather be playing golf."

"How do you see your problems?" the doctor asked, once I was seated in the chair facing his desk. Doctor Grant smiled mischievously as he waited for my answer. A white toy poodle darted in and out of his office as he questioned me.

"Bill's jealousy," I said, glancing up at the doctor. I noticed that he wore a toupee and steel rimmed glasses. And after every sentence he wet his lips with his tongue.

"Why is he jealous?"

I told him that I'd had an affair and all about A.D., and that ever since Bill found out, he'd been dogging my every step. I also told him about the violent scene in the bar a week earlier.

He smiled knowingly at me across the desk. "It's cocktail time, dear," he said. "Would you like a drink? It'll relax you." He took my arm and escorted me in to the well appointed kitchen at the rear of his office. He had restored a mansion just around the corner from my own office. The toy poodle followed us.

"Is it wrong for me to be friendly with another man?" We carried the drinks back into his private office. I sat down in the chair and sipped from the glass.

"Why don't you sit on my lap?" Dr. Grant said every woman should have tender loving care. I declined his offer and finished my drink. The poodle lay curled up beneath his desk.

Dr. Grant scheduled our next visit for a later hour than the first one. "It's cocktail time again, dear," he said.

"I want to smoke a joint," I challenged. I was wearing blue jeans, boots, and my old gray fedora, cocked jauntily on my head. I had just come from visiting Burt Reynolds, who was shooting a scene for a movie that he was making in Savannah. I rested my feet on the desk and tilted the chair to its back legs.

"I see you're wearing your movie star clothes." Dr. Grant smiled at me and without flinching, he opened a desk drawer, looked at me slyly, and began to roll a joint. "It's legal," he said with a wry smile, "for patients and medicinal purposes."

Of course, the best medicine he could have prescribed would have been the simplest: an explanation of my depression, endless tears, and an understanding that my roller coaster emotions were the direct result of the loss of the man I had substituted for my father, and my immediate need to try and replace him.

He might have reassured me that I was menopausal and that menopause didn't mean the end of beauty, or sexual appeal, or sexual enjoyment. How it can be a time of readjustment and then renewal. He seemed unaware that women go through far more than one change of life.

We inhaled deeply on the joint before walking up a winding set of stairs to see his library, taking with us a bottle of sherry. He put on the record player and we danced. He instructed me to listen carefully to the lyrics, as "To Dream The Impossible Dream," began playing.

It was obvious that Dr. Grant was obsessed with Don Quixote. He called me his Dulcenea. In his office, over the mantle, were several carvings of the Impossible Dreamer. Through the haze of marijuana I remembered Andrea telling me she had been to a psychiatrist in Atlanta, who asked her to dance naked with him and had requested she give him a blow job. Perhaps, I thought fuzzily, this is what psychiatry really is: rhythm and head.

Dr. Grant unrolled a blanket and set it in the middle of the floor, removed my boots, and guided me to sit on the blanket. He dipped my toes into his glass and licked off the sherry. Erotic feelings rose from the points where his lips brushed my skin. He had succeeded in arousing me to the point of sexually desiring him that minute. I felt I was going to burst. But Dr. Grant was impotent.

Deflated and frustrated, I curled up in the fetal position on the blanket and started to cry. He said his impotency was caused by where he was, in his office, not in neutral territory. Maybe he's falling in love with me, I thought. At that moment I didn't know what I wanted from sex, nor did I have a sense of who I was. I was just plain downright confused and in pain. I was as hollow as a shell.

"Come, my Dulcenea. Let's tidy up, and I'll take you to the Chatham Club for dinner." He leaned over and stroked my arms, pulling me up from the floor.

"I can't. Bill's jealous. He might kill us."

"Don't worry, Naomi, I have a gun." He spoke with complete assurance and control. "Just pick up the phone and tell him that I've asked you to dinner."

"I'm afraid of him," I said, my voice trailing off like a four year old, whose doll had fallen to the floor and shattered. "Do it for me, please?"

"Now, Naomi, you're a big girl, he coaxed. "I'll be right here with you but you have to call him on your own."

My fingers could not dial the number.

"If you want to conquer your fear just walk over to the phone and do it," Dr. Grant said firmly. "Call him."

"I better just go home," I said in a vacant voice, that sounded like a ghost's.

"Andrea, something must be wrong with me. Dr. Grant couldn't get an erection." We were sitting in Andrea' beautifully manicured garden, on her new white and yellow lawn chairs, when I popped that bit of news to her.

Andrea's coffee sprayed out of her mouth. She jumped up from her chair. "Are you crazy?" she shouted. "You shouldn't be having sex with your psychiatrist!"

"I must be losing any appeal I ever had," I said, ignoring my friend's shock and dismay.

"Naomi," Andrea said, shaking my shoulders, "the S.O.B. can't get it up because he knows damn well he's taking advantage of you. Why the hell do you think it's your fault if his cock doesn't get hard? Women always blame themselves for whatever goes wrong with the man."

"I must be undesirable. Jesus, I'm giving him a soft-on." I didn't hear a word Andrea said, caught up in my own guilt and frustration.

After a couple of visits Bill wanted to know why my appointments with Dr. Grant were always scheduled for late afternoon. I explained that he liked to give me extra time, and that he held his last appointment of the day for me. But quietly I worried that there was something wrong with me, that I was flawed.

A few weeks later Dr. Grant took me to Hilton Head for a medical conference. He packed a bottle of rare French wine and arranged to drive to the island in my car. The reservations were held in the names of Dr. and Mrs. Henderson Grant. I began to wonder what it would be like to be married to a psychiatrist. I still lived in that childish world of fantasy, that if I was having sex, then surely that spelled marriage. I had never been able to separate the two.

"You're insatiable, Naomi," Dr. Grant said, during a moonlit walk on our last night together. Here, away from his medical practice and my husband, he had no trouble sexually at all.

Back in the hotel room I brought up the indelicate subject of his fees for my "analysis." He feigned shock. "I'll tell my bookkeeper to cancel them." It seemed unfair to be charging Bill while he slept with me.

"Andrea, I think we're in love," I said after recounting my Hilton Head escapade. In my mind, sex, marriage and love were all links in the same chain.

"Naomi, don't be stupid." Andrea rolled her eyes and exhaled loudly.

"When I couldn't sleep, he shoved a pill in my mouth that took less than a minute to do the job. He pretended he hadn't done it. And he was so careful about getting ready for bed that I have no idea what he did with his toupee."

"Will you please stop seeing this man? He only wants to fuck you. And he's going to mess up your head worse than it is already." Andrea's exasperation was clear to me by then. She was worried that he might have given me a pill to induce sexuality, or even get me hooked into an addiction.

But my visits to Grant continued. One afternoon while waiting for my appointment I caught a glimpse of him through the slightly opened door. I wondered if my mind was deceiving me when I saw his nurse, Nancy, leaning over his desk and his hand patting her on the behind.

Dr. Grant began to see me on Saturdays for lunch-and-sex sessions. I noticed that the poodle was never in his office on the weekends. I cried less now that I was seeing him, but if I tried to phone him during those times when I was overcome with fear, with that raging angst, he avoided my calls. One night, I became insanely desperate. I couldn'. turn to Bill for comfort because he was out of town. I telephoned Grant's office but he was at the hospital. When I called him there he avoided me.

It was that night, lying alone in my bed, that an eerie animal scream escaped from my throat, rising from my lungs, from my stomach. It was the loneliest moment of my life, and the excruciating fear, the cutting edge of fright, lunged at me, a foul, hissing abomination from every corner of my room. I cringed there, feeling utterly abandoned.

The next day I grew furious that Dr. Grant had treated me so callously when he was the one person who should have shown me the compassion and wisdom to get me through the dark, brooding fear that was polluting my life. When I complained once more to Andrea she told me about a sad experience that she'd had.

"When I was recovering from Troy's death, our minister coerced me from my hospital bed and whisked me away to the church where he seduced me in the back of the social hall." My friend's story shed new light on what I was experiencing and I began to notice for the first time things that were inappropriate in my relationship with my analyst as though a veil was being lifted from in front of my eyes.

Savannah is a small town, and life is circular and somewhat inbred in the moss draped city. During one of my weekly visits to the beauty parlor, I sat next to a young woman with platinum blond hair who was having her nails painted a vivid shade of red. I couldn't help but overhear her conversation with Laurie, the manicurist.

"I don't understand what's going on," she said, then blew her nose into a tissue. "When my boyfriend and I broke up I was numb all over. When he said he'd pay for me to see a doctor, I didn't know that the doctor and I would fall in love on my second visit." She reached for another tissue and started to sob. As soon as she left the salon I asked the manicurist for the name of the doctor that the blond woman was talking about.

"Some crazy old shrink in town," Laurie said, as she filed my nails.

"Is his name Henderson Grant?"

"Yeah," Laurie said, looking at me. "That's it. My customer said they're falling in love. But she's confused. She wonders if it's normal for a patient to fall in love with her doctor."

I felt my stomach turn.

"And not only that," Laurie continued, "it's common knowledge that he brought his nurse to Savannah with him when he came here to open his practice. Then he bought an old building for his office and a house just across from his office for his nurse. At the same time, he bought a huge plantation in the country for his wife and kids."

The minute I got back to my office I phoned Dr. Grant. This time he took my call. "Whose poodle is that running around your office every time I'm there?"

"Why do you want to know?" He snickered into the phone.

"Is it your nurse's?"

"Yes, how did you guess?"

"You're a very cunning lover. I might be crazy but I'm not stupid." I hung up.

At home, lying in my bed, I came across a magazine article which read: "If any psychiatrist seduces his patient, he should be prosecuted for rape, not malpractice. A woman who goes to a psychiatrist, exposing her vulnerability and pain, should be treated like an innocent child — not a sexual object." I immediately cut it out, put it in one of my business envelopes with a note, "I thought you would enjoy reading this," and mailed it to Dr. Grant.

He was quick to respond. "Why, Naomi, you little devil," he said. "Are you blackmailing me?"

"If the shoe fits, wear it, you bastard." He asked if I'd like to meet him for a drink at the Hilton. He purred, he simpered.

"Just bring my medical records, you son of a bitch!" I slammed the phone down as hard as I could.

He was at the bar to greet me, all sweet, gentle smiles. He took a sheet of white paper from his inside jacket pocket and put it in my hand. "You always said you'd bet that I didn't have one written record in my file on you."

I looked at the paper. It was completely blank. He offered to refer me to another psychiatrist because he felt that I had experienced transference with him.

"If that means you fucked me, then yes, I did experience transference," I said, seething inside, wanting to rip the insipid smile off his face and the stupid wig from his head.

"Naomi, why don't you try leaving Savannah for a while?" He was finally giving me some worthwhile advice. The next morning I discussed the possibility at an office meeting with my newest sales agent. Cal Longbranch had a sister in New York and was looking for someone to sublet her apartment. Everyone offered to fill in while I was gone. And we'd be in touch daily by telephone. Cal had also become an associate broker and was perfectly capable of handling all transactions. I had come to count on him as an expert real estate broker and now as my friend.

Cal had moved to Savannah from Baltimore two years earlier. It had been seven in the morning when he called me at home in response to a For Sale sign in front of a downtown house. "Call tomorrow," I said. But Cal wanted to see the house right away. Of all the houses I had listed it seemed odd that he was calling about my birthplace on Charlton Street, now restored to a glory it had never known when I played there, swinging on John's foot.

Cal didn't buy the house — he and his male lover preferred a white-columned place on Victory Drive — but going through it was, for him, like going home again. Cal was the son of a Southern preacher and he knew that Southerners put great store in time and place. So did I. We had that in common from the first. Traipsing through the house on Charlton was for me, undiluted nostalgia. I pointed out the upstairs room where I had been born, and the kitchen where my grandmother had baked strudel. I walked around the spot in the backyard that had housed the small shop where I once bought penny candy.

After Cal had moved into his own home I persuaded him to sell real estate and join my firm. His good looks inspired people in Savannah to whisper that I had a young lover. Little did they know. By that time I had straight friends, gay friends, and some friends who weren't entirely sure. Cal was sure.

I felt a sudden surge of energy and optimism as I made my plans to go to New York in the fall of 1978. Cal's sister's sublet was on East Sixty-first Street, around the corner from Bloomingdale's. I rented it for one month. When I told Bill of my plans he seemed unconcerned. His response to most of my ideas was an unenthusiastic one.

Once in New York, I signed up for a two weekend EST, (Erhardt Seminar Training) course. It was the current rage in New Age self exploration, albeit a bit radical. Taught by Werner Erhardt, the charismatic, super salesman creator. It was guaranteeing to turn your life around, make you feel and see things in a whole new way in order to rid yourself of the past. Conventional psychiatrists thought it was bunk, even dangerous, and that Erhardt was a supreme snake oil salesman. He'd certainly become a millionaire from his seminars. But people in California and New York were swearing that he had changed their lives.

The group met on two consecutive weekends in the ballroom of a downtown hotel. Several hundred people, me among them, were herded into chairs and instructed not to get out of them. We were not allowed to go to the bathroom or have a drink of water. Near midnight, the trainer said we would not be leaving until six in the morning. He asked if anyone could offer housing to those that had none. I raised my hand. A young woman from Connecticut came back to my apartment with me just before daybreak so that we could get a few hours sleep before we were to report back at ten.

When the first weekend was over I became so disgusted watching grown men and women lie on the floor wailing in terror, vomiting and peeing on the floor because they weren't allowed to use the bathrooms. I knew I would never go back for the second weekend.

A New York friend invited me to an elegant dinner party at his loft in SoHo. During the evening he introduced me to some of the city's most interesting people, and soon I was accepting invitations to chic parties in Manhattan and Greenwich Village. I felt that I was making up for my dashed dreams of sharing an apartment in the city with Fern.

While I was in Manhattan, Bruce had called my office in Savannah and gotten my phone number. It was a pleasant surprise when he phoned and said he had to be in New York on business and would like to see me. One sunny afternoon we went to St. Patrick's Cathedral on Fifth Avenue and then rode the subway down to SoHo. We had lunch at the SoHo Charcuterie, walking the streets of Little Italy and holding hands. Late in the day, we stopped in Chinatown for tea and fortune cookies. New York was his hometown and he understood my love for the place. It was comforting to know we had established a mature friendship.

I didn't feel lonely in New York. The SoHo galleries became a favorite haunt of mine and on Sunday mornings, after lazily reading *The New York Times* over coffee and bagels, I'd meet friends at the Metropolitan Museum, which became a ritual for me. What I also discovered in New York was that instead of seeing a shrink with a wig, I would restore my townhouse. Little else, other than my children, mattered as much as the careful refurbishing of that antebellum house.

The broken dreams of A.D., my unhappy bond to Bill, and the mouthing of a perverted psychiatrist who had once told me I needed to learn how to fake orgasms, were temporarily forgotten, replaced by architectural and design details. There was a restoration of my soul in the process of returning what was once lovely back to its original glory. In my house, nothing would be faked.

My friend, Alan, who had the loft in SoHo, was a well respected and successful architect. He agreed to fly down to Savannah with me and help with the restoration.

On my next trip to New York to complete the details, Alan walked with me through the antique shops of Greenwich Village, carefully selecting traditional pieces that would complement the soft earth colored tiles planned for the floors of the kitchen and bathrooms. I trailed happily behind him through one showroom after another as we studied swatches of muted suede for the sofas on which I could curl up and stare into the fireplace in my living room. After lunch, we examined paint colors for the walls, colors so that my life would seem embraced by nature. I intended to nurture myself in an ambiance of colors and soft fabrics that soothed.

Together, we selected huge pale vases that would hold dozens of fresh flowers that I vowed to order for myself every Friday for the rest of my life. I felt I deserved them.

However, December of 1978 brought on an unexpected deluge of sadness and unhappy memories. Isaac had died in December, my wedding anniversary was in December, and, in recent years, the boys came home on their holiday pilgrimage to watch their parents pretend at marriage. Yet, the year was somehow different this time. I knew that even though my home was still in the suburbs with Bill, in planning the restoration of the townhouse, I was in essence planning my future, alone.

But I also knew that my plans had to take back seat because Alex and his fiancee were to be married in her hometown that December. Alex had asked if we objected to his wedding taking place on Isaac's birthday. Our family was pilgrimiging to Boston for the gala celebration. My heart was filled with joy for my son and his bride. Tears moistened my eyes when he picked her up and carried her through the snow, when they left for their honeymoon.

Chapter Twenty Six

My life now centered around real estate and restoration. When Cal and I went to Hilton Head to close a sale, we got what we went for. On the way back, Cal hummed as he drove. I stretched out across the back seat of my white Cadillac and gazed numbly at the passing marsh, the live oaks, the Low Country architecture. The gray opacity of the evening matched my mood. That's why the day was — well, it was ordinary. And I was bone weary of ordinary days. Had anyone asked I would have said I was weary of every damn thing: the city of Savannah, the South, my real estate business, my husband, myself.

I thought how the Southern lifestyle no longer struck me as viable. I had quit curtsying to latter-day Rhett Butlers. Nor was I willing to make small talk with aspiring Scarletts. All too often people had told me how like the belle of Tara I was. Why it was meant as a compliment in these changing times I could never understand.

This was the Southern coast, I thought, staring out the window of the car. This was my share, as the poet put it, of summer and smoke and sleepy air. The aromas of the salt marsh, the intoxicating land that had inspired James Oglethorpe to build a city on Yamacraw Bluff were as much a part of me as my Russian, Jewish grandmother's massacre of the English language.

As we drove toward home I explained to Cal how the white women of the South were told to emulate Scarlett O'Hara from the day she was thrust upon a forgiving world in 1936. Scarlett was a survivor, we were told. She used her wits, her beauty, and the feeblemindedness of the men in her life to ascend, like the phoenix, out of the ashes of Atlanta.

"Well, why not be like Melanie?" Cal said.

"Are you crazy? You know what I think about Melanie Hamilton? She was so delicate you just knew a swift kick in the ass would break her into a thousand porcelain slivers." In fact, Melanie was projected as a twin role model to Scarlett. *Gone With the Wind* became the white South's favorite novel during my young womanhood. And I, along with all the other daughters of the Lost Cause, had been given the impossible chore of becoming a blend of the book's heroines.

"Well, frankly, my dear, I think I'm more like Scarlett," Cal said. He pretended to brush a mane of hair off his face.

"Just think about it, Cal, she was a murderer, a closet boozer, a chronic liar, a conniver, a hotheaded swindler, and a primrose whore." I suddenly shot up in the back seat, ignoring every word Cal had uttered.

"Belle Watling did it for the Yankee dollar, but good old Scarlett did it to spite the man she loved, to spare her dipso father's farm, and, twice the careless widow, to get filthy rich," Cal said, giggling.

"Listen, she married a simpering boy, a puling old goat, and a womanizing war profiteer. Remember, Rhett first made Scarlett his plaything, not unlike A.D. did with me, then dumped her when she stopped being daddy's little girl. Not unlike me again."

The car was on Talmadge Memorial Bridge, which links Georgia and South Carolina, when I caught sight of Savannah. I revered the city. I reveled in its 250 year history. I knew its architectural glories; I had, in fact, helped to preserve them. But that evening, close to darkness, the city's customary magic didn't work. I felt a terrible melancholy that the sight of a beautiful city could not shake off.

Cal suggested we stop for a drink, hoping to change my mood.

"No thanks," I said. Although I dreaded going home to Bill I couldn't think of anything else. My sadness was debilitating.

"There are a lot of good-looking men there," Cal said, licking his lips.

"I'm tired, Cal. Please, just drive me home. When do you think I'll get the courage to do what I really want with my life?"

"Let's stop for a drink, Naomi. A game of backgammon will cheer you up. Really, it will do us both good." He ignored my question.

"Well, one drink and then home." I wanted nothing more than to go home, soak in a hot tub, and slip between crisp, clean sheets. Loud disco music and a backgammon club held no appeal.

Cal parked the car in a space reserved for the handicapped when we got to Club Les Amis. Inside, Cal pointed to a darkly handsome man who looked foreign. "He's the real reason I wanted to come, dear heart. I fell in love with him last night when I stopped here."

"What's his name?" I followed Cal to a small cafe table.

"I didn't meet him, darling, I only fell in love."

I caught a glimpse of the man Cal described as "my gorgeous Frenchman." He had the musky air of the southern European; his genes drenched in machismo, his trousers too tight, his Italian shoes pinch-toed. His shirt was open to the navel to show off a gold cross that hung around his neck. His clothes turned me off.

"Well, what do you think?" Cal asked and motioned for a cocktail waitress to come to our table.

"Go ask him to play backgammon."

"Oh my God! You do it for me." Cal feigned shyness.

"I'll do it for myself."

Walking over to the handsome stranger I suddenly felt revived. It was clear that desire had not abandoned me. I smiled across the table at him.

"Do you want to play?"

"But of course," he answered, staring straight at me. "I'm a master at the game." He walked around to help me up on the high stool. I liked the way he walked, the way he talked — rather the way he did not talk. There was a reason. His teeth needed repair. I didn't notice his teeth. If I had, I wouldn't have noticed his riveting eyes, which were studying me.

His name was Spyros. His last name was so long I couldn't pronounce it. I caught half of what he said, he caught half of what I said. His English was spotty. He was Greek, not French, and my Greek was nonexistent. Instead, I used all the tricks of flirting that are imbedded in Southern woman. It was half habit, and half to show Cal that I could, if I chose, take the Greek to my bed. That was not my choice.

Spyros told me about himself. He was from Athens, the chief engineer of two ships whose home port was Savannah. He needed a small apartment in the city. I thought about the amount of time it would take to find something for him to rent. There was so little commission involved in a rental that I didn't want to be bothered. Nevertheless, I slipped one of my business cards into his hand, purely out of habit.

He seemed not to know what I was doing.

"I'm in real estate," I explained. He looked blank.

"Meet me at five tomorrow in the bar of the DeSoto Hilton."

He hesitated.

"Five o'clock. The Hilton Hotel." I spoke slowly, deliberately.

He smiled. "Okay."

On the way home Cal pouted and sulked. "Damn you, Naomi, you took my Frenchman!"

"Look, Cal, my pet, you must realize that some men still prefer women." I gave him a conciliatory kiss on his cheek.

Driving to meet Spyros the next afternoon, I felt that Savannah was the most picturesque city in North America, rivaling Quebec and San Francisco. For all its veneer, Savannah with its quarter million population was a small town — fueled by gossip and the fact that everyone knew everyone else's business. Men had gone bankrupt, women crazy, and every survivor had a juicy tale to tell. Savannah drank, Savannah fornicated, and enjoyed midday trysts, but you weren't supposed to do it in the streets and scare the double-standard Bible Belters. What I did tonight would be fodder for breakfast tomorrow. No matter that I could have been at the Hilton on business. I was there with a man, a handsome, younger man, who was not my husband.

"*Allo*, Naomi," Spyros said as he stood to greet me.

"I wasn't sure you understood which hotel I meant." I held out my hand to shake his.

"How I can forget where to meet such exciting lady, eh?" He leaned over to kiss me on the cheek. "Ah, is most sexiest perfume I ever smell." He said he had kept me in his thoughts all day. He said he adored the way my hair fell over my shoulders. He liked my soft coastal accent. "Every word you say has a little smile."

As corny as his bullshit was I hung on to every syllable.

"How many bedrooms do you need?" I pulled out my list of rental properties to show him.

"One," he said. He smiled to acknowledge the word bedroom, as though it would be the most important room in his house.

"Do you have family?"

"Mother in Greece. Old, too old to visit." He told me that she still smoked cigarettes as he chain smoked through the evening. He said I would love Greece and described the beautiful islands to me. We went off to do some apartment hunting and after we'd seen the fourth apartment we said goodnight.

Three days later Spyros called me at the office and invited me to have a drink. He hadn't decided on an apartment yet he said.

197

"Should I show you property at the beach?"

"But of course." I picked him up in front of the John Wesley hotel, and as we drove towards Tybee he told me how unlike his native Athens this area was. Though he liked the sea he complained that it wasn't as beautiful here as where he came from.

Two weeks into apartment hunting I realized that he wasn't a serious client. He was definitely serious about his sex.

Once again, he asked me to meet him at the Hilton bar.

Carefully selecting my clothes, I knew that I wanted the attention, yet I was afraid of being noticed. As I carefully put on makeup and a favorite pair of gold hoop earrings all I could think of was romance, soft lights, and hot kisses. I told myself it was permissible to have cocktails with a man. After all, I was a businesswoman and he was a client, sort of.

There was little doubt that sex would be the bottom line. It always was. Romance was definitely my drug of choice, the drama of feeling that if I didn't sleep with him I would die. I blocked out all thoughts of Bill and whatever bond we still shared. Since Bill and I had stopped having sex two years earlier a thick tension existed between us.

Spyros rose, bowed, and kissed me on the lips. He had ordered a glass of champagne for me.

"I'm going to a party," I said. "Do you want to come?"

"But of course," he said with an air of total confidence.

"A local Greek friend is giving it," I said and told him that Savannah had a large Greek-American community.

"Sounds fun." He raised his glass to his lips.

I promised that it would be as I smiled squarely into his face.

A man who'd bought Pinkie's, a saloon in the Tammany Hall tradition, was giving the party. Jimmy Carter had stood on one of the stools at Pinkie's when he announced for president. Pinkie himself then worked the night away in a rear room of the bar, painting campaign signs that would decorate the town in the morning. His funeral brought Georgia's political bigshots to town. After Pinkie's death the ownership changed. The new owner was having a grand opening.

Spyros was a hit. The mayor, Pahno Papalakis, talked to him in Greek, delighting him. They both laughed, looked at me, then laughed again.

"What's going on?" I said. The only Greek words I could come up with were Melina Mercouri and baklava.

"Oh nothing," Mayor Papalakis said.

"Tell me," I insisted. I had known Pahno since we were children.

"I asked Spyros if you were baby-sitting, that's all." He had a smirk on his face. I turned purple with rage. His insult burned through me like a pair of hot fire tongs. Papalakis turned again to Spyros, they spoke rapidly in Greek, and then started laughing again.

I went into the ladies' room, checked my lipstick, eyeliner, and hair. My tight sweater reemphasized how many men had lusted after me since the summer of my fourteenth year. Baby-sitting, his ass. Yes, Spyros was younger, but I had worked hard to keep my body in shape and now, looking at my reflection in the mirror, I felt a surge of confidence. I knew that I could compete with any woman at the party.

Spyros was waiting for me. "I invite you to best restaurant in city." We drove to the 17 Hundred 90, an old Federal style house, with an engaging dining room and warmed by a giant fireplace. The glow from the fire cast huge shadows on theaged brick wall. All of the tables were set with bone china and sparkling crystal. Candles with dripping wax adorned the white linen tablecloths.

Spyros ordered wine. Good wine.

I had to admit the man was schooled in the art of seduction. He'd been in exotic ports, drunk exotic wine, bedded exotic women. But I also knew I was teetering on the edge. The last thing I needed was a young foreigner to complicate my life, and the thing I needed most was a lover to make me feel alive again. In the interior of my mind I could hear Andrea's warning to me, but to no avail.

Spyros ordered our food casually, confidently. What a contrast to the good old boys who washed down greaseburgers with a six-pack of beer.

I eased my foot across the slate floor and our toes touched. Spyros reached toward me, caressed my arm, the top of my hand, my fingers. Out of the corner of my eye I saw a couple who were business associates.

"You not eat," he said. "Why you not eat, eh?"

"I guess I'm not as hungry as I thought," I said. I clasped his hand and put the wine glass slowly to my lips. Romance was taking hold.

And romance was bred in my bones, a combination of my Russian and Southern blood. Romantic poets, romantic composers, romantic novels — the South had a history of grand passion — so did the Russians. I could smell Spyros's cologne, I could almost taste his wet kiss. We shared long looks over good food, wine, and candlelight. Once again, romance was conquering my sixth sense: reason.

At dinner, putting any thought of reason aside, I toppled.

"My God, I haven't felt like this in years," I said in a faint voice. Spyros stared across the table. Our eyes locked, and neither of us was able to look away.

I wasn't willing to deny myself the pleasures that my heart and flesh cried out for. I had lived in my head, fantasizing about men. And now, tonight, I didn't intend to fantasize any more.

I had lovers. Several lovers. And A.D.

Then, I had Spyros.

Chapter Twenty Seven

As we walked out of the restaurant, he pressed against me, and at the car he pushed me against the door, moving his body against mine so that I could feel his hardness. As he drove, we sat huddled. I allowed my mind and body to roll with the sensations. The trip to my house in the suburbs took forever.

"Is palace your home?" he said, as we walked through the rooms. "Where's bedroom?"

I was beginning to feel a sense of panic. Across the movie that was playing in my mind, I saw Bill slapping A.D. If Bill were to come home from Chicago this would be far more than a slap. I hadn't yet told Spyros that I shared the house with my husband.

We sat down on the sofa. Spyros began lighting one cigarette after another. He offered me one. I took it and inhaled deeply. He reached over and fingered the buttons at my breasts, and started to tug at my pants. To hell with self image, to hell with danger, I thought as I steered him to my bedroom.

"Wait," he said. He undressed me, then drew me to him.

"Yes," I said, "Yes." I unbuckled his belt and reached for him. I was Molly Bloom saying yes a thousand times yes. I was Sadie Thompson never saying no. "Spyros," I whispered, "Make love to me."

I reached one orgasm, then another, and satisfied, I held his head to my breasts through the night. I did not know what hour it was when, lying beside him, I told myself I was mad about him, crazy with uncomplicated lust. His youth and freshness were a new beginning for me.

"Sagapo," he whispered, half asleep. From the tone of his voice I understood: *I love you.*

"Sagapo," I answered.

While drinking my third cup of coffee the next morning the tug of war between my heart and head began as soon as Spyros's taxi picked him up. I recognized that old gnawing feeling in the pit of my stomach, that constant need to merge myself with another human being. For a week, Spyros and I met clandestinely. Even after Bill returned I managed to think up excuses to get out of the house almost every night. Each time we were together our sexual hunger for each other was met with the same excitement, the same joy.

In our first six days, before Spyros left on a trip for Trinidad, he guided me into sexual pleasures I didn't know existed. Cal and Andrea both liked Spyros. I would regale them daily with my romantic interludes. Andrea was living vicariously through me. Cal was happy to see me in love. One weekend the four of us had dinner at Andrea's beach cottage. She had decided to test her culinary skills in Greek cuisine. She produced a superb *spanakopeta*. And when she served *galactbourekok* for desert, Spyros squealed like a pig and grinned like a Cheshire cat.

"Nice friends, Naomi," he said as the two of us headed back to town at the end of the evening. I dropped him off at his hotel.

When Spyros took off for the West Indies, I cried, certain that he would find a younger woman and I'd never see him again. I waited for the letters he said he would write. "I miss being in arms through night," he wrote. "I don't know can call you home because of . . . ." He had been reluctant to mention the word husband. "Wait my telephone call between 21 and 24 December. I call you from where I am. With much love, Spyros." *With much love.* Slowly one day surrendered to the next and insidiously the tiredness returned.

His youthful energy made me look at myself differently. He brought back the lost excitement I had felt with other men. He symbolized youth and romance. I dreamed of his olive skin next to mine and I counted the minutes until we'd meet, touch, kiss, and everything else he had taught me.

Alone in my house, I sat in the middle of my bed waiting for the telephone to ring. It did, before Spyros's ship reached the mouth of the Savannah, fifteen miles down river. Bill had gone to Atlanta for a professional basketball game.

"Ship enter Savannah River from ocean," he said through the choppy connection of a ship-to-shore call. "Over."

"Wonderful," I said.

"Say 'over'."

"Over." I giggled.

"Why you laugh, love?"

"Because I love you, Spyros."

"Me, too," he said, adding, "Over."

I dashed wildly about the room throwing my sexiest nightie, a pair of brown corduroy slacks, and a cashmere sweater into a small suitcase. I scribbled a note for Bill saying I'd be out of town overnight, hoping that I would get back before he found it. Not caring if he did.

We met at our usual spot, the Hilton. I paused at the door to the bar and looked around for him. My heart was beating like an African drum. He was sitting at the far end of the bar, his back toward the room as he stared straight ahead. I walked to his end of the bar, my shoulders brushing against the green palms that were planted in huge copper buckets. Spyros turned on his stool, stared into my eyes, then broke into his boyish grin. He ordered a glass of wine for me.

We talked about his trip, his family, his travels, while I ached to be in bed next to him. He paid the bill, then walked with me to get the car from the underground garage.

Spyros grinned as he drove over the Talmadge Bridge.

"Are you laughing at me?" We were on the road to Beaufort.

"No, I thinking how nice to live in your beautiful house. We make love in different room every night." When I caught a glimpse of my expression in the mirror above the visor, I saw, instead, my mother's face staring at me. In the nadir of her life, during my father's romance with the bottle, with horses, and with other women, my mother went to her mother for advice. My grandmother had urged Mother to divorce and bring my sister and me to live with them. But divorce had never happened in their family, not in Russia, not in America. Minna stayed with Avram. Could I find the courage that she hadn't?

Spyros rubbed the palm of his warm hand just inside my thigh and glanced at me. "If so unhappy, why you not divorce?"

It wasn't like divorce had never entered my mind. I'd thought about it a thousand times, especially during the fifteen years with A.D. But I hadn't yet figured out what would replace marriage. I wanted someone to be there waiting for me when I took the final leap.

"Yes, I will, Spyros. I will divorce," I said, lapsing into the little girl voice that most men I'd known had liked.

He didn't believe me. No wonder. I didn't believe myself.

"I will do it," I said and slid my fingers to entwine with his. "Now the time is right."

"How's different?"

"I'm not afraid now."

"What you fear before, eh?"

"I don't know. Nothing." But that wasn't the truth. I was afraid of everything, of being alone, not having a husband, how could I take care of myself, and a whole bunch of other questions about survival.

Spyros raised my fingers to his lips. My courage rose as though I thought he would be there forever to give me his strength. I wallowed in the fact that I had this handsome young man. It renewed my worth just knowing that a man fifteen years younger had fallen in love with me. This time, damn it, I told myself, I will actually leave. I did know how to take care of myself. I had been as financially secure by the time I was fifty as most men of the same age, probably more so. One of the reasons I had stayed with A.D. was because he had showed me that I had the right to personal achievement and success. But, of course, his idle promises were always for the future.

Spyros and I lived in the present tense but it only took ten minutes for my brain to hopscotch into the future. Once again, I became inordinately ambitious for the man in my life to have his place in the sun, and we talked about his future. Spyros fell in step with my dreams: I saw him as Savannah's Onassis, the master of a fleet. And I would be his Jacqueline, sultry, desirable, the woman he came home to.

That night we made love with our usual wild passion, but the next morning when we walked along the riverfront I looked for some clue that he was the man capable of taking care of me. Until Spyros arrived with his youthful dreams, romance, and hints of marriage I had lacked the incentive for leaving Bill.

Silently, I wondered why Bill was willing to stay in our marriage. He seemed to have gotten used to the lovelessness, the hypocrisy of our relationship. And he couldn't bear the thought of divorce. Whenever I mentioned divorce to him or tried to get him to discuss it with me he'd run the other way.

And while my own feelings of guilt tore at me, for fifteen years I had been so consumed by A.D. that I rarely considered my marriage rationally. When that love affair ended I had tried to fill the void with other men. I was cold to my husband, angry at myself and at Bill for failing to take charge and change our lives. I was rude and sarcastic. My mother said I was too hard on Bill.

I worried how I would break the news to Mother. Divorce, I knew, would reduce me once again to the Naomi I had been at age four. I would be told again how unworthy I was. While I held a private conversation with Mother in my head, Spyros was dressed and ready to leave; he was getting impatient. He headed for the cocktail lounge. Spyros always felt at home sitting in a bar. Any bar. Drying my legs with the soft towel, I smiled into the bathroom mirror, with promises of a new life.

Between Christmas and the New Year Spyros and I met every day at my restored townhouse. For two years I had worked on it. No furniture yet but the floors were carpeted. Spyros spread beach towels, popped bottles of champagne, and we pretended we were on the sands of Mikonos, making love in an Agean moonlight. What we didn't drink he poured on my nude body — on my breasts, in my navel, down my belly, and oh God, yes, over my mons itself. And Spyros was never one to let good champagne go to waste.

The days before the year ended were idyllic for me. But for Spyros they were melancholy. He was far from his home, his family, his friends. To ease his loneliness I promised we'd celebrate New Year's Day at Cal's house. Bill would be on the golf course with his cronies and would never question where I was. Cal would roast a leg of lamb, Greek style, and I would make Hoppin' John, a traditional Southern dish for the New Year, made of ham hocks, rice, and black-eyed peas, cooked together for good luck.

Spyros and I snuggled in front of an open fire while Cal busied himself in the kitchen. Cal slammed the kitchen door to let us know he was aware of what was going on. "Damn it, you two, what about me?" Cal asked.

Cal wore a white Victorian apron tied around his waist. His tight, black leather pants seemed glued to his skin. His white tee shirt clung to his muscular chest. I walked into the kitchen as he was slicing the coconut cake topped with gooey icing.

"I can't help myself when I'm with him." I ran my finger through the thick creamy topping and licked it.

"Well, here I am cooking your damned dinner, why don't I get a turn?" Cal said with mock jealousy.

"Cal, Spyros ain't that way, now stop it." We sparred good-natured-
ly every time we got together. If a good-looking man passed us by, Cal
would poke me and ask, "Is he for you or me?"

I suggested a movie for Cal, a matinee.

"You bitch," he retorted, "first, you have me cook your dinner, and
now you want me to get out of my own house so you can fuck in my
den. I think I'll spend the night with Bill. I'd make a much better wife
than you, my little precious. This is one hell of a way for me to begin
nineteen eighty!" He untied the apron and threw it across the kitchen
counter. Spyros laughed at our friendly exchange.

Sex with Spyros was so exciting because what we felt for each other
was so mysterious. Based on passion, our feelings went beyond mere
arousal. I filled his need for home and family, he filled my obsession for
romance. He let me cling to him and that was all I thought I needed.

"Just think, I'm going to be living alone soon. The divorce is defi-
nite," I said as we drove toward his hotel. But I was just testing Spyros.
Nothing had been discussed with Bill.

"Do it for you, not me," Spyros barked with uncharacteristic irritation. He said earlier that if I stayed married, he would see me only during the day. Greek code of honor, no doubt. You romanced a married
woman in the light of day, never after dark. He had added, "If you stay
married, I see someone else at night." His blackmail made up in gall
what it lacked in subtlety. I didn't know if Spyros was implying that he
wouldn't be there at all, but I didn't want to know. He had been divorced
five years earlier after a brief marriage, he made it sound so easy, so
simple, like discarding an old pair of shoes.

I wondered again why I, of all people, was having such a hard time
with the decision. I, who had always done everything I wanted to do.
Well, that's the fable I told myself. And now I needed Spyros by my side
to make the decision stick.

My promise to Spyros and myself was met.

Chapter Twenty Eight

Two weeks later, during a fierce winter thunderstorm, I sat opposite Bill at the dinner table. I stared at the huge chunks of hail as they bounced from the windows. I took several deep breaths before I could speak.

"I want to move to the town house for a while and live there by myself." My heart pounded as though to drown out my own words.

"How long?" Bill carved his roast beef slowly, never taking his eyes from his plate.

"While this house is up for sale." The house was legally in my name, and the equity would go toward payment on the town house. Over and over I justified my actions, that because the house was mine, I could sell it when I wanted.

"Are you talking divorce again?"

"I'm saying I want to be alone long enough to get the downtown house set up." I was hurting from living a lie.

"Naomi, you've crushed me." Bill grimaced as though he had been punched in the stomach. But I didn't feel victorious, only bewildered and anxious.

"We've been married for thirty-two years, had three sons, and Ross says the only thing he remembers about us as a couple is the bickering. I'm tired of this life. We're not the same two people who married each other," I said.

"It may not be perfect, but what we have is better than most." Bill had convinced himself of that.

I had set out to be the perfect wife. Bill had set out to be whatever my cajoling inspired him to be. For years I had been trying to explain my unhappiness to Bill and to myself. It was as though I spoke one language and he another. It was beyond my understanding, so how could I explain it to him.

The following week Bill watched as I loaded my car with pots, pans, and clothes. Dora hauled the vacuum cleaner into the trunk.

"So, you're really leaving me?" Bill said. I was doing something that was incomprehensible to him.

"Please, Bill, don't." I needed every ounce of courage just to get into my car and drive away. For some unfathomable reason, at this moment, I felt as if the thirty odd years spent with this man was the same as being married to my mother. That afternoon, movers brought a bed, a chest of drawers, and the refrigerator from the house to my newly renovated place. As the movers carted in the refrigerator, I realized that Bill would have no ice for his martini that night.

On my first night alone in the new house I went to a nearby Chinese restaurant. Sipping a crisply-chilled Tsingtao beer, nibbling a tender eggroll, I savored my sense of exhilaration at being alone. After the meal I strolled through the lobby of the Hilton hotel, looking in the windows of the shops, feeling completely liberated. Finally, unable to think of any way to extend the evening, I bought a newspaper, strolled through the squares on Bull Street, and walked back to my house. That night, I fell asleep quickly and slept soundly.

Two nights later I was back in the suburban house, sleeping on the living room sofa. Within days my excitement had degenerated into confusion and terror. Bill cooked a thick juicy steak and baked potatoes for our dinner. His face wore a sad expression, but at the same time, I knew he felt hopeful that I wouldn't be able to make it without him. I wondered the same thing. A shock wave went through me upon seeing the emptiness of my bedroom. All the furniture was in the town house. Just through the dressing room Bill's room remained intact. He didn't offer to share his bed. Sleeping on my own living room sofa, during the few hours that I managed any sleep at all, I dreamed of falling into a dark cave and being unable to climb out. Never before had I lived in a house unless a man was under the same roof.

"I'm living alone, please call," I cabled Spyros, who was away for six weeks.

"I love you," he wired back. "I miss you."

I dissolved; I soared. The lump of fear that I had carried for the last several days melted away. I moved off the sofa, back to town. There wasn't a man in my house, but there was the essence of one — a man who loved me. That was enough for me. He was a new challenge. His life as a sailor, while not exotic in Savannah eyes, was the added spice to our affair. It also took him away for long periods. I ached to have him constantly underfoot, the centerpiece of my life. He was the catalyst for my separation and divorce.

At first being alone was exciting. At the end of a work day I would often leave my office stopping in at a bar with other business executives. It offered me a chance to get away from the house and my business, before the climb upstairs for another night alone.

At the 17 Hundred 90 bar, Bill's best friend came over to me one night as I sat with a group of women friends to ask if I would go home with him. He said his wife was out of town visiting her mother and their marriage was on the rocks.

"You should've gone with her," I said. News of the Kramer separation had spread. No longer the married woman, I was now considered easy prey. People who for years had been friends of mine and Bill's now invited only him to parties and dinners. I was becoming as socially acceptable as a leper.

However, the separation didn't change my relationship with my single women friends. And Andrea acted as though she were single most of the time.

One night as Beckie, my friend from my campaign days, and I sat in Teeple's restaurant she asked if I was having a hard time being alone. She had been very supportive during my struggle to separate. She telephoned regularly.

"I don't think I could've eaten one more meal alone," I told my friend, as I cracked open a crab claw and sucked the tender meat from the shell.

As Beckie pushed the crab shells through the hole in the middle of the table to the bucket underneath, she looked over at me and smiled sweetly. She had constantly urged me to try living alone to be sure that's what I really wanted, while Andrea encouraged me to divorce, if only for her own vicarious thrill. Beckie was the new Southern woman, in love with tradition, yet ever mindful that women's roles had advanced since James Edward Oglethorpe settled Savannah.

Beckie was thirty, unmarried, and happy that way. She was a magazine illustrator who had dreams of being a painter. She was constantly urging her friends to follow their dreams. The two of us shared confidences and quiet laughter.

When Beckie excused herself to go to the ladies' room, she returned with a roll of toilet paper she had pilfered and stuck into her huge tote bag. I rolled my eyes toward the ceiling. It wasn't that she couldn't afford the absolute necessities, it was just that she had her own self-acclaimed system of justice. She felt that life owed her a little something every now and then.

Beckie offered to spend the weekend with me. She had as much understanding of the burdened heart at age thirty as I did in my fifties. Outside the restaurant's windows, the shrimp boats sailed rhythmically up the Thunderbolt River, their shredded colored flags blowing in the wind.

Giving in to my guilty visions of Bill sitting home alone, I invited him over for brunch that Sunday. It was his first visit to the town house since its completion and his eyes slowly took in all the details, including Beckie, who was in the kitchen sitting at the wooden counter. Her short, fluffy blond hair curled softly around her freckled face. He gaped at her curvy behind in tight jeans as she walked outside to get the Sunday paper from the porch.

"So, you're sleeping with women now?" he said as soon as Beckie was out of earshot.

"For God's sake, Bill, don't be such an ass!"

Recalling that I had only invited him out of pity, I now felt something inside me come unglued. When Beckie walked back to the kitchen counter I grabbed her small hand for strength; it was harder having Bill around than I had imagined. His face was ashen as he stared at our clasped hands. He'd never be able to understand that Beckie's friendship at that time in my life was more important to me than an empty marriage.

"How about lunch tomorrow, Bill?" Beckie said, after sizing up the inharmonious situation.

"Maybe. Uh...I don't know. Where?"

He agreed to meet her. I felt instant relief that Beckie would explain it all to him. How sad that Bill and I could not say what we felt, not without a fight, not without name calling and accusations. We both still needed someone else to put order into our lives.

On the day that Bill and Beckie were meeting for lunch, Cal and I headed down Jones Street toward Mrs. Wilkes'. We sat at one of the large oilcloth covered tables, reaching for pieces of juicy fried chicken. Cal smiled at the man next to him. The seating was random and no one knew if the person at his right was a truck driver or a bank president.

I dipped my knife into the dish of pure butter and spread it in the middle of a hot biscuit, then poured hot gravy over the biscuit. I realized how much I missed the family I used to have, little boys who could hardly wait for the food I cooked to come off the stove and onto their plates. And of the happy years that Bill and I shared in the beginning of our marriage, when he had been my whole future. I remembered how, in those early days, I ate, slept, dreamed, worked, and thought Bill.

Beckie was reluctant to tell me of her lunch with Bill, but I insisted.

"He said that you've always been spoiled. That you're the one who wanted him to own his own business. That he was never ambitious, but you are."

"What else?"

"He's very sad, Naomi. He said you've crushed him."

Bill began making the rounds of bars, night after night, with other men who ended their day of stress by sharing a few drinks and some laughter. Bill drank more and more, grumbling to anyone who would listen to his misery. "She crushed me," became his trademark comment accompanied by his double martini.

A couple of days later, as I sat in my office checking and double checking a closing statement for an office complex, the secretary buzzed me on the intercom.

"I can't stand what people are saying about you!"

"Hello, Mother. What are people saying?" I shuffled through my papers, thinking, *Oh, God, here it comes.*

"People are saying that you're separated. Separated from that good man!"

"Well, I am living in one house and Bill's in the other. I guess you could call that separated."

"People are saying terrible things and I don't like it."

"What kind of things?" Could she have heard about Spyros? He was younger, he wasn't Jewish, he wasn't my husband. I was three times damned in Mother's way of seeing things.

"People are saying you're out dancing every night," she accused. I considered that a lucky break. At least they hadn't said out screwing. "With men!"

"What, with who?" I cradled the telephone between my chin and my ear as I continued working with the papers on my desk.

"With men!"

"Oh," I said. For a moment I wondered if my mother had imagined the alternatives.

"Your aunt Sadie and uncle Bob said everybody's talking about you." My mother and her sister talked on the phone everyday. As far as my mother was concerned every word Aunt Sadie uttered was pure gospel.

"Well, I don't give a damn what everybody says about me. Who the hell's everybody?"

"You better care!"

"In case you haven't noticed, Mother, I'm now over fifty. I also own and operate my own business. And I run my own life." My mother had hung up the telephone and didn't hear my sarcasm and anger.

"Patience, child, patience. You can't just change overnight and not bring on repercussions from the people around you. Things just don't happen that way," Beckie said. We were sitting in the living room on a Sunday morning, sipping black coffee and reading *The New York Times*. I had just told her about my mother's accusations.

Beckie had long kept daily journals of her life in the South, and as an artist, had recorded her thoughts in clear images. She had taken time to reflect on her surroundings, to list her priorities for her future. I realized, listening to my young friend speak, that, yes, I had imagined I could leave Bill, move into the new house alone, live by myself for the very first time, and simultaneously conceal my passionate affair with a man fifteen years my junior — all without fear or pain. For the first time I saw how confused I was, believing that I could make changes in my life without hurting others or myself.

The jangle of the telephone interrupted our conversation.

"I've been. . . awake all night," my mother said, gasping.

"What's wrong?"

"I got up . . . at seven . . . and started . . . to bake cookies." She paused. "And I thought . . . I would . . . feel better." Her voice faded.

"Have you called a doctor?"

"I don't know . . . what . . . to do."

Cold fear caught my chest. I turned to Beckie. "I think my mother is having a heart attack."

We sped the car through Sunday morning church traffic, on the way to my mother's small apartment. She was on the couch, gasping. I placed a coat over her shoulders and Beckie and I helped her down the stairs, through the musty entrance hall, and to my car. We drove straight to the hospital. Minna had never been ill in her life. She was small, frail, faded. But ill? No. I couldn't help but wonder if all this was happening because of what I thought were the unwarranted changes I was making in my own life.

"There's a great deal of fluid around her heart," announced the intern. "She may be having some heart failure and we're going to run a series of tests on her." He's crazy as hell, I thought. Not my Mother; she's strong.

Hours later, I tiptoed into my mother's room. Tubes connected Minna's tired body with life. I put a hand on hers to comfort her. I smiled and mouthed "hello." I wanted to tell her she could have all of my jewelry, my furs, my car. I would promise to live the way she wanted me to.

My mother fixed her eyes on me. Her first words were, "You did this to me."

Chapter Twenty Nine

For five months Spyros and I were lovers while I adjusted to single life. He had to leave on three different occasions for trips around the world while I practiced becoming a martyr. To early Christians the word passion meant suffering. Was it any wonder that I felt out of control as though I was experiencing my last supper?

Beckie mothered me constantly, while Cal served as surrogate father and mother. Andrea invited me to her house often for meals with her family. My mother was in and out of the hospital regularly during the next few months. Bill was constantly calling for dinner dates in an attempt at reconciliation. I was drained.

"Bill," I said calmly into the phone one morning, "I want to get a divorce."

"You won't get a damn cent from me, I can tell you that," he screamed into my ear.

"All right. Let's just set a date and get it done."

"I've seen a lawyer and I'll fight you all the way," he yelled.

"I can take care of myself. My business is doing well."

"I put a lot of materials in your office and house thinking I'd be living there. I should've known you'd do a sneaky thing like this."

"Bill, let's just agree on a lawyer, one we both know, and let him take care of the legalities. I won't ask for one thing."

We agreed to divide our art collection. Because I had new furniture for my historic house, Bill kept what we had. When I phoned my sister to tell her that I was going through with the divorce she seemed surprised. "You've talked about it for so many years and now that you're actually doing it I can't believe it."

"Mother is not taking it very well," I said.

"Well, she thinks Bill's the perfect husband. I always thought he was, too. She'll get over it, don't worry." My sister said that she planned to drive to Savannah some time during the next week to visit Mother and asked if she could stay with me.

Alex never mentioned the word divorce when I spoke to him on the phone. He was completely involved in being a new father. In January, during the middle of the night, Alex had called to announce the birth of his daughter. He and Dianne had been married for two years. My son with a baby of his own. It hardly seemed real. He told me that he had watched the entire birth.

I had replied sleepily into the receiver how happy I was to finally have a little girl in our family, trying to imagine in my mind the pink and perfect little girl, the one I had always dreamed of having, being. But instead, I felt more tired than ever, too depleted to be the elated grandmother. My mother was dying, I was getting a divorce, and found myself involved in a torrid love affair with a man fifteen years younger. Everything was jumbled together and it was more than I could handle emotionally or mentally.

Early the next day, I began telephoning everyone to announce that I had a granddaughter. Visions of this precious child standing around watching me in my kitchen, the way I had watched my grandmother, spun my heart into smells of strudel, cocoa, and bread rising, wrapped in a long-ago Russian accent.

Later that day, talking to Ruth, I wondered aloud if I were supposed to experience some special feeling that hadn't surfaced. Ruth assured me that the real love between grandmother and granddaughter comes as the friendship buds and blossoms, as hers was doing with her own granddaughter.

Ross reacted differently and asked me for details when I told him about the divorce. While he pretended that it didn't bother him, I knew deep down that he was upset.

"Well, Mom, what bothers me," Ross said, "is that you're the only one that can get Dad to do things." He had no idea how tired I was of living a life where I had to manipulate to be heard. It was not only exhausting, it was also demeaning.

It was much easier for me to talk to Bill with a phone between us. Looking at him made me feel guilty and at the moment my eyes were for Spyros alone. *This is happiness*, I told myself, but I didn't feel happy unless my young lover was with me.

After Spyros returned to Savannah in early July we went on holiday to Key West via Disney World. I had packed a picnic basket of gooey egg salad sandwiches with homemade mayonnaise and Greek olives. There was a bottle of Dom Perignon wrapped in bright red tissue. While the car swerved down Interstate 95, I fed Spyros bits of food, loving the way he nibbled the remnants from my manicured fingertips. I held the plastic goblet to his laughing lips.

On the day we did get back to Savannah a letter from the divorce lawyer was waiting for me. I had to be in court in thirty days, to appear before a judge who was a good friend. He was the first black Superior Court judge in Georgia; we knew each other from my campaign days. When I ran for the State Senate he had helped me win the endorsement of the NAACP.

On the night before the court appearance Spyros and I were at the supermarket, shopping for *moussaka* ingredients. Tanned and rested, we talked happily of our future.

"I want my own place," Spyros said. "I can't live in yours. It's your personality." But at least he said he was tired of living like a gypsy and wanted to know if I'd let him leave his clothes at my house. I was elated. It was the first sign of the commitment I had dreamed of.

"I want you wear this, love," he said, as he slipped a gold ring with a large onyx and a diamond in the middle, off his hand onto the third finger of my left hand.

Walking beside Spyros and the grocery cart, I suddenly caught sight of Bill at the dairy case. As he raised his head, our eyes met, and he took in Spyros. A slow smile, the false one I had come to know very well, spread across his face. I softly touched Spyros's arm, whispering, "I'll be right back, baby."

"Who's that with you?" Bill asked when I came up to him.

"Just a client." Outwardly calm, my insides were in a panic. Thank God, I thought, all this pretense will soon end. At last there seemed to be an end to lying and hiding. But at that moment, standing in the supermarket, I was terrified of what Bill might do.

"Would you like to go somewhere nearby and have a drink?" he asked. I shook my head and looked down at the cold floor.

I started walking away and Bill pushed his cart into me. "Oh, excuse me," he said, pretending innocence. I had seen him play dirty too many times on a basketball court. I said nothing and hurried back to Spyros.

"Who was that man?" he asked.

"Nobody special."

"Tell me. Tell me who was that man!"

"You know," I murmured reluctantly.

"Love, I want to know who was that man. Who pushed you?"

"My husband," I whispered.

"I thought so." Spyros's face clouded, his eyes narrowed. "Go, now, put groceries in car," he ordered. "I will talk to him."

"Please, baby, let's just go."

"No. I buy cigarettes and talk to him. He can't push you like that."

I left the supermarket and placed the bags in the car, praying silently that the two men were not locked in mortal combat inside the supermarket. A couple whose car was parked next to mine were putting their groceries in the trunk when I heard the man say, "Did you hear those two men yelling at each other? One threatened to punch the shit out of the other just as we were leaving the checkout counter." I locked my car and hurried back into the market to find Bill shaking his fist in Spyros's face.

"Goddamned, son of a bitch, you think you can fuck my wife and get away with it?" Bill took a swing at Spyros.

Spyros ducked and missed the punch. He shoved Bill out of the aisle with both hands. I pulled Spyros by the arm, urging that we leave immediately.

"That man is jealous mad, love. He's dangerous."

When we got into the car, Spyros drove. I was shaking against my seat. Bill had managed to get into his car and catch up with us as we were heading down Habersham Street. He maneuvered his car around to the passenger side of mine and signaled for me to roll down the window. He brushed his shiny new green Jaguar against my car. I rolled down the window as Bill screamed, shaking his fist, "You won't get that damned thing in the morning!"

"I'll go to hotel tonight," Spyros said. "It will be safer." Bill's car made a turn and screeched off in the opposite direction.

"No, please," I said, desperate not to be alone. "Don't leave me alone tonight. I need you."

From a pay phone near my house, I called Bill. I wanted to be sure he was in his house before I entered mine. "What the hell was that all about?" I said, injecting a note of righteous anger into my voice.

"I sure as hell am not going to support you when you're shacked up with some young *schmuck*," he lashed back.

At home there was a call on my answering machine from the lawyer telling me that the divorce proceeding was being postponed. Bill was not willing to sign the papers. He had been looking for any excuse to stop me.

That night, my dreams were a specter of Savannah murders. I feared I might become another statistic. Savannah had always accepted murder as an ordinary daily event. Only recently one of my real estate clients had been tried for the murder of his young gay lover. A prominent antique dealer, he had sold me the house on Gaston Street. Now he was known to send out daily from his jail cell for his lunch, from Mrs. Wilkes' restaurant.

When my client was released on bail, I saw him at a brunch given by a mutual friend. I stood in the corner with a Bloody Mary in my hand as the tall handsome parolee walked toward me. He smiled graciously, stirring the gin and tonic that he held. We had done business together many times and I knew that I couldn't completely ignore the circumstances he now found himself in.

"I would be remiss," I said, "if I didn't tell you how terribly sorry I am about this whole damned mess." With that he asked me to sit at a table with him, then went on to explain exactly what had happened between him and his lover. It was as though we were discussing an ordinary piece of property that had just gone up for sale.

Two days later, I still hadn't been assigned a date to appear in the judge's chambers. Spyros was growing nervous and was impatient with me as we waited. He didn't want an enemy with political influence while he still had only a green card.

Finally, I urged the lawyer to tell Bill that I would forfeit my rights to alimony or other moneys that might be due me if we could just sign the papers. Not having to give me alimony appealed to Bill. Andrea offered to go with me to the judge's chambers the morning of the divorce.

"I always hoped that marriage would guarantee eternal happiness," I said naively as Andrea drove toward the courthouse. Andrea shrugged her shoulders as she pulled into the parking garage.

"You think I'll make it on my own?" I asked Judge Gladdon when he walked around to my side of his desk and put a comforting arm around my shoulders. I searched his kind brown eyes for an answer. He stood tall in his judicial robe, his graying hair added a note of dignity.

"Of course. No doubt about it," the judge said. "You're a survivor. I've always known that about you." Bill did not have to appear. The judge read a lengthy document, I replied "yes" and "no" several times, and suddenly I was free. But the day turned out to be far more difficult than I could possibly have anticipated. Seeking more assurance, I called Spyros from the courthouse lobby.

"I'm single, baby," I said, expecting a joyful response. Instead, he announced that in a few days he would be leaving for another trip, a long one. I felt scared again and shaky. It took all my emotional strength to get through the divorce proceedings, but to Spyros it seemed almost trivial, ordinary.

At the posh Oglethorpe Club, where Andrea treated me to lunch, I toyed with my shrimp creole and listened to Andrea trying to convince me that there were worse divorces than mine. Hers in fact.

"I had a young child, just one year old and no one offered to go with me to court." Her parents had turned away and left her to handle her divorce alone.

That night, I sobbed in Spyros's arms.

"What's the matter, eh, love?" he asked. There was irritation in his voice. I knew in order to hold his love I would have to control my fears now that my needs were out from behind the protective barrier of my marriage. I muffled my sobs. However sad or insecure, I felt I'd have to hide my feelings from Spyros. Or take the chance of losing him. Freedom was new to me, and I couldn't appreciate it yet.

I drove Spyros to his ship. I had carefully packed a bag full of foods he liked: feta cheese, his favorite chocolate cookies, his beloved olives, and pickles. He took the large shopping bag from me like a small boy getting his brown bag lunch from Mommy.

"This is hard part," he said. "Hard for me like for you." He put his arms around me as tears spilled down my cheeks. "Don't cry, Naomi. Seeing my girl cry when I leave make me to feel bad and hurt also."

During the time that Spyros was away Cal, Beckie, and Andrea were there to comfort me. I seemed to sleepwalk through my daily business routines. Within the week, Spyros called before dawn, he was drunk after a night out in the French Quarter of New Orleans, a stopover on the way to Panama. He said, "I love you, I miss you, I need you."

We discussed a rendezvous, but Spyros only wanted me to meet him if he could provide a glamorous setting. Before we hung up, I said, "I love you, too."

Being separated from Spyros wasn't my only problem.

Chapter Thirty

Each morning as I entered my office, I seemed to confront an arena in which I was the matador and my career was *el toro*. The drive needed to maintain my status in the real estate market took more energy than I was able to summon. Would I defeat the bull, leave the arena unscathed, or would the beast hurl me onto the ground? I tasted dust in my mouth when I read ads by competitors which made outlandish claims. "We're number one," trumpeted one. "We outsell everybody else in the city!" said another. Why couldn't they just be satisfied with doing a job well? Why was it so important to be Number One? What did Number One really mean?

My office had become a testing ground for women on the way to independence. Calls came in every day from Savannah housewives who had real estate licenses and wanted to work for my company. I wasn't the only woman living alone. There was Beckie, who had successfully learned how to be by herself. I was still in the middle of that struggle. When Zelda's husband died after a long terminal illness I hastened to her side to help her make similar adjustments.

"One of us is a grass widow, Naomi," Zelda said, "the other a sod widow." She spoke in a quiet voice as we stood in her kitchen unpacking the groceries I had brought over. Zelda and I kept busy by cooking for each other. And Beckie and I talked on the phone into the wee hours of the morning to stave off loneliness.

Alex called often from Atlanta, usually on Saturday mornings just before his golf game, to talk about an interesting legal case, or was joyous with news of his daughter, never asking about my personal life. Ross was living a wild and crazy college life. He seemed to be accident prone and I was afraid to say anything to him for fear he'd turn on me and challenge my lifestyle. I was apprehensive about my sons meeting Spyros and managed to keep them apart. But then I had become quite expert in compartmentalizing my life.

Watching Mother's failing health precipitated a family meeting. We decided that she would be much safer in a high rise building that provided twenty four hour monitoring. But my mother became extremely thin, and she didn't enjoy the tiny apartment in a building geared for the elderly.

Every member of the family took turns bringing her meals. But she missed her familiar surroundings, and she blamed me and Ella for talking the others into thinking that this move would be best for her. I always grew anxious when I visited the apartment, imagining that at the entrance downstairs I'd meet an ambulance arriving to carry away another of the forgotten elderly who occupied the complex, this halfway house to death.

It was four in the morning, mid September, when the jangle of the telephone shattered my dreamless sleep. I awoke and grabbed the receiver.

Dial tone.

Collapsing into my pillows, I dozed for a few minutes, and again the grating ring of the phone awakened me.

Dial tone.

I slept fitfully, my mind echoing the ring of the telephone. At eight a.m. the insistent ringing wrenched me from sleep.

"Ain't nobody answering Amma's door," Hattie, the woman who stayed with my mother during the day, said on the other end. I called my aunt Shirley, who lived near Minna's apartment. She had an extra key.

"Mother isn't answering her door," I said.

Minutes later Shirley called me back. "Naomi, Minna's dead."

"What happened?" I could feel my skin turning clammy.

"It looks like she fell backward on her bed while trying to get to the phone," Shirley said. Mother had died during the night, alone, surrounded by her meager possessions, a bitter reminder of her lifelong disillusionment. The threadbare rug, the faded couch, and her worn cedar chest were the only material remnants of her life.

I went to meet my aunts and uncles at Mother's apartment. I sat on the couch, avoiding the sight of Minna's frail body behind the bedroom door, not wanting to see or accept the fact that I had given my mother

her fatal heart attack. To the mortician, I spoke calmly, matter-of-factly, while fighting the almost uncontrollable urge to run away, to howl at the unfairness which had been my mother's parcel in life.

At the funeral, the rabbi spoke of the family gathered for the sad duty of paying their last respects to a very dear and sweet Orthodox Jewish lady, Amma, as she was known. In the Jewish calendar, it was the Festival of Succos, and the rabbi was not allowed to deliver a lengthy eulogy because it might evoke excessive grief and detract from the joyous mood of this happy holiday.

As Ruth and I stood so the rabbi could cut the black ribbon pinned to our clothes, in traditional Jewish fashion, Ruth began crying. Then she ran toward the coffin as the pallbearers lowered the box, next to Avram's, in front of Zelig's and Eva's graves. Ella pulled Ruth away and helped her into the funeral limousine.

Afterwards the family came to my house for lunch. No one would have loved the ritual more than Mother. For a while, after the burial, the family exchanged loving stories of Minna, then everyone rose to say good-bye. When the last aunt had kissed my cheek, and after the door was finally closed, the shrill loneliness of my big house seemed palpable.

Carefully, I put away the dishes in my hi-tech kitchen and communicated in whispers with the lingering presence of the woman whose life forces had created my own. My hand was poised over the phone, set to dial her number. *But now I can't even call, there is no number, there is no you!* A Waterford goblet slipped from my hand and splintered on the floor.

A shrill voice filled my head as I walked through the foyer and up the curving wooden staircase to the silence of my bedroom. With clammy fingers I unbuttoned my blouse, unsnapped my bra. I tore off my black skirt, stepped out of my panties, and threw myself across the bed. "Mother, I'm scared!" I screamed.

The next day, I walked through my mother's small apartment, choking as if the building were on fire. The cheap costume jewelry piled into boxes atop an inexpensive fake mahogany dresser reminded me that while I had real diamonds and emeralds, my mother owned paste. Once when Mother was dressing for a party, I remembered her putting on every piece, playing with each one like a little girl at the five-and-dime. Ruth and I had chided her, saying so much jewelry was tacky.

Now, I fingered a solid gold pin, the circles encrusted with cultured pearls, which A.D. had insisted on buying for me to give to Minna as a Mother's Day gift. Next to the jewelry boxes were photographs of the babies, teenagers, marriages, Mama and Papa. I thought of how old ladies spread out pictures of their families and made a mental note to remove some of the pictures in my own house.

Packing my mother's belongings, I thought of her diminutive form. Had she been afraid? Had she tried to call for help or had it been a dream? Had she dialed my number at four in the morning? Were her solitary cries in the still night the sounds which had stirred me from sleep? Over and over, as I fingered Mother's meager possessions, I felt as though I'd been slashed with a sword, no less cruel for all its being imaginary.

"I'm an orphan. An unmarried orphan," I said aloud to no one. Just being where my mother had once lived stirred in me the compassion I now felt toward her. Minna had given all that she was capable of giving. I was determined to remember the bits of love that had filtered through, no matter what. The cupcakes that we had baked together when I was five, the potato latkes when I was fifty. How proud she was when I made her a grandmother.

Ross had agreed to meet me and help close up Mother's apartment after Ruth and the others had claimed what they wanted. There stood the old cedar chest, where Minna had stored her nostalgia. Faded ribbons from years ago, yellowed letters and cards, bits and pieces from her life that I didn't understand.

"What do you want me to do with this stuff. I don't have a truck," Ross said. He wanted an old dining room cabinet that he had always remembered and liked.

"Just get it out of here," I said, not wanting to linger a minute longer than necessary.

"Mom, I don't know what to do with it," he insisted.

"Goddamn it, I'm tired," I shouted. "Can't one of you do something for me?" I felt flooded with irritation and exhaustion overwhelming me.

Ross looked at me in bewilderment before he went into the other room and dialed his father. From the other room I overheard him say, "Something's wrong with Mom," on the phone to Bill.

Yes, I thought bitterly when Bill called later on to say he would send a truck and dispose of Minna's furniture for me, from his and Ross's point of view there was something wrong with me. I was human, after all. I looked in the mirror and saw myself as a giant breast with all of them — Ross, Alex, Bill, even Spyros — sucking the life out of me.

Spyros hadn't hurried to see me when he returned to the States two months later. This created another emotion I could not deal with: suspicion. I pictured Spyros in the arms of other women. Of all the emotional tortures, jealousy had to be the most insidious. I was disgusted with myself for still wanting love, for still craving everything that goes with it. I felt that I should have outgrown that need by this time in my life. The power of my sexuality had given me a lot of courage as though it validated my being on the earth. But now that I was over fifty it seemed dangerous to me.

My jealousy was sporadic. It was exacerbated by the physical distance between my lover and me. Spyros couldn't leave his ship; there were problems with the engine and the boat had to be docked in Florida for repairs. My constant attempts to reach him were frustrating. He was never in his motel room and he didn't return my calls. I located him by getting in touch with the president of his shipping company. Then the day came when my worst fears were realized. I phoned Spyros's room and a woman answered. When I finally got through to him, I was shaking.

"I can't believe you cheated on me. I've been calling, hoping you and I could arrange a place to meet and what do I find? Another woman in your room."

"But, Naomi, it is nothing, just sex. It's you I love." I could hear Spyros puffing on his cigarette.

"That's bullshit!"

"Why you call so many times?"

I caught my breath and answered, "Spyros, my mother died while you were away. I needed you."

"I don't know what to do. I don't know what to say. I'm not good for things like that. But, I call you when I get to Savannah."

Because sex with Spyros had been the most rewarding of my life, I couldn't stand the thought of his touching another woman, or the thought of sharing him. I was tormented by the idea that perhaps I wasn't as good in bed as the women he met in other ports. I knew that I was sexy and that together we were terrific, but I also knew I was competing with faceless, nameless, and probably, younger women. It was rewarding that Spyros was always so gentle and eager to please me. Whenever I complained about the extra ten pounds I had gained, he would assure me time and again that he liked his woman with some meat on her.

None of what he had said, or lovingly done, mattered at that moment. I screamed, "Get your fucking clothes out of my house or I'll throw them out." I banged down the receiver and fell back on my bed, remembering such temper tantrums directed at my sister Ruth over forty years ago.

Life for the next few weeks took me from my office, to my bedroom, and en route from the first to the second floor, my kitchen, where I stopped long enough to fix a meal.

"It's over. I no want your anger," Spyros said when he came to my house eight weeks after my mother's death. He sat across from me at the kitchen counter with a sad look in his eyes. In my heart I knew this was coming. Spyros's reaction to my mother's death was too callous, and my jealous rages were frightening to both of us. My possessiveness was more than he wanted to deal with.

"But, Spyros," I said, desperately, as I reached out to rescue our sinking relationship. "Don't you understand how sad I am? I miss my mother. You can't leave me now. Besides, how will you get over me?" I smiled meekly.

"I will press hard my insides," he said, his voice like granite. "Think of something you have done that made me mad. That will help. And you, you must do also."

As he spoke, I felt as if I'd been shelled. I had helped him adjust to American life, manipulated a judge to get his drivers license and I had been faithful. I had waited. I had divorced for him.

We finished dinner in silence. Afterwards, I watched as he emptied his drawers of clothes and put them into suitcases. When he finished packing, he kissed me on the forehead and went out the front door, closing it quietly behind him. I remained motionless, sitting on the couch, my hands folded, for hours after he left. I knew that I would smell him for months from the scent that his heavily perfumed clothes left behind in the closet.

I lowered my head and closed my eyes. I suddenly realized that while I had deserted God, God had not deserted me. For the first time in years, I felt a force that was on my side.

When November came I found it hard to believe that so many changes had taken place in my life in the short span of eight months. I had left Bill in January of 1980 and moved into the house in town so eager for adventure and a new life. But divorce and death, and an end to my exaggerated ideas of romance had left me exhausted and unsure of what to do next. I did not, however, regret any of the changes or the pleasure and love I had gotten from my young Greek god.

That night, as I lay silently in my king size bed, I thought: For a pioneer woman alone the worst hours are at night when she can't see beyond the darkness but knows the wolves are howling. Again and again she says to herself, "The day will dawn tomorrow and I will be all right, I will be all right."

One relationship, as Spyros proved, cannot give you life or remove it. I promised myself I would stop thinking about Spyros. But thoughts were all I had of him. I told myself how lucky I was that for a shining year we had been lovers. I told myself that what I needed was a magic word to erase the memory of him so the hurting would stop. I hoped that he hurt as much, but I knew he did not. Men forget, women remember. The culture we live in doesn't take the time for grieving death or loss. Denial seems to be the socially acceptable way for most people to deal with grief.

I discovered in the months that followed, how my dependency on A.D. was gone; however, the love I had felt for him, for my mother, Bill, and Spyros had left a space, enlarging and maturing inside of me. And I found out that life goes on no matter what. Alex was married, living in Atlanta, and building his law practice. Ross had graduated college and gone to work for Bill in his Atlanta store, turning into quite a success-ful salesman. It seemed to me that both my sons harbored some anger toward me for leaving their father.

There were mornings during the next six months when Dora arrived for work, witnessed my red swollen eyes, and served me breakfast in bed. She would bring up the wicker tray, setting the newspaper in the slot on the side, a mug of steaming hot coffee alongside a plate of bacon and eggs.

"Miss Naomi," she said, "you just gotta quit cryin' over them mens. They ain't worth it." She told me about her husband and how she got over him.

"I loved him so much. I loved the breeze that cooled that man. Honey, the onliest way I got over him was to get on my knees." As always her candor was an inspiration. "And, you got to ask that man upstairs for peace, 'cause he's the onliest man that's gonna help any of us womens."

I didn't think I was quite able to do that; instead I looked at life from a peripheral vision. Knowing that I was free, the time had come for me to reinvent myself. Somehow I knew that even the pain of breaking up might be put to use in a positive way. Or as Beckie said jokingly, "Maybe you're being prepared for greatness." Iintuitively , I knew if I continued to grow, to love, to achieve, to round off the edges of my life, the shocks and pains that we are all heir to would not be killing ones.

Chapter Thirty One

Work began to hold very little interest for me, but I needed the routine of my office. It was the glue that held me together.

Somewhere in the remnants of my reasoning I still believed I had to have a man in my life or I wouldn't be whole. I suppose if Atilla the Hun had come along at that time, I would have bestowed upon him all the love that was stored up inside of me, begging to be used.

"You're never going to meet anyone if you don't step out of your everyday routine. Try going to different places," Beckie lectured to me during dinner one night.

Listening to Beckie's suggestion, the next day I decided to walk through the lobby of the Hilton Hotel on my way to the Post Office. It was on that day that I met up with that enduring Southern species: the good ol' boy. He came into my life in the form of Bubba Strickland, a card-carrying GOB, and a dedicated practitioner.

I saw Bubba as he stepped out of the elevator, coming from his office on the top floor of the DeSoto Hilton. He was an investment broker, and although we hadn't done business together, we'd known each other casually for years. In fact, my old beau Bruce, had once been his boss.

Bubba walked straight toward me, gave me a big bear hug, and smiled the crooked smile I recalled from cocktail party conversations. "I just love hugging big bosomed gals!" he said too loudly, then asked me to meet him for a drink later that afternoon.

Bubba was tall and at least twenty pounds heavier than I had remembered him. His wiry, gray hair suggested that it might have once been curly. A shock of it stood at an angle away from his forehead as though it didn't belong to the rest of his head. He had a chipped tooth in the very front of his mouth.

"So, say I get to your house at five, what about five, will five be okay?" Bubba spoke in fast nervous tones. He seemed not to want the conversation to end.

"I have to close my office first."

Later that afternoon he came over just as I was going upstairs for the day. We sat on the green stools in my kitchen. He asked if I would join him for dinner.

"My best friend is coming in from Pensacola, Florida, and I want him to meet you."

"I have to shower and wash my hair but I'll join you later," I promised, less than enthusiastically, yet thinking that an evening at a nice restaurant, laughing with old acquaintances, would be better than a Friday night alone with the frozen dinner I planned to eat in front of the T.V.

"I'll just wait for you," he said. "You can carry your curlers, and whatever else you need with you to my house. I don't want him to get there and not find me home."

As I soaped my thighs in the shower, I wondered if I'd had the wrong impression of this guy. Perhaps Bubba was really a racy bon vivant, used to women depositing their curlers, tampons, and old mascara containers, at his apartment. Suddenly the evening seemed slightly more interesting than I had imagined.

I stepped from behind the shower curtain to find him sitting on the edge of the gray tiled Jacuzzi. "Jesus, Bubba, you move right in, don't you?"

"I think I'll spend the night with you," he said peremptorily, behaving as though the thick white towel I had jerked around my body was an outfit no more provocative than the gray pin striped suit I had worn that afternoon when we saw each other in the hotel lobby. The idea was amusing. I collected my curlers, bobby pins, and makeup and went off with him to his apartment. He was fun, I decided. A fun loving good ol' boy, a side of him I'd never noticed.

He did as he said and spent the night with me, in my guest room. The next night, he invited me to have dinner again. This time, we slept together in my king-size bed. Bubba's approach to sex was passive, but I liked the cuddling and the quietness. In the morning, he padded downstairs to make coffee. Vaguely hearing the sounds from the kitchen, I stretched luxuriously, contentedly, between the sheets. When he came back upstairs to set the pot of fresh coffee and the Sunday *Savannah*

New Press on the table, he brushed his lips across my forehead, then pulled on his clothes. His touch was maternal. Through half closed eyes, I watched him get into his boxer shorts with the design of a *Wall Street Journal* financial page imprinted on them. I couldn't make up my mind whether to read his shorts or the newspaper.

At last, an uncomplicated man, an uncomplicated romance. He may not have been Mr. Wonderful, but at least he was Mr. Okay. A man from my own hometown, one near my own age, and — if Waspish rather than Jewish — still someone from a similar social set. We began meeting for drinks, going to movies, and cooking dinner together. And it was nice to have such a big teddy bear, a cuddly and affectionate, if pale and paunchy, body in bed alongside mine. Indeed, it seemed to me that his pale softness was a part of what drew me to him, as though sucking at his almost womanly breasts, in the middle of long, satisfying nights took me back to some primal hunger.

Bubba and I rose early on the morning of March 17th. In Savannah everyone is Irish on St. Pat's, and even the public schools close for the celebration. We set out for the first of a round of parties, a breakfast in a row house on Gordon Street.

"Look, Bubba," I whispered as our plates were served, "the grits are green."

"Well, sugar, so are the scrambled eggs, the biscuits, and even the butter," he said handing me a Bloody Mary. "Let's fix a to go cup and watch the parade," Bubba added, steering me out the front door. He poured our drinks into green plastic cups. Bubba seemed to need the sustenance of a drink to get from one destination to another. In fact, most of the people in Savannah made their way, after working hours, from one destination to the other with the assistance of that cup.

As we walked through Chippewa Square to watch the huge parade, he pointed to a stately house. Bubba rambled on about a true Southern Gothic tale that I only half heard. I was too busy counting the For Sale signs in the Historic District as we walked toward the next party.

"The fellow got involved with a nightclub singer who was the mistress to Willie Somebody, the gambling czar of Tybee Island. When old Willie discovered that his beloved singer was cheating on him with none other than Ansley, he had his henchmen cut off old Ansley's balls. And then when Ansley's mother answered the doorbell, guess what? They threw his testicles in her front hall." Bubba laughed as if that was the funniest thing he'd ever heard. "What do you think of that?"

"I think if the queen had balls, she'd be king," I said, grabbing his arm and guiding him across the street, through the throngs of people lined up to see the parade. After the parade, as we finally were heading back to my house, we passed the prestigious Oglethorpe Club, the elite private club for business men only. Women were accepted in the dining room for lunch and dinner. They had to sign their husband's name on the bill. Debutantes were regaled there at parties, and it was often used for wedding receptions.

"You know Griffin Bell resigned as a member of this club because it discriminates against Jews and Blacks," I said, recalling all the hoopla during his appointment as Attorney General while Jimmy Carter was president.

"Yeah, sugar," Bubba said, "and he rejoined the club as soon as he resigned from the Carter Administration." Racial and religious prejudice had not disappeared, it had only temporarily gone underground.

That afternoon we went to another big party, this time a political bash being given by the tax commissioner, a woman I had helped to gain political office. She wielded more influence in Chatham county than most men, but at heart, I discovered she was another frightened little girl. Many nights she would call me, crying, hurt by the bullies she had to deal with on a daily basis. That fact alone made me glad that I hadn't won the Senate race, in the long run. More and more, I saw how phony and hypocritical those in elected positions were.

The crowd at the party was a curious mix. Savannah's political structure was diverse to say the least. I introduced Bubba to the police chief, who was Jewish and married to a Chinese woman. On top of that, the assistant police chief was an Afro-American who had converted to Judaism. And the mayor was Greek — all of which made Savannah different from the white bread and mayonnaise ambiance of many Southern cities. We ended the day at the riverfront, where Bubba and I watched the last of the Savannah River flow out to sea, with its waters colored green for the day.

I began to love Bubba despite the fact that he was fat, sloppy, and a premature ejaculator. In fact, I turned his shortcomings into endearing qualities. I decided he was exactly what I needed at the time: a combination of maleness, flabby breasts, and soft, comforting girth. I was sinking, and Bubba was my life raft, bobbing across my sea of troubles. He was good in bed, sleeping.

I had always hungered for a man who was both gifted with endurance and comfortable once the lights were out and the eyes were closed. Bubba filled the latter need: he didn't snore. Crowded close to him, nestling my head against his broad, chubby frame, my fears of tomorrow were lessened by his protective presence. I was caught up in the worship of illusion. The illusion of what we expected life with a man to become.

But that didn't change the fact that he was still a good ol' boy who, for many people in other parts of America, epitomized the white male Southerner. Beckie teased me about falling for a good ol' boy.

"Listen, Beckie, if you take the sequins off every singing plowboy in Nashville, all you've got left are good ol' boys," I said over dinner one night, as we cracked crab claws with a wooden mallet.

"You know Jimmy Carter wasn't a good ol' boy, but Jody Powell and Hamilton Jordan were. So's Joe Namath, even though he's from Pennsylvania and models pantyhose. Lyndon Johnson certainly was. Hubert Humphrey sometimes tried to be. Franklin Roosevelt wasn't, but he was the sort of man good ol' boys look up to." Beckie giggled wildly as she explained her point of view to me.

"A good ol' boy drinks his Bud from a can, listens to Willie Nelson and cries, likes to kick ass, and nuzzling up to the unattached woman at the bar, complains that the old lady, who is at home, barefoot, pregnant and cooking a supper that her old man will be late sitting down to, doesn't appreciate him," I said, further defining the Southern phenomena. Beckie and I drank another beer, and got sillier and sillier as we continued to describe our versions of southern manhood.

"Let me tell you, he drives too fast, spits a lot, and likes his mama. No finer man than his daddy ever lived, he will tell you, but his mama was a saint. A good ol' boy won't let his sons play with dolls or his daughters with footballs. He'd rather be with his buddies than any woman alive, but he'd crack your head open with a beer bottle if you hinted anything was funny about him.

Sex is wham bam thank you ma'am. And when he rolls off, sucking his teeth, he'll ask you if it was good for you, too. A good ol' boy'll do anything in the world for you — except go out of his way to make you happy. Feelings scare him. Emotions embarrass him. A soft heart

233

spells weakness." When I finished that monologue I shoved a hunk of lump crab meat into my mouth.

"As far as I'm concerned, a good ol' boy's mostly *boy* and rarely all that *good.* Usually what he lacks in heart he makes up in protruding gut," Beckie said. She slapped the table and raised her hand into a fist over her head.

Not to be outdone, I added, "And space between his ears."

Later that week Bill phoned and asked me to drive to Hilton Head with him for dinner on Saturday night. I accepted but didn't feel good about doing so. Just hearing his voice brought up enough guilt to flood my body.

"I always hoped we'd ride into the sunset together. I wanted us to be together at the end our lives, as husband and wife. Is there still a chance for that to happen?" Bill said, as he piloted his Jaguar down the oak-lined road toward the island. I knew the evening was all wrong.

"I wanted that, too." I leaned my head against the window.

"Why did you stop loving me?"

"I needed to learn to love myself and I don't know how." I was finally being honest with him.

"I'm so lonely without you, Naomi."

"Please, stop. You make me feel like I'm supposed to stay in the shallow end of the swimming pool for the rest of my life."

Yet something inside of me remained broken. I felt guilty each time I looked at Bill's sad profile above the steering wheel and was unable to shake off my regrets that we hadn't tried harder to make our marriage work. Even over dinner we couldn't relax and just be friends. The pain was too new, too fresh. As he badgered me for reasons for our broken marriage, all of my old resentments spilled out.

"You and my mother, neither of you ever cared about me! No one ever asked why I hurt," I said. "Nobody gives a damn about me. I never had any encouragement from either of you," I added bitterly, then looked up into his eyes, stopped short by the melancholy I saw there.

"I thought I gave you everything you wanted. I tried, I really did," he said gently.

"Bill," I said softly, patiently, "you've never listened to a thing I've said. I might as well be talking to the wind."

Tears stood in his eyes. Grabbing my napkin, feeling a desperation

I didn't think I could bear, I rushed to the ladies' room. When I had regained enough composure to return to the table, I found Bill standing beside his chair; he had already paid the check. Silently, we rode the dark forty-five minutes back toward Savannah. As Bill pulled up in front of my house I jumped out of the car murmuring a shaky good night.

"Just a minute, Naomi." Bill called me back to the side of the car.

"What is it?"

"I want you to know that the absolute worst fuck I've ever had in my entire life was Andrea." He smiled sheepishly. I wondered if he was trying to get even, but even so, I found it shocking and unbelievable that they would have had a sexual liaison.

"When? Where?"

"In our bed, just after you two came home from that Bahama trip." He started the ignition and drove away. It was hard for me to believe that Andrea could have remained my best friend throughout the years and kept that from me. She usually took my side in any argument concerning Bill. What A.D. had said about her disloyalty rung in my head. I unlocked the back gate, and slowly, heavily, climbed the stairs to my house.

On the days when I felt the ball of fear heaviest in my stomach, I would say to Beckie, "Perhaps I should have stayed married to Bill. If I had persevered, I could have overcome my boredom and wouldn't be so uncertain about myself and confused about my life." I was getting good at blaming myself for everything that went wrong.

One such day, while visiting Andrea, I looked at her sitting across from me, wearing her familiar shirtwaist dress and pearls She was still captive in her rigid, loveless marriage, afraid to upset her position with the Savannah social structure. Her house was filled with expensive antiques. She had heirlooms from her family in addition to what she regularly collected. She shopped endlessly for clothes and antiques. Needlepoint pillows that she had carefully crafted were lined up on every chair and sofa.

Andrea set out a silver tray with chicken salad sandwiches for lunch. They were cut diagonally and the crust was trimmed. Then she handed me a cup of coffee in a Haviland cup. I had decided not to bring up her one night stand with Bill. Not just yet anyway. Sometimes I wondered if Bill had been making it up. I didn't want to be like Andrea, with her afternoon lovers, lies, and hypocrisies. Now that I was past fifty, I wasn't sure which part of the old Naomi was going to survive.

I had my business, lots of friends, and I even had something to call a lover. But something inside of me told me that the substance of my existence wasn't thick enough to stretch out and carry me through the rest of my life. I wanted to feel that what I did with my life would be important enough to me so that I wouldn't see myself as a throwaway person just because I was getting older.

Beckie recommended a psychologist, David Willis, someone she knew and trusted.

"Is it an emergency?" he had asked when I called him.

"Yes, my life is one huge emergency." We made an appointment for that very afternoon and I hung up the receiver with relief.

I liked his boyish face and graying hair. David smiled and invited me to have a seat on his sofa. He said nothing, just waited. David Willis had the kind of warm male strength that made me think that only a man had the power or knowledge to make things better in my life. Be it Doctor, Daddy, or God.

"Do you know who I am?" I didn't know what made me ask him that. I suppose on some level it was a question that I was asking myself.

"Yes, I've heard of you," David said.

Sinking into the deep maroon couch I began my soliloquy: "I'm tired of emptying my guts to men, tired of being taken by them. I've been to a psychiatrist before. He fucked me. Literally."

Tears began to roll down my cheeks and I reached for a tissue from the box on the table next to me. "I'm recently divorced, my mother died a year ago, my oldest son died of a brain tumor when he was not yet fifteen. I had a love affair for fifteen years with a married man who promised to marry me but didn't. I had an abortion. I felt married to two men at once. Now I'm trying to get over a love affair that ended badly and my business is driving me crazy."

I heard my voice weakening, running down. "I feel as though I'm stuck in a revolving door. Every time I try to step out, the door slams me back again." I gave a final gasp. "I'm tired. Oh God, so tired."

David held his hand up like a traffic cop, motioning for me to stop. He shuffled his feet as though applying brakes in his car.

"Just a minute, woman," he exclaimed, "you've only been in my office for twenty minutes and I'm already tired, too."

I looked up at him in surprise and with a touch of relief.

"How many people do you think, especially women, have done and achieved what you have?" he asked. The question caught me off guard. Me, a success? I had never thought of myself in those terms. I had thought of myself only as the appendage to a successful husband, and as an ultimately rejected lover, and an irritating and embarrassing daughter.

"Do you really, honestly, want to make changes in your life?" David fixed his eyes on me.

"Yes! Very much!"

"Naomi," David said, in a kind firm voice, "I can invite you to change, offer you help with change, but you will have to do the work. It won't be easy."

At that moment David's words had no practical meaning for me, but I clung to them as if they were a mantra, and they registered somewhere deep inside my brain.

"You can pretend that I'm on your shoulder if you ever have the need to talk to someone," David said with a quick smile.

"I would like to not make decisions for a while in my life," I told him. "I've always been the one to take charge. I'm tired. My husband left all the responsibilities of raising our sons to me. I was the one that made the family work. It's as though I pulled the plug and a family died. I feel that it's my fault for not having a family. I miss having family. But I'm too tired to do the work. If only one of them would hear me, be here to comfort me, it would help so much. But I can't count on any of them."

Unlike Dr. Grant, David was effective and came to have a tremendous influence on my life. Self-awareness had eluded me until then. It would, I decided, elude me no longer.

We decided on a weekly schedule of one hour, every Thursday afternoon, at four o'clock. It became the most important hour of my week. Many days I felt terribly fragile and confused. When that happened I would call David and he would see me in between our Thursday sessions.

I told Beckie how pleased I was with my therapist and that I felt as though I was looking at somebody else's life when I talked about my childhood. I even suggested that she start seeing him, just on general principle.

By now Bubba and I were spending nearly every weekend together. One particular Sunday evening he was taking me to a party at the Savannah Golf Club and later we decided to spend the night in his apartment. I loved his place. It had a Greenwich Village charm about it, with a small courtyard beyond the double glass French doors of his bedroom. I felt safe there, a womblike safety, in his dark rooms. He held me close when we were in bed, as if I were his child. Next morning, he leaped from bed, whistling and happy.

"Just stay in bed today, sugar. Don't get up." Bubba said as he brought me a cup of fresh coffee. He looked handsome in his pale blue sports jacket.

"Bubba, my car's in the shop," I said. "How will I get home?"

"Use mine. I'll walk to my office." He dashed to the kitchen for more coffee. Bubba always seemed to be rushing no matter what he was doing. "You know you can use anything I own," he said, coming back into the bedroom.

I, teasingly, reminded him that he wouldn't let me use his steam iron when mine had broken. He was adamant about not lending this precious appliance of his. I had never known a man who did ironing before and I liked that about him. But Bubba could be cheap at times, wanting to spend money only on things that he thought important.

He hated expensive restaurants, yet he believed in buying the most expensive whisky and the best grade of toilet paper. His answers were his typical ones, though they made no sense to me. "Well, hell, I ain't going to put rot gut in my belly," he'd yell. Or, "I sure ain't gonna wipe my ass with cheap paper that cuts."

As I bustled about my own kitchen that afternoon, my front doorbell rang. It was Todd, Bubba's fourteen year old son. He had seen his father's car at my house, and thinking his dad was there, stopped by. As he licked peanut butter and jelly from his fingers, after finishing the sandwich I had made for him, he telephoned Bubba. The Bubba who arrived a half hour later was very different from the sweet, gentle man that had served me coffee in bed that morning.

"Why the hell did you have to stop here, Todd?"

"I saw your car," the boy said. He looked at his father in a curious way, wondering what he did that might be wrong.

"Naomi, couldn't you have given him a ride for Christ's sake?"

"What's the matter with you?" I said after Todd ran down the steps.

"My damned ex gave me a ration of shit, just like all women do." He explained that he had talked to her that day about a bill she wanted him to pay. It angered me that after six years as a divorced man Bubba still let the woman manipulate him.

She was the typical spoiled Southern belle, graduated into the role of nagging wife, constantly blaming Bubba for what went wrong in her unfulfilled life. During my next session with David I realized I had done the same thing in my marriage: when I had been dissatisfied with life, unable to create change, I blamed Bill. I began to realize that Bubba's ex-wife wasn't the only one who had a lot of growing up to do.

Chapter Thirty Two

It wasn't long before Bubba's misplaced anger began to spoil our time together. Sometime I would feel like a yo-yo on his string. After every intimate hour, he withdrew. It hurt when he left after we made love, when he didn't call, when he treated me like his lover one day, and as a nuisance the next. I was beginning to reel from his off-again-on-again behavior, never knowing what to expect and unable to communicate with him about it.

In David's office, I asked for help.

"It's not like a Chinese menu, Naomi," he said. "You don't get to choose one from column A and one from column B. Bubba comes with all of his stuff, and that means his ties to his ex-wife, his sons, and whatever baggage he hasn't dealt with from his childhood. He's gotten used to having his wife lash out at him, it's familiar, something he understands."

"Well, why the hell did she leave him? They were perfect for each other," I said sarcastically. And hadn't a number of my friends posed the same question to me about my divorce.

David urged me to pay attention to the things I wanted to change about Bubba, as an indication of what I really needed to change in myself. Some of it was beginning to make sense.

"Every time he pushes your buttons, Naomi, that's a clear sign that something inside of you needs change. Otherwise, it wouldn't bother you so much."

"I feel so much resentment," I said. "I should stop seeing Bubba. I know that. When I leave here I feel strong and ready to break up with him, but when I get home and start to feel lonely, I want him."

"Have options," David advised. "Life isn't an either/or situation. If you have options, you haven't failed if one of them doesn't materialize. You still have others to choose from."

I looked at him, puzzled. I didn't understand a thing he had said. When I left his office I felt more tired than I had in years. But my obsession didn't end in David's office.

"Tell me what to do about Bubba," I asked Cal when I called to get reassurance from my friend.

"Naomi, darling, I'm on the sun porch having a Bloody. It's a beautiful windy evening. There just ain't no time in my life for dear old *Blubber*. He works hard at being a son of a bitch. Will you please forget that ass!" But of course I didn't listen to Cal.

Not satisfied with Cal's assessment, I phoned Ruth in Atlanta, who said, "Men just don't change." Ruth had been struggling through some of her own crises. She had changed jobs several times and had given up smoking three months earlier. .

"What do you miss most about smoking?"

"Everything. I miss going to the store and buying the cigarettes, then opening the pack. I miss pulling out the cigarette and tapping it against my finger. I miss putting it in my mouth, lighting it and drawing the smoke down as far as it will go. And there ain't nothing in the world like a cigarette with a cup of coffee." I was proud of her; she never smoked again in her life.

My last call was to Beckie, who proved to be a better listener and didn't lash out at me. "Go out with other men. Sounds like Bubba's afraid of a real relationship. There's nothing you're doing wrong, you just need to find someone who's not afraid to love you."

I knew Beckie had hit upon the truth but there was still a part of me that believed I could seduce Bubba into changing. It was as though I had forgotten David's words. He had said to me one day in his office, "Remember, Naomi, insanity is going back again and again to the same thing or the same person and thinking it will change."

But I felt there was no better way to entice Bubba to change than with a five course dinner. To celebrate his forty-sixth birthday, I invited some of his friends from The Savannah Golf Club over for dinner. Bubba had a habit of arriving late. He, of course, arrived late.

But when he kissed me and told me that the food smelled delicious, and how happy I made him, I melted. He put on the tape from *A Chorus Line* and whirled me around the floor to the tune of *Kiss The Day Goodbye*. Inside I glowed, relinquishing every doubt about Bubba, eating up his warm, generous words.

I took pride in the rare standing rib roast cooked to perfection. I placed it before him to carve. The eight guests seated around my dining room table were happily anticipating the evening's celebration.

"Bubba, please pour me another glass of wine," I said, as I put the silver Tiffany ice bucket on a serving trolley next to him.

"Woman, you're pushy! You've got a handful of gimmee and a mouthful of much obliged." He scooped up a spoonful of caviar as though it was peanut butter. Still, it was obvious he enjoyed staying at my home, presiding over a fine dinner party. With Bubba, male supremacy was a set piece. With Bubba, I stayed confused.

And though I prided myself on being a liberated woman, totally independent, I still subconsciously succumbed to that pernicious fiction of the South, that men were the superior sex. Yet if anyone accused me of needing a man I would have been the first to deny it.

Back on David's couch, still frustrated, I asked, "Why am I hanging on to that ox?"

"Why do you think?" David always encouraged me to find my own answers.

"Well, for one thing, he's familiar. Familiar's safe. But I've been dreaming a lot of moving away. For years I've thought of living in New York. I have a whole network of fascinating people there.

"I've heard you say over and over that you want change in your life. But some people have to hang on to their neurotic needs until they're totally finished. The time frame is different for each of us. It takes what it takes to be done with the old, Naomi. And Bubba definitely scratches your itch.

I suggest you hang in there. Sometimes it's two or three steps backward and only one step forward. Sort of like dancing the cha cha."

But I wasn't patient; I wanted things to happen immediately. I had been that way all of my life. That was what made me a good real estate salesperson. I persevered.

"Why don't you put Bubba on a back burner while you decide what it is you want to do and where it is you want to move?"

"I don't have a back burner. All of mine are at full blast." David looked at me with a startled glance. Yet, I knew that inside of myself was a dormant energy, one that had been held captive for a very long time. How possible would it be for a woman my age to go back and capture some of my dreams? Could I do it?

"You know you can do anything you decide to do," David said with a loving smile. "Let's just hope to God you don't decide to become a brain surgeon."

Closing my office would be extremely hard, that much I knew. Not only was I an employer, I had also become a surrogate mother to many of my sales agents. When I discussed my ideas about moving away and shutting down the company at my weekly office meeting I immediately sensed the staff's fear and tension

"Just remember they're afraid, too," David said. "They're like children whose mother is deserting them."

In need of some loving support, I called Bubba. Rarely did he call me. He responded warmly to my voice.

"I love you, Bubba. I need to be with you tonight."

"You do? Do you want to jump my bones again?" Sometimes it pleased him to say we could never have more than what we had.

"My children will always come first," Bubba said on more than a dozen occasions. On others, he said that I was Jewish, he was not, or that he was gun shy about commitments and constantly pleaded lack of money since the failure of his marriage. And he'd always manage to drift out of my life for days at a time after a night of especially romantic intimacy.

He wouldn't call, he wouldn't take my calls. Savannah is a small city, and I would see his car parked outside one of his drinking haunts. I'd go in and Bubba would do his glad-to-see-you routine, as if I were no more than a casual friend, like a woman he took to lunch occasionally.

Later, when I walked into Cal's office and sank into the chair opposite his desk he knew what was on my mind. He pretended not to notice me; he tried every thing he could think of to keep me from mentioning Bubba's name. But it didn't work.

"Maybe he's a closet gay," I suggested.

"Don't try to dump him on our team," Cal said and continued to scribble on the paper on his desk. "Stuff his fat ass back in the closet. We don't want him."

Surprisingly, Bubba did come over that night. He asked why I needed him. He had even preempted a gin rummy game to be with me. "Why in the world would you want to close a good business?" he said. My excitement at the thought of shutting it down and moving away from Savannah struck Bubba as completely ridiculous. He mixed himself a drink and settled into the suede sofa. I sat at the opposite end, kicked off my shoes and put my feet in Bubba's lap.

"I've dreamed of living somewhere other than Savannah all my life. Haven't you ever dreamed of moving away?" I even wondered for a mad moment if I might ask him to move with me.

"That's bullshit! I haven't lost anything in any other city," he said.

However, contentment engulfed me that night as I snuggled with Bubba under my blue down comforter. I whispered, "Bubba, isn't this cozy? Do you love me?"

He held me closer. "You know I love you, sugar. I'm not in love with you. I love you like a person."

"A person! For Christ's sakes, Bubba, I didn't expect you to love me like a fucking vacuum cleaner!" I threw my pillow over his head.

Bubba laughed, put his arms around me and said, "Come over here, little Hoover."

"Bubba," I said softly, trying again, "do you want this relationship to work?"

"Huh? We don't have any relationship," he answered.

"Jesus, Cal is right! You are an ass. You are the asshole of all assholes, you are CEO of Assholes of America. No, make that the world." I grabbed the pillow and went into the guest bedroom for the rest of that night.

Chapter Thirty Three

The next weekend Andrea invited Bubba and me to her Tybee Beach cottage for lunch. An old fashioned house, surrounded by huge screened porches facing the ocean, it had been in Andrea's family for many years. She loved to cook and Bubba loved to eat. As we were finishing the bowl of sliced fresh figs, swimming in sweet cream, I noticed Andrea begin to rub her hand across the back of Bubba's chubby neck. It made me queasy. Later I went down to the beach, to wade at the edge of the water.

Staring out at the sea always gave me a sense of comfort. I sat listening to the gulls sing as they swooped down on the white sand. Sailboats drifted lazily by. The smell of the sea, the sounds of the birds, and the rolling tides gave me a feeling of renewal. The moon had just come out and cast a glow across the sand. When I returned to the house I saw Andrea dash across the living room, nude. Bubba took his time coming out of the bedroom.

"I can't believe what I'm seeing," I said.

"You didn't see anything," Andrea said.

When Andrea came back into the room I could no longer contain the past incidents. I stared at her in shocked rage. "You betrayed me with my husband and now you want to do it with Bubba?" I didn't mention that A.D. had told me about the time she had come on to him.

"Are you that damned insecure?" Andrea asked, tying a terry cloth robe around herself.

"Yes," I said. "But this isn't just about insecurity. You seem to be insensitive to my feelings by wanting every man in my life." It felt like a major step for me to be able to say the truth about my feelings.

Andrea's betrayal shattered me, even though I'd known about her past behavior. But so did Bubba's. He wasn't behaving any better. In the flick of an instant I knew I didn't need either one of them in my life.

I also realized there was no need for me to get upset at the thought of losing them because what they had shown me wasn't my definition of friendship.

"Andrea, I think it would be best for both of us if you transfer your real estate license to another office," I said when I phoned her the next morning.

"I've already contacted two or three brokers," she said defensively. Then, as though she were berating one of her children, she shouted, "Just remember, Naomi, you've made your bed and you'll have to lie in it. Don't ever call me again!"

I shook my head and hung up the telephone. A.D.'s words were ringing in my head: "Remember, baby, the best defense is a good offense."

A week or so after that incident I began having vivid and disturbing dreams. One was of an avocado which I opened, then closed. Inside was a strange fetal object. I asked David what this meant.

"It sounds like an undeveloped species, perhaps a fetus," he said. I thought it might be myself.

In another dream I was in a hospital. Bill stood at the foot of my bed. Attached to my wrist was a leech. I begged Bill to remove it. It hurt. He would not. "Call a nurse," I begged.

David said I was still looking to my former husband for help.

The next dream was very alarming. I was opening a bottom drawer which was empty. I tried to crawl inside and stretch out. It was an impossible task. I had removed from the drawer all of my mother's things, things she had left, to clear the space for myself to lie down.

"Was I trying to get into my mother's coffin?" I asked David.

"It sounds more like you've been removing the sense of guilt for the failure you thought you were in your mother's eyes. Perhaps your drawer filled with guilt is now empty." David smiled.

"David, I'm tired of toting that two hundred forty pound Bubba ox around. Do you think I've been clinging to him because I'm actually afraid to let go of my own childish behavior? When he comes over he parks that damned broken-down truck in my garage as though he owns

246

my house."

"What? You didn't tell me that he drives a truck! You need to find a man with a Porsche, woman." David also told me that he thought it wise for me to see Bubba, that he was perhaps the best homework assignment I could have. "Obsession is a wild and defining force. Remember, Naomi, like fire, it can forge or destroy. The line between the two is thin."

Ironically, my son Ross gave me an insight into Bubba's refusal to grow up during one of our Atlanta/Savannah telephone conversations. It infuriated me that Ross always chose to see situations through Bubba's eyes.

"Do you ever want a mature relationship?" I yelled at him, bursting into anger.

"Well, what am I supposed to do," Ross said, "put an ad in the *Atlanta Journal*, saying I'm now ready for a mature relationship, it doesn't matter if the girl looks like shit, just be mature? Is that what you expect?"

"Darling, I think you ought to be mature first."

"Well, I sure don't want to get old and stale," Ross said.

"Ross, boyish fun can get stale," I said. "Sometimes it's painful to grow up, but pain's part of the process." Perhaps anatomy is destiny, I thought. Women have owned the childbirth pain which has taught them to survive. They somehow know that at the end of pain something beautiful is born.

To decompress, Cal and I went dancing at the Who's Who, a gay disco on Bay Street. I figured I could shake off Bubba and what he meant in my life. Cal and I had gone there after the opening performance of the Savannah Symphony. The music blared, the habitues of the place were having a wild time, laughing just to laugh, throwing off demons on the dance floor, giving the African rhythms as much unrestrained feral movement as whites can.

I threw myself into the dance, trying to free myself of the frustration I had felt ever since I had gotten involved with Bubba. Past midnight, I pulled off my skirt and danced in my long, white angora sweater, which ended just above my knees. The dancers passed vials of amyl nitrate from one to the other, taking in deep whiffs and sparking their energy to the frenzy level.

Later that night, after Cal and I had consumed half a bottle of Russian vodka, I decided to pay Bubba a visit. I took the bottle with me and drove to Bubba's house. I slammed it against the glass French doors off of his bedroom, breaking out a small pane. It was then easy to open the latch.

Bubba, scared out of his wits, looked at my wild eyes, the smashed bottle in my hand, and jumped up out of his bed. "You're out of your fucking mind, woman!" he shouted. He grabbed my wrists.

"Hallelujah, Bubba, you finally got something right!"

Bubba grabbed my arms, dragging me to the front door of his apartment, screaming, "Get out of here!"

"Bubba, my mother told me to tell you something."

"I thought your mother was dead."

"So what! She still has something for me to tell you." I giggled.

"What?"

"She told me to tell you that you ain't a *mensch*!" He threw the rest of the bottle of vodka on the sidewalk in front of his building. When he released me, I dashed to my car and drove home. In the morning, I woke up sore and bruised and hung over.

Riding out to the beach alone that afternoon, I said aloud, "Goodbye, little girl. You've had your way long enough. The rest of my life will be lived without your childish manipulation."

The words seemed to be coming from the mouth of another person, to float around my head. Yet, as I drove the car up the sand access road to the ocean's edge, cut off the ignition, and sat looking out over the dunes to the sea, I suddenly felt a vast sense of relief. As vast as the ocean itself.

That night I dreamed that Bubba and I were lying in my bed and I heard a strange noise downstairs. I shook Bubba, but he didn't wake up. I heard two people talking inside my house. They weren't trying to hide. They came up to the bedroom, and the woman, stylish and beautiful, acted very friendly. The man looked like Warren Beatty, the movie star. The woman insisted on having sex with me. I could actually experience sex with a woman; the dream was that real. Although I had not been turned on sexually, neither was I repulsed.

Then came the horror part of the dream. Bubba and I were forced at gun point to go downstairs. The couple feigned friendliness as they took all of my sterling silver, the art collection, and many of my antiques — everything that I considered valuable.

The man then suggested Bubba have sex with him. Bubba refused, then just sat and stared in bewilderment. The man said he'd have to kill us both because we might identify him. I begged him to spare our lives. Bubba continued to stare dumbly. Both of us were shot. My body was riddled with bullets. Blood poured from me.

Near the end of the dream, I read a newspaper article about my own murder. Next to it was a photograph of Bubba sitting on the sidewalk, unable to speak, slack-jawed. He was leaning against a building; it was the bakery that had been next door to the apartment where Bill and I lived when Isaac and Alex were born.

I shot up in bed, pains in every place where the bullets penetrated in the dream. I automatically dialed Bubba.

"Bubba!"

Before I said another word, he answered, "Yes, Naomi, I love you." Then he dropped the telephone and passed out, drunk.

"Bubba, listen! I've just had the most awful nightmare!" But he was gone. The phone hung off the receiver to the floor next to his bed.

I phoned Cal. From my voice he knew how frightened I was. Cal told me to come over to his house. I put on a robe, dashed through my backyard, and into my car. When I arrived at his house, Cal hugged me. As he led me to the four-poster bed in his guest room, he handed me a yellow legal pad and a pen, suggesting that I make notes of any further dreams. I finally slept peacefully through the rest of the night.

The next afternoon I sat across from David in his office, drained and weak.

"You've been dealing with an emotional midget," the therapist said. "Did you expect a cripple to run? Bubba is a cripple." He said he had no doubt that Bubba loved me. "The trouble is Bubba himself doesn't know how much he really loves you. It scares the hell out of him."

I reached for a tissue. The sadness I was feeling was for the many times I hadn't known what was happening in my own life. And for the reality of acknowledging how I continually fell in love with immature men, always wanting to save them. Also for the truth, that I could have never saved my father. I was finally facing my inner grief, grief for an unfinished childhood.

"Let's make your life easier," David said in a gentle voice. "Stop being so hard on yourself. Get some rest. I'm here whenever you need me."

A year of rapid change had left me weary. The exploration of my feelings, and making changes had been interesting, but I longed for peace. In business I had made quick decisions. Yet, in my personal life I approached change with panic. I listened as David explained.

"A sane person always criticizes herself but she has to be careful that self-contempt doesn't take charge. I want you to remember those words."

Chapter Thirty Four

One October afternoon in 1981, a woman reporter from the *Philadelphia Inquirer* called me at my office and asked me for an interview. She was writing a piece about Southern women and their views on feminism. Several people had suggested she interview me. She had just finished reviewing a book by Mary Anne Dexter, on the subject of suppressed women in the South.

The minute she asked me what the feminist movement had been like in Savannah during its height, I replied without a pause, "You're looking at it." I told her I had fought for myself and other women, both in politics and in the real estate business. I hadn't wanted the lifestyle of most women my age — the comfortable stay-at-home lives that provided safety and convenience.

"Do you know Mary Anne?" the reporter asked. She was referring to the author who had recently moved to Savannah and whose poetry I had read and enjoyed. "You two should meet. You have such similar views about life and how women have fared in the South. Why don't we all meet tonight over a bottle of wine?"

"Feel free to come over to my house," I said. I hungered for interesting people in my life and in my home.

That night the three of us talked for hours. Mary Anne lived only a few blocks away in a small bohemian apartment and was working on a novel. She offered me a new kind of friendship, one where women are really supportive of each other. Listening became a new habit. Listening wholeheartedly was not a part of my family history. Mary Anne instilled trust once more in the bond of friendship.

Later that week, I sat in my office watching the familiar sight of leaves dropping from trees in my backyard, and once more dreamed of being away from the familiarity and starting anew. I would never be with another man like Bubba, who too many times had complained I was oversexed. He had accused me of being too aggressive when all I had done was stop being submissive. It was time to start taking charge of my own sexuality, my own life. With Mary Anne, it was possible to discuss desire and sexuality. It was a giant hurdle toward my quest for total independence.

Often Beckie joined me for dinner with Mary Ann. One night when she came to my house, just before we headed toward River Street, she said she needed to talk to me alone.

"Well, you sure won't believe what I have to tell you," Beckie said with a startled tone in her voice. "My father's a bigamist."

She had just found out that during the last few years of her parents' long marriage, he had been married to another woman. Beckie was extremely shaken and had decided that she was going to leave Savannah and the lie of her parents' lives. Indeed, she had called that very afternoon for an application to Columbia University. As Beckie made plans to get a fellowship, I felt ashamed that for over twenty-five years I had wanted to leave Savannah. Now my friend had the courage that I could never find. What was that strange tie that had kept me bound to this city.

"I don't understand how anyone can go on living in the same place generation after generation," Beckie said.

With Mary Anne I had found a friend who heard what I said and was sympathetic to my feelings. Once when I told her about Bubba, how I felt that he might have been my last chance to have a man in my life, and how scared that made me feel, she took my hand and smiled.

"Naomi, I've found that dating other men is a great way to get over a disappointing relationship." Mary Anne's voice was soft and tender. "Besides, you're too good for him. You know, you could look at him as another house that you've restored. If you don't like it just get rid of it. Or sell it as an FHA repossession." Her remark softened the mood and I broke into laughter.

I told her about the bumper sticker on the back of Bubba's car that says *How 'Bout Them Dawgs!* It was a reference to the University of Georgia's football team, and its official mascot, a bulldog named Uga.

"Naomi, if that's the extent of Bubba's self-identity, I'd think twice about the man and his goofy bumper sticker."

"What's wrong with me?" I felt his shortcomings were my fault.

"It bothers me that women always think there's something wrong with them when things go wrong," Mary Anne said. "One night stands are good enough for me. I have my days free to write and I can pick and choose at night. It's like a sexual smorgasbord." She seemed to cherish her apartment alone, after three failed marriages.

During a restless night, a night of tossing and turning, I dreamed of Isaac. He seemed so small and alone, yet peaceful. It became clear that one of the reasons I hadn't left Savannah was my fear that I might be deserting him. It took me a while to understand that my love for Isaac would always be in my heart. There can be new loves, or different loves, and other kinds of love. But in the summation of it all, I had to finally learn to live with that deep and ·lingering loss. There would forever be scar tissue across my heart.

Chapter Thirty Five

Not only was I changing, the world around me was also. Once I thought men were strong, but now many of them ran away from the togetherness I'd always dreamed of, to homosexuality, impotence, booze, or all three. The men in my hometown seemed afraid when Southern women came of age. My growth into womanhood was leaving me less and less of a choice for a mate.

Ever since I had started jogging forty-five minutes down to the riverfront and home again every morning, I felt an immediate and almost scary sense of physical relief. I began to sense freedom in a way I'd never felt before. It was on such a morning that I arrived home and found a message from Fern on my answering machine.

"Girl, where in the world are you at the crack of dawn? I thought I'd find you lolling over coffee and the newspaper. Please call." She had left a number. When I caught up with her she was at her sister's house.

That night, Fern came to visit and we talked for hours. She was now living in Orlando, and working for the federal government in an agency connected with the space program. Fern had become a born again Christian; she was, heart-and-soul, a child of the church. They even talked in tongues at her congregation. At the end of almost every subject we discussed, she espoused a quote from either Matthew, Luke or John.

"What about your sex life, Fern?"

"I've given up sex. It leads toward violence," she said.

"I don't think sex and violence are necessarily one and the same."

"The bible says it's immoral to sleep with someone if you're not married. From my experience, that turned out to be true."

"Well, then I must confess, I'm immoral," I said smiling at Fern.

But Fern quickly changed the subject and asked, "Are you sorry that you divorced Bill?"

I thought about her question for a few moments before answering. "Sometimes I really wish it had worked. The fantasy of growing old together grabs at my heart. But I'm glad to be on my own. It's something I needed in my life. Yes, I'm quite clear."

Occasionally I would bump into Bill at a party or out at a restaurant. He always seemed uncomfortable when we met. Once when I had been at a dinner party with Bubba, Bill had walked up to me and extended his hand, in a business acquaintance kind of handshake. I felt like one of his constituents. It was obvious that Bill and I weren't going to have a friendship. Perhaps if we had been good friends, we would have still been married.

It had been a few years since I'd seen A.D. Our phone calls had also stopped, but I'd heard that he was quite ill. On the phone, just after his heart attack, he told me that he had left his law practice and that he was scared to be alone. Nurses had been hired to stay at night. He not only had high blood pressure, he was also diabetic, and had been in the hospital. I suddenly wanted to see him, to know what was happening with this person who had played such an important role in my life. I was forever trying to tie life into neat little packages.

While on a shopping trip to Atlanta with Cal, he urged me to stop wondering about A.D. "Just call him and we'll pay him a short visit." Cal wanted to meet the man that I had talked so much about. A.D. asked us to his house late in the afternoon. When we arrived, pulling up to the rear of his garage, Cal parked his van behind A.D.'s chocolate brown Rolls Royce. We had come in Cal's faded white van so he could load a recently purchased antique dining table. Next to the Rolls was a brand new red Cadillac Seville. But both cars were seldom driven by their owner. I rang the back doorbell.

A.D. greeted us, clad in blue silk pajamas, a robe, and slippers at four in the afternoon. My former knight in shining armor was now a tired, sick old man. He shuffled across the floor of his musty library and took us into the living room. The heavy drapes were pulled shut and the room was dark and eerie. Stacks of old newspapers littered the floor.

When he spoke there was no doubt that his mind was as keen as it had always been. Only his spirit had died. But the sight of him shocked me. His health was failing fast.

"Mazik," he said, "you know where everything is, why don't you fix a drink?" As he rose to pour himself a glass of water he peered out his kitchen window and saw Cal's van.

"What's that crazy thing you're riding in, baby?"

"Well, when you abandoned me, I just had to give up all the good things in life." It was a feeble attempt at being witty.

"That's foolish talk," he said. His eyes looked sad, lonely, and desperate.

"Why did you let me down?" I asked. There was no anger in my voice, nor had I planned to say that.

"I never meant to hurt you," he said in a hushed whisper. Tears formed in his small, glassy eyes. I paced nervously around his room and picked up a copy of Thoreau's Walden. I read aloud: "Rather than love, than money, than fame, give me truth."

A.D. fixed his eyes on me and said, "I thought money was love."

"I guess you did. You really did."

"You don't understand. That's not what I meant to say." He stammered, reaching out of habit for his lawyer language to mend my hurt.

"I know exactly what you meant," I said, no longer his demure baby doll. "Tell me, A.D., did I ever hurt you? Ever?"

"No, baby, never," he answered. "I'm sorry." They were the same words my father had uttered on his death bed.

A.D. walked haltingly toward his bedroom and stayed there for a few minutes. When he returned, he handed me a piece of paper. "Buy yourself something extravagant, baby."

"No thank you."

Two weeks later I received a package from Neiman Marcus. I knew before I opened it who it was from. Inside the black jewelers box, that I had grown accustomed to receiving, was an exquisite amethyst ring surrounded by diamonds. I took it from the box and slipped it on my ring finger. I smiled and felt warm all over. My head was filled with pleasant memories of A.D. This man had always loved to shower me with beautiful gifts and he couldn't resist this one last time.

Chapter Thirty Six

In the summer of l983, I liquidated my business. Although I had talked to several local firms that I thought might buy my company, I didn't want to wait, I was impatient. Once I had made up my mind to leave Savannah I was in a hurry to move on, to find a new life. Closing my business was effortless I thought, compared to all the changes I had undergone.

Several people in the office had suggested I take a one year leave of absence. Cal decided to go back to school and get another degree. He wanted a teaching position at the Savannah College of Art and Design. Zelda planned to open a small real estate firm, taking several of the agents with her to her new company.

With the business closed I no longer had to rush to my office every day. I awoke to quiet, to emptiness, to loneliness. There were days when my mind and body were immobile. There were days when I lay staring into open space. Other days I ran up the stairs just to get away from myself, only to race down again.

"I told you that change is brought about through hard work," David said. He added that pain was necessary. "You're not going crazy. You're not scared to death." I was having growing pains; I was grieving my business. Loss is loss, even when it's self-imposed.

My aunt Ella called one morning to ask how I was getting along without the challenge of my real estate business. "I feel like there's something I should be doing for you," Ella said, with a quiver in her voice. She added, "I don't know what you need."

"Oh, I'm fine," I said in response to my aunt's kindness. It had been so long since anyone in my family had offered me a loving word that I wept with joy. The time had come to replace those tears of anguish.

Having loving grandparents, aunts, and uncles had been my salvation as a child. I laughed suddenly at the memory of my sister and me dashing into Pinkerson's Drugstore, just after dancing class, to order a "dope with vanilla." Scenes of my childhood —Mama's *kreplach*, my summer in New Canaan, our father teaching us to slug down a jigger of rye whiskey chased by ginger ale — were the tonic that gave me strength. More and more, the family revealed itself as the security that had been mine as a child. The older I got, the more pronounced was the void it had left.

In early fall, a dear friend of mine invited me to visit Los Angeles to attend the premiere of a film her husband had produced, I jumped at the opportunity to see what life was like on the West Coast. Abigail picked me up at the airport, and the two of us drove to the Oaks Health Spa in Ojai for five days. There, I met other women who were in the midst of major changes in their lives and I felt right at home. When we got back to Los Angeles, I decided to look at rental properties. Malibu instantly appealed to me and I could see myself walking the beach among the gulls, across the scraggy rocks, and being lulled to sleep by the ocean's tides.

When I returned to Savannah the air was cool and brisk, almost time for another Thanksgiving, which had always been my favorite holiday. The autumn leaves of rust and gold laced the trees in filigree patterns. Outside of my house strange shapes cast animal figures on the ground. I told Cal that I would love to cook a traditional Thanksgiving dinner and invite friends. He was readily agreeable and immediately designed the menu.

As soon as I called to invite Mary Anne she insisted we cook the meal together. Thanksgiving morning, I jumped from bed, set the table, seasoned the turkey, and turned on the oven. Mary Anne brought oyster dressing, pecan pies, and fresh greens. Cal supplied the wine. Mary Anne's daughter and Mary Anne's young lover, a local photographer, were coming, too. And Cal's mother was visiting from North Carolina. It would be festive and happy.

The smell of turkey filled the kitchen with rich and pungent fragrances. There was a feeling of extended family and mutual thanks for this gathering as we sat around the huge wooden counter preparing drinks, carving turkey, and placing the food on serving platters. Zelda and her youngest daughter dropped by unannounced when the meal was finished and joined us for coffee and dessert.

I bustled from the kitchen to the dining room, wearing a starched white apron over my long burgundy velvet skirt. This particular Thanksgiving was comforting and heartwarming because it swept away so many past memories.

Alex called from Atlanta to wish me a happy holiday and to say how much he missed our family celebration. I described my group of friends to him and told him that I had fallen in love with the thought of living on the beach in Malibu.

"For God's sake, Mom! Act your age. That's what teenagers do." When I rejoined the festive group in my living room, I told Mary Anne what Alex had said.

"Naomi, sons are that way about their mothers. Get used to it. He still sees you slaving over a hot stove and waiting to wipe away his tears. Tell him to grow up."

Then Cal made a toast: "To the best new family in the world, God bless!"

"I'll drink to that," I said. I missed family gatherings, and this seemed absolutely perfect. I lifted my brandy and took a long drink as I looked toward the smiling faces of my newly chosen family.

Mary Anne, who was different from the women I had spent time with, believed that a woman could open herself up to new directions in life if she could truly become sexually free. And I was quick to grab on to her notion.

"Women have a difficult time separating love from sex," Mary Anne said. "Often they deny themselves the sex that they truly need, just as they need to eat when hungry, sleep when tired."

I confessed to Mary Anne that I was beginning to feel empty: depression was foreshadowing many of my days. I kept thinking that a man could solve that problem.

"Look, Naomi," Mary Anne said, late one afternoon. "Do you want to get laid, or are you looking for a husband?"

"I want to be part of a couple," I answered.

"Well, what about just getting yourself satisfied? You never know whether or not the real thing will be the result." Mary Anne was certainly the freest woman I'd ever known.

That weekend Mary Ann insisted that I go to a local bar with her. She thought a round of drinks and some casual flirting might be good for the two of us. Perhaps just a little more than casual fun might surface. When we entered Spanky's, I saw a number of fellow realtors already relaxing at happy hour. When one handsome young man in the group asked to be introduced to Mary Anne, we joined him and some of the others.

"You sure do fill out that sweater and do it justice!" the Young Realtor of the Year said when he held the chair for Mary Anne to be seated.

"Well, it's just too bad you don't do the same for the crotch of your trousers," Mary Anne demurred, ordering a Jack Daniels on the rocks. After the men left the club the two of us continued our conversation. She said that I might like to join a writing group that met at her house on Saturday afternoons.

"One of the women wrote a poem about her fear and guilt concerning sex, having been brought up in the Bible Belt." Mary Anne said she'd met hundreds of Southern women who said they suffered from sexual hang-ups.

"A woman I knew from high school days — she's now married to a prominent New York lawyer — every time she comes home to Savannah, she rolls up her car windows when she drives through town," I said. "Her excuse is always: 'I'm afraid a big black'll get me.'"

"That's pretty revealing," Mary Anne said with a flickering smile. "Probably her secret fantasy. And not a bad one at that." I admired her for never being afraid of who she was. Although she was a few years younger than me, she was very much my teacher. She, along with David, was having a great impact on my life and my changing perceptions.

I might have been a slow learner, but at last I knew I had to take full responsibility for my womanhood. It's better late than never, I told myself.

Chapter Thirty Seven

Finally, my decision to leave Savannah was made. I invited Cal, my neighbor Malcolm, and Mary Anne, for Sunday night dinner and told them my plans.

"Look, I've listened to Mary Anne's advice and I think she ought to teach classes for women, how sexual freedom can be a stepping stone to independence." I passed around a tray of Camembert and ginger snaps to my guests.

"Naomi is my prize pupil," Mary Anne said. "She's taken to the home-work assignments like a duck to water."

"I'll bet you five bucks right this minute that Naomi moves to Paris," Malcolm added.

"I'll take that bet, my dear, and up you one," Cal stated, with a smile. "If I know my little precious, she's going to New York, New York!" He got up and did a few tap steps across the floor.

Cal, Malcolm, and Mary Anne raised their glasses to me.

"To you getting to do whatever the hell you want," Cal shouted.

"Hallelujah," we all cried in unison.

"And I want to toast my friend Naomi. To tell her that she's no longer Scarlett. No longer Melanie. She's a middle-aged woman and her mother's daughter." Mary Ann raised her glass.

I didn't have the energy for life in New York I told my friends. I wanted a quiet place. I needed the sea. A place to reflect, a place to heal. They talked of wonderful cold rainy afternoons in Provincetown, and the tropical sun in Key West. We even discussed San Miguel de Allende, a popular place in Mexico where many creative, retired older Americans had settled.

I took a long breath and said, "Calm down, all of you. I'm going to lease my house to a suitable tenant and move to Malibu. I've already found a small house on the beach to rent. It's like a gift from God; it's perfect for me. My family think I'm nuts, but at long last I get to do it my way."

I had no idea what to expect when my sons said they would drive down to Savannah to see me before I set out on my journey. I told them about my plans to place most of my things in storage and invited them to each choose a few pieces for themselves.

"I'd like your tea set, Mom," Alex said, as he wandered through my house, fingering bric-a-brac and various antiques. He chose a miniature set of china cups and saucers with handpainted figures of Mickey Mouse on them. I was surprised at his selection. My father had bought the set for me when I was six years old.

In the meantime, Ross, while watching me sort out various pieces of jewelry asked if he could have the onyx and diamond ring that Spyros had given me. He slipped it on his finger. It was a perfect fit. Since Ross had recently taken up cooking as a hobby he wanted some of the pots and pans I had accumulated through the years.

An international court reporter rented my house and office on Gaston Street as soon as it went on the market. When the leases were signed, I told my real estate agent in California to write a three year lease on the beach house in Malibu. My landlord was head of a famous theatrical agency.

During my last visit to my therapist, I told David that there seemed to be something inside of me, very deep rooted, that still needed to come out. I felt shaky.

"Let me remind you that freedom is the hardest thing to handle," he said. "Just take it a little at a time."

"You know, Naomi, when a cold, unloving mother denies her child what she needs, the child becomes grasping, demanding, always hoping that the mother will change and give her what she wants so desperately. It takes a long time to learn that you will not get those baby needs met, because you are no longer a baby. You have to serve your own needs, adult ones," David said. "And be kind to the child inside."

This time I knew exactly what he was saying.

"But quit blaming the past," David said lovingly. "You've divorced Bill; now it's time for you to divorce your mother. The time has come for you to grieve your unfinished childhood. You know there will be parts of your old self that you'll miss terribly."

"I feel rejuvenated, David. I feel as though I've witnessed my entire life, my death and rebirth." As soon as I'd uttered those words it felt like tons of heaviness being released from my body.

"You have. You've become strong enough to deal with hurt. You certainly don't have to be a martyr. You don't have to analyze or justify your feelings. You just need to feel them and try not to let them control your actions."

I wasn't a bit surprised when he explained how I had acted out my relationship with my father through my love affair with A.D. But it did come as a surprise when he told me that I'd done the same with Bubba, only this time it was my mother I was acting out.

"I guess it's never too late to grow up, is it? It seems that school's in session until the day we die." My heart felt gratitude for this man who had guided me toward being able to let go.

I got up from David's sofa for the last time, reached toward him and gently touched his arm. I opened the door, walked out of his office, and closed the door behind me, realizing that I was no longer defined by being someone's mother, another's wife, or someone's daughter. My definition of self would now be based on how I saw myself, how I defined myself. A sense of triumph swept over me.

It took me less than six weeks to get organized. Bill, once he accepted that I was really leaving, decided to cut all ties. He demanded that I sign a document in front of a rabbi giving him a *GET*: a Jewish divorce in which a husband dismisses his wife, leaving him free to choose another. This religious divorce terminates a marriage among Orthodox Jews only if both husband and wife agree.

"That's pure witchcraft," I said, when Bill insisted that I appear before an orthodox rabbi, who with a group of specially trained men, would perform the ceremony.

"Just show up, please," he urged.

"You get a *GET*! I get alimony." I still hadn't lost my ability to cut a deal.

"You know I like to chisel," Bill said with a sly smile. He nodded and agreed to have his lawyer draw up the necessary papers, then added that he would only give me half of what I had asked for. He hadn't said it but I suspected Bill was going to remarry.

It was a brisk Sunday afternoon when I appeared at the door of the rabbi's office. I was wearing blue jeans and cowboy boots. The time worn gray fedora sat like a trusty old friend, jauntily on my head.

"Well, you certainly don't look like a woman who was married for thirty years," the Rabbi said, looking me over.

"It seems that aggravation agrees with me."

Bill was asked to walk around the room, waving a white handkerchief several times. He was giving me my freedom the Rabbi explained. By virtue of my husband I was now allowed to feel free. I could barely keep from laughing. It was a very complex proceeding, all in Hebrew, and I hadn't the faintest idea what was being said.

The Jewish laws follow the same dogma for centuries. My hands were to be cupped like a vessel, but the papers must touch flesh, so my rings had to be removed and the papers placed in my two hands. The men had on prayer shawls and yarmulkes and were bent over their prayer books. After forty-five minutes of ritual and prayer it ended. When it was over and Bill had thanked the rabbi and his *GET* group, we left the office and each of us headed to our separate cars. At home I glanced at the document and noticed the last paragraph.

"This certifies that Mrs. Naomi Kramer has been divorced from her husband Bill Kramer on Sunday, 11 Shevat, 5744, according to the law of Moses and Israel. Mrs. _____ will be permitted to marry again to any Jew except a Kohen after a waiting period of ninety-two days from the above date, and only after obtaining her civil divorce." They hadn't even filled in the blank.

"To a wedding, walk; to a divorce, run." This was the old folk saying that made me laugh as I folded the paper and shoved it into a desk drawer.

Chapter Thirty Eight

I opened my blue striped suitcases and placed them around the bedroom floor. My clothes lay strewn on chairs and across the bed. As I began packing for the drive to California, the phone rang. It was Ruth calling from Atlanta.

"I have sad news for you," she said.

"What?" My heart began to pound.

"It's about A.D. He died last night. I just read his obituary. The funeral's tomorrow at two. Do you want to come? I'll go with you."

I said nothing, holding the receiver away from my ear.

"No," I replied, after a long pause.

I sank down on the side of my bed. I gazed around the room, at the paintings that A.D. had bought for me, the silver antiques that he had encouraged me to collect. I recalled his pleasure in frequenting the chic shops in Charleston and Georgetown. I realized how much he had contributed to my life.

But that was a lifetime ago, so it seemed. I felt no need to stand over his barren grave. My memories of the man with whom I'd shared such a deep love would suffice.

I fingered the amethyst ring on my finger.

"A.D.," I said as though he was in the room with me, "God knows I loved you and I know deep in my heart how much you loved me. I no longer need a mentor, Daddy. Your little Mazik has come of age."

The morning I was to leave, Cal and I had breakfast at Clary's.

"Are you afraid?" he asked, holding my hand as we left the drugstore.

"Of course, a bit," I said. Actually, I couldn't wait to settle into the dollhouse I had rented on the beach in Malibu. I knew that living on the

West Coast meant pushing myself to my absolute limits, probably hanging on by my fingernails. I'd be forced to live alone, to take stock of my life, and in Los Angeles, a town built on fantasy, perhaps I'd find my own reality. I had always, it seemed, done things backwards.

"In California nobody gives a damn. You're accepted no matter who or what you are. I can do what I like, feel what I want; nobody's gossiping behind your back, nobody cares. Out there everybody's a stranger from Iowa or Kansas." I felt I was making a speech of encouragement to myself.

Cal laughed. "I'm sure going to miss you."

Cal and Dora helped me load my car. Cal carefully placed my typewriter in the trunk against the full length dark mink coat that A.D. had given me. Dora carried my chest of sterling silver flatware to the car and shoved it under the many books that were lying helter-skelter in the front seat and spilling over into the back.

"As you can see, I'm only taking the necessities," I said and struggled to fit the vacuum cleaner between my jewelry case and a huge beloved teddy bear.

Dora put her arms around me awkwardly, then pulled me to her with a crushing hug. "Just remember, Miss Naomi, courage is fear what's done said her prayers."

Cal leaned through the window, and kissed me on my forehead. Then he whispered, "God bless, Naomi."

I slid into the driver's seat, blew him a kiss, flicked on the ignition, and headed for the highway out of Savannah. I glanced back, smiling over my left shoulder, toward Cal and Dora, and toward Savannah. Leaving my hometown was like shedding a final skin. But I knew that the beauty of the Spanish moss, the piney woods, and the smells of the marshes were embedded in my soul.

"Listen, listen," I shouted, opening the window wider so my voice could rise above the limbs of the live oaks, so that my words could be heralded up through the sunny spaces that shimmered through the tree tops. I whipped my car onto the interstate, settling against the soft leather upholstery.

"We're going to have a blast, God. I promise!"

I thought the book was interesting in the way a personal story would be. I did not find much value in the dependence she fought for as a housewife & mother. I did sympathize that she was treated so badly by her mother & that her father did not measure up to father standards (though most fathers don't). I found Ruth and Bill to be pillars in her life & felt no sympathy that A.D. did not marry her. I found her choice of friendship with Andrew sad at best but found Cal, Beckie & MaryAnn more deserving of a friendship & of confidence.

I think Naomi was spoiled in
her expectations of always having
what she wanted "Now" though
I didn't begrudge her of her
desires - just the way she
went about getting them.
The again with the shrink
should have been nipped in the
bud As soon as it started.
The relationship with Daniel was
a little more reasonable.
The younger man thing was
disgusting only in that she
felt more desirable by being
able to have the love & attention
of a younger man. He was completely
free to tell her whatever she
wanted to hear & carry on
with others should he desire
to do so while away on his
Trips.

978-0-595-38382-5
0-595-38382-3

In general I found the book salacious but without much real meaning — entertaining only.